William Winter

Life and Art of Joseph Jefferson

together with some account of his ancestry and of the Jefferson family of actors

William Winter

Life and Art of Joseph Jefferson
together with some account of his ancestry and of the Jefferson family of actors

ISBN/EAN: 9783337423506

Printed in Europe, USA, Canada, Australia, Japan

Cover: Foto ©Andreas Hilbeck / pixelio.de

More available books at **www.hansebooks.com**

Elmer A. Allen
Christmas 1894

JOSEPH JEFFERSON IN 1894.

With his Grandson.

WARREN JEFFERSON.

LIFE AND ART OF JOSEPH JEFFERSON

TOGETHER WITH SOME ACCOUNT OF HIS
ANCESTRY AND OF THE JEFFERSON
FAMILY OF ACTORS

BY

WILLIAM WINTER

" O that I had a title good enough
to keep his name company !"
— SHAKESPEARE

New York

MACMILLAN AND CO.

AND LONDON

1894

TO

John Lawrence Toole

THE REPRESENTATIVE COMEDIAN OF ENGLAND

IN THE PRESENT GENERATION

I DEDICATE THIS MEMORIAL OF

Joseph Jefferson

THE REPRESENTATIVE COMEDIAN OF AMERICA

IN THE SAME PERIOD

THUS UNITING

IN AN HUMBLE TRIBUTE OF LOVE AND HONOUR

MEN LONG SINCE UNITED

IN PERSONAL AFFECTION AND PUBLIC ESTEEM

WILLIAM WINTER

February 20, 1894

PREFACE

ABOUT fourteen years ago, at the kind suggestion of my thoughtful friend Laurence Hutton, I wrote an account of the Jefferson Family of Actors, which was published in 1881, under the name of The Jeffersons, as one of the American Actor Series, projected and supervised by him. The present Memoir is a complete revision of that biography. The story has been rectified, augmented, re-arranged, and in part re-written, — so that this work is, practically, new. It certainly is more ample and more authentic than its predecessor, and therefore more worthy of its interesting subject and of the public favour. In the composition of it I have drawn upon my dramatic writings in the New York Tribune, since 1865, and in other publications, notably my Brief Chronicles. The beauty and greatness of the dramatic art and the possible dignity and utility of the stage are better known and understood now than they were in former times, and I have assumed that the achievements of an exceptionally talented family of actors may be deemed worthy of commemoration. The Jefferson family has been upon the stage, continuously, for five generations, and in this narrative an effort has been made to trace its history along one unbroken line, throughout that time. The English historic period traversed by this biography begins with the reign of George the Second, in 1727. The American period extends from 1794 to the present day. The first Jefferson had his career in England, in the time of Garrick. The second was famous in the days of the old Chestnut Street theatre, in Philadelphia. The third did not attain to eminence. The fourth is the Rip Van Winkle and the Acres of contemporary renown, whose sons are also on the stage. Other members of the race have been distinguished actors, and their names and deeds are recorded in this chronicle. The Garrick period has been so fully described by many writers that, in recounting what is known of the first Jefferson, I have preferred not to linger upon it. Select quotation from old chronicles has, however, been deemed essential, as a basis of authority. The career of the second Jefferson recalls the storied days of the Chestnut Street theatre,—an institution which has not been surpassed, if ever it was equalled, in the history of the American stage, for dignity, intellectual resource, stateliness of character, and opulence of association. Ample materials exist, no doubt, in the manuscript journals of the elder Warren, for a minute account of that theatre and its dramatic luminaries; but they are not accessible. The third Jefferson, his sister Elizabeth, his wife, and his stepson, Charles S. T. Burke, are commemorated in this book, and mention is herein made of all the known scions of the Jefferson race. The design has been to portray this family in its relation to the times through which it has moved, and thus to make an authentic basis for the researches and illustrative embellishments of future inquirers. Attention has been chiefly given to the career of the fourth Jefferson, and to his impersonation of Rip Van Winkle,—an artistic achievement which has fascinated the public mind for thirty years. No single dramatic performance of our time, indeed, — not Edwin Booth's Hamlet, nor Ristori's Queen Elizabeth, nor Lester Wallack's Don Felix, nor Marie Seebach's Margaret, nor Charles Kean's Louis, nor Adelaide Neilson's Juliet, nor Henry Irving's Mathias, nor Ada Rehan's Rosalind, — has had more extensive popularity, or has in a greater degree stimulated contemporary thought upon the influence of the stage. The wish to honour it will be recognised in these pages, although the power may be missed. Every writer upon the history of the drama in America must acknowledge his obligation for guidance to the thorough, faithful, and suggestive Records made by the veteran historian, Joseph N. Ireland. In the composition of this biography reference has frequently been made to that work. Other authorities, likewise, have been consulted, and they are duly mentioned. I have profited by the personal recollections of several members of the Jefferson family, and by useful suggestions of friendly correspondents, — among whom should be named Thomas J. McKee of New York, L. Clarke Davis and George P. Philes of Philadelphia, and my old, honoured, and lamented friend, the late John T. Ford of Baltimore — by whose sudden death I am admonished that the number of persons to whom any writings of mine can appeal with the confident expectation of sympathy is growing smaller every day.

> *" Like clouds that rake the mountain summits,*
> *Or waves that own no curbing hand,*
> *How fast has brother followed brother*
> *From sunshine to the sunless land!"*

W. W.

March 25, 1894.

✠

*" In giving an account of the stage a good story may sometimes be admitted on
slender authority, but where matters of fact are concerned the history of the stage
ought to be written with the same accuracy as the history of England."* — GENEST.

" The longest life is too short for the almost endless study of the actor." —
BARTON BOOTH.

" A name
Noble and brave as aught of consular
On Roman marbles." — BYRON.

" First, noble friend,
Let me embrace thine age ; whose honour cannot
Be measured or confined." — SHAKESPEARE.

" Noble he was, contemning all things mean,
His truth unquestioned and his soul serene.
Shame knew him not, he dreaded no disgrace,
Truth, simple truth, was written in his face;
Yet, while the serious thought his soul approv'd,
Cheerful he seem'd and gentleness he lov'd ;
To bliss domestic he his heart resign'd,
And with the firmest had the fondest mind.
Were others joyful, he looked smiling on,
And gave allowance where he needed none.
Good he refused with future ill to buy,
Nor knew a joy that caused reflection's sigh.
A friend to virtue, his unclouded breast
No envy stung, no jealousy distress'd ;
Yet far was he from stoic pride remov'd, —
He felt humanely, and he warmly lov'd." — CRABBE.

" He is insensibly subdued
To settled quiet : he is one by whom
All effort seems forgotten ; one to whom
Long patience hath such mild composure given
That patience now doth seem a thing of which
He hath no need."

" He is retired as noontide dew,
Or fountain in a noon-day grove ;
And you must love him, ere to you
He will seem worthy of your love."
— WORDSWORTH.

*" We are a queen (or long have dreamed so), certain
The daughter of a king."* —SHAKESPEARE.

" Upon my word, thou art a very odd fellow, and I like thy humour extremely." — FIELDING.

---

*" With all the fortunate have not,
With gentle voice and brow.
— Alive, we would have changed his lot—
We would not change it now."*
— MATTHEW ARNOLD.

" If he come not, then the play is marred." — SHAKESPEARE.

" It is difficult to render even ordinary justice to living merit, without incurring the suspicion of being influenced by partiality, or by motives of a less honourable nature. Yet, as what I shall say of this gentleman, whose friendship I have enjoyed for many years, and still possess in unabated cordiality, will be supported by all who are acquainted with him, I am under no apprehension of suffering by the suggestions of malice." — JOHN TAYLOR.

---

*" I marvel how Nature could ever find space
For so many strange contrasts in one human face :
There's thought and no thought, and there's paleness and bloom,
And bustle and sluggishness, pleasure and gloom.*

*" There's weakness and strength, both redundant and vain ;
Such strength as, if ever affliction and pain
Could pierce through a temper that's soft to disease,
Would be rational peace, — a philosopher's ease.*

*" There's indifference, alike when he fails or succeeds,
And attention full ten times as much as there needs ;
Pride where there's no envy, there's so much of joy ;
And mildness, and spirit both forward and coy.*

*" There's freedom, and sometimes a diffident stare,
Of shame, scarcely seeming to know that she's there :
There's virtue, the title it surely may claim,
Yet wants heaven knows what to be worthy the name.*

*" This picture from nature may seem to depart,
Yet the Man would at once run away with your heart :
And I for five centuries right gladly would be
Such an odd, such a kind, happy creature as he."*
— WORDSWORTH.

✠

CONTENTS

LIST OF ILLUSTRATIONS.

LIFE OF JEFFERSON

I

THOMAS JEFFERSON

1728–1807

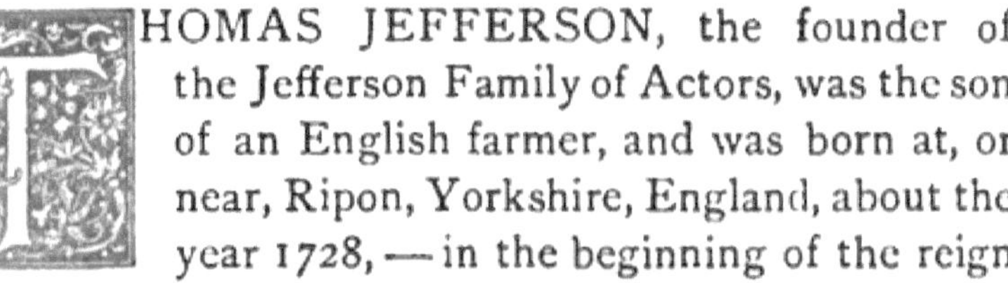

THOMAS JEFFERSON, the founder of the Jefferson Family of Actors, was the son of an English farmer, and was born at, or near, Ripon, Yorkshire, England, about the year 1728, — in the beginning of the reign of George the Second. Little is known of his parents, or of his childhood, and stories of him that have survived are meagre and contradictory. One person, however, who had seen him, lived to our time, dying in 1869, and gave an account of the beginning of his stage career. That person was Mr. Drinkwater Meadows,[1] a respected actor, who saw Thomas Jefferson, at Ripon, in 1806, a feeble old man, sitting by the

---

[1] MR. DRINKWATER MEADOWS, long a useful and esteemed comedian on the London stage, made his first appearance in London, at Covent Garden, in September, 1821, acting Scrub, in *The Beaux' Stratagem*. He was the original Fathom in *The Hunchback* (1832). His last appearance on the London stage was made at the Princess's theatre, in 1862, and he then retired from the profession. He occupied, for a time, the office of Secretary of the Covent Garden Theatrical Fund, discharging its duties with probity and courtesy. He died at his residence, Prairie Cottage, Barnes, on Saturday, June 5, 1869, at about the age of eighty.

fireside, ill with gout, and tended by his relatives. Mr. Meadows was at Ripon, on a visit to one of the aged actor's sons, Frank Jefferson, a lieutenant aboard a royal yacht in Virginia Water, at Windsor; and from him he learned something of old Thomas Jefferson's life, which he lived to relate to Thomas Jefferson's great-grandson, whom he saw upon the stage as Rip Van Winkle, and personally met, in London, in 1865. According to the narrative of Mr. Meadows, Thomas Jefferson, when young, was a wild lad, dashing and gay, and capable of any intrepidity. His person was handsome, his bearing free and graceful, his intelligence superior, his temperament merry; he was a frolicsome companion, a capital equestrian, and a general favourite. A time presently came when his skill in horsemanship, his good spirits, and his excellent faculty for singing a comic song were the means, if not of making his fortune, at least of prescribing his career. The rebellion of 1745, for Charles Edward Stuart, appears to have been a motive to his prosperity. A dispatch was to be conveyed from Ripon, or perhaps from neighbouring York, to London, and young Thomas Jefferson — who could ride well, and whose thriving father could mount him on a thoroughbred steed, for the journey — was chosen to be its bearer. He undertook the task, and he accomplished it, — through what perils it were idle to conjecture; but an equestrian trip of two hundred and twenty miles, through wild parts of the kingdom, what with bad roads and highwaymen, was a serious business;[1] and it may be supposed that

---

[1] " In 1707 it took, in summer one day, in winter nearly two days, to travel from London to Oxford, forty-six miles." — *Haydn's Dictionary*. The

Thomas Jefferson was a man well satisfied with himself and with fortune, when at length his mission had been fulfilled, and he was taking his rest at a London inn. He had arrived just in time to grasp the extended hand of a singular good-fortune. On that night David Garrick, the wonder and delight of London, was feasting with a party of friends at that inn; and presently to the merry circle of Roscius in the parlour, a laughing servant brought word of the jovial young fellow from the country, who was singing songs and telling stories to the less select revellers in the tap-room. A proposition to invite this pleasant rustic, for a frolic over his bumpkin humour, met with the favour of Garrick's companions, and so it chanced that Thomas Jefferson was asked to sit at the table of David Garrick. Fancy dwells pleasurably on the ensuing scene of festal triumph for the sparkling country lad. He charmed his fastidious acquaintances of the parlour as much as he had charmed his careless comrades of the tap; and the fancy that Garrick took for him, on that night, was destined not only to ripen into a lasting friendship, but to mark out his pathway in life. He returned no more,

ride from Ripon to London, in 1746, could not have been made in less than five summer days. — "In the year 1763 the roads were so bad at particular seasons of the year that they were, for want of proper forming, almost impassable; and it has been known, in the winter, to have been eight or ten days' journey from York to London." — Tate Wilkinson's *Memoirs*, Vol. III., p. 142. — Travel was not the expeditious business, in old times, that it is now. In the spring of 1623 Prince Charles, afterward Charles I. of England, being then at Madrid, to woo the Infanta of Spain, apprised his father, James I., that he had come safely from London to Madrid "in less than sixteen days." See Howel's *Familiar Letters*, Book I., Letter xv.

for a long time, to Ripon; but, with Garrick's advice and aid, he adopted the stage, and was embarked in professional occupation.

There is a romantic air about that narrative which, possibly, implies a fiction; but such is the story, as transmitted by Mr. Meadows, and so it remains. Another account says that Jefferson was educated for the bar, and began the practice of law; but soon, by accident, discarded that profession, for the stage. According to this tale, he chanced one day to stroll into a barn in the neighbourhood of Ripon, where some wandering players had undertaken to enact Farquhar's comedy of *The Beaux' Stratagem*, and there and then volunteered his services, in place of an actor suddenly disabled by illness, to perform Archer. His offer was accepted. He had previously acted the part at a private theatrical club, and his success in it was so cheering that he determined to renounce the law and adopt the theatre. This legend furthermore states that Garrick, when accosted by the new-comer, promptly bestowed upon him an engagement, together with his personal friendship, and that Jefferson subsequently for a term of years shared the honours of the stage with its chieftain. The student of theatrical history, however, without reference to the comparative sterility of existing records of Jefferson's career, remembering what is authentically recorded of Garrick's temperament and habits, will prefer to accept the more rational and pleasing story related on the authority of the veteran of Covent Garden.

Jefferson, it is certain, never at any time in his professional career divided honours with his great leader. The earliest record of his appearance at Drury Lane assigns it to October 24, 1753, when he performed Vain-love in *The Old Bachelor*.   He acted Horatio, and also King Claudius, to Garrick's Hamlet ; the Duke of Buckingham, to Garrick's Richard the Third ; Paris, to Garrick's Romeo ; Colonel Britton, to Garrick's Don Felix ; and the Duke of Gloster, to Garrick's John Shore ; and this showing indicates his place in Garrick's company. He was "a well-graced actor" ; he gained and held a good rank, when rank was hard to gain ; and he possessed Garrick's regard more fully than probably he would have done had he ever been, or seemed to be, a rival to that illustrious but not always magnanimous genius.   Jefferson seems to have been early captivated by the idea of theatrical management in the provincial towns, and he may have left Garrick's company either as a strolling player, or with this vocation in view.   There is an anecdote, treasured by his descendants, that when he sought that great actor to say good-bye, Garrick, who had just ended a performance of Abel Drugger, in Ben Jonson's comedy of *The Alchemist*, took off his wig, after exchanging words of farewell, and threw it to him, saying, "Take that, my friend, and may it bring you as much good as it has brought me."   This relic survived for a long time ; was brought to America by Joseph Jefferson, in 1795, passed into the possession of the next Joseph Jefferson, father of our Rip Van Winkle, and ultimately was destroyed, together with other articles of stage wardrobe, which had been entrusted by the latter to the care of Joseph Cowell,[1] the comedian, in a fire that burnt down the St. Charles theatre, New Orleans, in 1842.

[1] JOSEPH LEATHLEY COWELL was born at Kent, England, August 7, 1792, and passed his youth at Torquay, where he saw Nelson, of whom

There is another version of Thomas Jefferson's exodus from Ripon, the details of which are sanctioned by several authorities. This account states that when a youth he was, for a short time, employed by an attorney in Yorkshire, presumably at Ripon, and that he went to London as an adventurous fugitive. The attorney had ordered him to prepare for a journey up to the capital, and this, to the gay lad, was a joyful prospect ; but, to his disappointment and mortification, he was presently apprised that the plan had been changed, and that the attorney himself would make the trip. Young Jefferson, not to be thus defeated, thereupon determined to go to London on his own account. A fortunate chance seemed to favour his flight. A fine charger had been bought, in the neighbourhood of Ripon, for a military magnate named General Fawkes, and Jefferson got permission to ride the horse to London. Thus provided, he bent

---

he can find nothing better to say than that he was "a mean-looking little man, but very kind and agreeable to children." Cowell made his first appearance on the stage, at Plymouth, in 1812, as Belcour, in Cumberland's comedy of *The West Indian*. He afterwards was on the York circuit, — Tate Wilkinson's old ground, — and eventually he became a member of the company at Drury Lane. In 1821 he came to America, under engagement to Stephen Price, for the New York Park theatre, and he remained in this country till 1844, when he returned to England. He was in New York in 1850, and appeared at the Astor Place opera house; and on April 23, 1856, at the old Broadway theatre, he took a farewell benefit and left the stage. His autobiography, entitled *Thirty Years among the Players*, was published by Messrs. Harper and Brothers, in 1844. He went back to England with his grand-daughter, Kate Bateman, and died in London, November 14, 1863, in his seventy-second year. He was popular as Crack, in *The Turnpike Gate*, — a musical piece, by T. Knight, first acted at Covent Garden, in 1799, — and his portrait, in that character, painted by Neagle, is one of the illustrations of Wemyss's *Acting American Theatre*.

his course toward the capital, arriving there in January, 1746 or 1747. In the spring of 1747 he was an inmate of the Tilt-yard coffee-house, when that building chanced to be blown up with gunpowder, — a large quantity of which had been served to certain soldiers who were to guard that old reprobate, Simon Fraser, Lord Lovat, on his way to Tower Hill.[1] Several persons were killed by that explosion, but Jefferson was saved by the fortunate intervention of a falling timber, which protected him from being crushed. A little later he happened to attend a performance at Drury Lane, where he saw the fascinating Peg Woffington, as Ruth, in Sir Robert Howard's comedy of *The Committee;* whereupon his fancy was so captivated that he could think of nothing but the stage, and he determined to devote himself thereafter entirely to its pursuit.

Thomas Jefferson's professional career was various and devious, but in general it was successful, and it seems to have been attended with happiness. He was a theatrical manager at Richmond, Exeter, Lewes, and Plymouth; he frequently made strolling expeditions, and he acted at Drury Lane, intermittently, from about 1750 to 1776. Soon after his first meeting with Garrick, he appeared at the Haymarket, London, as Horatio, in *The Fair Penitent.* The exact date of that meeting is unknown. Garrick made his great hit[2] in London,

---

[1] LOVAT, born in 1667, perished beneath the axe, on March 20, 1747. The other noted Scotch lords who suffered death in the cause of the Pretender — Balmerino and Kilmarnock — were beheaded earlier, August 18, 1746. The axe and block that were used in those executions are shown at the Tower.

[2] DAVID GARRICK, 1716-1779. — In John Bernard's *Retrospections of the Stage*, Vol. II., chap. 6, mention is made of a spectator of the first

at Goodman's Fields theatre, when he was twenty-five years old, on October 19, 1741, afterwards went to Dublin, and then was engaged by Fleetwood, for Drury Lane, where he remained till 1745. In that year he was again in Ireland, acting with Thomas Sheridan, father of the famous Richard Brinsley, in the theatre in Smock alley. But in 1746 he was acting, under the management of Rich, at Covent Garden, and it was not till the winter of 1747 that he became the manager of Drury Lane. Jefferson's meeting with him occurred in 1746 or 1747. It is likely that, through Garrick's influence, Jefferson was early attached to the stage. He may at first have gone on a country circuit, and afterwards joined the Drury Lane company, when Garrick had become its manager, quitting that theatre at a later time to manage for his own benefit in the provinces. He must soon have learned, as others did, that it was

appearance of Garrick in London. That was Philip Lewis, uncle of the English comedian, William T. Lewis. "He was the only man of my acquaintance," says Bernard, "who remembered the début of Garrick; and it was . . . when sitting at my table, with Charles Bannister and Merry, he uttered an impromptu I have since heard attributed to others : —

> "'I saw him rising in the east,
>   In all his energetic glows;
> I saw him sinking in the west
>   In greater splendour than he rose.'"

Hannah More [1745-1833], certainly a shrewd observer, came up to London, from her home at Bristol, to see Garrick's farewell performance, 1776, and after her return she wrote these words: "I pity those who have not seen him. Posterity will never be able to form the slightest idea of his perfection. The more I see him, the more I admire. I have seen him within these three weeks take leave of Benedick, Sir John Brute, Kitely, Abel Drugger, Archer, and Leon. It seems to me as if I was assisting at the obsequies of the different poets."

DAVID GARRICK.

well-nigh impossible, in that epoch, for any actor to win a pre-eminent success, at the. British capital, in face of the overwhelming ascendency which Garrick then maintained.

A reprint of the Drury Lane play-bill, which, following the authority of Genest, appears to assign Jefferson's first appearance at that theatre, under Garrick's management, to October 24, 1753, will here be appropriate. It is a reduced fac-simile from an original. Almost every name in it is distinguished in theatrical history. Mrs. Pritchard was Dr. Johnson's "inspired idiot," — the great Lady Macbeth of the eighteenth century, prior to Mrs. Yates and Mrs. Siddons. Foote was "the English Aristophanes." Woodward — superb as Mercutio and fine as Touchstone — was deemed the model of every grace. Palmer and Blakes are complimented even by the exigent Churchill — in *The Rosciad.* Yates was the original Sir Oliver Surface, and died in 1796, in his 97th year. Mrs. Davies was the lovely wife of Thomas Davies, the actor, author, and bookseller, the man who introduced Boswell to Dr. Johnson; and it is sad to think that, being left a widow, she fell into misfortune and died in an almshouse. Miss Macklin was Maria, daughter of Charles Macklin (1690–1797), the first great Shylock of the stage. William Havard, a conscientious actor and an estimable man, was the author of several successful plays,—one of them on Charles the First,—and he rests in Covent Garden Church, commemorated by an epitaph from the pen of Garrick.

Theatre Royal in *Drury-Lane*,

This prefent *Wednefday*, being the 24th of *October*,
Will be *Revived* a COMEDY, call'd

The OLD BATCHELOR.

Fondlewife by Mr. FOOTE,
Bellmour by Mr. PALMER,
Sharper by Mr. HAVARD,
Vainlove by Mr. JEFFERSON,
Heartwell by Mr. BERRY,
Sir *Jofeph Wittol* Mr. WOODWARD,
Noll Bluffe by Mr. YATES,
Setter by Mr. BLAKES,
Belinda by Mifs HAUGHTON,
Araminta by Mrs. DAVIES,
Sylvia by Mrs. COWPER,
Lucy by Mrs. BENNET,
Lætitia by Mrs. PRITCHARD.

In Act III. a *DANCE* proper to the Play, by
Monf. *GERARD*, and Mad. *LUSSANT*.

To which will be added a COMEDY in Two Acts, call'd

The Englifhman in PARIS.

Buck by Mr. FOOTE,
Lucinda by Mifs MACKLIN,
(*Being the* Third *Time of her appearing upon that* STAGE.)

With a NEW Occafional PROLOGUE,
and the ORIGINAL EPILOGUE.

Boxes 5s.　Pit 3s.　First Gallery 2s.　Upper Gallery 1s.

PLACES for the Boxes to be had of Mr. VARNEY, at the Stage-
door of the Theatre.

† *No Perfons to be admitted behind the* Scenes, *nor any Money to be
returned after the* Curtain *is drawn up.　Vivat REX.*

A period of about twelve years of itinerant acting and perhaps of desultory theatrical management, after Jefferson's arrival in London, is accordingly to be supposed. In 1758 he went to Ireland, and in 1760 he was a member of the Crow Street theatre, acting with a company which included Barry, Dexter, Foote, Heaphy, Macklin, Mossop, Sowden, Vernon, Walker, Woodward, Mrs. Dancer, Mrs. Fitzhenry, and Mrs. Kennedy. In that year, or a little later, he left Dublin, in order to assume the management of the Plymouth theatre, with which his name was afterward long associated. In 1764, still holding the Plymouth house, he joined with Mrs. Pitt, in the direction of a theatre at Exeter, and in 1765, conjointly with Josiah Foote, a tradesman of that town, he purchased Mrs. Pitt's interest in that property and renewed the lease ; but in 1767 he sold his share of the estate to his partner, Foote, and after that time he concentrated his attention upon the care of the Plymouth theatre. He managed, indeed, at one or two other places, and he appeared at Drury Lane, — his name being occasionally found in the casts of plays that were presented there, during the period from 1753 to 1776. But he never appeared in that theatre after Garrick left it — June 10, 1776 ; and after Garrick's death, January 20, 1779, when that resplendent career, of thirty-five years, was ended, he seems never to have cared again to associate himself with London theatrical life. He was now about fifty years of age, with his children growing up around him, and his circumstances had assumed a character such as naturally restricted him to the safe fields of unadventurous industry.

The rank of Thomas Jefferson among the actors of

his time was with the best, — setting aside the names
of Garrick, Barry, Henderson,[1] and Mossop as exceptional, and far above their comrades. The dramatic
period was a storied one, and only a man of fine talent
could have held a conspicuous position in the shining
group of players which then adorned the British stage.
Theatrical powers and enterprises in those days were
more closely concentrated than they have been since,
except, perhaps, in the best period of the Chestnut and
the Park, in America, and were subjected to a more
exacting attention, on the part of the public, than they
receive, or, generally, are calculated to inspire, at present.
The stock companies were few, and they were composed
of performers who, for the most part, in the vastly
extended theatrical area, and the vastly increased demand and remuneration for theatrical entertainments,
would now be "stars." Jefferson's repute, if not sur-
passingly high, like that of Garrick, was, nevertheless,
that of sterling merit. He ranked with Barry in comedy,
— excelling Mossop, Sheridan, and Reddish, — but he
was not half so good as Barry in tragedy. His tragedy,

[1] "HENDERSON (1747–1785) was the legitimate successor to Garrick's throne, — the only attendant genius that could wear his mantle.
Though it is difficult to compare the others, owing to the peculiarities of
their paths, Powell was best in the Romans and fathers; Holland, in the
ardent spirits of lovers and champions, the Hotspurs and Chamonts; and
Jefferson in the kings and tyrants. Of the four, Powell and Reddish were
the cleverest. But Reddish was differently situated; he lived in Garrick's
time, and was one of the many stars, in that Augustan era of acting, whose
radiance was absorbed in the great luminary's. Powell, Holland, and
Jefferson were all in the same predicament: Mossop, Barry, and Sheridan
were the only ones who rose into notice from a collision with the Roscius;
but even their memories are fading." — John Bernard's *Retrospections of
the Stage*, Vol. I., p. 15.

however, was accounted equal with that of Macklin, the first great Shylock of the British stage; and he must have been important, if he could hold his rank against that competitor. The *Thespian Dictionary* (1805), recording, perhaps, the testimony of a contemporary, says that he "possessed a pleasing countenance, strong expression and compass of voice, and was excellent in declamatory parts." His abilities, obviously, were considerable, and they must have been versatile, for the chronicles show that he was sometimes accepted as a substitute for Garrick; that he was even thought to resemble him in appearance; and that he was accounted a competent actor throughout a wide range of parts.

An indication of the professional rank of Thomas Jefferson, and also of that of his first wife, Miss May, is given in a Scale of Merits of the Performers on the Dublin stage, made about 1760–1763. This document was published in the *London Chronicle*, Vol. XV., and is quoted in Malcolm's *Anecdotes of the Manners and Customs of London, during the Eighteenth Century*, Vol. II., p. 247.

Men.	Tragedy.	Comedy.
Mr. Barry	20	10
" Mossop	15	6
" Sheridan	15	6
" Macklin	8	15
" Sowdon	13	12
" Dexter	10	12
" T. Barry	10	8
" Ryder	6	12
" Stamper	0	12
" Sparks	0	12
" Jefferson	8	10
" Heaphy	6	8
" Reddish	6	8
" Walker	0	8
" Glover	4	8
" Mahon	4	6

Women.	Tragedy.	Comedy.
Mrs. Dancer	14	16
" Fitzhenry	14	6
" Abington	0	18
" Hamilton	10	12
" Kennedy	8	10
" Kelf	8	10
" Barry	8	10
" Jefferson	6	8
" Ambrose	0	8
" Mahon	0	6
" Roach	0	6
" Parsons	0	6

Thomas Jefferson was twice married. His first wife, Miss May, was the daughter of a member of the British Navy, and, according to Gilliland's *Dramatic Mirror*, he agreed, in marrying her, to forfeit £500 to her father, in case she should ever appear upon the stage. That was at Lewes, where Jefferson acted for two seasons, under the name of Burton, in the dramatic company of a manager named Williams. A number of the ladies of that place, on a subsequent occasion, wished that Mrs. Jefferson should appear in a dramatic performance, and, finding Mr. May's bond an obstacle to their desire, they succeeded in persuading him to cancel it. Mrs. Jefferson thereupon acted Lady Charlotte, in Sir Richard Steele's comedy of *The Funeral* (1702). " The ladies," says the *Mirror,* " provided the females of the company with dresses for the piece, and it was played three nights, each person's share amounting to six guineas." The first appearance of Mrs. Jefferson on the London stage was made at Drury Lane, October 6, 1753, as Anne Bullen.

Mrs. Jefferson was a beautiful woman, and of a lovely disposition, and that part of the married life of Thomas Jefferson which was passed in her society was happy She bore two sons, — John and Joseph. The former became a clergyman of the established church, and went as a missionary to some part of Asia, where he was presently slain by persons who opposed him in religious opinion. In Ryley's *Itinerant* (1808), mention is made of John Jefferson, a son of Thomas, who, it is said, " was very tall, very slim, very sallow, and a very poor actor " ; and it is further stated that he was of a religious turn of mind, and was called " The Parson."

That may have been the pious John. The latter son, Joseph, became an actor, and, after a brief career in England, emigrated to America, and established the family in this country. The mother of those boys, whenever named in old theatrical chronicles, is named not merely with honour and affection, but with evident wonder that so much beauty could coexist with so much goodness. Even her death bore witness to the sunshine of her nature ; for she died of laughter. Davies, in his *Life of Garrick*, records the incident, and describes the heroine : —

" Britannia was represented by Mrs. Jefferson, the most complete figure, in beauty of countenance and symmetry of form, I ever beheld. This good woman — for she was as virtuous as fair — was so unaffected and simple in her behaviour that she knew not her power of charming. Her beautiful figure and majestic step, in the character of Anne Bullen, drew the admiration of all who saw her. She was very tall, and had she been happy in ability to represent characters of consequence, she would have been an excellent partner in tragedy for Mr. Barry. In the vicissitudes of itinerant acting she had been often reduced, from the small number of players in the company she belonged to, to disguise her lovely form and to assume parts very unsuitable to so delicate a creature. When she was asked what characters she excelled in most, she innocently replied, ' Old men in comedy,' — meaning such parts as Fondlewife, in *The Old Bachelor*, and Sir Jealous Traffic, in *The Busybody*. She died suddenly at Plymouth, as she was looking at a dance that was practising for the night's representation. In the midst of a hearty laugh she was seized with a sudden pain, and expired in the arms of Mr. Moody,[1] who happened to stand by, and saved her from falling on the ground."

---

[1] JOHN MOODY. — He established a theatre in the island of Jamaica, in 1745, and was thus the means of introducing the acted drama into America. He was considered exceptionally fine as the Irishman Teague, in *The Committee*. In the print of *The Immortality of Garrick* he is represented as Adam.

That is said to have occurred on July 18, 1766. It is
a tradition in the Jefferson family that the proximate
cause of the catastrophe was a rehearsal of Dicky Gossip, by Edward Shuter. That comedian, the original
representative of Mr. Hardcastle, in *She Stoops to Conquer*, and of Sir Anthony Absolute, in *The Rivals*, was
thought by Garrick to be the greatest comic genius
of his time. "I remember him," says John Taylor,
(*Records of My Life*), "as Justice Woodcock, Scrub,
Peachum, and Sir Francis Gripe. . . . His acting was
a compound of truth, simplicity, and luxuriant humour.
Never was an actor more popular than Shuter." "He
was more bewildered in his brain by wishing to acquire
imaginary grace, than by all his drinking," says Tate
Wilkinson; "like Mawworm, he believed he had a call."
Shuter, a devout Methodist, was also a fine Falstaff.
The part of Britannia, mentioned by Davies as allotted
to Mrs. Jefferson, occurs in a masque by David Mallet,
first produced at Drury Lane in 1755. The music was
composed by Dr. Arne (1710–1778). A prologue to the
piece, written by Mallet and Garrick, and spoken by the
latter, made a hit, by presenting a tipsy sailor reading a
play-bill, with allusions to war with the French. Mrs.
Jefferson is mentioned by Genest as having played
Mrs. Fainall, in Congreve's comedy of *The Way of
the World* (1700), at Drury Lane, on March 15, 1774,
for the benefit of Mrs. Abington. Her attributes and
rank as an actress may be inferred from those facts.
Her death is said by one authority to have occurred
in 1766; by another, in 1768. The birth of Joseph
Jefferson is assigned to 1774 or 1776. It is known that
he had a step-mother; one cause of his leaving home

and emigrating to America, indeed, was his dissatisfaction with his father's second marriage ; and there is no record that Thomas Jefferson was married more than twice. It is not questioned that the mirth-making race of Jefferson has descended from the lovely lady who died of laughter on the Plymouth stage ; but either the date of her death or that of Joseph Jefferson's birth has been incorrectly stated. The true date of her death, probably, is 1776. One account says that Joseph Jefferson was born literally upon the stage, and that his mother died shortly afterward. It is a coincidence, bearing on the question of descent, that the Jefferson of our day, Rip Van Winkle, suffers agony at the base of the brain, from inordinate laughter.

Tate Wilkinson,[1] in his agreeable *Memoirs* (1790), a work containing several allusions to Thomas Jefferson, pays a tribute to the first Mrs. Jefferson, when referring to the Exeter episode of Jefferson's career as a manager : —

"Early in December, 1764, I set off for Exeter, where Mr. Jefferson, my old friend and acquaintance in Dublin and London, was then become the manager, and everything then promised most flatteringly that he would soon make a fortune. But the substance is often changed for a shadow, nor are managers' gains so easily amassed as the public can gather it for them. His invitation had double allurement : first, novelty, which was ever prevalent ; and next, to see so pleasant and friendly a man as he had ever proved to me. I joined him and his new troop. Mr. Jefferson was at that time endeavouring — not without encouragement — to bring that theatre into a regular and established reputation. He had engaged Mr. Reddish[2] and many other good performers. Mrs.

---

[1] TATE WILKINSON was born on October 27, 1739, and he died on December 1, 1803.

[2] SAMUEL REDDISH. — He was born in 1740, became insane in 1779,

B

Jefferson, his first wife, was then living. She had one of the best dispositions that ever harboured in a human breast; and, more extraordinary, joined to that meekness, she was one of the most elegant women ever beheld."

Jefferson's second wife was Miss Wood, sister to a public singer of that name, then distinguished in London. She was a worthy lady, though apparently less amiable than her predecessor, and though unpropitious toward her step-son. She did not attempt the stage. The children of that union were two sons, Frank and George, and two daughters, Frances and Elizabeth. Frank has been mentioned, as at one time an officer of a royal yacht in Virginia Water, at Windsor. George became an actor, and a respectably good one; and he also displayed talent as a painter. It is said that a titled lady, resident near Ripon, established in her house a gallery of his works, and bought everything that he painted, — binding him not to sell his productions to any other person. Elizabeth died in youth. Frances was married to Mr. Samuel Butler,[1] manager of the Harrowgate, Beverly, and Richmond theatres, Yorkshire; and in after time was known upon the

and died in 1785, in an asylum at York. John Taylor, who saw and knew him, records that he chiefly distinguished himself in the Shakespeare characters of Edgar, Posthumus, and Henry the Sixth.

[1] In St. Mary's Church at Beverly, Yorkshire, is a tablet bearing this inscription : —

" IN MEMORY OF

SAMUEL BUTLER.

' A poor player, that struts and
frets his hour upon the stage, and
then is heard no more.'

Obt. June 15, 1812.

Æt. 62."

stage, both as manager and actress. F. C. Wemyss, when a youth of eighteen, joined Mrs. Butler's dramatic company (April 12, 1815) at Kendal, in Westmoreland ; and he records in his *Theatrical Biography*, that he there was introduced by the lady to George Jefferson, her brother, who was stage manager. That branch of the Jefferson family, however, contributed nothing of great importance to the stage. Reference, though, should be made to the professional career of Samuel W. Butler, son of Mr. and Mrs. Samuel Butler above mentioned, and grandson of Thomas Jefferson. That actor appeared at the Bowery theatre, New York, on December 14, 1831, as Coriolanus, and subsequently he played Virginius, and other parts. On November 4, 1841, he came forward at the Park theatre, as Hamlet, and on November 9, he acted Walder, in *Walder, the Avenger*. Ireland says that, although "handsome in person, graceful in action, and correct in elocution, he still lacked the inspiration necessary to rank him as an artist of the first class." His wife, who accompanied him in America, surpassed him in public favour, — acting Louisa, in *The Dead Shot*, and also Gil Blas. Mr. and Mrs. Butler returned to England. Samuel William Butler died on July 17, 1845, aged forty-one, and was buried in Ardwick cemetery, Manchester. Charles Swain wrote his epitaph, which is here transcribed from a valuable collection of *Curious Epitaphs*, made by the learned antiquary, William Andrews, of Hull, England, and published in 1884. Mr. Andrews mentions a sketch of the life of Butler, written by Mr. John Evans and printed in *Papers of the Manchester Literary Club*, in 1877. This is the epitaph :—

"Here rest the mortal remains of Samuel William Butler, Tragedian. In him the stage lost a highly-gifted and accomplished actor, on whose tongue the noblest creations of the poet found truthful utterance. After long and severe suffering he departed this life the 17th day of July in the year of our Lord, 1845. Aged 41 years.

> "Whence this ambition, whence this proud desire,
> This love of fame, this longing to aspire?
> To gather laurels in their greenest bloom,
> To honour life and sanctify the tomb?
> 'Tis the Divinity that never dies,
> Which prompts the soul of genius still to rise.
> Though fades the laurel leaf by leaf away,
> The soul hath prescience of a fadeless day;
> And God's eternal promise, like a star,
> From faded hopes still points to hopes afar;
> Where weary hearts for consolation trust,
> And bliss immortal quickens from the dust.
> On this great hope the painter, actor, bard,
> And all who ever strove for fame's reward,
> Must rest at last; and all that earth have trod
> Still need the grace of a forgiving God."

Thomas Jefferson had a long career. He was on the stage from about 1746 to almost the day of his death, in 1807, — a period of sixty years. At first a rover, he saw many parts of the British kingdom, and became a favourite in the theatrical circles of many communities. He then settled into the groove of theatrical management, and there he remained till the last. His most prosperous days were those that he passed at Plymouth, where he was established by chance. He had been asked to become the manager of the Plymouth theatre, for a salary and one-third of the profits, and he agreed, — on condition that the interior of the theatre should be renovated. This was promised, and he there-

OLD PLYMOUTH THEATRE.

upon sent forward carpenters and painters, from the theatre at Dublin, where (about 1760) he happened to be acting, to do the work. Before those artisans reached Plymouth, the owner of the theatre, Mr. Kerby, had died; nevertheless they were permitted, by his representative, to proceed in their task. Jefferson soon followed, with his theatrical company, but on arriving was astonished to learn that the building materials used by his mechanics had been supplied on the credit of his name, which was well known and highly respected, and that he now already owed £261 to the tradespeople of the town. The heir-at-law refused to assume that debt, or undertake any responsibility in the matter; and, thus hampered, Jefferson determined to secure a lease of the theatre, — buying its scenery and wardrobe, — and to make Plymouth his permanent residence. That project was fulfilled. He remained sole proprietor till 1770, when he sold one-third interest to Mr. Foote, of Exe-. ter, with whom, in the mean time, he had been associated in the ownership of the Exeter theatre, and another third to Mr. Wolfe, of Pynn. This partnership lasted till 1784, when, upon the death of Foote, Jefferson inherited half his share, and Wolfe the other half, in trust. Three years later, in the winter of 1787, John Bernard[1] purchased from Jefferson a third interest in

---

[1] JOHN BERNARD. — This actor, famous in his day for the perfection of his dry humour and finished manners, and equally excellent in the lines of acting typified by Lord Ogleby and Dashwould, was born at Portsmouth, England, in 1756. He went on the stage in 1774, and left it in 1820. After a time of provincial tribulation, he succeeded in winning a good rank on the London stage, and was long a favourite at Covent Garden. Wignell engaged him to come to Philadelphia in 1797, and he was there connected with the Chestnut Street theatre until 1803, when he removed to Boston,

the Plymouth theatre, for £400, and thereafter Jefferson, Bernard, and Wolfe were partners in its management, till the season of 1795-96, when Bernard sold his share, apparently to another Mr. Foote, and emigrated to America. Jefferson, a sufferer from gout, had become infirm, — so that he had to be helped in and out from house to theatre, — and after Bernard's departure he did not long retain his Plymouth property, but sold it for the consideration of an annual benefit, clear of expenses, as long as he should live. That contract was fulfilled, and the veteran received a testimonial each year till his death.[1] He derived support, also, as an annuitant, from the Covent Garden Theatrical Fund, of which he had long been a member. His last days, notwithstanding illness and trouble, were marked by cheerful resignation. He was an entertaining companion, and was always in good spirits. His last appearance on the stage was made in Aaron Hill's tragedy of *Zara*, as the aged, dying monarch, Lusignan, a character that he represented, seated in a chair. Wood mentions

where he remained three years. In 1807 he appeared at the New York Park, and he was last seen in New York in 1813 at the Commonwealth theatre, corner of Broadway and White street. He returned to England, and died in London, November 29, 1828, aged seventy-two. His *Retrospections of the Stage*, edited by his son, William Bayle Bernard, is a charming book, and one of the best contributions that have been made to the history of the English stage. He left papers, also, from which his son compiled and edited *Early Days of the American Stage*, first published in Tallis's *Dramatic Magazine* (December, 1850, *et seq.*). Bayle Bernard died in London, August 9, 1875. He was the author of many plays, notably of two versions of *Rip Van Winkle*.

[1] "JEFFERSON'S benefit (at Plymouth) is always well and fashionably attended, and we are happy to add the last two years have been particularly lucrative." — Gilliland's *Dramatic Mirror*.

that incident, in his *Personal Recollections*, and refers to
an acquaintance of his, who witnessed the ceremony of
Jefferson's final retirement.   (The tragedy of *Zara*, produced at Drury Lane in 1736, was borrowed from Voltaire's *Zaire*.)   At the time of his death, which speedily
followed his farewell, Jefferson was at Ripon, on a visit
to his daughter Frances, Mrs. Samuel Butler, and it
was there that he was seen by Drinkwater Meadows.
His residence in Plymouth was a house adjoining the
theatre.   A view of those premises occurs in James
Winston's *Theatric Tourist*, and Winston directs attention to the comedian's bedroom window, which is visible
in that print.   It was in this theatre that the first Mrs.
Jefferson died ; and it was in this house, no doubt, that
Joseph Jefferson was born, — the actor who first made
the name conspicuous in American theatrical history.
The old Plymouth theatre, — a queer little two-story
building, having two small doors and seven small windows, — was burnt down in 1863.

In Bernard's first season with Jefferson (1787) at
Plymouth, the dramatic company, he says, was "more
select than numerous.   Jefferson, in the old men, serious
and comic, was a host.   Wolfe, my other partner, was
a respectable actor, and Mrs. Bernard and myself were
established favourites, from the metropolis.   Among
the corps was a Mr. Prigmore," — who afterwards came
to America.   The same writer describes, in a sprightly
strain, the average audience with which the actors at the
Plymouth theatre were favoured : —

"Sailors in general, I believe, are very fond of play-houses.   This
may be partly because they find their ships work-houses, and partly
because the former are the readiest places of amusement they can

visit when ashore. I remember, on my first trip to Plymouth, I was rather startled at observing the effect which acting took on them, as also their mode of conducting themselves during a performance. It was a common occurrence, when no officers were present, for a tar in the gallery, who observed a messmate in the pit that he wished to address, to sling himself over and descend by the pillars, treading on every stray finger and bill in his way. When his communication was over, and before an officer could seize him, up again he went like a cat, and was speedily anchored alongside of 'Bet, sweet Blossom.' The pit they called the hold; the gallery, up aloft, or the main-top landing; the boxes, the cabin; and the stage, the quarter-deck. Every General and gentleman they saluted as a skipper; every soldier was a jolly, or lobster; and the varieties of old and young men who were not in command they collectively designated swabs. Jefferson, being the eldest, was a Rear-Admiral, and I was a Commodore."

The merry temperament of Jefferson and the drifting kind of life that he led, in common with his comrades of the sock, are suggested in this anecdote, from the same book : —

"On arriving at Plymouth (1791) I found, to my great surprise, the company collected, but no preparations for the opening of the theatre. Wolfe and Jefferson were away, on one of their temporary schemes, and their precise point of destination I could not ascertain, till Jefferson came over from the little town of Lostwithiel, bringing with him the pleasing intelligence that the result of the speculation had placed all our scenery and wardrobe in jeopardy.[1] I agreed to

---

[1] The cost of conducting a theatre, however, was much less, in old days, than it is now, because the salaries paid to actors were smaller. About 1680 the highest salary paid to an actor was six shillings and threepence a day. About 1773 the total payment, for a week, at Drury Lane, amounted to about £523. In 1750 Quin was paid £1000 a year, by Rich, at Covent Garden, — the highest salary given to any actor on the English stage, up to that time. Dunlap states his total expenses, at the Park theatre, New York, in the season of 1798–99, at less than $1200 a week.

go back with him and play for his benefit, taking with me our singer, a very pleasant fellow, of the name of West.

"On crossing the ferry we bought a quantity of prawns, which we agreed to reserve for a snack at an inn, where Jefferson said there was some of the finest ale in the country. West and myself, however, could not resist our propensities towards a dozen of the prawns, which, lying at the top, happened to be the largest, in the manner of pottled strawberries, to cover a hundred small ones. Coming to a hill, West and I jumped out of the coach, leaving Jefferson to take care of the fish. We had just reached the summit when we heard a great bawling behind us, and looking round perceived the coach standing still at the foot of the ascent, and Jefferson leaning out of the window and waving his hand. Imagining some accident had happened, down we both ran, at our utmost speed, and inquired the matter. Jefferson held up the handkerchief of diminutive prawns to our view, and replied, 'I wished to know if you wouldn't like a few of the large ones.' There was so much pleasantry in this reproof that we could only look in each other's face, laugh, and toil up the hill again."

Ryley's *Itinerant*[1] gives pleasant glimpses of Thomas Jefferson : —

"Tom Blanchard came to play a few nights, and with him Jefferson of Exeter. During their stay we received an invitation to perform *The School for Scandal* and *An Agreeable Surprise*, at Torr Abbey, on some grand public occasion which now slips my memory. Three chaises conveyed the major part of the company. Jefferson rode his own horse, and I walked, with my dogs and gun. During the journey, we thought of nothing but British hospitality and good cheer. Rich wines and fat venison were descanted upon, with epicurean volubility: when, behold, we were shown into a cold, comfortless servants' hall, with a stone floor. Jefferson, who was a

---

[1] SAMUEL WILLIAM RYLEY, born 1755, died 1837. Author of a musical farce, called *The Civilian, or Farmer turned Footman* (1792), a comic opera on the subject of Smollett's novel of *Roderick Random* (1793), and a monologue entertainment entitled *New Brooms*, which contains several songs. His *Itinerant, or Genuine Memoirs of an Actor*, was published in 1808.

martyr to the gout, looked around him with disgust; and when the
servant unfeelingly inquired whether we *chose* any dinner, he replied:
' Tell your master, friend, that after his death he had better have a
bad epitaph than the players' ill report while he lives.' So saying
he remounted his horse, and left us to do the play as well as we
could without him. This rebuke had a good effect, for the butler
soon made his appearance, with an apology, and the players received
courteous entertainment during their stay at Torr Abbey."

One of the anecdotes told by Ryley, has been illustrated with an etching by Cruickshank, published in
The Humourist : —

" The last night of Jefferson's engagement, he played *Hamlet*, for
his own benefit ; and Tom Blanchard, ever accommodating, agreed
to double Guildenstern with the Grave-Digger. When Hamlet
called for ' the recorders,' Blanchard, who delighted in a joke, instead
of a flute brought on a bassoon, used in the orchestra. Jefferson,
after composing his countenance, which the sight of this instrument
had considerably discomposed, went on with the scene : —
   ' *H.* Will you play upon this pipe?
   ' *G.* My lord, I cannot.
   ' *H.* I pray you.
   ' *G.* Believe me, I cannot.
   ' *H.* I do beseech you.
   ' *G.* Well, my lord, since you are so very pressing, I will do my
best.'
   " Tom, who was a good musician, immediately struck up *Lady
Coventry's Minuet*, and went through the whole strain, — which fin-
ished the scene ; for Hamlet had not another word to say for him-
self."

Bernard speaks of Benjamin Haydon, father of the
painter, as a resident of Plymouth, in the days of his
management with Jefferson, and as his friend and agent.
The elder Haydon was in the habit of meeting Jefferson
and Wolfe, for consultation with them on the business
of the theatre, and regularly communicating with Ber-

nard, in London. When Bernard lived at Plymouth, he often dined with Haydon, and he tells this story of the boy who afterwards became so distinguished as an artist : —

"His son, the present artist of celebrity, a spirited, intelligent little fellow about ten years of age, used to listen to my songs, and laugh heartily at my jokes, whenever I dined at his father's. One evening I was playing Sharp, in *The Lying Valet*, when he and my friend Benjamin were in the stage-box; and, on my repeating the words, ' I have had nothing to eat, since last Monday was a fortnight,' little Haydon exclaimed, in a tone audible to the whole house, ' What a whopper! Why, you dined at my father's house this afternoon.' It was on this occasion, I believe, Mr. B. R. Haydon [1] first attracted the notice of the public."

The memory of Thomas Jefferson is associated by Victor (*Secret History of the Green-Room*) with that of the brilliant actress, Frances Abington. That siren seems to have had many worshippers, and she remained, to the end of her days, a fascinating woman. She was born in London, in 1737, and died there, in Pall Mall, in March, 1815, and was buried in St. James's, Piccadilly. A life-like glimpse of her is given by John Taylor, in his *Records of my Life*, p. 230 ; and another by Henry Crabb Robinson, in his *Reminiscences*, p. 214. Her maiden name was Frances Barton. She married a musician named Abington. Her first appearance was made at the London Haymarket, in 1755, as Miranda, in *The Busybody*, and her last public appearance occurred on April 12, 1799. She was accounted a great Beatrice,

---

[1] BENJAMIN ROBERT HAYDON, born in 1786, committed suicide in 1846. His grave is in old Paddington churchyard, London, a little way from that of Sarah Siddons. *The Lying Valet*, mentioned by Bernard, is a comedy by David Garrick, first produced in 1741, at Goodman's Fields theatre.

in *Much Ado*, and she was the original Lady Teazle, in *The School for Scandal*, — a part that she made a fine lady, with no trace of rustic origin. Garrick referred to her as a " most worthless creature, as silly as she is false and treacherous." Robinson's picture of her is more agreeable : —

"June 16, 1811. — Dined at Sergeant Rough's, and met the once celebrated Mrs. Abington. From her present appearance one can hardly suppose she could ever have been otherwise than plain. She herself laughed at her snub-nose ; but she is erect, has a large, blue, expressive eye, and an agreeable voice. She spoke of her retirement from the stage as occasioned by the vexations of a theatrical life. She said she should have gone mad, if she had not quitted her profession. She has lost all her professional feelings, and when she goes to the theatre can laugh and cry like a child ; but the trouble is too great, and she does not often go.

"It is so much a thing of course that a retired actor should be a *laudator temporis acti*, that I felt unwilling to draw from her any opinion of her successors. Mrs. Siddons, however, she praised, though not with the warmth of a genuine admirer. She said : ' Early in life Mrs. Siddons was anxious to succeed in comedy, and played Rosalind before I retired.' In speaking of the modern declamation and the too elaborate emphasis given to insignificant words, she said, ' That was brought in by them ' (the Kembles). She spoke with admiration of the Covent Garden horses, and I have no doubt that her praise was meant to have the effect of satire.

"Of all the present (1811) actors Murray most resembles Garrick. She spoke of Barry with great warmth. He was a nightingale. Such a voice was never heard. He confined himself to characters of great tenderness and sweetness, such as Romeo. She admitted the infinite superiority of Garrick, in genius. His excellence lay in the bursts and quick transitions of passion, and in the variety and universality of his genius. Mrs. Abington would not have led me to suppose she had been on the stage, by either her manner or the substance of her conversation. She speaks with the ease of a per-

MRS. ABINGTON.

son used to good society, rather than with the assurance of one whose business it was to imitate that ease."

The Covent Garden horses, mentioned by Mrs. Abington, were a number of steeds exhibited at that theatre, in 1811, in processions, in *Blue Beard* and *The Forty Thieves*. Sheridan referred to them in this couplet : —

> " How arts improve in this degenerate age !
> Peers mount the box, and horses tread the stage ! "

Thomas Jefferson's life seems to have been simple, industrious, and kindly. Although he was well known, he never filled a place of great prominence in the public eye or in the records of his time. The man was, obviously, more than the actor. To us, as his figure glimmers forth in the dim retrospect of the vanishing past, he is far less remarkable for what he achieved than for the associations that cluster around his name, and for what we are enabled to perceive of those charming characteristics which have survived in his living descendants. It was a romantic period through which Thomas Jefferson lived. It was a time, in theatrical annals, of varied and brilliant activity. The old story of Garrick's dethronement of the classic style of acting makes its background. The great Newton, in science, and Betterton and Elizabeth Barry, in art, had but lately died, when Jefferson was born. Congreve was still alive. Cibber, with the courtly graces of the age of Queen Anne, was just passing from the scene, while Quin,[1]

---

[1] JAMES QUIN, 1693-1766. — The great Falstaff of the eighteenth century, and a man of sturdy intellect, imperious character, and caustic wit. He was buried in Bath Abbey, where the visitor may see his epitaph, written by Garrick. " I can only recommend a man who wants to see a

with his Roman dignity and pompous declamation,
was soon to follow. Fielding was writing his novels.
and Sheridan his comedies. It was the time, in acting,
of Garrick, Barry, Henderson, Woodward, Macklin,
Foote, Weston, Mossop, Shuter, King, Mrs. Pritchard,
Mrs. Cibber, Mrs. Woffington, and Mrs. Yates. It was
the time, in poetry, of Cowper, Crabbe, Gray, Goldsmith,
and Robert Burns. Burke and Fox and Pitt were treading the stately heights of oratory, and the terrible Earl
of Chatham was swaying the rod of empire. To Thomas
Jefferson must have come, as news of the passing day,
the thrilling martial story of Clive's exploits in India,
and the strange and startling tale of Washington's auda-
cious and successful rebellion in America. He might
have heard of the glorious death of Wolfe, upon the
Plains of Abraham, and his gaze may have followed the
funeral cortege that bore that young hero to his grave
in Greenwich church. He could have noted, as an
incident of the hour, the suicide of Thomas Chatterton,
in Brook street, Holborn. He possibly saw, in Westminster Hall, the historic pageant of the trial of Warren

character perfectly played to see Quin in *Falstaff*." — *Foote*. "His sentiments, though hid under the rough manner he had assumed, would have
done honour to Cato." — *George Anne Bellamy*. One of his intimates
was James Thomson, the poet, who wrote of him, in *The Castle of Indolence*, Canto I., stanza 67 : —

> " Here whilom lagged the *Esopus* of the age:
> But called by fame, in soul yprickéd deep,
> A noble pride restored him to the stage,
> And roused him like a giant from his sleep.
> Even from his slumbers we advantage reap:
> With double force the enlivened scene he wakes,
> Yet quits not nature's bounds. He knows to keep
> Each due decorum. Now the heart he shakes,
> And now with well-urged sense the enlighten'd judgment takes."

Hastings, and, in Westminster Abbey, the grief of a nation over the burial of David Garrick, and afterwards of Samuel Johnson. Some of the greatest men of the eighteenth century witnessed his acting, in the theatres of London and Dublin. Living from 1728 until 1807, he could have seen, as contemporary publications, the later writings of Pope and the earlier writings of Wordsworth and Sir Walter Scott. He lasted until close upon the regency of George the Fourth, and passed away just as the accumulated force of Goethe and Niebuhr and the new powers of Coleridge, Byron, and Shelley were opening a great era in human thought. It cannot be otherwise than instructive to muse upon the experience of a man before whose vision such memorable scenes and persons arose, and into whose life so much was crowded of impressive spectacle and admonitive fortune.

One of the clearest impressions derived from the story of Thomas Jefferson's life is the impression of his docile amiability and droll humour. A manly, independent spirit, a gentle disposition, and an inveterate love of fun seem to have been the principal attributes of his character, and those attributes have marked his race. The apostles of heredity are somewhat overfond of telling us about transmitted evil. It is a comfort occasionally to remember that good also can be inherited. Jefferson was scrupulously honest, but he had no economy. The will of the facetious Weston,[1]

---

[1] THOMAS WESTON, 1727–1776, was a son of the chief cook to George the Second. After a wild, roving youth, he became an actor. He was in Garrick's company, at Drury Lane, and he was with Foote, at the old Haymarket. His excellence was shown in Scrub, Drugger, and Jerry

that droll comedian, who almost rivalled Garrick in
Abel Drugger, and for whom Foote wrote the character
of Jerry Sneak, contains this clause : "*Item*. I having
played under the management of Mr. Jefferson, at
Richmond, and received from him every politeness;
I therefore leave him all my stock of prudence, it being
the only good quality I think he stands in need of."

"I acted Bayes, at Exeter," says Tate Wilkinson,
"and spoke a speech or two in the manner of old
Andrew Brice, a printer of that city, and an eccentric
genius. It struck the whole audience like electricity.
Mr. Jefferson, who performed Johnson, was so taken
by surprise that he could not proceed for laughter."

Elsewhere in Wilkinson's *Memoirs* (Vol. III., p. 193)
the reader sees Jefferson, in the full tide of innocent,
sportive mischief, demurely chaffing the pompous and
truculent Henry Mossop, — a man of great ability, but
one who lacked the sense of humour, and therefore was
the easy prey of the joker. Both were members, at that
time, of the Smock Alley theatre, in Dublin : —

"Jefferson, who loved a little mischief, said to Mossop one day,
'Sir, I was last night at Crow Street, where Wilkinson, in *Tragedy
à-la-Mode* and in *Bayes*, had taken very great liberties indeed,' and
added that the audience were ill-natured enough to be highly entertained; on which Mossop snuffed the air, put his hand on his sword,
and, turning upon his heel, replied. 'Yes, sir; but *he only takes me
off a little*,' and made his angry departure. After which Jefferson
never again renewed the subject; but was astonished, after his
repeated and open threats of vengeance, he had not acted more

---

Sneak. He seems, personally, to have been a compound of Charles
Surface and Dick Swiveller. He was merry, comic, improvident, and too
fond of the bottle for his own good. An interesting sketch of him is given
in John Galt's *Lives of the Players*, Vol. I., p. 232.

consistently. And after the said Jefferson's telling me that circumstance I never heard more of Mr. Mossop's sword, pistol, or anger." Mossop had previously, in a comic interview with Wilkinson, in the street, threatened him with violence. "'Sir,' said Mossop,[1] 'you are going to play in Crow Street theatre with Barry, sir, and, sir, I will run you through the body, sir, if you take the liberty to attempt my manner, by any mimicry on the stage. You must promise me, sir, on your honour, you will not dare attempt it. If you break that promise, sir, you cannot live; and you, Mr. Wil-kinson, must die, as you must meet me the next day, and I shall kill you, sir.' I told him it was impossible to comply with that his mandate."

A reference to Thomas Jefferson, showing how near, for the second time, he came to a sudden, accidental death, occurs in a sketch of Theophilus Cibber, published in the *Biographia Dramatica*. Theophilus, the profligate son of the poet laureate, Colley Cibber, was drowned, in 1758, aged fifty-five, on a voyage from England to Ireland. In recording that catastrophe, the *Biographia* makes allusion to Jefferson : —

"Mr. Cibber embarked at Parkgate, together with Mr. Maddox, the celebrated wire-dancer, who had also been engaged as an auxiliary to the same theatre,[2] on board the Dublin trader, some time in the month of October; but the high winds which are frequent at that time of the year in St. George's channel, and which are fatal to many vessels in the passage from this kingdom to Ireland, proved particularly so to this. The vessel was driven to the coast of Scotland, where it was cast away, every soul in it (and the passengers were extremely numerous) perishing in the waves, and the ship

---

[1] Mossop (1729–1773) died in London, in great penury, — which, however, he kept a secret, — and was buried in or near Chelsea church. I tried, in 1885, to find his grave, but without success. It is unmarked.

[2] Those performers were on their way to join the Theatre Royal in Smock alley, Dublin, managed by Thomas Sheridan, who needed recruits, as he had been much pressed, in that year, 1758, by the opposition of the new theatre in Crow street. Indeed, it ruined him there.

C

itself so entirely lost that scarcely any vestige of it remained, to indicate where it had been wrecked, excepting a box containing books and papers which were known to be Mr. Cibber's, and which were cast up on the western coast of Scotland. [So said Mr. Baker,[1] but this was a mistake; for we have since found that in this ship, in which Theoph. Cibber, Maddox, and others perished, Mr. and Mrs. Jefferson, Mr. Arthur and family, Mrs. Chambers, and some others were passengers, and, by leaping into a small boat, were saved."]

A peculiarity in Thomas Jefferson's character, and a singular incident in his experience, are thus stated by his grand-daughter, Elizabeth Jefferson, in a letter to the present biographer : —

"My grandfather had a great aversion to litigation and lawyers. I remember having been told of an instance of this. He had paid a large sum of money to a creditor, but had mislaid the receipt; and it happened that in time this same bill was again presented for payment. He explained and protested, but his creditor was positive, and finally my grandfather was sent to jail. My father voluntarily went there, along with him, to take care of him, and for a whole year they endured imprisonment. At last the missing receipt was found, and their prison doors were opened. My grandfather was now urged to bring an action for damages, and, doubtless, he might have recovered a large sum; but his invincible repugnance to litigation restrained him, and he resolutely refused to proceed, being content with his liberty and with the contrite apology offered by his hard creditor. My father's devotion to him was never forgotten; nor — by his step-mother — was it ever forgiven."

Thomas Jefferson died at Ripon, January 24, 1807. Contemporary records of the event offer a strong contrast to the kind of chronicle which is made, in modern journals, of the death of a notable man. The *Gentle-*

---

[1] DAVID ERSKINE BAKER, who projected and began the *Biographia*, bringing the record to 1764. ISAAC REED, F.A.S., subsequently continued this useful chronicle to 1782, and STEPHEN JONES brought it onward to 1811.

man's Magazine, for March, 1807, presents, for example, the subjoined obituary notice: —

"Died. — At Ripon, County of York, while on a visit to a daughter, Mr. Jefferson, comedian, — the friend, contemporary, and exact prototype of the immortal Garrick. He had resided many years at Plymouth; and as often as his age and infirmities permitted, he appeared on that stage, in characters adapted to lameness and decay, and performed them admirably, particularly at his last benefit, when he personated Lusignan and Lord Chalkstone. We know not whether Mr. Hull or Mr. Jefferson was the father of the British stage; they were both of nearly an equal standing. To the Theatrical Fund,[1] of which the former is founder and treasurer, the latter owed the chief support of his old age."

---

[1] THE THEATRICAL FUND of London was instituted at Covent Garden, December 22, 1765, and confirmed by act of Parliament in 1766. The plan of it was suggested by George Mattocks, and was carried into practical effect by Thomas Hull. In the churchyard of St. Margaret's, near the north porch of Westminster Abbey, could once be read, on a gravestone, this inscription, — the lines by John Taylor: —

" Also to the Memory of
THOMAS HULL, Esq.,
Late of the
Theatre Royal, Covent Garden,
who departed this life
April 22, 1808,
In the 79th year of his age.

" Hull, long respected in the scenic art,
On this world's stage sustained a virtuous part;
And some memorial of his zeal to shew
For his loved Art, and shelter age from woe,
Founded that noble Fund which guards his name,
Embalmed by Gratitude, enshrined by Fame."

At Chingford in Essex, within the precincts of a most interesting old church, now in ruins, I one day came upon a weather-beaten tombstone, bearing this inscription: —

" In memory of Mr. John Jefferson, late of this parish, who departed this life January 27, 1794, in the 71st year of his age. Also of Mrs. Mary Jefferson, wife of the above. June 2, 1775. Aged 48. Tom Jefferson. 1804. 81."

These may have been relatives of old Thomas Jefferson. It seemed worth while to copy the records.

A passing reference to the same bereavement is made in the *Annual Register*, for 1807 : —

"Mr. Jefferson was on a visit to a daughter, who is settled in Yorkshire, when death closed the last scenes of this honest, pleasant, much esteemed man."

These notices of the life of Thomas Jefferson cannot better be embellished than with the suggestive reflections made by Mr. James Smith, of Melbourne, a diligent and appreciative student of theatrical history, and one of the most sprightly and ingenious writers of the Australian world : —

"What times to have lived in," that moralist exclaims, "and what men and women to have known ! He saw Old Drury in the height of its glory, and Garrick in the zenith of his renown. He flirted with Kitty Clive, and supped with Fanny Abington. He listened to the silver tones of Spranger Barry, and was melted by the pathos of Susanna Cibber. He chuckled at the sight of Sam Foote mimicking everybody, and of Tate Wilkinson mimicking Sam Foote. He saw the curtain rise before an audience that included Lord Chancellor Camden and Lord Chief Justice Mansfield, William Hogarth and Charles Churchill, Edmund Burke and Edward Gibbon. He heard Goldsmith's child-like laugh and Dr. Johnson's gruff applause. He saw the courtly sarcasm sparkle in Horace Walpole's eyes, and the jest quivering on Selwyn's lip. He recognised the quaint figure of Sir Joshua Reynolds in the boxes, and the brilliant, homely face of Thomas Gainsborough in the pit. And, above all, he trod the same stage with the English Roscius, and was privileged to watch every movement of that marvellous face. This was, indeed, an uncommon and a happy fate! What pleasant hours he must have spent with Garrick, at Hampton, and what a fund of anecdote he must have accumulated, with which, in his age, to charm his cronies at Plymouth! He had seen King carry the town by storm as Lord Ogleby in *The Clandestine Marriage*, and Garrick take his farewell of the stage. He could recall the airy flutter of Dodd ; the rollicking Irish humour of Moody ; the well-bred ease

THOMAS JEFFERSON

of Palmer; the eloquent by-play of Parsons; the versatility of Bannister; the strong, melodious voice of Holland; the ardour of Powell; the whimsical drollery of Reddish; Mossop's harmonious delivery, and Macklin's rumbling growl. He had seen the Abingtons, the Baddeleys, the Cibbers, the Clives, and the whole splendid phalanx of the Garrick dynasty, pass from the scene; and he had lived to view the rise of the Kembles, and to hear the thrilling accents of Mrs. Siddons, and the sweet, bubbling laugh of Dora Jordan. What reminiscences might have been written by Thomas Jefferson!"

Dramatic art is not the assumption of disguises, but the idealised exposition of nature and the poetic interpretation of character, by means of action. Human capacity in that art — as experience and observation have amply shown — is sharply limited; for, in acting, everything centres in the personality of the individual. The best success of the best actor is gained in only a few characters, and those such as comprise, however intermingled with other ingredients, attributes sympathetic with his own. Thomas Jefferson acted parts of every description, from the Bleeding Soldier up to Macbeth, and from Katherine's music-master up to Hamlet. In the course of the twenty-five years during which, at intervals, he performed in Drury Lane, he presented about sixty characters. In all of them he was efficient; in some of them he was excellent; in no one of them did he make an impression that has endured. Garrick is remembered as Don Felix and King Lear; Kemble, as Coriolanus and Penruddock; Edmund Kean, as The Stranger, Sir Edward Mortimer, and Othello; Cooke, as Sir Giles Overreach; Junius Brutus Booth, as Richard the Third; Macready, as Macbeth; Forrest, as Damon; Edwin Booth, as Hamlet and Richelieu; Henry Irving, as Mathias in *The Bells*, Becket, Lear, Hamlet, Louis, and Dr. Primrose : but of Thomas Jefferson, the memory is simply that of a clever, versatile actor, who followed the natural style of Garrick, excelled in the representation of kings and tyrants, and loved his joke. Some of the parts that he played, together with the titles of the plays in which they occur, and with occasional comment, are named in this catalogue.

REPERTORY OF THOMAS JEFFERSON

A.

Aubrey, in *The Fashionable Lover*. Comedy. By Richard Cumberland. Drury Lane, 1772.

B.

Balance, in *The Recruiting Officer*, — one of the fine comedies of Farquhar. Drury Lane, 1705. The scene is Shrewsbury. Farquhar was once a recruiting officer, and he is thought to have drawn his own character in that of Captain Plume. His Justice Balance was designed as a compliment to Mr. Berkely, then recorder of Shrewsbury; and Sylvia was drawn from Mr. Berkely's daughter. Jefferson acted Balance, on occasions of his benefit, in 1775 and 1776.

Belford, and also Baldwin, in *The Fatal Marriage, or The Innocent Adultery*. Tragedy. By Thomas Southerne. 1694. Altered by Garrick, and called *Isabella, or The Fatal Marriage*. Drury Lane.

Blandford, in *The Royal Slave*. Tragi-comedy. By William Cartwright, 1639. First acted in 1636, at Oxford, before Charles the First.

Buckingham, in Cibber's alteration of Shakespeare's tragedy of *Richard the Third*. Drury Lane, 1700.

C.

Chalkstone, in Garrick's farce of *Lethe*, first produced at Drury Lane, in 1748. It had been presented three years earlier, in a different form, at Goodman's Fields theatre, under the title of *Æsop in the Shades.* Garrick was the original Lord Chalkstone.

Cubla, in *Zingis.* Tragedy. By Alexander Dow. Drury Lane, 1769.

Captain Worthy, in *The Fair Quaker, or The Humours of the Navy.* Comedy. By Charles Shadwell, 1710. Altered by Captain Edward Thompson. Drury Lane, 1773.

Carlos, in *The Revenge.* Tragedy. By Dr. Edward Young, author of *Night Thoughts.* Drury Lane, 1721.

Careless, in *The Committee, or The Faithful Irishman.* Comedy. By Sir Robert Howard. 1665.

Careless, in *The Double Gallant, or The Sick Lady's Cure.* Comedy. By Colley Cibber. Haymarket, 1707.

Colonel Britton, in *The Wonder.* Comedy. By Susanna Centlivre. Drury Lane, 1713-14.

Colonel Rivers, in *False Delicacy.* Comedy. By Hugh Kelly. Drury Lane, 1768. Jefferson acted this part for his benefit, in 1773.

Colonel Lambert, in *The Hypocrite.* An alteration of Cibber's play of *The Nonjuror*, 1718, which, in turn, was based on Molière's *Tartuffe*, made by Isaac Bickerstaff, 1768. The chief part in *The Nonjuror* is Dr. Wolf, a priest, who pretends to be an English churchman. In *The Hypocrite* Mawworm is the principal part, and that was acted, with great ability, by Thomas Weston. Drury Lane.

Cleomenes, in *Florizel and Perdita.* Pastoral Drama, in three acts, altered from Shakespeare's lovely comedy of *A Winter's Tale*, by Garrick, and produced at Drury Lane, in 1756.

Clytus, in *Alexander the Great.* Altered from Nathaniel Lee's tragedy of *The Rival Queens, or The Death of Alexander the Great.* Theatre Royal, 1677. Produced at both Covent Garden and Drury Lane, 1770. Roxana and Statira are in that play. Revived at Drury Lane, 1795. The author, a brilliant genius, died, at thirty-five, in 1691 or 1692, shortly after being released from Bedlam.

D.

Dolabella, in *All for Love, or The World Well Lost.* That is the tragedy in which Dryden imitated Shakespeare's *Antony and Cleopatra*, and which he said was the only one of his plays that he had written for himself. Theatre Royal, 1678. Dr. Johnson remarks of this play that the author, "by admitting the romantic omnipotence of love, has recommended as laudable and worthy of imitation that conduct which, through all ages, the good have censured as vicious, and the bad despised as foolish."

Don Frederick, and also Don John, in *The Chances*. Comedy. By Beaumont and Fletcher, 1647. Altered by the Duke of Buckingham, 1682. Altered by Garrick, 1773, who acted Don John. Drury Lane.

Dunelm, in *Athelstan*. Tragedy. By Dr. John Browne, once Bishop of Carlisle. Drury Lane, 1756.

E.

Earl of Devon, in *Alfred*. Tragedy. By David Mallet. Altered by Garrick. Drury Lane, 1773.

Emperor of Germany, in *The Heroine of the Cave*. Tragedy. Begun by Henry Jones, and finished by Paul Hiffernan. Acted, for the benefit of Samuel Reddish, March 19, 1774.

F.

Friar John, in Shakespeare's *Romeo and Juliet*. This part is usually omitted: it was, however, restored by Irving (1882).

Fairfield, in *The Man of the Mill*. 1765. A burlesque opera, written by "Signor Squallini," in satire of *The Maid of the Mill*, by Isaac Bickerstaff, — a comic opera, on the subject of Samuel Richardson's novel of *Pamela*. Covent Garden, 1765.

G.

Gloster, in *Jane Shore*. Tragedy. By Nicholas Rowe. Drury Lane, 1713.

Mrs. Siddons told Dean Milman that one line in Rowe's tragedy of *Jane Shore* was the most effective she ever uttered: "'Twas he — 'twas Hastings."

In 1772 Mrs. Canning — mother of the statesman, George Canning (1770–1827), then a child of two years — made her first appearance on the stage, acting Jane Shore in that piece. Garrick acted Shore. An allusion to that incident occurs in Bernard's *Retrospections*, Vol. I., p. 13 : —

"At Drury Lane I remember seeing *Jane Shore*, on the evening that Mrs. Canning, the widow of an eminent counsellor, made her début, as the heroine. She was patronised by numerous persons of distinction, and the house was very favourable towards her. But, independently of the personal interest which attended her attempt, Mrs. Canning put forth claims upon the approbation of the critical. One thing, however, must be admitted; she was wonderfully well supported. Garrick was the Hastings, and Reddish (her future husband), the Dumont. I little thought as I sat in the pit that night, an ardent boy of sixteen, that I then beheld the lady who was destined, at some fifteen years' distance, to become the leading feature in a company of my own; nor that in the Gloster of the night, — admirably acted by Jefferson, — I beheld my partner in that management. (Plymouth.)"

Goodwin, in *The Brothers*. Tragedy. By Dr. Edward Young, author of *Night Thoughts*. Drury Lane, 1753.

Gratiano, in Shakespeare's comedy of *The Merchant of Venice*.

H.

Heartfree, in *The Provoked Wife*. Comedy. By Sir John Vanbrugh. Lincoln's Inn Fields, 1697. Quin was distinguished in it, as Sir John Brute.

Horatio, in *The Fair Penitent*. Tragedy. By Nicholas Rowe. Lincoln's Inn Fields, 1703.

I. AND J.

Iachimo and also Cloten, in Shakespeare's *Cymbeline*, altered by Garrick, 1761.

Jarvis, in *The Gamester*. Comedy. By Susanna Centlivre. Lincoln's Inn Fields, 1705; Drury Lane, 1758. There is an earlier play, with this title, by James Shirley (1637), which was altered by Garrick, and brought out at Drury Lane, in 1758; and there is a later one, by Edward Moore (1753), in which Mrs. Siddons acted Mrs. Beverley, and John Palmer was great as Stukeley. Moore died in 1757, and his grave is in the burial-ground which was given to London by Archbishop Tenison, in what was once called High street, Lambeth.

Johnson, in *The Rehearsal*. This capital comedy, by George Villiers, second Duke of Buckingham (1627, 1688), was produced at the Theatre Royal, in 1672, and in after years it afforded to Garrick, in the character of Bayes, originally Bilboa, an opportunity, which he brilliantly improved, for satirical imitation of the noted actors of the time. *The Rehearsal*, as is well known, suggested to Sheridan the admirably humourous farce of *The Critic*.

Jaques, in Shakespeare's comedy of *As You Like It*.

K.

Kathel, in *The Fatal Discovery*. Drury Lane, 1769. A tragedy by the Rev. John Home, author of *Douglas* — so amusingly described by Thackeray (*The Virginians*, chap. 11). Mr. Home was so unpopular, on political grounds, at the time of the production of this tragedy, that, when the fact of its authorship became known, the malcontents threatened to burn the theatre, if the piece was not withdrawn ; and Garrick, accordingly, withdrew it, after the twelfth night.

King Claudius, in *Hamlet*, — the Dane being acted by Garrick.

L.

Leonato, in Shakespeare's comedy of *Much Ado About Nothing.*

Littlestock, in *The Gamesters*, a comedy by Garrick, 1758, altered from *The Gamester*, by James Shirley.

Lord Morelove, in *The Careless Husband*. Theatre Royal, 1705. This is Colley Cibber's most polished comedy, and by some judges is considered his best. Lady Betty Modish occurs in it, — in which part Mrs. Oldfield "excellently acted an agreeably gay woman of quality, a little too conscious of her natural attractions." Lord Morelove is her devoted lover.

Lord Trinket, in *The Jealous Wife*. Comedy, by George Colman. Drury Lane, 1761.

Lovemore, in *The Way to Keep Him*, a three-act comedy by Arthur Murphy. Drury Lane, 1760. Jefferson acted this for his benefit, in 1771.

Lyon, in *The Reprisal, or The Tars of Old England*. Farce. By Tobias Smollett, the novelist. Drury Lane, 1757. Garrick had rejected a play by that author, entitled *The Regicide*, and Smollett had subsequently satirised him, as Brayer, in Mr. Melopyn's story, in *Roderick Random*. Garrick's acceptance of the poor farce of *The Reprisal* was, therefore, viewed as an act either of magnanimity or prudence.

M.

Mathusius, in *Tamanthes*.

Megistus, in *Zenobia*. Tragedy. By Arthur Murphy. Drury Lane, 1768. Adapted from the French of Crébillon.

Mirabel, in *The Way of the World*. Comedy. By William Congreve. Drury Lane, 1700. Jefferson acted this part for the benefit of Mrs. Abington.

Mercury, in *Amphytrion*. This piece is from the Latin, of Plautus. It was adapted by Molière, and afterwards by Dryden. An alteration of Dryden's piece, made by Dr. Hawkesworth, at Garrick's request, was produced at Drury Lane, in 1756.

Music-master, in Shakespeare's comedy of *The Taming of the Shrew*.

Myrtle, in *The Corsican Lovers*.

O.

Orsino, in Shakespeare's comedy of *Twelfth Night*.
Oswald, in *King Arthur*.

P.

Palamede, in *The Frenchified Lady Never in Paris*. Comedy. By Henry Dell. Covent Garden, 1757. Based on plays by Dryden and Cibber.

S.

Sir Tan Tivy, in *The Male Coquette, or Seventeen Hundred Fifty-seven*. Farce. By Garrick. Drury Lane, 1757.

Siffredi, in *Tancred and Sigismunda*. Tragedy. By James Thomson, author of *The Seasons*. The plot of this piece is found in *Gil Blas*. Drury Lane, 1745.

Sunderland, in *The Note of Hand, or A Trip to Newmarket*. Farce. By Richard Cumberland. Drury Lane, 1774.

Sir Epicure Mammon, in *The Alchemist*. This piece was an alteration of Ben Jonson's comedy. Garrick acted Abel Drugger, and was famously good in the character. A fine painting of Garrick as Abel Drugger is in the club-house of the Players, — presented to that institution by Joseph Jefferson (1890). Garrick's performance of Abel Drugger was so good that an infatuated young lady, who had begun matrimonial negotiations with him, became disgusted and abandoned her project; while a gentleman from Lichfield, who had brought from Garrick's brother a letter of introduction to the

great actor, would not deliver it, after seeing that impersonation, —
so great was his contempt for the person he then saw.

Garrick's acting of the part is described as follows, by a contemporary observer, Mr. Lichtenberg, who wrote some account of what he saw as a traveller in England, and whose observations were translated by Tom Taylor : —

"Abel Drugger's first appearance would disconcert the muscular economy of the wisest. His attitude, his dread of offending the doctor, his saying nothing, his gradual stealing in further and further, his impatience to be introduced, his joy to his friend Face, are imitable by none. When he first opens his mouth, the features of his face seem, as it were, to drop upon his tongue; it is all caution, — it is timorous, stammering, and inexpressible. When he stands under the conjuror, to have his features examined, his teeth, his beard, his little finger, his awkward simplicity, and his concern, mixed with hope, and fear, and joy, and avarice, and good nature, are beyond painting."

T.

Trueman, in *The Twin Rivals*. Comedy. By George Farquhar. Drury Lane, 1703.

Tullius Hostilius, in *The Roman Father*. Drury Lane, 1750. Tragedy, by William Whitehead, who succeeded Cibber, as Poet-Laureate, in 1757. It is based on the Roman story of the Horatii and the Curiatii, treated in *Les Horaces*, by Corneille, and made immortal by Rachel.

V.

Velasco, in *Alonzo*. Tragedy by the Rev. John Home. Drury Lane, 1773.

Vainlove, in *The Old Bachelor*. Comedy. By William Congreve (his first piece). Theatre Royal, 1693.

Thomas Jefferson's character developed itself along a conventional line. He had, indeed, the boldness to adopt the stage, — against which, in his time and for many years afterward, the respectable British parent is found protesting with severity and contempt. But when he did that he was an adventurous lad, with no position to lose, and the vocation of the actor no doubt consorted as well with his necessities as with his humour and talents. It does not appear that there was either moral courage or mental prescience in the choice. He was a bold, high-spirited youth. He was fascinated by the playhouse, and he drifted into acting as a source of pleasure and a means of advancement. When thus embarked, he soon sobered to the practical English view of duty, and thereafter he ambled calmly in the beaten track. Through what is known of his intellectual life, the inquirer discerns no impulse of positive originality, no exercise of creative power. His style as an actor was based on that of Garrick, and he could not have had a better model ; but he was scarcely more than a shadow of his great original. He took the parts as they came, and he applied to their illustration dramatic instinct of a fine quality and dramatic faculties of a good order. But he struck out no individual path. He resembled Garrick, as Davenport resembled Macready, or as Setchell resembled Burton : he was of the Garrick school, and that was all. His influence on the stage was not the influence of genius ; he did not come to destroy, but to fulfil, the tradition which he found. That he followed the lead of Garrick, and not of Quin, was significant rather of temperament than of deliberate choice : brilliancy and warmth allured him more than scholarship and formality : but, had he been attracted to the school of Quin rather than to that of Garrick, he still would have remained a disciple. His services to the stage, accordingly, were those of an able and generous man, working by conventional methods in a traditional groove. He sustained at a high level the dignity of his profession, and he was the more scrupu-

lously careful of the integrity of the theatre because
sensitive to the reproach under which it laboured.
While he did not reject Archer, Careless, Woodall,
Belmour, Scandal, and kindred shining scamps of old
English comedy, he, evidently, was the kind of man
who must have acted them, not from sympathy with
vice, not from immoral intent, but because experience
had shown them to be useful, and because they were in
possession of the stage.   He played them as he played
everything else, — as he played Jaques, and Horatio, and
Orsino, and as, had he lived in our day, he would have
played, with equal impartiality, Master Walter and
Joseph Surface, Ludovico and Adrastus, Alfred Evelyn
and Captain Bland.   He was a thorough actor ; he
helped to build up the British stage : he held, to the
end of a long life, the esteem of the public ; and he left
to history and to his descendants an interesting and
honourable name.

II

JOSEPH JEFFERSON

1774-1832

Joseph Jefferson, the second of the Jefferson Family of Actors, and one of the most honourably distinguished performers that have graced the theatre, was born at Plymouth, England, in 1774. His education was conducted with care, and he received, under the guidance of his parents, a thorough training for the stage. While yet a lad he acted in the Plymouth theatre, — after Bernard had become associated with his father and with Mr. Wolfe in its management. His youth, so far as can be judged from the little that is known of it, was commendable for patience, industry, and filial devotion. He appears to have matured early, and to have been capable of far-sighted views and the steady pursuit of a definite purpose in life. He did not find his home comfortable after his father's second marriage, and also he sympathised with the republican drift of feeling, which, at that disturbed period, — between the revolt of the British colonies in America and the French Revolution, — was, to a slight extent, rife in England. Those causes of discontent impelled him to emigrate to America. The opportunity was afforded by C. S. Powell, of Boston, who had come to England, in 1793, to enlist actors for the new theatre in that city. Powell agreed to pay the passage money, and a salary of $17 a week. Jefferson came over in 1795, and from that time his lot was cast with the people of this land. He never returned to England. His American career lasted thirty-seven years, and he deserved and received every mark of honour that the respect and affection of the community could bestow upon genius and virtue. His character was impressive, and at the same time winning. His life was pure. His professional exertions were well directed, and for a long time his name retained a brilliant prestige. Domestic afflictions and waning popularity, indeed, overshadowed his latter days ; but, when we remember this, we must also remember that the fifth act of life's drama cannot be otherwise than sad, and that this actor, before it came, had enjoyed, in ample abundance, the sunshine of prosperity.

The advent of Joseph Jefferson in America is associated with the infancy of the Republic and with an early period in the history of the American stage. In coming upon this incident, accordingly, the observer's thought is prompted to dwell for a moment upon the beginning of the theatre in this country. The acted drama came into America by way of the island of Jamaica, and the pioneer, if not the actual founder, of the American stage was the Irish comedian, John Moody, originally a barber, who, about the year 1745, came over from England to Jamaica, where, after a preliminary experiment with amateurs, he presently established a theatre, which he conducted with prosperity for four years. Moody had been an unsuccessful aspirant in tragedy, but subsequently he became distinguished as a comedian. On his return to London, in 1749, he was employed in Garrick's company at Drury Lane, and he then leased his theatrical property at Jamaica to a theatrical company headed by David Douglas and inclusive of Mr. Daniels, Miss Hamilton, Mr. Kershaw, Mr. Morris, and Mr. Smith. Those successors to Moody came across the Atlantic in 1751. It was a year of destructive hurricanes in Jamaica, yet the adventurous actors prospered there; and soon the news of their prosperity, finding its way back to England, stimulated other active spirits to follow in their track. So far the drama had not yet made a genuine lodgement upon the mainland. Such spirits were the more willing to venture because goaded by the spur of necessity. Garrick, who had defeated and overwhelmed the elocutionists in acting, was in complete possession of the dramatic field in London, and, for a time, no theatrical enterprise or aspirant could withstand the sweep of his extraordinary power. Among other competitors who went down in the struggle was William Hallam, who had succeeded Garrick at Goodman's Fields theatre, but who could make no headway against the new dramatic chieftain, and who, therefore, in 1750, retired from the contest, a bankrupt and £5000 in debt. The creditors of Hallam, however, being satisfied with his conduct, discharged him from debt, and presented to him the wardrobe and properties of the theatre. He was then enabled to begin business anew; but, despairing of prosperity at home, and allured by tidings of theatrical success abroad, he determined to begin it in America. He collected a dramatic company, and setting sail from Bristol, aboard the *Charming Sally*, on May 17, 1752,

D

landed at Yorktown, Va., in June of that year. The Governor of the Province was Dinwiddie. Hallam's company, led by himself and his wife, included his two sons, Lewis and Adam, and his daughter, Miss —————— Hallam. The other members of it were Mr. Adcock, Mr. and Mrs. Clarkson, Mr. Herbert, Mr. Malone, Miss Palmer, Mr. and Mrs. Rigsby, Mr. Singleton, and Mr. Wynell. Hallam, proceeding to Williamsburg, obtained for his theatre a building in the outskirts of the town. It stood, indeed, so near to the woods that whenever he wished to have pigeons for his repast, the manager could, and often did, without leaving his doorstep, shoot them on the tree-tops. There, on September 5, 1752, occurred the first dramatic performance on the continent of America, given by a regular company at a regular theatre.[1] The plays performed were Shakespeare's comedy of *The Merchant of Venice* and Garrick's farce of *Lethe*. Lewis Hallam, the second, afterwards highly distinguished in American dramatic life, making his first appearance in that representation, totally failed from stage fright.

The Hallam Family will always be named with respect in American theatrical history. The name is first asso-

---

[1] One authority declares, however, that the first regular theatre erected in America was at Annapolis, Md., — a neat brick building tastefully built, which would contain about five hundred persons, — and that a performance was given there on July 13, 1752, the first in our history of which any record has been found. The plays there acted were *The Beaux' Stratagem* and *The Virgin Unmasked*. The company included Mr. Wynell and Mr. Herbert, probably members of Hallam's company, who had repaired thither from Williamsburg. The prices charged were: boxes, ten shillings ($2.50); pit, seven shillings and sixpence ($1.87); gallery, five shillings ($1.25).

ciated with a melancholy incident in the life of Charles
Macklin, who, in 1735, accidentally killed Thomas Hallam, of the Lincoln's Inn Fields theatre, London, by
thrusting a walking-cane into his eye. Thomas Hallam
was an actor, and so was his brother Adam ; and three
sons of the latter, William, Lewis, and George, adopted
the same profession ; a fourth son entered the navy and
rose to the rank of admiral. William Hallam came
over to America in 1752 and established the family
here ; but this adventurer remained only a little while
in the American field ; for, shortly after 1754, he sold
his business to his brother Lewis, and returned to England. Lewis Hallam remained here, and so far prospered in management that for a time he was the leader
of the American stage. He had been the principal low
comedian at Goodman's Fields theatre ; his wife — a relative of Rich, of Covent Garden, and a woman of great
beauty and talent — had been leading lady there ; and
both were experienced performers. They brought to
America three of their children, a daughter and two
sons, Lewis and Adam, but left their fourth child, another daughter, in the care of relatives in England.
The immigrant daughter, then fifteen years old, at first
played juvenile ladies, and in time she rose to a position
of some prominence ; but she did not become a remarkable figure on the stage, and in 1774 she returned to
England, and so vanished from the chronicle. The
younger sister, who had remained here, went on the
stage and became the celebrated Mrs. Mattocks. Lewis
Hallam, the second, notwithstanding his disastrous first
appearance, at Williamsburg, rose to eminence and had
a brilliant career. He was the first theatrical manager

in New York after the Revolution, swaying, in association with John Henry and Thomas Wignell, the fortunes of the John Street theatre. Lewis Hallam, the first, his father, did not long survive his American expedition. He succeeded, however, in carrying forward the work that William Hallam had planned, — in planting the dramatic standard upon this continent; for, in the face of many and serious obstacles, he opened theatres in Williamsburg, Yorktown, Annapolis, New York, and Philadelphia. But, after all his efforts, he did not find himself adequately rewarded, and eventually he withdrew to the island of Jamaica, and there, in 1756, he died. His widow presently became the wife of John Moody's theatrical successor in the West Indies, David Douglas; and, as Mrs. Douglas, she was the most distinguished actress of her time in the western world. Douglas removed from Jamaica to New York in 1758, and opened theatres in that city and in Philadelphia, Newport, Perth-Amboy, Charleston, and Albany; and throughout the extensive circuit thus indicated he reigned in affluence until the storm-clouds of the Revolution began to gather, and all the arts and graces of peace were submerged by the flowing tide of war. Mrs. Douglas died at Philadelphia in 1773, and soon after that calamity her husband abandoned the American dramatic field, and returned to Jamaica, where he became a magistrate, and so ended his days. His stepson, Lewis Hallam, had accompanied him, and so had Thomas Wignell, who was Lewis Hallam's second cousin: indeed, all the actors in the colonies, finding their occupation gone, were obliged to seek other places or new pursuits, and many of them went to

Jamaica : but when the war was ended Lewis Hallam returned to New York, and, in association with John Henry, re-opened and established, in 1785, the John Street theatre, an institution which, during the next thirteen years, with some changes of management, led the American stage.

Charles Stuart Powell,[1] under contract to whom Jefferson came to America, was the first manager of the Boston theatre, in Federal street, which he opened on February 3, 1794 ; but sixteen months of bad business sufficed to make him a bankrupt, and on June 19, 1795, he closed his season and left the theatre ; so that Jefferson, when he reached Boston, found the house in strange hands, and ascertained that his services were not wanted. The new manager, however, had engaged the company of Hodgkinson and Hallam, from the John Street theatre, New York, which acted at the Boston theatre, from November 2, 1795, till January 20, 1796 ; and with those players Jefferson seems to have formed an early alliance. There is a tradition that Hodgkinson and Hallam, before their return to New York, on this occasion, gave performances at a few intermediate towns, and that Jefferson, who had accepted employment with them as scene-painter, on condition that he might have one night for a trial appearance, acted La Gloire, in Colman's play of *The Surrender of Calais*, at one of those places, and made so brilliant a hit that Hodgkinson at once engaged him for the John Street theatre. But the authentic record of his first

---

[1] C. S. POWELL, the Boston manager, died in Halifax, in 1810. SNELLING POWELL, his brother, also a manager, died in Boston, April 8, 1821, aged sixty-three.

important appearance[1] in America assigns it to that theatre, in New York, on February 10, 1796, when he came forward as Squire Richard, in *The Provoked Husband*. That was the opening night of the season, and Mr. and Mrs. John Johnson, Mr. and Mrs. Joseph Tyler, and Mrs. Brett, — all from England, — were also then seen for the first time in the American capital. William Dunlap, the manager, saw that performance, and in his *History of the American Theatre*, made this mention of Jefferson : —

"He was then a youth, but even then an artist. Of a small and light figure, well formed, with a singular physiognomy, a nose perfectly Grecian, and blue eyes full of laughter, he had the faculty of exciting mirth to as great a degree, by power of feature, although handsome, as any ugly-featured low comedian ever seen. The

---

[1] JEFFERSON IN BOSTON. — Reference to the advertisements in the *Columbian Centinel* (1795) elicits the information that, on December 21, in that year, *Macbeth* was acted at the Federal, with " Mr. Jefferson " as one of the witches; that, on December 23, *The Tempest* was given, with " Mr. Jefferson " in a minor character; and that on December 28, for the benefit of M. de Blois, " Mr. Jefferson " appeared, and sang the comic song of " John Bull's a Bumpkin." The minor character acted by Jefferson in *The Tempest* was Mustachio, a sailor mate. That part is one of several interpolations, made by Dryden and Davenant, in their version of Shakespeare's comedy, acted at Dorset Gardens, and published in 1670. Dorinda, a sister to Miranda, Sycorax, a sister to Caliban, and Hippolito, a youth who has never seen a woman, are among the persons introduced. That piece was long in use, but ultimately it gave place to John Philip Kemble's adaptations, made in 1789 and 1806. Garrick made an opera of *The Tempest;* so did Sheridan; and there is a rhymed version of it by Thomas Dibdin. Mr. W. W. Clapp [1826–1891], whose careful and thorough record, *The Boston Stage*, covering the period from 1749 to 1853, is of permanent value to theatrical inquirers, apprised me that no particular mention of the name of Jefferson occurs in any of the papers that he consulted in making his chronicle of that time; while the only Jeffersons mentioned in his book are of the fourth generation.

Squire Richard of Mr. Jefferson made a strong impression on the writer. His Sadi, in *The Mountaineers*, a stronger; and, strange to say, his Verges, in *Much Ado About Nothing*, a yet stronger."

Among the references to Jefferson's career in New York is an anecdote told by Dunlap respecting the attempt of Mr. J. D. Miller, a young baker, to play Clement, in *The Deserted Daughter:* —

"Miller's début is connected with the admirable acting of Jefferson, in the character of Item, the attorney, whose clerk Miller represented. Worked up to a phrensy of feigned passion, Jefferson, a small-sized man, seized Miller by the breast, and, while uttering the language of rage, shook him violently. Miller, not aware that he was to be treated so roughly, was at first astonished; but as Jefferson continued shaking, and the audience laughing, the young baker's blood boiled, and, calling on his physical energies, he seized the comedian with an Herculean grasp, and violently threw him off. Certainly Miller never played with so much spirit or nature on any subsequent occasion.

"This may remind the reader of John Kemble's regret at the death of Suett,[1] the low comedian, who played Weasel to Kemble's Penruddock. The lament of the tragedian is characteristic, as told by Kelly: 'My dear Mic, Penruddock has lost a powerful ally in Suett. Sir, I have acted the part with many Weasels, and good ones too, but none of them could work up my passions to the pitch Suett did. He had a comic, impertinent way of thrusting his head into my face, which called forth all my irritable sensations. The effect upon me was irresistible.' Such was the effect of Jefferson's shaking upon Miller, and Jefferson found the Yankee's arm equally irresistible."

---

[1] RICHARD SUETT died in 1805, at a ripe age. The date of his birth is not recorded. He was a native of London. He first acted in London in 1781, as Ralph, in *The Maid of the Mill*. He became a favourite at York. Anecdotes of him may be found in Bernard's *Retrospections*. Charles Lamb says that "Shakespeare foresaw him when he framed his fools and jesters." Penruddock occurs in the comedy of *The Wheel of Fortune*, by Richard Cumberland; acted at Drury Lane in 1795.

The John Street theatre — first opened on December 7, 1767, and finally closed on January 13, 1798 — was the precursor of the Park. Jefferson was associated with it for nearly two years, and when it closed he transferred his services to "The New Theatre," as the Park was at first styled, which was opened on January 29, 1798, under Dunlap's management. He received a salary of $23 a week, which, in the next season, was increased to $25. Hallam and Cooper, in the same company, received $25 each. The highest salary in Dunlap's list was $37, paid to Mrs. Oldmixon. The manager's main-stay, in tragedy, was Cooper, and in low comedy, Jefferson.

On his arrival in New York, Jefferson had found a lodging in the house of Mrs. Fortune, in John street, adjoining the theatre. That lady, whose ashes, together with those of her husband, rest in the churchyard of St. Paul's, at the corner of Broadway and Vesey street, New York, was the widow of a Scotch merchant, and she had two daughters, who were residing with her at this time. One of those girls, Euphemia, soon became the wife of Jefferson. The other, Esther, about eleven years later married William Warren, — being his second wife, — and in that way the families of Jefferson and Warren, both highly distinguished on our stage, were allied. Warren,[1] born at Bath, England, in 1767, had

---

[1] WILLIAM WARREN, after the wreck of his fortunes at the Chestnut Street theatre, rapidly declined in strength and spirits, and soon died. His death occurred at Baltimore on October 19, 1832. His age was sixty-five. Five of his children became members of the stage: I. HESTER, first Mrs. Willis, afterwards Mrs. Proctor, died in Boston, Mass., in 1842. II. ANNA, who became the wife of the celebrated comedian, Danford Marble, and died in Cincinnati, March 11, 1872. III. EMMA, first Mrs.

acted under the management of Thomas Jefferson ; and now, arriving in America in 1796, he was destined to become the brother-in-law of Joseph Jefferson, the son of his former manager. Warren's son, William Warren, born of this marriage, in 1812, was long a favourite and much honoured and beloved in Boston. Mrs. Jefferson made her first appearance on the stage, December 22, 1800, at the Park, as Louisa Dudley, in *The West Indian*. She was then twenty-four years old. She subsequently went, with her husband, to Philadelphia,

Price, afterwards Mrs. Hanchett, died in New York, in May, 1879. IV. MARY ANN, who married John B. Rice, afterward mayor of Chicago, one of the most honoured and beloved of men. She retired from the stage in 1856. V. WILLIAM WARREN. He was born at his father's residence, No. 12 (now, 1894, No. 712), Sanson street, Philadelphia, on November 17, 1812. He made his first appearance on the stage, at the Arch Street theatre, in his native city, in 1832, acting young Norval, in Home's tragedy of *Douglas*. He subsequently led a roving theatrical life in the West, till at length he settled in Buffalo, where he became a favourite comedian, at Rice's Eagle theatre. From Buffalo he went to Boston, — making his first appearance there, as Sir Lucius O'Trigger, in *The Rivals*, on October 5, 1846, at the Howard Athenæum, under the management of James H. Hackett. In that theatre he acted for twenty weeks, but in August, 1847, he joined the Boston Museum, and with that house he was associated until nearly the end of his life. He acted almost all the chief parts, of their day, in the lines of low and eccentric comedy and old men. The finest Touchstone on the stage of his period, — grave, quaint, and sadly thoughtful behind the smile and the jest, — an admirable Polonius, great in Sir Peter Teazle, and of powers that ranged easily from Caleb Plummer to Eccles, and were adequate to both extremes of comic eccentricity and melting pathos, Warren presented a shining exemplification of high and versatile abilities worthily used, and brilliant laurels modestly worn. He had a long career, crowned with prosperity and honour. He died at No. 2 Bulfinch Place, Boston, September 21, 1888, and was buried at Mount Auburn. Another of the elder Warren's children was HENRY WARREN, — a theatrical manager, in Buffalo and elsewhere, but not an actor. He died at Chicago, on February 21, 1894, aged eighty.

where she was long an ornament to the theatre and society. She died in January, 1831, aged fifty-six.

Jefferson's career at the Park extended through five regular seasons, ending in the spring of 1803. One of his hits was made as Peter, in *The Stranger*, which was performed for the first time in America in December, 1798. Dunlap had obtained a sketch of the plot, together with a portion of the dialogue of Kotzebue's play,[1] then successful in London, as adapted and re-written by Sheridan, for Drury Lane ; and he promptly wrote a piece, upon the basis of those materials, telling no one but Cooper his secret. The work was produced anonymously, with the following cast : —

The Stranger	Mr. Cooper.
Francis	Mr. John Martin.
Baron Steinfort	Mr. Giles L. Barrett.
Solomon	Mr. William Bates.
Peter	Mr. Jefferson.
Mrs. Haller	Mrs. Barrett.
Chambermaid	Mrs. Seymour.
Baroness Steinfort	Mrs. Hallam.

Cooper produced a great effect ; Mrs. Barrett was powerful and touching ; Martin was correct ; and Bates and Jefferson pleased the lovers of farce, — "for such," says Dunlap, "the comic portion of the play literally

---

[1] AUGUSTE FREDERICK FERDINAND VON KOTZEBUE, 1761-1819. — "One of his plays, *The Stranger*, I have seen acted in German, English, Spanish, French, and, I believe also, Italian. He was the pensioner of Prussia, Austria, and Russia. The odium produced by this circumstance, and the imputation of being a spy, are assigned as the cause of his assassination, by a student of Jena. He was living (at Weimar, 1801), like Goethe, in a large house and in style. I drank tea with him, and found him a lively little man with small black eyes." — *Reminiscences of Henry Crabb Robinson*, Vol. I., p. 74.

was." *The Stranger* insured the success of the season, and the manager was so much pleased that he immediately learned the German language, and thereupon opened upon the Park stage a sluice of the sentiment of Kotzebue. The actors sneered at it as "wretched Dutch stuff," and well they might; yet, for a time, it was almost as epidemic as the yellow fever, which in those days devastated, at intervals, the whole Atlantic coast.

Many other low-comedy parts and old men fell to Jefferson during his five years at the Park. He played them in the most conscientious and thorough manner. Among his characters were Kudrin, in *Count Benyowski;* the Fool, in *The Italian Father;* John, in *False Shame;* and Michelli, in Holcroft's *Tale of Mystery.* As La Fleur, in Dunlap's opera of *Sterne's Maria,* a singing part, he was especially brilliant. Mrs. Oldmixon, Miss Westray, Mrs. Seymour, Cooper, Tyler, young Hallam, and John Hogg[1] were in the cast. The ladies were singers, but only Jefferson and Tyler among the males could sing. Another of his admirable delineations was that of Jack Bowline, the Boatswain, in an adaptation from Kotzebue, blessed with the engaging title of *Fraternal Discord.*[2] Hodgkinson, who had

---

[1] JOHN HOGG, 1770–1813, a native of London, made his first appearance in New York, at the John Street theatre, in 1796. His grave is in Trinity churchyard, near the front porch. His son obtained a change of name, from Hogg to Biddle; and his grandson, George Edgar Biddle, has been pleasantly known on the contemporary stage, as George Edgar, in the characters of Othello and King Lear.

[2] Some of the old-fashioned, once popular, but now faded and forgotten melodramas bore wonderful titles. Sol Smith produced a piece entitled *The Hunter of the Alps, or The Runaway Horse that Threw His Rider in*

joined the Park company in the autumn of 1799, acted
Captain Bertram, a gouty mariner, and was accounted
wonderfully fine.   The two comedians seem to have
been well matched, but Hodgkinson was the better of
the two. " Jefferson's excellence," writes Dunlap, " was
great, but not to be put in competition with Hodgkinson's, even in low comedy."

John Hodgkinson seems to have been the prince of
actors, in that period.   He was born at Manchester,
England, in 1767, being the son of an inn-keeper, named
Meadowcraft.   In youth he was bound an apprentice to
a trade; but he ran away from home, adopted the name
of Hodgkinson, and went on the stage, and his prodigious
talents soon raised him to a position of importance.   He
was early joined to Mrs. Munden, whom it is said he
alienated from the famous comedian, Joseph Shepherd
Munden (1758-1832), and subsequently to Miss Brett,
of the Bath theatre, whom, however, he did not wed till
after they had come to America, — in September, 1792.
Hallam's partner, Henry, found them at the Bath theatre, and engaged them for this country.   Hodgkinson's
first American appearance was made in Philadelphia, as
Belcour, in *The West Indian*, and on January 28, 1793,
he acted at the John Street theatre, New York, as
Vapid, in *The Dramatist*, — that comedy, by Frederic
Reynolds, first given in 1789 at Covent Garden, which

the Forest of Savoy.   That, probably, was William Dimond's play, *The
Hunter of the Alps*, — presented at the London Haymarket in 1804, —
embellished with an extended title, for the provincial market.   There is in
print a play called *The Lonely Man of the Ocean*, which was acted with
the supplementary title of *The Night before the Bridal, with the Terrors
of the Yellow Admiral and the Perils of the Battle and the Breeze*.   Melodrama was introduced upon the English stage in 1793, by Thomas Holcroft.

JOHN HODGKINSON.

has been called the precursor of "the numerous family by which genteel and sprightly comedians have been converted into speaking harlequins." He was one of the managers of the John Street theatre, from 1794 to 1798, and he acted in the principal cities along the Atlantic seaboard, from Boston to Charleston, and was everywhere a favourite. He died suddenly, of yellow fever, near Washington, on September 12, 1805, aged thirty-eight. Hodgkinson's life was sullied by wrong actions, and his last hours were very wretched. "He was in continual agitation," we are told, "from pain and excessive terror of death, and presented the most horrid spectacle that the mind can imagine. He was, as soon as dead, wrapped in a blanket and carried to the burying-field by negroes." So, prematurely and miserably, a great light was put out.

Bernard, in his *Early Days of the American Stage*, pays a tribute to the memory of that great actor, as follows:—

"When I associate Hodgkinson with Garrick and Henderson (the first of whom I had often seen, and the latter had played with), I afford some ground for thinking he possessed no common claims. . . . Hodgkinson was a wonder. In the whole range of the living drama there was no variety of character he could not perceive and embody, from a Richard or a Hamlet down to a Shelty or a Sharp. To the abundant mind of Shakespeare his own turned as a moon that could catch and reflect a large amount of its radiance; and if, like his great precursors, it seemed to have less of the poetic element than of the riches of humour, this was owing to association, which, in the midst of his tragic passions, would intrude other images. An exclusive tragedian will always seem greater by virtue of his specialty, by the singleness of impressions which are simply poetic. Hodgkinson had one gift that enlarged his variety beyond all competition; he was also a singer, and could charm you in a burletta, after thrilling you

in a play : so that through every form of the drama he was qualified
to pass. . . . I doubt if such a number and such greatness of requisites were ever before united in one mortal man. Nor were his
physical powers inferior to his mental ; he was tall and well-propor-
tioned, though inclining to be corpulent, with a face of great mobility,
that showed the minutest change of feeling, whilst his voice, full and
flexible, could only be likened to an instrument that his passions
played upon at pleasure."

In the summer seasons of 1800 and 1801, while the
Park theatre remained closed, Jefferson and his wife acted
at Joseph Corré's Mount Vernon Gardens, situated on the
spot which is now the northwest corner of Leonard street
and Broadway. That theatre was opened July 9, 1800,
with *Miss in Her Teens, or The Medley of Lovers*, and
Jefferson acted Captain Flash. In the regular seasons
at the Park, which rarely opened before the middle of
October, Jefferson's professional associates were Mr. and
Mrs. Hodgkinson, Mr. and Mrs. Hallam, Mr. and Mrs.
John Hogg, Mr. and Mrs. S. Powell, Mr. and Mrs. J. Harper, Mr. Tyler, Mr. Fox, Mr. Martin, Lewis Hallam, Jr.,
Mr. Crosby, Mrs. Melmoth, Mrs. and Miss Brett, Miss
Harding, and Miss Hogg. There, and afterwards at the
Chestnut, he ranked with the best of his competitors ;
and in looking back to those days of the stage, it
should be remembered that at some seasons it would
happen that every man in the company was a classical
scholar.

Jefferson's conspicuous hits, even at an early age,
appear to have been made in old men ; and an anecdote
which he related attests his success. A sympathetic
lady called at the John Street theatre, with a subscription list, to entreat the managers "to withdraw that poor
old Mr. Jefferson from the stage." She said she had

seen him play Item, in *The Steward*,[1] — a wonderful performance, — and she thought it would be only a Christian charity to remove such an aged person from public life, and to provide for him. She had headed her list with a liberal gift, and she was now on her way to get additional subscribers, in order to provide a respectable home for the infirm actor. Cooper,[2] who chanced to be present, told her, in reply, that such a scheme had been considered, and that the manager would gladly cooperate in any charitable effort to relieve the hardships of the aged Jefferson's condition. Just then Jefferson entered the room, and Cooper straightway introduced him to the lady, calling her his "kind friend and protector, who had charitably undertaken to find him a home." Her amazement at seeing a slender, handsome young fellow instead of a senile mummy, was excessive. She stammered out a word of explanation, and tore her subscription paper in pieces; and the scene ended in a laugh.

The year 1803 was a crisis in Jefferson's life. Theatrical enterprise at that time was about equally divided

---

[1] An alteration of *The Deserted Daughter*. Comedy. By Thomas Holcroft. Covent Garden, 1795. Jefferson acted Grime as well as Item, in that piece.

[2] THOMAS COOPER, one of the best and most admired tragedians of his time, was born at Harrow, near London, in 1776-77. He was educated under the care of William Godwin, the philosopher who figures in the life of Shelley, and he was befriended by Holcroft. He early adopted the stage (1792), but for some time was unsuccessful. He came to America in 1796. He received and used the middle name of Abthorpe, to distinguish him from another Cooper. He was the original Damon in America, and was deemed great in that character and in Virginius. He was famous also as Hamlet, Mark Antony, and Leon. He died at Bristol, Pa., April 21, 1849, and his grave is at that place.

between Philadelphia, New York, and Boston. The
Chestnut Street theatre, Philadelphia — which city had
only in 1800 ceased to be the capital of the Republic
— held the lead. The Park theatre, in New York,
under Dunlap's management, was second; while the
Federal Street theatre, in Boston, — rebuilt after the fire
of 1798, and now managed by Snelling Powell, brother
of C. S. Powell, — was, for the first time, successful. On
the New York stage Jefferson must have found himself
as much overshadowed by Hodgkinson, who came and
went like a comet, as his father had been, on the London stage, by Garrick. The opportunity of a new field
now came to him, and, apparently, came at just the right
time. Mrs. Wignell, left a widow by the sudden death
of the great manager, was obliged, in the spring of 1803,
to assume the direction of the Chestnut Street theatre,
and a proposal was made to Jefferson to join the company there, taking the place of John Bernard, who had
repaired to Boston. At first he hesitated, being reluc-
tant to leave a community where he had been much
admired, and where he possessed many friends; and
also, perhaps, — for he was a man of extreme modesty, —
apprehensive of being compared, to some disadvantage,
with his accomplished predecessor. In the end he
accepted the 'Philadelphia engagement, for his wife as
well as himself : and, after a summer season of about two
months, passed at Albany,[1] he finally left the New York

[1] JEFFERSON IN ALBANY. — Mr. H. P. Phelps, in his compendious and
useful record of the Albany stage, entitled *Players of a Century*, notes that
Jefferson was with Dunlap's company from the New York Park theatre,
which acted in that city, in the Thespian Hotel, in 1803, the season lasting
from August 22 till October 27. He reappeared in Albany, June 9, 1829,
acting Dr. Ollapod and Dicky Gossip; but then he was in his decadence.

stage. He was seen at the old Park, though, as a visitor, in the spring of 1806, when he acted, with splendid ability, the favourite characters of Jacob Gawky, Jeremy Diddler, Bobby Pendragon, Dr. Lenitive, Toby Allspice, and Ralph ; and he came again in 1824, when, on August 5, at the Chatham Garden theatre, he took his farewell of the metropolis, acting Sir Benjamin Dove, in *The Brothers*, and Sancho, in *Lovers' Quarrels*. The story of his life, after the year 1803, is the story of his association with the Chestnut Street theatre.

Mrs. Wignell was the famous actress first known in London as Anne Brunton. That beautiful and brilliant woman, born at Bristol, England, in 1770, had made a hit at Covent Garden, October 17, 1785, before she was sixteen years old, and she was accounted the greatest tragic genius among women, since Mrs. Siddons. In 1792 she became the wife of Robert Merry, author of the Della Crusca verse, to which Mrs. Hannah Cowley, as Anna Matilda, had replied in congenial fustian, and which was excoriated by William Gifford, in his satires of *The Baviad* and *Mæviad*. Mr. and Mrs. Merry came to America in 1796, the lady being then in her twenty-seventh year, under engagement to Wignell, for the Philadelphia theatre. It is mentioned that the ship in which they sailed made the voyage to New York in twenty-one days. Wignell himself was a passenger by her, and so was the comedian Warren, whom also he had engaged. All those persons, surely, would have been amazed could they have foreseen the incidents of a not very remote future. Merry died in 1798, at Baltimore, and on January 1, 1803, his widow married Wignell. He, in turn, died suddenly, seven weeks after their marriage, and on August 15, 1806, the widow married Warren. She had a bright career on the American stage, and was greatly admired and esteemed. Her death occurred at Alexandria, Va., June 28, 1808, and her tomb is a conspicuous object in the Episcopal churchyard of that place.[1] Her sister, Louisa Brunton, who was seen on the London stage in 1785 as Juliet, became the Countess of Craven.

When Jefferson joined the Chestnut Street theatre, the dramatic company was the strongest in America, and one of the best ever formed. Warren and Reinagle were directors, — the former of affairs in general, the latter of the department of music. William B. Wood, who had been to England for recruits, was the stage-manager. The company comprised Francis Blissett, J. H. Cain, —— Downie, John Durang, Gilbert Fox, William Francis, —— Hardinge, Joseph Jefferson, —— L'Estrange, C. Melbourne, Louis J. Mestayer, Owen

---

[1] In the Dramatic Censor department of *The Mirror of Taste*, March, 1810, was published an elegiac poem on Mrs. Warren, closing with the subjoined lines : —

> " Although no civic aim was there,
>   Yet not in vain that voice was given,
>   Which, often as it bless'd the air,
>   Inform'd us what was heard in heaven.
>
> " Sure, when renew'd thy powers shall rise,
>   To hymn before th' empyreal throne,
>   Angels shall start, in wild surprise,
>   To hear a note so like their own."

This is suggestive of Dr. Johnson's couplet, —

> " Sleep, undisturbed, within this peaceful shrine,
>   Till angels wake thee with a note like thine " ;

and also, perhaps, of Dr. Johnson's remark on epitaphs : " The writer of an epitaph should not be considered as saying nothing but what is strictly true. Allowance must be made for some degree of exaggerated praise. In lapidary inscriptions a man is not upon oath."

Morris, William Twaits, Luke Usher, William Warren, —— Warrell, William B. Wood, Mrs. Downie, Mrs. Durang, Mrs. Francis, Miss Hunt, Mrs. Morris, Mrs. Oldmixon, Mrs. Shaw, Mrs. Snowden, Mrs. Solomon, Mrs. Wood (late Miss Juliana Westray), and Mrs. Wignell. The union of powers thus indicated, for comedy acting, was extraordinary. The weight, dignity, and rich humour, with which Warren could invest such characters as Old Dornton and Sir Robert Bramble made him easily supreme in that line. He held the leadership, also, in the line of Falstaff and Sir Toby Belch. Blissett's fastidious taste, neat execution, and beautiful polish, made him perfection, in parts of the Dr. Caius and Bagatelle order, which he presented as delicate miniatures. Francis (1757–1826), a superior representative of comedy old men, was finely adapted for such boisterous characters as Sir Sampson Legend and Sir Anthony Absolute. Jefferson, conscientious, thorough, and brilliant, ranged from Mercutio to Dominie Sampson, from Touchstone to Dogberry, and from Farmer Ashfield to Mawworm, and was a consummate artist in all. Wood was the Doricourt and Don Felix. And Twaits, a wonderful young man, brimful of genius, seemed formed by nature for all such characters as Dr. Pangloss, Lingo, Tony Lumpkin, and Goldfinch.

Dunlap observes that Twaits was an admirable opposite to Jefferson, and his description of that prodigy sharpens his apt remark : —

" Short and thin, yet appearing broad ; muscular, yet meagre ; a large head, with stiff, stubborn, carroty hair ; long, colourless face ; prominent hooked nose ; projecting, large, hazel eyes ; thin lips ; and a large mouth, which could be twisted into a variety of expression, and which, combining with his other features, eminently served the purpose of the comic muse, — such was the physiognomy of William Twaits."

William Twaits, born April 25, 1781, at Birmingham, England, died in New York, August 22, 1814, of consumption, precipitated by his convivial habits. Twaits married Mrs. Villiers (Miss Eliza Westray), and he was manager of the Richmond theatre at the time of the fire that destroyed it, — and with it at least seventy-one lives, — December 26, 1811.[1] The mother of Rip Van Winkle Jefferson, who received instruction from him, and often acted with him, spoke with enthusiasm of his brilliant mental qualities and the fine texture of his dramatic art. A three-quarter length painting of Twaits as Dr. Pangloss long existed among the possessions of the Jefferson family, but ultimately it disappeared.

Another remarkable figure in that group was Francis Blissett, one of the most charming actors of that delightful dramatic period. Blissett was born in London, about the year 1773, and spent his early days at Bath. His father was a favourite comic actor, and the son early exhibited dramatic talent. He was taught music, and at first destined to that pursuit; but, at the age of eighteen, he made such a successful dramatic essay, — appearing

---

[1] The Richmond theatre was so built that persons in the boxes could not escape from them except by a long, winding passage, and a small, angular staircase. The catastrophe was awful. Many accomplished and beautiful women were among the victims. The governor of Virginia (George W. Smith) and other leading citizens perished. The public mind was everywhere deeply affected. The citizens of Richmond wore mourning for thirty days, and amusements of every kind were prohibited by law, for a period of four months. See the *Mirror of Taste*, for December, 1811.

as Dr. Last, on the occasion of his father's benefit, —
that it was thought best to devote him to the stage. He
came to America in 1793, and joined Wignell's company,
at the Chestnut, and with that company he was associated
for twenty-eight years. In 1821, having, upon the death
of his father, come into possession of a considerable
inheritance, he withdrew from public life and established
his residence in the island of Guernsey, where he died,
in 1848, aged seventy-five. He was a thoughtful man, of
melancholy temperament and reserved demeanour, fond
of books and of music, and a skilful player of the violin.
His style of acting was marked by exquisite delicacy
and finish. He preferred to act little parts and make
them perfect, rather than to exercise his powers upon
those of magnitude. His humour was dry and quaint.
He could speak with a capital Irish brogue, or with a
French or a German accent. He was excellent as Dr.
Caius, the Mock Duke, in *The Honeymoon*, the Clown,
in *As You Like It*, Crabtree, David, in *The Rivals*, Crack,
Verges, Dr. Dablancour, Sheepface, Dennis Brulgrud-
dery, and the First Gravedigger. He was averse to
society, seldom spoke, and was observed to be usually
melancholy in manner. It is said he was born out of
wedlock, and that this misfortune bred in him an
habitual reserve. He was benevolent, but by stealth,
and shunned ostentation. He cultivated but few friendships, yet was greatly respected and liked. No character
of the group is more interesting than that of Blissett.

Among authentic sources of information respecting
the life of Jefferson after he settled in Philadelphia are
William B. Wood's *Personal Recollections of the Stage*,
and Francis Courtney Wemyss's *Theatrical Biography*.

The former volume, published in 1855, in its author's seventy-sixth year, covers, discursively, the period from 1797 to 1846, in Philadelphia theatrical history; the latter, published in 1848, in its author's fifty-first year, traverses, in part, the same ground, from 1822 to 1841, though, in the main, it is Wemyss's autobiography, beginning in 1797 and ending in 1846. Those writers were associated for several years. Wood, who had long been employed in Wignell's company, became stage-manager of the Chestnut in 1806, and a partner with Warren in the management in 1809. Wemyss was engaged for the Chestnut company, by Wood, in 1822, and after Wood had retired he became the stage-manager under Warren, in 1827. To both writers, accordingly, the affairs of the theatre were well known. They were not harmonious spirits, as their respective memoirs show; but they concur, with reference to Jefferson, in admiration for his character and for his great abilities as an actor.

Jefferson's first appearance under Mrs. Wignell's management was made as Don Manuel, in Cibber's comedy of *She Would and She Would Not*. He was seen at Baltimore [1] as well as at Philadelphia, " at once establishing," says Wood, " a reputation which neither time nor age could impair." During the season of 1808 he acted ten times, as Sir Oliver Surface, Charles Surface, and Crabtree. His personation of Sir Peter Teazle was

---

[1] The managers of the Chestnut had a theatrical circuit which included Baltimore and Washington, and they were accustomed to make regular, periodical visits to those cities. Cowell, in his *Thirty Years*, makes a characteristic jibe, in referring to this fact: " Baltimore had for years been visited by Warren and Wood, with the same jog-trot company and the same old pieces, till they had actually taught the audience to stay away." The allusion is to a later period.

highly approved, but it appears to have been accounted inferior to that of Warren, — probably because it excelled in quaintness and sentiment, rather than in the more appreciable qualities of uxorious excess and rubicund humour. In 1810–11 the performance for his benefit, at Baltimore, yielded $1403; in 1814, $1221; in 1815, $1618; in 1816, $1009; in 1822, $697. "The starring system," Wood says, "now began to show its baleful effects on the actors, whose benefits, after a season of extreme labour, uniformly failed." In the season of 1815–16, *The Ethiop* and *Zembuca*[1] were among the pieces presented at the Chestnut, and Wood records that —

"Much of their success was owing to the taste and skill of Jefferson, in the construction of intricate stage machinery, of which, on many occasions, he proved himself a perfect master, not unfrequently improving materially the English models. These valuable services were wholly gratuitous, all remuneration being uniformly declined. He felt himself amply repaid for the exercise of his varied talent by the prosperity of the establishment of which for twenty-five years he continued the pride and ornament. . . . *The Woodman's Hut*,[2] with an effective conflagration scene designed by Jefferson, produced several houses of $700 each. . . . Holcroft's admirable comedy of *The Man of Ten Thousand* was revived for Jefferson's benefit, with unusual effect, to $1009."

The first Philadelphia performance of Charles Lamb's farce of *Mr. H.* was given at the Chestnut Street theatre on February 19, 1812, with Wood as Mr. H., and Mrs. Jefferson, the grandmother of our Rip Van Winkle, as Melesinda. Lamb's farce was originally presented on December 10, 1806, at Drury Lane, with Elliston as

---

[1] *Zembuca*, a melodrama, by Isaac Pocock, was first produced on March 27, 1815, at Covent Garden. Emery and Liston were in the first cast.

[2] *The Woodman's Hut*, melodrama, by Samuel James Arnold, son of Dr. Arnold, the musician. First produced at Drury Lane, April 12, 1814.

Mr. H. and Miss Mellon as Melesinda, and it was hissed, — the author participating in the sibilation.[1]   It is, nevertheless, a droll composition, and it has long been valued as one of the curiosities of the theatre.   The first American edition of it was published in Philadelphia, in 1813, — that, indeed, being the first production of Lamb's printed in this country.   That edition is exceedingly scarce.   A copy of it was recently (1894) bought by an admirer of Lamb, who paid $25 for it, and who said he had been searching for it more than ten years.   The following is a fac-simile of the title-page, and to that are appended, as dramatic curiosities, the cast with which it was acted at the Chestnut, and the official advertisement of its production : —

[1] On the next day Lamb wrote to Wordsworth: "*Mr. H.* came out last night, and failed.   I had my fears : the subject was not substantial enough. John Bull must have solider fare than a letter.   We are pretty stout about it ; have had plenty of condoling friends ; but after all we had rather it should have succeeded.   You will see the prologue in most of the morning papers.   It was received with such shouts as I never witnessed to a prologue. How hard ! — a thing I did merely as a task, because it was wanted, and set no great store by ; and *Mr. H.!!*   The number of friends we had in the house — my brother and I being in public offices, etc. — was astonishing, but they yielded at length to a few hisses.   A hundred hisses (damn the word, I write it like kisses — how different !), a hundred hisses outweigh a thousand claps.   The former come more directly from the heart.   Well, 'tis withdrawn, and there is an end." — The hissing is thus described : "By this time I had become acquainted with Charles Lamb and his sister ; for I went with them to the first performance of *Mr. H.* at Covent Garden. . . .   The prologue was very well received.   Indeed, it could not fail, being one of the very best in our language.   But on the disclosure of the name [Mr. Hogsflesh], the squeamishness of the vulgar taste in the pit showed itself by hisses ; and I recollect that Lamb joined, and was probably the loudest hisser in the house.   The damning of this play belongs to the literary history of the day, as its author to the literary magnates of his age." — Henry Crabb Robinson, *Reminiscences*, chap. x.

[THE FIRST AMERICAN EDITION OF CHAS. LAMB'S FARCE.]

MR. H.

OR,

BEWARE A BAD NAME.

A FARCE IN TWO ACTS.

[Anonymous.]

As performed at the

PHILADELPHIA THEATRE.

————

PHILADELPHIA:

PUBLISHED BY M. CAREY, 122 MARKET STREET.

A. Fagan, Printer.

1813.

18mo *pp.* 36.

DRAMATIS PERSONÆ.

MEN.

Mr. H.	Mr. Wood.
Mr. Belvil	Barret.
Landlord Pry .	Blisset.
1st Gentleman	Spiller.
2d Gentleman	Downie.
David . .	Harris.
Jonathan	Durang.

Waiters, Messrs. F. Durang, Lucas, Jones, &c.

WOMEN.

Melesinda	Mrs. Jefferson.
Old Lady	Simpson.
1st Lady	Blisset.
2d Lady . . .	Seymour.
3d Lady	Miss White.
4th Lady	Mrs. Bray.
5th Lady	Miss Pettit.
Betty, *maid to Melesinda* .	Mrs. Francis.

SCENE — *Bath.*

[Copy right secured according to act of Congress.]

[From *The Aurora*, Philadelphia, January 5, 1812.]

NEW THEATRE.

Mr. JEFFERSON'S BENEFIT.

THIS EVENING, [*Monday.*] February 17. [1812.]
Will be presented, (not acted here these seven years)
an Historical Play, interspersed with Songs, called

THE HERO OF THE NORTH.

Founded on the Life of Gustavus Vasa, the Swedish Hero.

Written by Mr. Dimond *Junr.*

End of the Play — the comic song of " *The Tidy One*," by Mr. Jefferson.

An Epilogue on Jealousy, by Mrs. Twaits.

" *How to Nail 'Em*," a comic song by Mr. Jefferson.

To which will be added a Comic Opera (never performed here) called

THE COMET;

Or, He Would Be An Astronomer.

Written by the late Wm. Milne, Esq.

On Wednesday, (not acted here these 5 years) the celebrated
play of THE CURFEW — or, The Norman Barons, with
(*for the First Time*) the new Farce of

MR. H;

OR, BEWARE A BAD NAME,

for the Benefit of Mrs. Wood.

[The Aurora, Philadelphia, Monday, February 17, 1812.]

NEW THEATRE.

Mrs. WOOD'S BENEFIT.

Wednesday Evening, February 19. [1812.]
Will be presented, (not acted here these five years)
a celebrated Comedy, in 5 acts, called

THE CURFEW;

OR, THE NORMAN BARONS.

Written by the late JOHN TOBIN, author of the HONEY-MOON,
performed at the Theatre Royal, Drury Lane,
with the most unbounded applause.

NORMANS.

Hugh de Tracey, a Baron .... Mr. Calbraith.
Robert, his son .... Mr. Jefferson.
Walter, toller of the Curfew .... Mr. Blissett.
Matilda, the Baron's wife .... Mrs. Twaits.
Florence, his daughter ` .... Mrs. Mason.

DANES.

Fitzharding, leader of a banditti .... Mr. Duff.
(His second appearance here.)

To which will be added, *a New Farce, in 2 acts, never acted here,*
(performed in London and N. York, with great applause.)

CALLED

Mr. H;

OR, BEWARE A BAD NAME.

Mr. H .... Mr. Wood.
Mr. Belville............................... Mr. Barrett.
Landlord Pry .... Mr. Blissett.

Melesinda ....Mrs. Jefferson.

On Friday [Saturday], a Comedy (translated from the French)
called THREE & DEUCE, with (by desire) the BRIDAL RING.

For the Benefit of *Mrs. Twaits.*

"MR. H." was performed "for the 2d time here, by desire of many ladies and
gentlemen," for the Benefit of MRS. TWAITS, which occurred *Saturday* evening
(not on Friday as previously announced), February 22, 1812.

One of the Chestnut casts of *The School for Scandal*
shows the great strength of its company : —

Sir Peter Teazle	Warren.
Sir Oliver Surface	Francis.
Charles Surface	Wood.
Joseph Surface	H. Wallack.
Sir Benjamin Backbite	Johnson.
Crabtree	Jefferson.
Rowley	Hathwell.
Moses	T. Burke.
Careless	Darley.
Trip	John Jefferson.
Snake	Greene.
Lady Teazle	Mrs. Wood.
Lady Sneerwell	Mrs. Lafolle.
Mrs. Candour	Mrs. Francis.
Maria	Mrs. H. Wallack.
Maid	Mrs. Greene.

This is given according to Wood's record. That of
Wemyss also gives it, assigning Sir Benjamin Backbite
to Thomas Jefferson.

Sol Smith, in his *Theatrical Management in the West
and South for Thirty Years*, mentions a memorable
Chestnut cast, which he saw in 1823. "I witnessed
that night," he says, "the performance of *The Fortress*[1]
and *A Roland for an Oliver*. The afterpiece was a rich
treat to me. How could it be otherwise, with such a
cast as the following : —

Sir Mark Chase	Warren.
Fixture	Jefferson.
Alfred Highflyer	Wemyss.
Selbourne	Darley.
Maria	Mrs. Darley.
Mrs. Selbourne	Mrs. Wood.
Mrs. Fixture	Mrs. Jefferson."

[1] *The Fortress* is a musical drama, by Theodore Edward Hook, first
acted at the Haymarket, London, in 1807.

The company engaged at the Chestnut, for the season that opened on December 4, 1826, with *The Stranger*, included: —

—— Bignall.
Joseph L. Cowell.
John Darley.
William Forrest.
—— Garner.
John Hallam.
Hamilton Hosack.
Lewis J. Heyl.
James Howard.
Joseph Jefferson.
John Jefferson.
William Jones.
—— Klett.
—— Meer.
—— Murray.
—— Parker.
Charles S. Porter.
George Singleton.
William Warren.
William B. Wood.
F. C. Wemyss.
Charles Webb.
J. Wheatley.

Mrs. Anderson.
Mrs. Cowell.
Mrs. Darley.
Mrs. Greene.
Miss Hathwell.
Mrs. Joseph Jefferson.
Mrs. John Jefferson.
Mrs. Meer.
Mrs. Murray.

N. M. Ludlow, in his *Dramatic Life as I Found It*, published in 1880, glances thus at the character of Jefferson's acting: —

"While in Philadelphia, in 1826, I had the pleasure of beholding a performance of 'Old Jefferson,' as he was then called. . . . I had seen him in New York when I was a youth of seventeen, early in the year 1812, when Wood and Jefferson came to New York to perform, while Cooper and others went from New York to Philadelphia for a like purpose. I was delighted with Jefferson when I saw him then, as a boy. I was not less so when I now beheld him with professional eyes and some experience. The comedy that I saw played in Philadelphia was by Frederic Pillon, and entitled *He Would be a Soldier*, with the following cast of characters: Sir Oliver Oldstock, Warren; Captain Crevett, George Barrett, for many years well known as a genteel comedian; Caleb, Jefferson; Charlotte, the beautiful Mrs. Barrett. All are now dead. In Jefferson's acting there was a perfection of delineation I have seldom, if ever, seen in any other comedian of his line of character; not the least attempt at exaggeration to obtain applause, but a naturalness and truthfulness that secured it, without the appearance of any extraordinary efforts from him. The nearest approach to his style is that of his grandson, of the same name."

Macready came to act at the Chestnut in the season of 1826–27, and on the day of his arrival was entertained at dinner by the manager, Wood, — Jefferson being one of the guests. The next morning a rehearsal of *Macbeth* occurred, and Jefferson, who was lame with gout, appeared with a cane. That was an infraction of a well-known rule, but it was understood in the company that Jefferson was ill, and therefore the breach of stage etiquette was not regarded. The comedian was to enact the First Witch. Macready, — a very tyrannical and passionate man, with a talent for profanity seldom equalled, — observed the cane, and, with his customary arrogance, determined to assert himself. "Tell that person," he said, "to put down his cane." The prompter, thus commanded, delivered his message. "Tell Mr. Macready," said Jefferson, "that I shall not act with him during his engagement"; and he left the stage. "Mr. Macready had a right," he afterwards remarked, "to object to the carrying of a cane at rehearsal; but it was obvious to me that this was not his point. He chose to disregard the fact that we had

met as social equals, and to omit the civility of a word
of inquiry, which would have procured immediate explanation. His purpose was to overbear and humiliate
me, so as to discipline and subjugate the rest of the
company. It was a rude exercise of authority, and its
manner was impertinent."

It is recorded of Joseph Jefferson and Euphemia
Fortune, whom he wedded, that they were born on the
same day of the same month and year, — one in England, the other in America. Their marriage proved
fortunate and happy. They were blessed with nine
children (Cowell erroneously says thirteen), and the
death of the husband followed that of the wife,
within eighteen months. All their children, with
two exceptions, adopted the stage. One died in infancy. The following is a record of those descendants : —

1. THOMAS, the eldest son, went on the stage in his fourteenth
year, rose to a good position, and died, in 1824, at the age of
twenty-seven. He was never married.

2. JOSEPH, 1804-1842. He was the father of Rip Van Winkle
Jefferson. His career is made the subject of a separate chapter.

3. JOHN was accounted the most brilliant of this family. He
was remarkably handsome and athletic. He received a careful
education, and he displayed astonishing talents. Had he lived, and
continued to improve, he would have become a great actor; but he
was prematurely broken down by conviviality, and he died, suddenly, at Lancaster, Pa., in 1831, aged twenty-three.

4. EUPHEMIA, her father's favourite daughter, was correct and
pleasing on the stage, and a most estimable woman. She married
WILLIAM ANDERSON, — described by Ludlow as "a good actor in
heavy characters, tragedy villains, and the like," — but he was an
unworthy person, and he embittered her life. Her marriage was
a grief to her father. She was a member of the dramatic com-

pany at the New York Park theatre in 1816, and of the Chestnut Street theatre, Philadelphia, in 1817. "Mrs. Anderson, late Miss Jefferson," says Wood, in his *Personal Recollections*, "was now added to the company, and shortly reached a high place in public favour." She died in 1831, leaving two daughters, Jane and Elizabeth. — JANE ANDERSON, born in February, 1822, appeared at the Franklin theatre, New York, August 15, 1836, as Sally Giggle, in *Catching an Heiress*. She had a bright career on the stage, beginning in 1829, and she was a superior representative of old women. She became MRS. GREENBURY C. GERMON, and was long a resident of Baltimore. She retired from professional life in 1889–90. MISS EFFIE GERMON, born at Augusta, Ga., on June 13, 1840, and long a sparkling soubrette of Wallack's theatre, is her daughter, and thus a descendant of Thomas Jefferson. The father, G. C. GERMON, the original Uncle Tom, in *Uncle Tom's Cabin*, died at Chicago, in April, 1854, aged thirty-eight. — ELIZABETH ANDERSON began at the Franklin theatre, August 1, 1836, as Mrs. Nicely, and she also had a good theatrical career. She was married in 1837, to Jacob W. Thoman, and subsequently, as MRS. THOMAN, she became a favourite in Boston. She accompanied Thoman to California, where she obtained a divorce from him; and afterwards she again married, becoming MRS. C. SAUNDERS. Both Jane and Elizabeth Anderson had played, as early as 1831, in the theatre at Washington, managed by their uncle Joseph. Elizabeth, although very young, acted old women. She was at the Walnut Street theatre, Philadelphia, in 1835. — WILLIAM ANDERSON, the father of those girls, after a career of painful irregularity, ending in indigence, died, in 1869, at a hospital in Philadelphia. Cowell remarks that Jemmy Bland's answer, — when adrift in the words, — to the question, "Who is this Coriolanus ?" exactly describes Anderson : "Why, he's a fellow who is always going about grumbling, and making everybody uncomfortable."

5. HESTER became MRS. ALEXANDER MACKENZIE, first wife of the actor and manager of that name, once prominent in the West. Mackenzie was a cousin to Joseph Neal, author of *Charcoal Sketches*. Mrs. Mackenzie began to act in 1831, and attained to a good rank as a general actress. She died at Nashville, Tenn., February 3, 1845, much lamented.

F

6. ELIZABETH. Mrs. CHAPMAN-RICHARDSON-FISHER. A brilliant and popular actress at the New York Park, in its great days. Her story is told in a separate chapter.

7. MARY ANNE. She became the wife of DAVID INGERSOLL, a tragedian, of great promise, who died at St. Louis in 1837, aged twenty-five. She subsequently married JAMES S. WRIGHT, for many years prompter at Wallack's theatre. She was a member of the Bowery theatre company, New York, in 1834, and she was a favourite in theatres on the western circuit. James S. Wright died, in New York, June 27, 1893, aged 79. Mrs. Wright is still living (1894).

8. JANE is remembered as a lovable girl, devoted to her family. She never went on the stage, but died, aged seventeen, in 1831.

Lives that do not imprint themselves on the passing age are lost so quickly and so irretrievably that it seems as if they never had existed. There is something forlorn in the few slight and scattered memorials that remain of those persons; all of them at one time auspicious, and actuated, no doubt, by a high ambition. Thomas Jefferson, as a lad, appeared at the Park theatre, New York, on May 27, 1803, as the Boy, in *The Children in the Wood*, — a drama by Thomas Morton, the music by Dr. Arnold, first acted at the London Haymarket, in 1793, and made memorable by the great success of John Bannister as Walter, — and he was seen at the Chestnut, Philadelphia, January 1, 1805, as Cupid, in the pantomime of *Cinderella*, his father playing Pedro and his mother Thisbe; but his first important effort was made on October 7, 1811, in his fifteenth year. The play was *The Merry Wives of Windsor*. Warren acted Falstaff; Jefferson, Sir Hugh Evans; Blissett, Dr. Caius; Mackenzie, Ford; and young Thomas Jefferson came on as Master Slender. The result was recorded by a contemporary writer,

S. C. Carpenter, the dramatic censor of *The Mirror of Taste* (Vol. IV., p. 297) :—

"The chief novelty of the night, and on many accounts a most pleasing one, was Mr. Jefferson's eldest son, in Master Slender. . . . A fine boy, and the son of one of the greatest favourites of the people of Philadelphia. . . . There was no blind, undistinguishing enthusiasm exhibited on the occasion. . . . The audience chose rather to reserve their praise till it would do the youth substantial credit, by being bestowed only on desert; and in the full truth of severe criticism we declare that of the loud applause bestowed upon the boy there was not a plaudit which he did not deserve. From this juvenile specimen we are disposed to believe that he inherits the fine natural talents of his father."

In 1817 the three brothers, Thomas, Joseph, and John, acted together, in *Valentine and Orson.* In 1821 James H. Caldwell (1793–1863), the pioneer theatrical manager in the South and West, — next after "old man-Drake," [1] as the actors commonly called him, and likewise after the veteran Ludlow, — had a good dramatic company, at Petersburg, Va., which included (according to James Rees, *Dramatic Authors*, p. 58) Mrs. Anderson, Mrs. Benton, Mr. Cafferty, Mr. Gray, Mr. and Mrs. Hughes, Mr. and Mrs. Hutton, Mr. Jefferson, Mr. Ludlow, Miss Eliza Placide, Mr. and Mrs. Russell, Mr. Scholes, Miss Tilden, and Mr. West. Miss Eliza Placide, sister to Henry and Thomas Placide, became Mrs. Mann and mother of Alice Placide Mann. The Mr. Jefferson, no doubt, was Thomas. In 1825, at Washington, the elder Joseph Jefferson and his son John acted in *Cherry and Fair Star*, which was set in

---

[1] SAMUEL DRAKE, 1772–1847, was the only manager in the West, as late as 1816. He made his first appearance on the American stage, in 1809, at the Federal Street theatre, Boston.

scenery painted by the younger Joseph. *Bombastes Furioso* was likewise presented, the elder Jefferson acting Bombastes, and both John and Joseph co-operating as actors in the performance. Joseph, our Jefferson's father, was then regarded as mainly a scenic artist.

The untimely death of Thomas Jefferson was caused by an accident on the stage, when he was doing a service for a brother actor. That was the vocalist and comedian John Darley (1780–1858), father of the artist Felix O. C. Darley, both of whose parents were ornaments of the early American theatre; his mother being Miss Ellen Westray. John Darley was playing Paul, in the opera of *Paul and Virginia*, and, not wishing to make the leap from the rock, he asked young Jefferson to make it for him. The youth, who was playing the slave Alhambra, acceded to his request, plunged from the scenic precipice, and in so doing broke a blood-vessel in his lungs. That injury resulted in consumption, and, after a lingering illness, he died in Philadelphia on September 16, 1824. "He had been afflicted for some time," said a writer in the *National Intelligencer* (September 21), "with a pulmonary complaint, which he bore with fortitude. His end was calm and resigned. . . . His friends valued him; their regret is mingled with the tears of his family; and his remembrance is drawn on a tablet whence passing occurrences cannot easily efface it."

Hester Jefferson, Mrs. Mackenzie, seems to have possessed the same patient, submissive nature. A Nashville journal, recording her death, says that "she bore a severe illness with Christian serenity," and that she was "a lady graced by many accomplishments, but still more by virtues which conciliated the esteem and affection of all who knew her." "There are many friends of her late father," adds that obituary tribute, "and of his family, in different parts of the Union, to whom this brief notice will recall many affecting associations. It will be a solace to them to know that she passed to the portals of the tomb in the full and joyous assurance of a blessed immortality."

The Chestnut Street theatre, established by Thomas Wignell, in 1792–94, stood in Chestnut street, next to the west corner of Sixth street, and was the pride of Philadelphia. In April, 1820, it was burnt down, and the accumulations of the finest dramatic temple in America were lost. It was rebuilt and reopened, but it never recovered its former glory.[1] A change in the public taste as to theatrical matters was maturing at about that time, and players who had long been favourites, were losing their ·hold upon popularity, in the gradual waning of the generation to which they belonged. Jefferson, a continual sufferer from hereditary gout, had begun somewhat to decline, alike in personal strength

---

[1] An article in the New York *Clipper*, 1893, descriptive of the veteran actor John Roland Reed, 1808———, records that about 1824 " Mr. Reed contracted to light the three principal theatres in Philadelphia, — the Chestnut, under the management of Wood & Warren; the Arch, under the management of 'the three Bills,' William Forrest, brother of Edwin Forrest, William Duffy, and William Jones; and the Walnut, under the management of Wemyss. The lamps were made in acorn shape, the footlights representing one hundred and fifty lamps. All were filled with oil. When a dark scene was necessary, at a signal from the stage-manager the lights were lowered under the stage. Around the boxes there were chandeliers, presenting three lamps on three prongs. When severe cold weather came, the oil would freeze, and the lights would go out. Then Mr. Reed had to go around with hot irons and thaw the oil."

and popular favour. During the season of 1821, Jefferson, Francis, Wheatley, and others of the Chestnut company, were ill almost one-third of the time, and could not appear. In the season of 1823–24, at Baltimore, Jefferson was ill nine nights, and did not act. The final scenes of his life's drama were ushered in by those warnings of decay. Wood refers to unfriendly machinations against himself, which presently parted him from Warren, who was thus left alone in the management, in 1826; and thereafter the business grew worse and ever worse, the receipts falling as low as $98, $90, $61.50, and even $20.75 a night, till at last Warren left the theatre, utterly ruined, in 1829.

" Jefferson's last benefit," writes Wood, " took place on December 23, 1829, and, being suddenly announced, failed to attract his old admirers to the house. He was now infirm and in ill spirits, from domestic distresses, as well as the breaking up of the old management, and the gloomy professional prospects which that event placed before him. The play, *A School for Grown Children*, had originally failed here, being remarkably local, and proved a singularly bad choice."

That was a comedy by Morton, which Burton once gave in New York, under the name of *Begone Dull Care*.

Similar testimony is borne by Wemyss : —

"Jefferson, whose benefit was announced with the new play of *A School for Grown Children*, could scarcely muster enough to pay the expenses, and resolved to leave the theatre. The manager, having demanded and received the full amount of his nightly charge on such occasions, offered him but half his income, at the treasury on Saturday. This was a blow the favourite comedian could not brook. The success of Sloman, an actor so greatly his inferior, had irritated him both with his manager and the audience. But what must have been the apathy of the public towards dramatic representation, when such a man, whose reputation shed lustre on the theatre to which he was attached, was permitted to leave the city of Philadelphia, with scarcely an inquiry as to his whereabouts ; two-thirds of the audience ignorant of his departure! The last time he acted in Philadelphia was for my benefit, kindly studying the part of Sir Bashful Constant, in *The Way to Keep Him*,[1] which he played admirably."

Cowell's *Thirty Years*, a useful though censorious book, contains a kindred reference to the last days and the character of Jefferson. Cowell was the father of Samuel Cowell, a once popular actor and comic singer, and of Sydney Frances Cowell, who, as Mrs. Hezekiah L. Bateman, became known as a dramatic author, and as the mother of "the Bateman children," Kate, Ellen, and Virginia. Cowell succeeded Wood, as stage manager of the Chestnut, and it is to that period he refers (Vol. II., chapter 8), when writing of Jefferson :—

"Jefferson was the low comedian, and had been for more than five and twenty years. Of course he was a most overwhelming favourite, though at this time drops of pity for fast-coming signs of age and infirmity began to be freely sprinkled with the approbation long habit more than enthusiasm now elicited. . . . Literally born on the stage, he brought with him to this country the experience of age with all the energy of youth, and in the then infant state of the drama, his superior talent, adorned by his most exemplary private deportment, gave him lasting claims to the respect and gratitude, both of the profession and its admirers. And, perhaps, on some such imaginary reed he placed too much dependence ; for the whole range of the drama cannot, probably, furnish a more painful yet perfect example of the mutability of theatrical popularity than Joseph Jefferson.

---

[1] *The Way to Keep Him.* Comedy, by Arthur Murphy: Drury Lane, 1761. "Sir Bashful Constant is a gentleman who, though passionately fond of his wife, yet from a fear of being laughed at by the gay world, for uxoriousness, is perpetually assuming the tyrant, and treating her, at least before company, with great unkindness."

"When Warren left the management, younger, not better, actors were brought in competition with the veteran, and the same audience that had actually grown up laughing at him alone, as if they had been mistaken in his talent all this time, suddenly turned their smiles on foreign faces; and, to place their changed opinion past a doubt, his benefits, which had never produced less than twelve or fourteen hundred dollars, and often sixteen, fell down to less than three. Wounded in pride, and ill prepared in pocket for this sudden reverse of favour and fortune, he bade adieu forever to Philadelphia. With the aid of his wife and children he formed a travelling company, and wandered through the smaller towns of Pennsylvania, Maryland, and Virginia, making Washington his headquarters.[1] Kindly received and respected everywhere, his old age might still have passed in calm contentment, but that 'one woe did tread upon another's heel, so fast they followed.' His daughter, Mrs. Anderson, and his youngest, Jane, died in quick succession, after torturing hope with long and lingering disease. His son-in-law, Chapman, was thrown from a horse, and the week following was in his grave. His son John, an excellent actor, performed for his father's benefit, at Lancaster, Pa., was well and happy, went home, fell in a fit, and was dead. And last, not least, to be named in this sad list, the wife of his youth, the mother of his thirteen [error: he had but nine] children, the sharer of his joys and sorrows for six and thirty years, was 'torn from out his heart.'"

To Wood the inquirer is indebted for an account of the closing days and the death of Jefferson, containing discriminative observations on his character. Though not a sympathetic man, Wood has no word for Jefferson, except of profound respect and cordial kindness.

---

[1] The comedian had long been accustomed to make periodical trips to Washington, and he knew his ground, therefore, on going into exile. "Washington city," says the same writer [*Thirty Years*, Vol. II., chapter 10], "could then (1827) boast of only a very small theatre, in a very out-of-the-way situation, and used by Warren and Wood as a sort of summer retreat for their company, where the disciples of Izaak Walton, with old Jefferson at their head, could indulge their fishing propensities."

" At an early age Jefferson anticipated the inheritance of his father's complaint, gout, and vainly endeavoured, by a life of the severest care and regimen, to escape its assaults. For many years the attacks were slight, but with increasing age they increased also, and at length became so frequent and violent as to undermine his health and spirits. The decline of Warren's fortunes greatly distressed him. His associates of thirty years were disappearing from his side, and he retired suddenly from a stage of which for a quarter of a century he had been the delight, ornament, and boast. . . . . I unexpectedly met him, subsequently, at Washington. He was engaged, along with John Jefferson, Dwyer, Mills, and Brown, in a temporary establishment, the manager of which had invited Mrs. Wood and myself to a short star engagement. The company was sufficiently strong to present a few plays creditably, but could not have afforded either a suitable recompense or scene for his remarkable and finished powers. On our final night at Washington, Jefferson roused himself to an effort which astonished us. Though now grown old and dispirited, and with a theatre very different from the one which had formerly inspired his efforts, his performance of Sir Peter Teazle in *The School for Scandal*, and of Drugget, in *Three Weeks After Marriage*, was nearly equal to his finest and early efforts. This was the last time we ever met. I understood, that, after this, he became engaged with a company at the town of Harrisburg, Pa., and appeared occasionally. . . . Many and severe domestic afflictions were added to his bodily sufferings, and, worn out with physical and mental distress, he there closed his pure and blameless life. . . . . Nobody of just feelings could know Jefferson as long and intimately as I knew him, and have any estrangement with him, about anything; for he was a man at once just, discreet, unassuming, and amiable. . . . . Studious and secluded in his habits, and surrounded by a numerous family, he had neither the wish nor leisure for general society. A few select friends and the care of his children occupied the hours hardly snatched from his professional duties. He felt an unconquerable dislike to the degradation of being exhibited as the merry-maker of a dinner party,[1] and sometimes offended by his perseverance on

---

[1] This was also true of his contemporary and associate, Francis Blissett, and the same trait has shown itself in the character of Joseph Jefferson, his grandson.

this point. He was frequently heard to observe that for any dinner entertainments there were plenty of amateur amusers to be found, without exhausting the spirits and powers of actors who felt themselves pledged to reserve their best professional efforts for the public who sustained them. To an excellent ear for music, he added no inconsiderable pretensions as a painter and machinist. Incapable alike of feeling or inspiring enmity, he passed nearly thirty years of theatrical life in harmony and comfort. It is painful to contrast those with the misfortunes of his later years."

Among contemporary opinions of Jefferson, that of John P. Kennedy, the novelist, author of *Horse-shoe Robinson*, etc., is significant : —

" He played everything that was comic, and always made people laugh until the tears came in their eyes. . . . I don't believe he ever saw the world doing anything else. Whomsoever he looked at laughed. . . . When he was about to enter, he would pronounce the first words of his part, to herald his appearance, and instantly the whole audience set up a shout. It was only the sound of his voice. He had a patent right to shake the world's diaphragm, which seemed to be infallible. When he acted, families all went together, old and young. Smiles were on every face ; the town was happy."

" In low or eccentric comedy," says Ireland, " he has rarely been equalled ; yet his success in other lines was very great."

"In the days of *Salmagundi*, in the days when the leaders of intellect and of society were frequenters of our theatres," said the poet N. P. Willis, " flourished Jefferson ; and there are some yet living who will speak to us with all the fondness of early recollections, connected with the freshness of life, of one who now lies mouldering beneath the sod."

Those tributes are examples of the general testimony of his time, with reference to Joseph Jefferson. He was a man of original mind, studious habits, fine temperament, natural dignity, and great charm of character, and his life was free from contention, acrimony, and reproach.

An instructive description of Jefferson as an actor is given by Wemyss : —

"Joseph Jefferson was an actor formed in nature's merriest mood. . . . . There was a vein of rich humour running through all he did, which forced you to laugh, despite of yourself. He discarded grimace as unworthy of him, although no actor possessed a greater command over the muscles of his own face, or the faces of his audience, — compelling you to laugh or cry, at his pleasure. His excellent personation of old men acquired for him, before he had reached the meridian of life, the title of 'Old Jefferson.' The astonishment of strangers, at seeing a good-looking young man pointed out in the street as Jefferson, whom they had seen the night previous at the theatre, tottering apparently on the verge of existence, was the greatest compliment which could be paid to the talent of the actor. His versatility was astonishing — light comedy, old men, pantomime, and occasionally juvenile tragedy. Educated in the very best school for acquiring knowledge in his profession, . . . Jefferson was an adept in all the trickery of the stage, which, when it suited his purpose, he could turn to excellent account. He was the reigning favourite of the Philadelphia theatre for a longer period than any other actor ever attached to the city, and left it with a reputation all might envy. In his social relations he was the model of what a gentleman should be, — a kind husband, an affectionate father, a warm friend, and a truly honest man."

A tribute to Jefferson and to his associate Francis, occurs in James Fennell's *Apology for the Life of an Actor*, pp. 418, 419 : —

"My next excursion was to Alexandria, where I completed my engagements under the direction of Messrs. Francis and Jefferson. I cannot reflect on the conduct of these gentlemen without comparing it with my own : nothing has impeached their characters during their residence in the United States, but much has occurred to exalt them. No instability has marked their dispositions; with steady industry, perseverance, and prudence, they have attached themselves closely to the profession they had chosen and the city which was originally their promised land, and in which they are now (1813) in happy possession of competency and respect; — the one, the friend and protector of the orphan; the other, the father of a numerous family, under the guardianship of himself and his amiable consort, well educated and well instructed. Neither one nor the other entered this new world (they will pardon the remark) with the advantages I possessed, nor has either of them received a fourth part of the sum of money that I have, from the patronage of Americans. What, then, has made them rich? Prudence. What has reduced my state? Imprudence. Jefferson! the amiable father of an amiable offspring; Francis! the protector of the unprotected, permit me to offer you, poor as it is, my homage."

Fennell seems to have been the Micawber of actors, long before the character was created. He was born in London, December 11, 1766; made his appearance on the American stage in 1794; and was excellent in the tragic parts of Zanga and Glenalvon. He lived a wild life, and wrote an account of it; and he died in Philadelphia, a pitiable imbecile, in 1816.

A Philadelphia writer, whose name is unknown, gives this glimpse of the personal appearance of Jefferson: —

"He was scarcely of medium height, not corpulent, elderly, with clear and searching eyes, a rather large and pointed nose, and an agreeable general expression. But never was a human face more plastic. His natural recognition of each personage in the mimic scene, his interest in all that was addressed to him, the plan or purpose of what he had to say, his coaxing, quizzing, wheedling, domineering, and grotesque effects, were all complete, without the utterance of words; yet it was said that in these particulars he never twice rendered a scene in precisely the same manner. In singing, his voice was a rich baritone, and in speech it was naturally the same. He was so perfect an artist that, although always faithful to his author, he could, by voice or face or gesture, make a point at every exit."

Edwin Forrest, who had known Jefferson and was familiar with his acting, spoke of him with earnest admiration: —

"One morning . . . he began relating to Oakes . . . his recollections of old Joseph Jefferson, the great comedian. He told how, when a boy, he had visited that beautiful and gifted old man; what poverty and what purity and high morality were in his household; how he had educated his children; and how at last he had died among strangers, heart-broken by ingratitude. He told how he had seen him play Dogberry, in a way that out-topped all comparison; how at a later time he had again seen him play the part of the Fool, in *Lear*, so as to set up an idol in the memory of the beholders, for he insinuated into the words such wonderful contrasts of the greatness and misery and mystery of life, with the seeming ignorant and innocent simplicity of the comments on them, that comedy became wiser and stronger than tragedy. — His listener afterwards said, 'We two were alone. Never had I seen him so deeply and so loftily stirred in his very soul as he was then, about Jefferson. His eulogy had more moral dignity and intense religious feeling than any sermon I ever heard from the pulpit.'" — *Life of Edwin Forrest. By William Rounseville Alger*, Vol. II., pp. 827–28.

Jefferson resided for many years at No. 10 Powell street, Philadelphia. The house is still standing, but a change in the enumeration of the houses in that street has made it number 510. In company with Rip Van Winkle Jefferson I visited that house, in September, 1880. Upon Jefferson's saying that his grandfather once lived there, the occupants courteously invited us to enter, and we passed a little time in the rooms on the second floor, which the comedian remembered as associated with his ancestor; and he recalled having been held up, at the front window, a child in his grandfather's arms, to watch the heavy raindrops pattering in the pools of water in the street below, — which drops the old gentleman told him were silver pieces, and said he should presently go and get them. That anecdote, told then and there, seemed very suggestive of the kind, playful nature always ascribed to "old Jefferson."

There was a strong personal resemblance between President Jefferson and the comedian, and this indication confirmed their belief that they had sprung from the same origin. They were friendly acquaintances and occasionally met ; but the actor, who shrunk with honourable pride from even the appearance of courting the favour of the great, was always shy of accepting the attentions of the President. A book had appeared, written by an Englishman, in which it was asserted, in a spirit of ridicule, that the President of the United States, while in the morning he would write state papers and attend to the affairs of the nation, could at night be seen at the theatre, with a red wig on his head, bowing responsive to the applause that he got while making the people laugh, in a farce. That was sufficiently childish satire, and it is not to be supposed that any person seriously regarded it. Yet it was not wholly without effect on the sensitive mind of the comedian. He entertained a profound respect for the republican ideas of his adopted country, and for the exalted office of its chief magistrate ; and this, conjoined with the self-respecting dignity of his character, made him extremely punctilious as to all social intercourse outside of his own class and rank. The President and himself were not able to trace their relationship, but both believed it to exist, although the ancestry of the former was Welsh, while that of the latter was English. The actor, however, said that his gratification in their alliance would be marred if the matter were made known, as an avowal of it might be misunderstood. President Jefferson presented to the actor a court-dress, as a mark of his respect and admiration. This was highly valued by the recipient, and was left by him to his son Joseph, who also inherited Garrick's Abel Drugger wig. Those relics formed part of the wardrobe entrusted to Joseph Cowell, and by him stored in the St. Charles theatre, New Orleans, which was burnt, with its contents, on Sunday night, March 13, 1842.

One of the biographers of President Jefferson describes that remarkable man in language which might equally well apply to the great actor who was his contemporary : —

"He was a tender husband and father, a mild master, a warm friend, and a delightful host. His knowledge of life, extensive travels, and long familiarity with great events and distinguished men rendered his conversation highly attractive to social visitors. His scientific acquisitions and the deep interest which he took in all branches of natural history made his society equally agreeable to men of learning. Many such visited him, and were impressed as deeply by his general knowledge as they were by the courtesy of his demeanour."

Jefferson was buried in the grounds of the Episcopal church at Harrisburg, at the rear of the building ; and there, in 1843, a memorial stone was placed over him, by Judge Gibson [1] and Judge Rogers, of the Supreme

[1] JOHN BANNISTER GIBSON was distinguished as a jurist of high ability. He was a native of Pennsylvania, born in 1780, being the son of Lieutenant-Colonel Gibson, who was killed in battle with the savage Indians, in St. Clair's expedition against them, in 1791. He was admitted to the bar in 1803, and subsequently was several times elected to the State legislature. In 1813 he was appointed presiding Judge of one of the judicial districts of Pennsylvania, and in 1816 he became Associate Justice of the Supreme Court of that State. In 1827 he became Chief Justice, succeeding Judge Tilghman. He was deprived of his seat in 1851, when a change in the Constitution of Pennsylvania made the judiciary an elective institution. He was, however, elected an Associate Justice in the same year. He died

Court of Pennsylvania.   The inscription upon it, written
by Judge Gibson, is as follows :—

✠

BENEATH THIS MARBLE
ARE DEPOSITED THE ASHES OF

JOSEPH JEFFERSON:

AN ACTOR WHOSE UNRIVALLED POWERS
TOOK IN THE WHOLE RANGE OF COMIC CHARACTER,
FROM PATHOS TO SOUL-SHAKING MIRTH.
HIS COLOURING OF THE PART WAS THAT OF NATURE, — WARM,
PURE, AND FRESH ;
BUT OF NATURE ENRICHED WITH THE FINEST CONCEPTIONS OF
GENIUS.
HE WAS A MEMBER OF THE CHESTNUT STREET THEATRE,
PHILADELPHIA,
IN ITS MOST HIGH AND PALMY DAYS,
AND THE COMPEER
OF COOPER, WOOD, WARREN, FRANCIS,
AND A LONG LIST OF WORTHIES
WHO,
LIKE HIMSELF,
ARE REMEMBERED WITH ADMIRATION AND PRAISE.
HE WAS A NATIVE OF ENGLAND.

WITH AN UNBLEMISHED REPUTATION AS A MAN,
HE CLOSED A CAREER OF PROFESSIONAL SUCCESS,
IN CALAMITY AND AFFLICTION,
AT THIS PLACE,
IN THE YEAR 1832.

"*I knew him, Horatio: a fellow of infinite jest; of most
excellent fancy.*"

✠

---

in Philadelphia in 1853, having been eminent on the bench for forty
years.   An eloquent eulogy on him was delivered by Chief Justice Jeremiah Black, which may be found in the seventh volume of Harris's *Pennsylvania State Reports.*

There is an authentic tradition that the clergyman who read the burial service over the remains of Jefferson, knowing that he had been an actor, and disapproving of that circumstance, altered the text of the ritual, substituting the phrase "this man" for "our deceased brother," in the solemn passage beginning "Forasmuch as it hath pleased Almighty God, in his wise providence, to take out of this world the soul of our deceased brother, we therefore commit his body to the ground — earth to earth, ashes to ashes, dust to dust." That proceeding, which was observed at the time, and which can only be viewed as an act of bigotry, done with intent to cast a sort of ecclesiastical indignity upon the dead, has been remembered by the descendants of the noble and blameless person whose dust was thus disparaged. The present Joseph Jefferson, whose spotless character and beneficent life are their own sufficient praise, is not a member of the church. It is by acts like that, with which its history has often been sullied, that the church has suffered the alienation of many true hearts.

After nearly forty years, the remains of Joseph Jefferson were removed from the Episcopal churchyard to the Harrisburg cemetery, and again laid in the earth. The same stone that marked their first sepulchre, marks their final place of rest. This disturbance of them was compelled, through the conversion of a part of the churchyard into a building plot. In the absence of the present Jefferson, the removal to a temporary sepulchre was effected by Attorney-General Benjamin F. Brewster and Senator Cameron, of Pennsylvania; but on returning from Europe, Jefferson personally supervised the final burial.

G

It is my privilege to present a compendium of PER-
SONAL RECOLLECTIONS OF JOSEPH JEFFERSON, given to
me by his daughter, ELIZABETH JEFFERSON, — Mrs.
Chapman-Richardson-Fisher. These recollections were
written at my request, in 1869–70. They came to me
in the form of rough memoranda, the manuscript being
entitled *Notes from Memory*, and they were found
to need revision. Accordingly, with their respected
writer's consent, I carefully pruned, condensed, and
paraphrased her narrative, preserving her facts, strictly
adhering to the spirit of her statements, and, where-
ever possible, using her words. A sketch of Elizabeth
Jefferson's life is given in a separate chapter of this
biography. Her reminiscences are appended : —

"My father was genial and social, but reserved in manner. He
never allowed theatrical matters to be discussed in his presence ;
not from dislike of his profession, but because his life was so entirely
wrapt up in it that he needed relief from reference to the subject of
his constant study and thought.

"Hodgkinson was most liberal to my father in professional business, and in a very little time after they came together gave up to
him the low-comedy parts. This soon made him a leading feature
of the John Street theatre, and a great favourite with the public.
One night, when it chanced that his first child was very ill, he had
gone to the theatre much depressed, though not apprehensive of
bereavement. While dressing himself for a farce, he received news
that his child was dead. The love of children was a ruling passion
with my father, and to lose his own and (then) only one, was an
overwhelming grief. Hodgkinson went before the curtain to state
the reason of the delay that had been caused by this news, and
to beg of the audience to allow another farce to be substituted
for the one announced ; but the whole house rose, and, with a
cry of 'No farce!' left the theatre. This was an unusual compliment.

"Considerations of economy were among the reasons that induced

my father to remove from New York to Philadelphia, where his name
became a household word.   No man ever held more esteem and
affection than followed him.   His wife lived but in him ; his children
idolised him ; his servants worshipped him ; his nature was one that
inspired not only respect but love ; his fondness for children was
extreme, and I have seen our parlour at home filled with little ones,
— children of neighbours, whose names even he did not know, —
but they flocked around him as if he were something more than mortal, and he never tired of amusing them.   A great tease he was to
them, — but they preferred to be teased by him rather than petted
by others.

"There was a simplicity in our household that I have seldom met
with since.   In affairs of business my father would often take us all
into his council.   One instance of this, which is singular and amusing, I particularly recall.   A neighbour of ours was in the habit of
lending money at interest, — a proceeding which we had been taught
to regard as almost as bad as robbery, — and a merchant of Philadelphia, who was in need of money, had come to him to borrow it.
The usurer chanced to be insufficiently supplied, and he mentioned
this exigency to my father, saying that a certain very high rate of
interest could be obtained upon a loan.   My father answered that
he would consider the proposition, and communicate his decision on
the morrow.   He then called a family council and apprised us of his
opportunity to profit by usury.   He dwelt long and earnestly on the
merchant's distress.   We all exclaimed in horror against the idea.
I vividly remember the impression I received that he was about to
become a Shylock, and that he might be tempted to end by cutting
a pound of flesh from the breast of the impoverished debtor.   But
we kept our father from that shocking crime, which, of course, he
had not dreamed of an intention to commit, and blessed him that
he was not a Shylock.   His waggish way of enforcing a moral lesson
was to be realised afterward, in memory.   I do not suppose that
there ever was a man who lived more entirely 'unspotted from the
world.'

"In matters relative to the stage he was scrupulously careful and
thorough.   His wigs were, with a few exceptions, invented and
made by himself.   He hit upon the idea of a wig that should be
practicable, — the hair upon it rising at fright.   He had undertaken

a part in a piece entitled *The Farmer*,[1] but not being particularly struck by it, he set about the study of what could be done to strengthen it. It was then that he hit upon the expedient of making the wig do what the part could not, and he was richly repaid by the laughter of the audience. I was present, and I remember hearing the people around me saying, 'Now look at Jefferson's wig,' in a certain scene of the piece; and, indeed, this comic wig saved the play.

"His varied talent was turned to every line of acting, except tragedy. On one occasion Mrs. Wood,[2] the leading lady of the Chestnut Street theatre, wife of the manager, William B. Wood, was joking with him, saying that he had mistaken his calling, and that his line was tragedy, and she persuaded him to play for his benefit Old Norval, in John Home's tragedy of *Douglas*. I have heard him declare that he really intended to act that part seriously, but he said that the audience had been so accustomed to laughing whenever he appeared that they would not accept him soberly, and when he made his entrance in this tragic character, he was greeted with a shriek of laughter. He tried to be solemn, but it was of no use. The spectators had determined to laugh at Jefferson, and laugh they did. Mrs. Wood always said that he did something on the sly to provoke the laughter, but he would not acknowledge this. I suspect him, though, — for his sentimental acting, as it occasionally occurred in comedy, was touching and beautiful.

"After my father's death, when I was alone in New York, I was requested to give permission for the removal of his remains from Harrisburg to Philadelphia, where it was said a monument should be erected to his memory. But, knowing what sorrow he had suffered at the neglect he received in Philadelphia, towards the end of his career, and knowing also his aversion to all disturbance of the grave, I refused to sanction this proceeding. His ideas were peculiar as to death. When I wished him to see my mother, after she was dead, he would not be persuaded. 'How can you ask me,' he said,

---

[1] *The Farmer.* A musical farce, in two acts. By John O'Keefe. Covent Garden, 1787.

[2] " January 30th, 1804. Married by the Rev. Dr. Abercrombie; Mr. W. B. Wood, to Miss Juliana Westray, both of this (the Chestnut) theatre." — *Wood's Personal Recollections*, page 101.

· to turn with disgust from a face which for so many years has been my pride and my pleasure?' And until a year before his death he never saw a corpse. The first and only dead face he ever looked on was that of his son John. His wish was to be buried in a village churchyard, with no stone to mark the place. But this, it seems, could not be, for two of his old friends, judges of Pennsylvania, erected a stone at his head, in Harrisburg, where he died.

"I never but once saw my father out of temper : and, indeed, he could not have borne to be so ; his naturally equable temper was essential to his health. During Mr. Wemyss's [1] stage management of the Chestnut Street theatre (1827–30), that gentleman went abroad to try to engage a company that, in fact, was not wanted. Among other importations that he brought back was Mr. John Sloman, a comic singer, together with his wife, as stars. Mr. Sloman was a good comic singer, but as an actor was execrable. In my father's contract with the theatre it was expressly stipulated, and had been so for years, that all plays or farces in which he was desired to appear should be sent to him, so that he might choose his part. This arrangement seemed to hurt the self-love of some of the actors ; but, as it was a rule, Mr. Wemyss did not attempt to break it. Nevertheless, after Mr. Sloman had made a hit with his comic singing, Mr. Wemyss harboured the idea that the American public would also accept him as an actor ; and so all the new pieces that came from England that season were given to Sloman, on the pretext that he was a new star, and that they were his property. My father made no protest, feeling sure that neither Mr. Wemyss nor Mr. Sloman could depose him from his place in the public regard. On an occasion of Mr. Warren's benefit, Sloman volunteered his services, and my father was to act in a new farce. I was in the green-

---

[1] FRANCIS COURTNEY WEMYSS (1797–1859), author of a *Theatrical Biography*. In chap. xiii. of that work Mr. Wemyss refers to this subject as follows : " We proceeded as usual to Baltimore for the spring season, and while there I was taken one morning by surprise, by an offer from Mr. Warren to accept the acting and stage management of the theatres under his direction ; to cross the Atlantic, and recruit his dramatic company by engaging new faces from England. . . . I therefore, on May 6, 1827, made an engagement for three years with Mr. Warren. . . . On June 20, I sailed from Philadelphia."

room that day, and I never shall forget my father's face when he saw the announcement. This proclaimed, first, a five-act tragedy; then six successive songs by Sloman; then a farce for Sloman; and finally his own feature, *The Illustrious Stranger*.[1] Mr. Wemyss happened to enter the room at this moment. My father said to him, 'Good morning, sir; that bill must be changed.' 'Why, Mr. Jefferson,' he replied, 'it is impossible: we could not have new bills printed by night.' 'I don't care what you do,' answered my father; 'I want the order of those pieces changed. I have spent time and thought upon my part, and, damn it, sir, I won't have it wasted.' The manager's face was a picture. An oath from the lips of Jefferson frightened us all; but his farce was placed immediately after the tragedy, and I remember that it was a success. I never heard my father use a profane word, except on that occasion.

"The Chestnut Street theatre was now declining in prosperity. Mr. Warren, my uncle, was soon declared insolvent. This new company, which his stage-manager, Mr. Wemyss, had engaged, was to have raised the theatre to the pinnacle of success; but it proved, as sensible observers had feared, the ruin of the house.[2] My father's benefit, always good before this, now turned out a failure. Edwin Forrest, then the rising star, chanced to be acting at the Walnut. On my father's benefit night the opposition managers had put up Forrest's name for a benefit, and the young favourite proved the success. While we were sitting that day at dinner, a letter was brought from Forrest, stating that the writer had not been aware of the employment of his name to oppose that of the elder actor, and that he hoped the blame might be laid where it was due; and he offered to give my father a night, whenever he might choose to name the time, to prove his respect and appreciation. My father deemed the young actor somewhat presumptuous, in taking so much for granted; but a few hours sufficed to teach him the bitter lesson of waning popularity. On the night of that last benefit in Philadelphia, he made up his mind to leave that city and never return to it.

---

[1] *The Illustrious Stranger, or Married and Buried.* Musical farce. By James Kenney. Drury Lane, 1827.

[2] The instructions to engage this company emanated from Mr. Warren, of whose plans Mr. Wemyss was the executor, not the originator.

"At a later time, when my father was acting and managing in Washington, Forrest came there as a star, and he then actually refused one night's emolument. He had said that he would play one night for Jefferson, and he insisted on keeping his word. The money was sent after him, when this was discovered, but he returned it, and positively refused to receive it. Efforts were made, from time to time, to induce my father to return to Philadelphia. Forrest's brother, at the Walnut, made him a most liberal offer, without conditions. Wemyss also came, offering anything. But this was in vain. The heart and the pride of the actor had been wounded to death. He never went back, and he soon died.

"Of all my father's children the most talented was John. He was the pride of our family. A classical scholar, proficient also in modern languages, a clever artist, an accomplished musician, a good caricaturist, an excellent actor, he was one of the most talented men of his day. Playing seconds to my father, he had caught his thoroughness of style, without becoming a servile imitator. He was a good singer and a graceful dancer. He possessed every attribute essential to an actor. But his attractive disposition and his brilliant talents soon gave him an exacting and perilous popularity. Gay company, and the dissipation that it caused, injured his health, though to the last he never was known to fail in professional duty. The last performance he ever gave was in Lancaster, Pa. When my father left Philadelphia, John, who had acted both at the Chestnut and Walnut, resolved to turn manager, and, for some time after that, he managed theatres at Washington and Baltimore, making summer trips to Harrisburg, Lancaster, Pottsville, and other places. It was while we were playing at Lancaster that John died. The pieces that night were *The School for Scandal* and *The Poor Soldier*. Part of the cast of the former was as follows : —

Sir Peter Teazle	Joseph Jefferson, Sr.
Sir Oliver Surface	John Jefferson.
Rowley	Joseph Jefferson, Jr.
Lady Teazle	Mrs. S. Chapman (Elizabeth Jefferson).
Mrs. Candour	Mrs. Joseph Jefferson, Jr.
Lady Sneerwell	Miss Anderson.
Maria	Miss Jefferson.

"The Miss Anderson was Jane (afterwards Mrs. Germon), the eldest daughter of my sister Euphemia ; the Miss Jefferson was my sis-

ter Mary Anne (afterwards Mrs. Wright) ; Mrs. S. Chapman was myself; so this was indeed a theatrical family party. In mounting the
stone steps of the hotel, on our return from the performance, my
brother John slipped on a bit of orange peel, and fell heavily, striking his head, and fracturing his skull. He was taken up insensible,
and he never spoke again. My father never rallied from the shock
of that calamity. In this son his chief hopes had been centred.
He believed that John was destined to great honour and fame, and
that he would keep the name of Jefferson distinguished upon the
stage. After this my father refused to act in any of the plays in
which John had been accustomed to act with him, and in less than
a year he, too, went to his rest.

"My nephew, Joseph Jefferson (Rip Van Winkle), bears a
striking resemblance to my father. He was a wonderfully precocious child: all who remember his childhood say this. When little
more than two years old he gave an imitation of Fletcher,[1] the

---

[1] JOHN FLETCHER, said to have been born in that part of London's
historic fortress called the Bloody Tower, appeared at the London Adelphi
in 1831, showing the Venetian statues; came to America; appeared at
Boston, November 28, 1831, — at the Bowery theatre, New York, December
13, 1831, and at the Walnut Street theatre, Philadelphia, January 5, 1832.
Joseph Jefferson (Rip Van Winkle) was born in Philadelphia, February
20, 1829, and consequently was less than three years old when Fletcher
first performed in that city. It must have been his own mother who observed his precocious endeavours and who made the statue dress for him,
— because Elizabeth Jefferson's mother died in January, 1831. The lad
was very early taken on the stage, at the theatre in Washington, as Cora's
Child, in *Pizarro*, — that being his beginning in the profession; but his
first regular appearance, in a speaking part, was made at the age of four,
1833, when he was carried on as little Jim Crow, by Thomas D. Rice, at
Washington. He then danced and sang. His appearance in the statues
preceded his appearance as little Jim Crow.

A passing glimpse of that juvenile statue episode is given in an article
that was published in the *New York Times*, June 5, 1881, descriptive of an
interview with the aged actor Edmon S. Conner, then 72 years old, since
dead : —

"Mr. Conner recalls a circumstance regarding Joseph Jefferson. He says that the
great comedian was a remarkably small child at the age of seven (?), being hardly larger
than other children at three, but that he was beautifully formed. A man named Fletcher

statue man, and it was indeed an astonishing feat. My mother
chanced to notice the child, in a corner of the room, trying this
experiment, and she called him to her side, and found that he had
got all the "business" of the statues, though he could not have pronounced the name of one of them. She made him a dress similar
to that worn by Fletcher, and he actually gave these imitations upon
the stage when only three years old. Rice came to Washington to
sing his Jim Crow songs, and little Joe caught them up directly,
and, in his baby voice, sung the songs, although he could not
correctly pronounce the words that he sung. His taste for drawing
and painting showed itself at an early age. My father could not
keep his drawing-box away from the boy. Joe was in his fourth
year when my father died. The old gentleman idolised him. I
remember his almost daily salutation would be, ' Joe, where 's my
paint ? ' ' It 's gone,' said the child. ' Yes, sir, I know it 's gone ;
but where ? where ? ' ' Him lost,' was Joe's reply. ' Yes, sir, I
know it 's lost and gone ; but how and where ? ' The boy would
look up, roguishly, and say, ' Him hook um '; and then his grandfather would prophesy what a great artist that child would one day
become, and say that he was ' the greatest boy in the world,' and
let him destroy any amount of anything he chose. The inheritance
of talent was never more clearly shown than in the case of the
present Joseph Jefferson : his habits, his tastes, his acting, — all he
is and does seems just a repetition of his grandfather."

The professional life of Joseph Jefferson exemplified
a wide versatility of shining intellectual power and great
and zealous artistic labour. The specification of some
of the parts that he acted will supply an eloquent testi-

had then just introduced into this country living tableaux representing renowned statuary of the Old World. They had created a great sensation. During a certain summer
season Mr. Conner, with others, was in Wilmington, Del. One of the most attractive
features of their entertainments was that furnished by little Joe, who, in white fleshings,
white wig, and chalked face, was placed upon a small round table, and gave imitations of
Fletcher's statuary, — ' The Discobolus,' ' Ajax Defying the Lightning,' etc. He was
hardly longer than the legs of the table, but so admirably he struck the attitudes, and so
perfectly proportioned was he, that the audiences were charmed with the graceful, lovely
boy."

monial to the force and brilliancy of his talents and to his studious energy. He appeared in more than two hundred characters, and the list is by no means complete. It is by records of this kind, carefully examined and considered, that the judicious observer is able to gauge the actors of the past,[1] and, at the same time, by remarking the changes which occur in the public taste, to trace the dramatic movement from age to age, and thus to sharpen his perception and broaden his grasp of the march of civilised society: for the accepted drama of a nation is always a significant sign of the condition of its people. Subjoined is a partial

REPERTORY OF JOSEPH JEFFERSON

A.

Adonis, *alias* Joe the Shepherd, in *Poor Vulcan, or Gods upon Earth*. Burlesque. By Charles Dibdin. Covent Garden, 1778.

Alibi, in *The Toy, or The Lie of the Day*. Comedy. By John O'Keefe. Covent Garden, 1789.

---

[1] The old theatrical chronicler, Downes, in a note to his *Roscius Anglicanus*, edition of 1789, p. 63, says, of Betterton : —

" Nothing shows the richness of this actor's genius so much as the variety of different characters that he represented. The first tragedian of the age acting the solemn coxcomb would appear surprising to us had we not seen Mr. Garrick perform Sir Anthony Branville, in *The Discovery*. The accomplished actor is master of the whole business in his profession, and no one excepting Mr. Garrick performed such a number of different characters as Betterton."

The veteran Macklin presented one hundred and sixty-five characters. The actor who has played the greatest number of parts, however, is Henry Irving, — who, between the time of his first appearance on the regular stage, September 29, 1856, at Sunderland, and that of his departure from Edinburgh, for the Princess's theatre, London, September 13, 1859, played four hundred and twenty-eight parts. [See *Biographical Sketch of Henry Irving*. By Austin Brereton. 1884.] Since 1859 the list of parts played by Irving must have been largely extended. Henderson played one hundred and fifteen parts.

Acres, in *The Rivals*. Comedy. By Richard Brinsley Sheridan. Covent Garden, 1775.

Apollo Belvi, and also Buskin, in *Killing No Murder*. Farce. By Theodore Hook. Haymarket, 1809. The elder Mathews was the original Buskin.

B.

Bluntly, in *Next Door Neighbours*. Comedy. By Elizabeth Inchbald. Haymarket, 1791.

Bombastes Furioso, in the burlesque tragic opera of that name.

Bobby Pendragon, in *Which Is the Man?* Comedy. By Mrs. Hannah Cowley. Covent Garden, 1783.

Block, in *Where is He?* Farce. By William Dunlap. 1801.

Bras de Fer, in *Tekeli, or The Siege of Montgatz*. Melodrama. By Theodore Edward Hook. Music by the elder Hook. Drury Lane, November 24, 1806.

Bribon, in *Columbus*.

C.

Cloten, in Shakespeare's tragedy of *Cymbeline*.

Cloddy, in *The Mysteries of the Castle*. By Miles Peter Andrews. Covent Garden, 1795.

Count Cassell, in *Lover's Vows*. Drama. Adapted from Kotzebue by William Dunlap. New York Park, 1799.

Clown, in *Harlequin's Vagaries*. — There are, of course, many old plays implicating the Italian masques. The *Biographia Dramatica* mentions no less than sixty, relative to Harlequin.

Charles, in *Know Your Own Mind*. Comedy. By Arthur Murphy. Covent Garden, 1777. The character of Dashwould, in this piece, was intended to portray Foote, the actor and dramatist.

Conrad, in *The Stranger's Birthday*, a sequel to Kotzebue's play of *The Stranger*.

Carlos, in *The Man of Fortitude*. Drama, 1797. Alleged author, Hodgkinson; but Dunlap claimed the piece as his, under the name of *The Knight's Adventure*, and said that Hodgkinson made use of his manuscript.

Carlos, in *The Blind Boy*. An alteration, made by Dunlap, of Kotzebue's *The Epigram*.

Cadi, in *Il Bondocani*. Comic Opera. By Thomas Dibdin, 1801. Music by Boieldieu. Afterwards played as *The Caliph of Bagdad*.

Colin, in *The Irish Mimic, or Blunders at Brighton*. Musical Farce. By John O'Keefe. Covent Garden, 1795.

Captain Copp, in *Charles the Second*. Comedy. By John Howard Payne.

Caleb, in *He Would Be a Soldier*. Comedy. By Frederick Pillon. Covent Garden, 1786.

Captain Flash, in *Miss in Her Teens*. Farce. By David Garrick. Covent Garden, 1747.

D.

Don Ferolo Whiskerandos, in *The Critic*. Farce. By Richard Brinsley Sheridan. Drury Lane, 1779.

Diego, in *The Virgin of the Sun*. Drama. Translated from Kotzebue. Jefferson also acted, later, Orozembo, in *Pizarro, or The Death of Rolla*,—another version of the same piece.

Dogberry, and also Verges, in Shakespeare's comedy of *Much Ado About Nothing*.

Davy, in *Bon Ton*. Farce. By David Garrick. Drury Lane, 1775.

Dickey Gossip, in *My Grandmother*. Farce. By Prince Hoare. Drury Lane, 1796.

Dorilas, in *The Whims of Galatea, or The Power of Love*. Jefferson painted the scenery for this piece, at the John Street theatre, New York, March, 1796.

Don Vincentio, in *A Bold Stroke for a Husband*. Comedy. By Mrs. Hannah Cowley. Covent Garden, 1783.

David Mowbray, in *First Love, or The French Emigrant*. Comedy. Drury Lane, 1795. Dora Jordan was admirably good as Sabina Rosni. The part was acted in America by Mrs. Hodgkinson.

Drugget, in *Three Weeks After Marriage*. Comedy. By Arthur Murphy. Covent Garden, 1776.

Don Manuel, in *She Would and She Would Not*. Comedy. By Colley Cibber. Drury Lane, 1703.

Doctor Last, in *The Devil upon Two Sticks*. Comedy. By

Samuel Foote. Haymarket, 1768. The original Doctor Last was Weston. Foote acted the Devil.

Dromio of Syracuse, in Shakespeare's *Comedy of Errors*. Cowell was the other Dromio.

Dubois, in *The Abbé de L'Épée, or Deaf and Dumb*. 1801.

Don Guzman, in *The Follies of a Day*. Comedy. By Thomas Holcroft. Covent Garden, 1785. Adapted from *La Folle Journée*. by Beaumarchais.

Dominique, in the opera of *Paul and Virginia*. By James Cobb. Music by Mazzinghi and Reeve. Covent Garden, 1800.

Dr. Smugface, in *A Budget of Blunders*. Farce. By Prince Hoare. Covent Garden, 1810. Jefferson, in Dr. Smugface, wore a false nose, skilfully made of wax, which increased the comicality of his aspect in that irascible character.

Dr. Lenitive, in *The Prize, or 2-5-3-8*.

Dominie Sampson, in *Guy Mannering*. Musical Play, on Sir Walter Scott's novel. By Daniel Terry. Covent Garden, 1816.

Dr. Petitqueue, in *The Toothache*. Farce. By John Bray.

E.

Edward, in *The Haunted Tower*. Comic Opera. By James Cobb. Drury Lane, 1789.

Endless, in *The Young Quaker*. Comedy. By John O'Keefe. Haymarket, 1783.

Ennui, in *The Dramatist*. Comedy. By Frederic Reynolds. Covent Garden, 1789.

Ephraim, in *The School for Prejudice*. Comedy. By Thomas Dibdin. Covent Garden, 1801. An enlargement of its author's previous comedy of *Liberal Opinions*.

F.

Frank, in *Half an Hour After Supper*. Haymarket, 1789.

Farmer Ashfield, in *Speed the Plough*. Comedy. By Thomas Morton. Covent Garden, 1800.

Ireland cites a critical opinion on Jefferson's personation of Farmer Ashfield, which is suggestively descriptive of his quality and style : —

" No man possessed such happy requisites for exhibiting this character in the true colours of nature as Mr. Jefferson. In the rustic deportment and dialect, in the artless effusions of benignity and undisguised truth, and in those masterly strokes of pathos and simplicity with which the author has finished the inimitable picture, Mr. Jefferson showed uniform excellence ; and as, in the humorous parts, his comic powers produced their customary effect, so, in the serious overflowings of the honest farmer's nature, the mellow, deep, impressive tones of the actor's voice vibrated to the heart, and produced the most intense and exquisite sensations." — *Mirror of Taste*, Vol. I., p. 75.

Ferrett, in *The Horse and the Widow*. Farce. Altered from the German of Kotzebue, by Thomas Dibdin. Covent Garden, 1799.

Fool, in *The Italian Father*. Drama. By William Dunlap. Park, 1799.

Frank Oatland, in *A Cure for the Heartache*. Comedy. By Thomas Morton. Covent Garden, 1797. This was among Jefferson's best performances.

Francis, in Shakespeare's *King Henry IV.*

First Witch, in *Macbeth*.

Fixture, in *A Roland for an Oliver.* Comedy, 1819.

G.

Gregory Gubbin, in *The Battle of Hexham*. Drama. By George Colman, Jr. Music by Dr. Arnold. Haymarket, 1789. Story of Margaret, Queen to Henry VI., befriended by a bandit.

Grime, in *The Deserted Daughter*. Comedy. By Thomas Holcroft. Covent Garden, 1795. This piece was sometimes acted under the name of *The Steward*. Item, in this, was also one of Jefferson's characters.

Gregory, in *The Mock Doctor, or The Dumb Lady Cured*.[1] Farce. By Henry Fielding. Drury Lane, 1732.

---

[1] That piece was taken from *Le Médecin malgré Lui*, by Molière, — originally named *Le Fagotier*. The story is that the wife of a wood-cutter, in order to be revenged on her husband for his ill treatment of her, told two strangers that he was a learned physician, who would not, however, give his medical knowledge and care, until he had been soundly thrashed; whereupon they compelled him first to attempt the cure of a girl who had been feigning dumbness in order to avoid an obnoxious marriage, and next to assist in an elopement. The situations had previously been used, in *Love's Contrivance* (1703), by Susanna Centlivre, and *The Dumb Lady* (1672), by John Lacy. The subject has been treated in an opera by

Guillot, in *Richard Cœur de Lion*. Historical Play. By Gen. John Burgoyne. Drury Lane, 1786.

Gil Blas, in pantomime play of *Gil Blas*.

H.

Hans Molkin, in *The Wild Goose Chase*. Translated by Dunlap.

Herbert, in *The Man of Ten Thousand*. Comedy. By Thomas Holcroft. Drury Lane, 1796.

Hurry, in *The Maid of the Oaks*. Farce. By Gen. John Burgoyne. Drury Lane, 1774. Covent Garden, with Mrs. Abington in it, 1782. The author was the British commander who capitulated to General Gates, at Saratoga, in 1777, — prompting Sheridan's couplet : —

> " Burgoyne defeated — oh, ye Fates,
> Could not this Samson carry Gates ! "

Humphrey Grizzle, and also Frank, in *The Three and the Deuce*. Comedy. By Prince Hoare. Haymarket, 1795. This piece is suggestive of both the *Comedy of Errors* and *She Stoops to Conquer*.

Gounod, produced at the Théâtre Lyrique, Paris, January 15, 1858, and at the Princess's theatre, London, early in 1865.

It is recorded that David Garrick, before he decided to adopt the dramatic profession, chose *The Mock Doctor*, to test his powers. The particulars are given as follows : —

" The place was the room over St. John's Gate, Clerkenwell. . . . The time was soon after Garrick's friend and tutor, Samuel Johnson, had formed a close intimacy with Cave, the printer and publisher of the *Gentleman's Magazine*, and while Garrick was still in the wine trade, with his brother Peter, and secretly meditating a withdrawal from it, in order to adopt the congenial, but, in the opinion of his friends, the disreputable, calling of an actor. The audience was composed, first of Cave himself, who, though not a man given to mirth, or with an idea beyond his printing presses, had been tickled by Johnson's description of his young townsman's powers. . . . Then there was the burly lexicographer, — in those days very shabby and seedy indeed, but proudly battling his way in the world. . . . Several of Cave's literary handicraftsmen were, doubtless, among the audience : Webb, the enigma writer, Derrick, the pen-cutter, and ' Tobacco' Browne, whose serious poetry even the religious Johnson himself confessed he was unable to read with patience. The actors who assisted Garrick were some of Cave's journeymen printers, who had, for the time, laid aside their composing sticks, and read or recited the parts allotted to them, as best they could. Garrick played the involuntary physician Gregory, as Fielding renamed him ; and we have all read how Johnson, in his later years, returning from the Mitre, or the Cheshire Cheese, with Boswell, in the early morning, would grasp the street-post by Temple Gate, and send forth a peal of laughter, which echoed and re-echoed through the silent streets, as he recalled the irresistible humour of his clever friend little Davy."

The comic effect is obtained by means of complications arising out of the bewildering resemblance between three brothers, — each being mistaken for another, and all displayed at cross purposes with the rest of the characters. Frank is a rustic, of the Zekiel Homespun stripe. Humphrey Grizzle is an opinionated, cranky, eccentric old servant, whose perplexity affords much amusement. The three brothers, — Percival, Peregrine, and Pertinax Single, — who " raise the Deuce " by being alike in appearance but diverse in character and conduct, are acted by one and the same person.

I.

Ibrahim, in *Blue Beard, or Female Curiosity.* Musical Extravaganza. By George Colman, Jr. Drury Lane, 1798.

J.

Jasper Lunge, in *A Good Spec — Land in the Moon.* Farce. 1797.

Jacob Gawky, in *A Chapter of Accidents.* Comedy. By Miss Sophia Lee. Haymarket, 1780.

Jaques. and also Rolando, in *The Honeymoon.* Comedy. By John Tobin. Drury Lane, 1805.

Jeremy Diddler, in *Raising the Wind.* Farce. By James Kenney. Covent Garden, 1803. Lewis was the original Jeremy. — " Diddler has been attempted by many celebrated comedians, but by none so successfully as by Jefferson, who exhibits the various dispositions of Jeremy with admirable effect." — *The Thespian Monitor.*

John Lump, in *The Review. or The Wags of Windsor.* Musical Farce. By George Colman, Jr. Haymarket, 1808.

Jargon, in *The Bulse of Diamonds, or What is She?* [By Dr. Doddrell ?]

John, in *The Wheel of Truth.* Farce. By James Fennell, the actor. New York Park, 1803.

Job Thornbury, in *John Bull.* Comedy. By George Colman, Jr. Covent Garden, 1805.

Jack Stocks. in *The Lottery.* Farce. By Henry Fielding. Drury Lane. 1731.

Justice Greedy. in *A New Way to Pay Old Debts.* Comedy. By Philip Massinger. Acted at the Phœnix in Drury Lane, 1633.

John, in *False Shame*. Drama. Adapted from the German, by Dunlap.

Jack Meggott, in *The Suspicious Husband*. Comedy. By Dr. Benjamin Hoadly. Covent Garden, 1747. Garrick was famously good, in this piece, as Ranger. George the Second sent the author one hundred pounds, as a compliment.

Jack Arable, in *Speculation*. Comedy. By Frederic Reynolds. Covent Garden, 1795.

James, in *Bourville Castle*. Musical Drama. By Rev. John Blair Linn. 1797.

Jack Bowline, and also Captain Bertram, in *Fraternal Discord*. Drama. Adapted from the German of Kotzebue, by Dunlap. John Street theatre, 1800.

Jack Acorn, in *Columbia's Daughters*. Drama. By Mrs. Susanna Rowson, author of *The Female Patriot, Slaves in Algiers, Charlotte Temple, Americans in England*, and other pieces. 1800.

Jew, in *Self-Immolation, or Family Distress*. Drama. Adapted from Kotzebue, by Dunlap.

K.

Kourakim, in *The Captive of Spilsberg*. Drama. By Prince Hoare. Drury Lane, 1799.

Kit Cosey, in *Town and Country*. By Thomas Morton. Covent Garden, 1807.

Kudrin, in *Count Benyowski*. Drama. By Dunlap. Park, 1799.

L.

Louis, in *The Robbery*. Drama. By Monvel. Translated by William Dunlap.

Lackbrain, in *Life*. Comedy. By Frederic Reynolds. Covent Garden, 1801.

Lord Listless, in *The East Indian*. Comedy. By M. G. Lewis. Drury Lane, 1799.

Launcelot Gobbo, in *The Merchant of Venice*.

Lord Grizzle, in *The Life and Death of Tom Thumb, the Great*. Burlesque. 1785.

La Fleur, in *Sterne's Maria, or The Vintage*. Opera. By Dunlap. Music by Pellesier. 1799.

H

Leopold, in *The Siege of Belgrade*. Comic opera. By James Cobb. Music by Stephen Storace. Jefferson painted scenery for this piece.

Lieutenant, in *The Archers, or The Mountaineers of Switzerland*. Opera. By Dunlap. Called, also, *William Tell, or The Archers*.

La Gloire, in *The Surrender of Calais*. Play. By George Colman, Jr. Haymarket, 1791. Based on a French novel.

Lord Dartford, in *The Fair Fugitive, or He Forgot Himself*. This was *The Fair Fugitives*, a musical extravaganza, by Miss Anna Maria Porter. Music by Dr. Busby. Acted at Covent Garden, 1803.

Lord Foppington, in *The Relapse*. Comedy. By Sir John Vanbrugh. Drury Lane, 1708. Altered, and named *The Country Heiress*.

Lodowick, in *Adelmorn, The Outlaw*. Drama. By M. G. Lewis. Drury Lane, 1801.

La Fleur, in *Animal Magnetism*. Farce. By Elizabeth Inchbald. Covent Garden, 1788. Of French origin.

M.

Michael, in *The Adopted Child*. Musical piece. By Samuel Birch. Drury Lane, 1795.

Memno, in *Abællino*. Drama. By Dunlap, from the German of Zsokke.

Motley, in *The Castle Spectre*. Drama. By Matthew Gregory Lewis. Drury Lane, 1798. — "A story has been told that about the end of the season (this piece having proved very successful), Mr. Sheridan and the author had a dispute in the green-room; when the latter offered, in confirmation of his arguments, to bet all the money which *The Castle Spectre* had brought, that he was right. 'No,' said Sheridan: 'I cannot afford to bet all it has brought; but I'll tell you what I'll do — I'll bet you all it is worth.'" — *Biographia Dramatica*.

Mercutio, and also Peter, in *Romeo and Juliet*. The former part Jefferson acted, for the first time, at the Chestnut Street theatre, Philadelphia, in the season of 1815–16.

Matthew Mug, in *A House to Be Sold*. Musical piece. By James Cobb. Music by Kelly. Drury Lane, 1802. Altered and enlarged from a French piece, entitled *Maison à Vendre*.

Michelli, in *A Tale of Mystery*. Melodrama. By Thomas Holcroft. Covent Garden, 1802. Jefferson also acted Francisco, in this piece.

Mawworm, in *The Hypocrite*. Comedy. By Isaac Bickerstaff. Drury Lane, 1768. An alteration of Cibber's *The Nonjuror*.

Mendoza, in *The Duenna*. Comic opera. By R. B. Sheridan. Covent Garden, 1775.

Muley Hassan, in *Fiesco*. Drama. From the German of Schiller. 1796, 1798.

Marshal Ingelheim, in *The Harper's Daughter, or Love and Ambition*. Called, also, *The Minister*. Drama. Adapted by M. G. Lewis, from *Love and Intrigue*, by Schiller.

N.

Nicholas Rue, in *Secrets Worth Knowing*. Comedy. By Thomas Morton. Covent Garden, 1798.

Nicholas, in *The Follies of Fashion*. Comedy. By Leonard McNally. Original title, *Fashionable Levities*. Covent Garden, 1785.

Nipperkin, in *The Sprigs of Laurel*. Comic Opera. By John O'Keefe. Covent Garden, 1793. Afterwards acted under the title of *The Rival Soldiers*.

O.

Osman, in *The Two Misers*. Farce. By Kane O'Hara. Covent Garden, 1775.

Officer, in *The Independence of America*. Pantomime. 1796.

Old Rapid, in *A Cure for the Heartache*. Comedy. By Thomas Morton. Covent Garden, 1797.

P.

Polonius, and Osric, in *Hamlet*. — "Jefferson was the best Polonius that ever trod the American stage. No other actor ever succeeded so well in combining the courtier and the gentleman with the humourist. He gave elegance and dignity to the character." — *Old N. Y. Spirit of the Times*.

Plainwell, in *A Quarter of an Hour Before Dinner*. Farce. By Rev. John Rose. Haymarket, 1788.

Peter, in *The Stranger*. Dunlap's version of Kotzebue's drama.

Pero, in *The Spanish Castle, or The Knight of Guadalquivir*. Musical Drama. By William Dunlap. Music by Hewitt. 1800.

Papillion, in *The Liar*. Comedy. By Samuel Foote. Covent Garden, 1762.

Paulo, in *The Italian Monk*. Drama. By James Boaden. 1797. Founded on Mrs. Radcliffe's novel of that name.

Precipe Rebate, in *Retaliation*. Farce. By Leonard McNally. Covent Garden, 1782.

Peter Postobit, in *Folly as It Flies*. Comedy. By Frederic Reynolds. Covent Garden, 1802.

Pedro, in *Cinderella*. Pantomime.

Philosopher, in *The Merry Girl, or The Two Philosophers*.

Q.

Quillet, in *Hear Both Sides*. Comedy. By Thomas Holcroft. Drury Lane, 1803.

R.

Robert, in *The Prisoner*. Musical Piece. By John Rose. 1792.

Realize, in *The Will*. Comedy. By Frederic Reynolds. Drury Lane, 1797.

Ralph, in *Lock and Key*. Musical Farce. By Prince Hoare. Covent Garden, 1796–97.

Roderigo, in *Othello*.

Robert Grange, in *Delays and Blunders*. Comedy. By Frederic Reynolds. Covent Garden, 1803.

S.

Sir William Howe, in *Bunker Hill, or The Death of Warren*. Drama. By John D. Burke. 1797.

Samuel, in *The Indians in England, or The Nabob of Mysore*. Drama. Adapted from Kotzebue, by Dunlap.

Stephano, in Shakespeare's comedy of *The Tempest*.

Soleby, in *The School for Soldiers*. Play, from the French, by Dunlap.

Sambo, in *Laugh When You Can*. Comedy. By Frederic Reynolds. Covent Garden, 1799.

Sir Matthew Maxim, in *Five Thousand a Year*. Comedy. By Thomas Dibdin. Covent Garden, 1799.

Sir Shenkin, in *Fontainebleau, or Our Way in France*. Comic Opera. By John O'Keefe. Covent Garden, 1784. The sub-title given to that piece when it was acted in America was *John Bull in Paris*. The part of Sir Shenkin Ap Griffin was subsequently changed by the author to Squire Tallyho.

Septimus, in *The Doldrum*. Farce. By John O'Keefe. Covent Garden, 1796.

Sir Samuel Sheepy, in *The School for Arrogance*. Comedy. By Thomas Holcroft. Covent Garden, 1791.

Sir Stately Perfect, in *The Natural Daughter*. Comedy. By Dunlap. 1799. New York Park theatre.

Stephen, in *Every Man in His Humour*. Comedy. By Ben Jonson. 1598.

Sir Peter Curious, in *The Telegraph*. Comedy. By John Dent. Covent Garden, 1795.

Silky, in *The Road to Ruin*. Comedy. By Thomas Holcroft. Covent Garden, 1792.

Sancho, in *Love Makes a Man, or The Fop's Fortune*. Comedy. By Colley Cibber. Drury Lane, 1701.

Sir Adam Contest, in *The Wedding Day*. Comedy. By Elizabeth Inchbald. Drury Lane, 1794.

Sadi, the Moor, in *The Mountaineers, or Love and Madness*. Play. By George Colman, Jr. Haymarket, 1795. Based on the episode of Cardenio, in *Don Quixote.* — "Jefferson as Sadi was universally admired and applauded. The music of the piece he is perfectly acquainted with, and his manner of delivering the duets, in conjunction with Mrs. Wilmot's [1] notes, in Agnes, communicated the highest gratification and delight." — *Thespian Monitor, December* 16, 1809.

---

[1] MRS. WILMOT, originally Miss Webb, was first known as Mrs. Marshall. She came from England in 1792, with Marshall, and both were speedily accepted as favourites. Mrs. Marshall was reputed the best chambermaid actress of her time. "A pretty little woman," says Dunlap, "and a most charming actress, in the Pickles and romps of the drama." She was much admired by Washington. She returned to England, left Marshall, wedded Wilmot, came back to America, and here died.

Sir Harry Harmless, in *I'll Tell You What*. Comedy. By Elizabeth Inchbald. Haymarket, 1785–86. Colman named this piece.

Sir David Daw, in *The Wheel of Fortune*. Comedy. By Richard Cumberland. Drury Lane, 1795.

Sebastian, in *The Midnight Hour*. Comedy. By Elizabeth Inchbald. Covent Garden, 1788. From the French of M. Damaniant.

Squire Richard, in *The Provoked Husband, or A Journey to London*. Comedy. By Colley Cibber. Drury Lane, 1728.

Sampson Rawbold, in *The Iron Chest*. Tragedy. By George Colman, Jr. Drury Lane, 1796.

Stave, in *The Shipwreck*. Comic Opera. By S. J. Arnold. Drury Lane, 1796.

Solus, in *Every One Has His Fault*. Comedy. By Elizabeth Inchbald. Covent Garden, 1793. A fine portrait of Jefferson, as Solus, appears in the Wemyss collection of theatrical portraits.

Sir Benjamin Dove, in *The Brothers*. Comedy. By Richard Cumberland. Covent Garden, 1769.

Sharpset, in *The Votary of Wealth*. Comedy. By J. G. Holman. Covent Garden, 1799.

Sir Robert Bramble, and also Dr. Ollapod, in *The Poor Gentleman*. Comedy. By George Colman, Jr. Covent Garden, 1802.

Sir Peter Teazle, Sir Oliver Surface, Charles Surface, Crabtree, and Moses, in *The School for Scandal*. By Richard Brinsley Sheridan. First acted, May 8, 1777, at Drury Lane.

Sheepface, in *The Village Lawyer*. Farce. From the French. 1795.

Sir Hugh Evans, in Shakespeare's *The Merry Wives of Windsor*.

Sir Owen Ap Griffith, in *The Welsh Girl*. Vaudeville.

Scaramouch, in *Don Juan*.

T.

Toby, in *The Wandering Jew, or Love's Masquerade*. Comedy. By Andrew Franklin. Drury Lane, 1797.

Toby Allspice, in *The Way to Get Married*. Comedy. By Thomas Morton. Covent Garden, 1796.

Tom Seymour, in *Fortune's Fool*. Comedy. By Frederic Reynolds. Covent Garden, 1796.

Tom Holton, in *Tell Truth and Shame the Devil*. Comedy. By Dunlap. John Street theatre, New York, 1797. Reduced to one act, and played at Covent Garden, London, May 18, 1799, for benefit of Mrs. Johnson.

Touchstone, Adam, Le Beau, and William, in *As You Like It*.

Toby Thatch, in *The London Hermit, or Rambles in Dorsetshire*. Comedy. By John O'Keefe. Haymarket, 1793.

Tagg, in *The Spoiled Child*. Farce. Drury Lane, 1790. Attributed to Isaac Bickerstaff.

Tallboy, in *The Spanish Barber*. Musical Farce. By George Colman, Sr. Haymarket, 1777.

Tristram Fickle, in *The Weathercock*. Farce. By J. T. Allingham. Drury Lane, 1806. — "Jefferson's Tristram, lively, active, and productive of real merriment." — *Thespian Monitor, December* 13, 1809.

Tim Tartlet, in *The First Floor*. Farce. By James Cobb. Drury Lane, 1787.

Tom Starch, in *The Wise Man of the East*. Play. By Elizabeth Inchbald. Adapted from Kotzebue. Covent Garden, 1799.

Thomas, in *The Good Neighbor*. Farce.

Timothy Quaint, in *The Soldier's Daughter*. Comedy. By Andrew Cherry. Drury Lane, 1804. Edwin Forrest, in his youth, often acted Malfort, in this piece. *The Soldier's Daughter* was revived in Boston, at the Globe theatre, in June, 1872, but it did not please the public.

V.

Varland, in *The West Indian*. Comedy. By Richard Cumberland. Drury Lane, 1771.

W.

Williams, in *He's Much to Blame*. Comedy. By Thomas Holcroft. Covent Garden, 1798.

William, in the opera of *Rosina*. By Mrs. Brooke. Covent Garden, 1783. Bible story of Boaz and Ruth.

Witzki, in *Zorinski*. Drama. By Thomas Morton. Haymarket, 1795.

Y.

Young Scharfeneck, in *The Force of Calumny*. Drama. Adapted from the German, by Dunlap.

Young Clackett, in *The Guardian*. Comedy. By David Garrick. Drury Lane, 1759, 1773. Based on *La Pupille*, by M. Fagan.

Z.

Zekiel Homespun, in *The Heir at Law*. Comedy. By George Colman, Jr. Haymarket, 1797.

Born in 1774, five years before the death of Garrick, and dying in 1832, one year before the birth of Edwin Booth, Joseph Jefferson's lifetime covered much of the period of the Kembles and Edmund Kean, in England, and of Dunlap, Wignell, Warren, Wood, and others who aided to build the foundations of the stage in America. He saw the rise and fall of Hodgkinson and of Fennell, and the advent of Cooper, Junius Brutus Booth, Maywood, Conway, Hamblin, and Forrest. He acted in the same company with the beautiful Anne Brunton and the wonderful Mary Duff.[1] He made his advent in

---

[1] MARY A. D. DUFF, 1794-1857. — She was, probably, the greatest tragic actress that ever trod our stage. It was to her that the poet Moore referred, in his lovely song, " While gazing on the moon's light." She was born in London; married John R. Duff, of the Dublin stage; came with him to America in 1810; and in subsequent years had a career of astonishing brilliancy, — darkened, however, by much misfortune. She died, of cancer, at No. 36 West Ninth street, New York, and is buried in Greenwood (lot 8999, grave 805). Her life has been affectionately written by Ireland. Ludlow describes her as " refined, yet powerful; not boisterous, yet forcible; graceful in all her motions, and dignified without stiffness." She had lived a Catholic all her days, but she became a Methodist toward the last, after her marriage with Mr. J. G. Sevier, of New Orleans. Her death and burial were obscure, and for many years her fate remained unknown, — some of her relatives being averse to the association of her name with the stage, and desirous of leaving the subject in oblivion. She was a

JOSEPH JEFFERSON, Sr., AND MR. BLISSETT

As Dr. Smugface and Dr. Dablancour in the Budget of Blunders.

the second term of the presidency of Washington, when
the American Republic consisted of only sixteen States
and contained a population of barely four millions,[1] and,
living through the terms of Adams, Jefferson, Madison,
Monroe, and John Quincy Adams, he died in the first
term of Andrew Jackson. It was a courtly period in
American history, and Joseph Jefferson was one of its
most conspicuous ornaments. He differed materially
from his father, not in worth or honour, but in important
personal attributes and in the general character of his
life. He was less sturdy, less bluff, less genial and com-
panionable, less a man of the world, and more a studious
recluse. His temperament was more delicate, his nature more reticent, his mind more ambitious, his faculties
more nimble and more brilliant ; and his life seems to
have been carefully planned and rigidly governed. He
saw at an early age both the direction of his talents
and the goal of his desires ; and thereafter, in a spirit of
simple self-devotion, he moved forward to the attainment
of high and honourable ends. He was essentially a
virtuous person, acting always from the monitions of
principle, never from the promptings of impulse or the
fickle whims of expediency or of social custom. His
consideration for others was an exact regard for their
rights and a tender sympathy with their feelings. He
was unselfish, devoid of conceit and affectation, and he
loved the dramatic art more than he loved himself. His
wish was to live the life of a good man and to win the

good woman as well as a great actress. See my *Shadows of the Stage,*
Vol. II.

[1] In 1790 the population of those States was 3,929,214. The city of
New York, as late as 1807, contained scarcely more than 80,000 persons.

success of a great comedian, and that wish was nobly accomplished.   For business enterprise he had but little either of taste or talent, and his mental constitution was such as required that personal advancement should be the result of personal desert and worthy achievement. His ambition was to grasp success itself, and not to grasp merely its emoluments, and he would have been made miserable by honour and wealth that he had not merited.   That fine nature, flowing into all his works and ways, inspired his acting with lovely and winning attributes, — those indefinable charms which far transcend words and actions, in the expression of the soul. His lack, if such it may be deemed, was one that is natural and usual in a comedian, — a lack of passion.   No deadly conflict could ever have raged upon the theatre of that serene spirit ; no pall of tempest could ever have lowered over its pure, pellucid depths.   He felt no wounds but those that strike the heart.   His private life was lived in the affections; his public life in that realm of dramatic art which requires, exclusively, observation mingled with invention, eccentricity tempered by fancy, and humour touched with tenderness.   As an actor his superiority appears to have consisted in his extraordinary thoroughness and felicity of treatment.   His genius did not overwhelm, but it always delighted and satisfied.   His contemporaries universally commended him as a natural actor.   His artifice, accordingly, must have been perfect, and must have been employed with consummate skill ; for no actor ever yet produced the effect of nature by being perfectly natural.   He possessed, in ample variety, the rich treasures of wise and safe tradition, but he used those treasures with the boldness of an original mind ; and therefore he left upon his age the impression, not of a copyist, but a creator. His artistic ancestors, if conjecture be not idle, were Robert Wilks (1670–1732) and Thomas Dogget (obiit 1721). He had the deep feeling, the delicacy, the versatility and the dash of Wilks, and he had more than Dogget's glowing humour and consistent and polished art. " I can only copy nature from the originals before me," said Sir Godfrey Kneller, to Dogget ; " but you can vary them at pleasure, and yet preserve the likeness." That was likewise true of Jefferson ; and there can be no testimonial more explanatory of his charm, or more significant of his exalted powers and achievements, alike in the conservation, the improvement, and the transmission of the best tradition of comedy-acting on the English stage, than the eloquent fact that the actors, who are habitually severe censors of each other, — actors like Hodgkinson, Cooper, Kean, and Forrest, — heartily, and with one accord, pronounced him the finest comedian of the age in which he lived.

III

ELIZABETH JEFFERSON

1810–1890

ELIZABETH JEFFERSON, whose recollections have been incorporated in my sketch of her father, was born in Philadelphia, about the year 1810, and in the spring of 1827, when seventeen years of age, was presented at the Chestnut Street theatre as Rosina, in *The Spanish Barber*.[1] She had a lovely voice, and had been carefully instructed and trained in music ; but her timidity and inexperience, on the first night, marred her efforts, and her attempt was accounted a failure. Cowell, who preceded Wemyss in the stage management of the Chestnut, when Warren and Wood dissolved their partnership, in 1826, had the superintendence of the effort, and he has left this record of it, in his *Thirty Years*, Vol. II., p. 9 :—

"During this season, 1826–27, I had the gratification of introducing two of the 'fairest of creation,' as candidates for histrionic fame — a daughter of old Warren, and a daughter of old Jefferson. They were cousins, and about the same age. Hetty Warren had decidedly the best of the race for favour at the start, but Elizabeth

---

[1] *The Spanish Barber.* Comedy, with songs, by George Colman. Haymarket, 1777. Taken from *Le Barbière de Seville*, by P. A. C. de Beaumarchais.

Jefferson soon shot ahead, and maintained a decided superiority. Poor girls! They were both born and educated in affluence, and both lived to see their parents sink to the grave in comparative poverty. Hetty married a big man named Willis, — a very talented musician, — much against the will of her doting father; and, like most arrangements of the kind, it proved a sorry one. Elizabeth became the wife of Sam Chapman, in 1828. He was a very worthy fellow, with both tact and talent in his favour, and her lot promised unbounded happiness."

Wemyss, who saw Elizabeth Jefferson's first appearance, gives concurrent testimony, in his *Theatrical Biography*, chap. 13 : —

"For the benefit of Mr. Jefferson, whose name was sure to fill the house, his daughter, Miss E. Jefferson, made her first appearance upon any stage as Rosina, in *The Spanish Barber*. If Miss Warren was the best *débutante* I had ever seen, Miss Jefferson was decidedly the worst. She spoke so low, and so completely lost all self-possession, that, had it not been for her father, she would scarcely have escaped derision. The only redeeming point was her song of *An Old Man would be Wooing*, in which she was feebly encored. From such an unfavourable beginning little was to be expected. But, in the race commenced between Miss Warren and herself, although distanced in the first attempt, she soon outstripped her rival, in her future career, rising step by step, until she became, as Mrs. S. Chapman, the leading actress of the American stage, in the Park theatre of New York."

After a dull beginning Miss Jefferson put forth her powers with augmented resolution, and, — at the Chestnut, and in those wandering theatrical expeditions with which her renowned father closed his professional career, — she soon acquired the experience essential to her success. Thus equipped, she came forward at the Park theatre, New York, on September 1, 1834, as Ophelia, and there was accepted as an actress of the finest powers. She had in the mean time been married, in Philadelphia, to Samuel Chapman, a young and clever actor, who seems to have been a favourite with "old Jefferson"; but he had died[1] shortly after their marriage, and she was now a widow. The bills announced her as Mrs. S. Chapman. The stock company in which she took her place included T. H. Blakeley, John H. Clarke, John Fisher, H. B. Harrison, Henry S. Hayden, John Jones, W. H. Latham, John Kemble Mason, Gilbert Nexsen, Henry Placide, Thomas Placide, T. Povey, Henry Russell, Peter Richings, William Wheatley, Mrs. Archer, Mrs. Durie, the lovely Mrs. Gurner, Mrs. Harrison, the Misses Turnbull, Mrs. Vernon, and Mrs. Wheatley. James William Wallack acted Hamlet, to open the season, and in its course Sheridan Knowles appeared, in a round of his own characters. Mrs. Chapman's success was uncommonly brilliant.

"No actress who ever preceded or followed her on the Park stage," says Ireland, "excelled her in general ability, and she was the last stock actress attached to the establishment fully competent to sustain equally well the leading characters in the most opposite walks of the drama. Devoid of stage trickery, artless, unaffected, and perfectly true to nature, not beautiful in feature, but with a coun-

---

[1] SAMUEL CHAPMAN. — "The Reading mail stage, with nine male passengers and the driver, was stopped by three foot-pads, a few miles from Philadelphia, in the middle of the night. . . . Chapman, who was extremely clever at dramatising local matters, took a ride out to the scene of the robbery, the better to regulate the action of a piece he was preparing on the subject, was thrown from his horse, and slightly grazed his shoulder. He had to wear, that night, a suit of brass armour, and, the weather being excessively hot, he wore it next his skin, which increased the excoriation, and it was supposed the verdigris had poisoned the wound. At any rate, he died, in a week after the accident. . . ." — *Cowell's Thirty Years*, Vol. II., chap. 9.

tenance beaming with beauty of expression, in whatever character
cast, she always succeeded in throwing a peculiar charm around it,
and in making herself admired and appreciated. Her performance
of Julia, in *The Hunchback*, first stamped her reputation as an artist
of the highest rank. Her engagement was a continued triumph,
and her retirement from the stage, in the spring of 1835, on her
marriage with Mr. Richardson, a source of deep and earnest
regret."

The marriage was contracted with Mr. Augustus
Richardson, of Baltimore. Cowell mentions him, as "a
clever young printer," whom he met, in company with
Junius Brutus Booth, at Annapolis, in 1829. Mr.
Richardson, like his matrimonial predecessor, died suddenly, in consequence of an accident ; and his widow,
returning to the stage, was again seen at the Park. She
subsequently went into the South, joining her brother
Joseph and other relatives and connections. After her
brother's death, in 1842, she managed for a time the
theatre at Mobile ; and at that place, in 1849, she
was married to Charles J. B. Fisher, — brother to the
famous vocalist, Clara Fisher, — whose death, in 1859,
aged fifty-four, left her again a widow. Those bereave-
ments were not her worst afflictions. One of her sons
was murdered in New Orleans, and another, Vernon,
became insane from a fall, and, after lingering for many
years in lunacy, expired in an asylum. Her own death
was stated, in Brown's *History of the American Stage*,
p. 310, to have occurred in 1853, but that was an error.
A strong will, an intrepid spirit, and a magnificent
constitution, sustained her, in patience and steadfast
industry, to a great age. For many years she was a
teacher of music ; and one of her daughters, — Clara
Fisher, named after her distinguished relative, now

(1894) Mrs. Maeder, — was favourably known as a vocalist. Charles J. B. Fisher's first appearance on the stage was made at the Mobile theatre, in 1842, as Dazzle, in *London Assurance.*

The musical style of Elizabeth Jefferson was based on that of the beautiful Garcia,[1] whom she saw at the New York Park theatre in the season of 1825, having been sent from Philadelphia to observe and study that incomparable model. When only eleven years old she was elected an honorary member of the Musical Fund Society, of Philadelphia. John Sinclair, the vocalist, father of Catherine Sinclair, who became the wife of Edwin Forrest, repeatedly designated her the best singer in America, and more than once offered her a star position in his musical company. Had she devoted herself exclusively to either the lyric or dramatic stage, and resisted the allurements of ideal domesticity, she might have reached the greatest eminence. Before she came to the Park theatre, Henry J. Finn, the comedian, had assured Edmund Simpson, the manager, that she was beyond rivalry as a comedy actress; and Finn had offered her the leading business, on her own terms, at the St. Charles theatre, New Orleans. Tyrone Power had also spoken of her, with unstinted admiration. Edwin Forrest, in

---

[1] SIGNORINA MARIA FELICITÉ GARCIA.—Born in 1808. Made her first appearance in 1823, at Covent Garden. Appeared at the Park theatre, New York, November 29, 1825, as Rosina. Was married on March 23, 1826, to Eugene Malibran. Made her last appearance in America, October 28, 1827, at the Bowery theatre, New York, as the Princess of Navarre, in *John of Paris.* Went to Europe and had great success as Mme. Malibran. Obtained a divorce from her husband and married the violinist De Beriot. Died September 17, 1836, at Manchester, England, in her twenty-eighth year, and is there buried. She was a wonder of genius and beauty.

PARK STREET IN 1830

whose support she had acted, at Washington, declared her to be the best tragic actress on the stage. " She is the best Lady Macbeth we have," he said, " and the only Pauline." Somebody asked Simpson how he had happened to hear of her as an actress. "I have heard of nobody else for two years," he answered. During the Park engagement of Sheridan Knowles, she acted in all the plays produced for him, — *The Hunchback*, *William Tell*, *Virginius*, *The Wife*, etc., — and the famous author was fascinated with her loveliness and her genius. Ever afterward, in writing to her from England, he addressed her as Lady Julia Rochdale, and signed his letters, "Your father, Walter." It was as Julia that she made her first hit at the Park; and her popularity there was so great that every omission of her name from the bill would cause a serious fall in the receipts. Yet she was only a member of the stock company, receiving a salary of $30 a week ; and the receipts from her farewell benefit performance were only $882. Elizabeth Jefferson (she acted as Mrs. Chapman in 1834, and as Mrs. Richardson in 1835 and 1837) was the original representative in America of several important characters in modern comedy, vaudeville, and burlesque· A few of those parts may be named : —

Bess . . . . in . .	The Beggar of Bethnal Green.
Eliza . . . . " . .	The Dumb Belle.
Gabrielle . . . " . .	Tom Noddy's Secret.
Gertrude . . . " . .	The Loan of a Lover.
Julia . . . . " . .	The Hunchback.
Lydia . . . . " . .	The Love Chase.
Lissette Gerstein " . .	The Swiss Cottage.
Marianne . . " . .	The Wife.
Oliver Twist . " . .	Oliver Twist.

I

Pauline . . . in . The Lady of Lyons.
Perseus . . . " . The Deep, Deep Sea.
Smike . . . " . Nicholas Nickleby.

Her repertory also included, aside from more conspicuous characters : —

Amina . . . in . The Somnambulist.
Cinderella . . " . Cinderella.
Esmeralda . . " . The Hunchback of Notre Dame.
Helen Worret . " . Man and Wife, or More Secrets than One.
Jenny . . . " . The Widow's Victim.
Maria . . . " . Of Age To-morrow.
Mimi . . . . " . The Pet of the Petticoats.
Mrs. Budd . . " . My Wife's Mother.
Mrs. Lynx . . " . Married Life.
Mme. de Manville " . Married Lovers.
Myrtello . . . " . The Broken Sword.
Rosina . . . " . The Barber.
Therese . . . " . Secret Service.
Vettoria . . . " . The Knight of the Golden Fleece.

A complete list of her embodiments would fill several pages. Her range extended from Little Pickle to Lady Macbeth, and in all that she attempted she was excellent. Time makes sad havoc with beauty and popularity. In those bright days of the old Park theatre when Elizabeth Jefferson walked abroad, her footsteps were followed by the admiring glances of hundreds of worshippers. There came a time when her slight and faded figure, clad in the sable garments of grief, would flit by unnoticed in the crowd. She passed some time, toward the close of her life, at St. John, Newfoundland, where she gave instruction in music. She died, at No. 139 West 20th street, New York, on November 18, 1890, closing in poverty and oblivion a career most sadly admonitive of the evanescence of human happiness, worldly fortune, and theatrical renown.

IV

JOSEPH JEFFERSON

1804-1842

JOSEPH JEFFERSON, the father of our Rip Van Winkle, lived an uneventful life, the story of which naturally takes the form of a tribute to beauty and worth of character rather than a narrative of achievements that concern the world. Joseph Jefferson, the third of the Jefferson Family of Actors, was born at Philadelphia, in 1804, and in that city he received his education and grew to manhood. While a boy he did not evince a taste for the stage, but preferred the study of architecture and drawing; and that he pursued diligently and with success. In those branches, and also in painting, he was instructed by Robert Coyle,[1] an English scenic artist, of repute at that period. There is no positive record of his first appearance upon the stage, but it is remembered that he sometimes played such parts as the First Murderer, in *Macbeth*, while yet a youth. His name appears in the playbills of the Chestnut Street theatre as early as 1814, and it is known that when finally he had adopted

---

[1] ROBERT COYLE was killed by an accidental fall from a wagon, his horse having suddenly started in fright. A performance for the benefit of his widow occurred at the Bowery theatre, New York, August 22, 1827.

131

the dramatic profession, he made himself a good actor in
the line of old men.   In 1824, he was a member of the
dramatic company of the Chatham Garden theatre, New
York, under the management of Henry Barrière.   That
company comprised Andrew J. Allen, George H. Barrett, Thomas Burke, John M. Collins, C. Durang, Thomas
Kilner, who was stage-manager, Henry George Moreland, William Oliff, once prompter at the old Park theatre, W. Robertson, Alexander Simpson, ———— Spiller,
———— Somerville, John Augustus Stone, — who afterward wrote *Metamora*, for Edwin Forrest, — Henry
Wallack, ———— Williamson, Mrs. Allen, Mrs. Burke,
Mrs. P. M. Clark, Mrs. Durang, Mrs. Entwistle (who
had been Mrs. Mason and who became Mrs. Crooke),
Miss Henry, afterward famous as the beautiful Mrs.
Barrett, Mrs. Kilner, Miss Oliff, Mrs. Spiller, Mrs. H.
Wallack, Mrs. Walstein, and Mrs. Caroline Placide Waring,[1] widow of Leigh Waring, and afterwards the wife
of William Rufus Blake.   The theatre was opened for
its third season on May 17, 1824, with *The Soldier's
Daughter* and *Raising the Wind*, and the casts of the
night set Jefferson's name against the characters of
Woodley and Fainwould.   His acting, on that and subsequent occasions, was thought to give a promise of
excellence.   He did not long remain in New York, but
went back to Philadelphia; and there, and in Washington, Baltimore, and the adjacent region, he fulfilled dis-

---

[1] ANN D. WARING, daughter of Mr. and Mrs. Leigh Waring, became
the wife of James W. Wallack, Jr., son of Henry Wallack, and by the marriage of Blake to Mrs. Waring, James W. Wallack, Jr., became Blake's
step-son-in-law, — a relationship between those actors which was ever the
cause of some mirth.   Ann D. Waring's first husband was William Sefton.

cursively his theatrical duties.   In 1826, at the age of twenty-two, he was married to Mrs. Thomas Burke, whom he had first met at the Chatham Garden theatre, and who was eight years his senior.   That was a love-match, and the marriage proved exceptionally happy and fortunate.   After his father left Philadelphia, in the season of 1829–30, he managed for him, in Washington, Lancaster, Harrisburg, and other cities, and he remained with him till the end.   During the season of 1831–32 he directed the theatre in Washington.   During the seasons of 1835–37 he was connected, successively, with the Franklin theatre, at No. 175 Chatham street, New York, and with Niblo's Garden.   At the Franklin he was scene-painter as well as actor.   *Mobb the Outlaw, or Jemmy Twitcher in France*, a version of *Robert Macaire*, was given there, on May 2, 1836, with new scenery painted by him.   On May 25, he acted King Arthur, in the travestie of *Tom Thumb*.   On June 1, *The Hunchback* was performed, for his benefit, with his sister Elizabeth as Julia, and with his wife in the bill, for a song.   The latter had been absent about ten years from the New York stage, and it was observed that her voice and person had been impaired by time.   On March 1, 1837, Jefferson took another benefit, the bill comprising *The Lady of the Lake*, *The Forty Thieves*, and a vaudeville entitled *The Welsh Girl*, in the latter of which pieces he represented Sir Owen Ap Griffith.   Mrs. Jefferson appeared as Blanche of Devon, and as Morgiana. Charles Burke, her son, then a lad of fifteen, took part in the exercises, singing a song entitled *The Beautiful Boy*.   The fourth Jefferson, Rip Van Winkle, then eight years old, was present at that performance.   For a few

weeks during the summer of 1837 Jefferson and John
Sefton managed a vaudeville company at Niblo's Garden,
and produced musical farces.   Miss Jane Anderson, Miss
De Bar (first wife of J. B. Booth, Jr.), Mrs. Bailey,
Alexina Fisher (afterward Mrs. Lewis Baker), Mrs. Gur-
ner, Mrs. Harrison, Mrs. Henry, Mrs. Knight, Mrs.
Maeder (Clara Fisher), Mrs. Richardson, and Mrs. Watts
appeared in that company, as also did T. Bishop, William
Edwin, William Henry, Joseph Jefferson, W. H. Latham,
—————— Lewellen, Cramer Plumer, John Sefton, Edward
Thayer, Jacob Thoman, J. W. Wallack, Jr., and P. Williams.   The season ended on September 16, 1837, and
that proved Jefferson's farewell of the New York stage.
He proceeded with his family to Chicago, there joining
his brother-in-law, Alexander Mackenzie; and the rest
of his career — made up of wandering and vicissitude
— was accomplished in the West and South, in a primi-
tive period of the American theatre.   He seldom met
with prosperity, but he possessed the Mark Tapley temperament, and his spirits always rose when his fortunes
were at the worst.   He was manager, actor, scene-painter,
stage-carpenter, — anything and everything connected
with the art and business of the stage.   He understood
it all, and in every relation that he sustained toward it
he was faithful, thorough, and adequate to his duties.
The dramatic chronicles give but little attention to his
proceedings; yet they bear invariable testimony to his
personal charm, winning simplicity, and intellectual and
moral worth.   His trials were bravely met; his hardships were patiently borne; and, to the end, he laboured
in steadfast cheerfulness and hope, making good use of
his talents and opportunities, and never repining at his lot.

"The father of our Rip Van Winkle " — so, in a letter to me,
wrote the veteran manager, John T. Ford — "was one of the most
lovable men that ever lived.   He acted occasionally, painted almost
constantly, and when he had a theatre, as sometimes happened, he
managed his business with that careless amiability, almost amounting to weakness, that was inseparable from his nature.   Once, when
he was managing in Washington, he was so poor that, wanting
Edwin Forrest to act there, he had to walk to Baltimore, forty
miles, and did so, to solicit him.   He enjoyed life, in a dreamy
way, and his only anxiety was for his children."

Another kindly picture of him is afforded by his sister Elizabeth, who wrote to me as follows : —

"My brother Joe was a gentle, good man, true and kind in every
relation of life.   He was very like his father, — so much so that, in
the play of *The Exile*,[1] when the latter had to dance in domino, Joe
would often, to save his father the trouble, put on the dress and
dance the quadrille, and no spectator could tell the difference, or
was aware of the change of persons.   He was fond of his fireside,
serene in adversity, humble in prosperity, affectionate in temperament, and beloved by all who knew him.   Painting was his great
passion.   He became a very good actor in old men.   He was an
inveterate quiz.   I have séen him, — when he was manager as well
as actor, — after making a mistake on the stage, fix his composed
and solemn gaze magisterially upon some one of the supers, till the
poor fellow came really to think that the blunder had been made by
himself, and trembled lest he might be discharged.   Joe married
Mrs. Burke, who was a great singer.   No voice that I ever heard
could compare with hers, except, possibly, that of Parepa.   My
father feared that, as Joe was so much younger than his wife, the
match might not turn out well; but there never was a happier
marriage.   Indeed, it could not be otherwise; for Joe was all sunshine, and she loved him, and that says all."

Jefferson was not self-assertive, and, apparently, one
reason why he did not take a high rank in the public

---

[1] *The Exile, or The Desert of Siberia.*   Musical Play, in three acts.
By Frederic Reynolds.   Covent Garden, November 10, 1818.

estimation was that he did not care to make the essential effort.   His philosophic, drifting, serene disposition is aptly illustrated in this incident.   An old friend of his, hearing that he had met with great misfortune in business, and, in fact, become bankrupt, called at his dwelling to cheer him, and was told by Mrs. Jefferson that her husband had gone fishing.   He expressed surprise, and, with some vague apprehension that all might not be well, went to the river in search of him. The object of his solicitude was soon found, sitting composedly in a shady nook on the bank of the Schuylkill, humming a tune, and sketching the ruins of a mill on the shore.   Cordial greetings having been exchanged, the sympathetic visitor could not conceal his astonishment that a crushing trouble should be accepted so cheerfully.   "Not at all," said Jefferson; "I have lost everything, and I am so poor now that I really cannot afford to let anything worry me."

A few of the characters that were acted by the third Jefferson are specified here : —

Admiral Franklin, in *Sweethearts and Wives*.
Baron Vanderbushel, in *The Sentinel*.
Baptisto, in *The Hunter of the Alps*.
Crabtree, in *The School for Scandal*.
Dogberry, in *Much Ado About Nothing*.
First Grave-digger, in *Hamlet*.
Gratiano, in *The Merchant of Venice*.
John Bull, in Colman's comedy of *John Bull*.
King Arthur, in *Tom Thumb*.
M. de Villecour, in *Promotion, or The General's Hat*.
Mr. Coddle, in *Married Life*.
Memno, in *Abællino*.
Naudin, in *Tom Noddy's Secret*.
Norfolk, in Cibber's version of Shakespeare's *Richard the Third*.

Polonius. In the unconsciously humorous sapience and half-senile prolixity of that part he must have been exceptionally excellent.

Raff, in *The Conquering Game*.

Reef, in *Ambrose Gwinett*. Melodrama. By Douglas Jerrold.

Sentinel, in *Pizarro*.

Sentinel, in *The Wandering Boys*. By M. M. Noah.

Sir Robert Bramble, in *The Poor Gentleman*.

Spinoza, in *Venice Preserved*. Tragedy. By Thomas Otway. 1682. It is interesting to consider that Garrick placed the plays of Otway next to those of Shakespeare, as to dramatic qualities.

Stanon, in *The Blind Boy*. By William Dunlap. Altered from Kotzebue.

Tapwell, in *A New Way to Pay Old Debts*.

Witch, in *Macbeth*.

Abællino was a conspicuous example of the "wretched Dutch stuff" that Dunlap's actors despised. In later days, at the Chatham Garden theatre, it gave occasion for a facetious exploit by Jefferson and his comrades, to the discomfiture of Andrew Jackson Allen (1776–1853), who was the guy of the company. That performer was a maker of ornaments, of gold and silver leather, for stage dresses; and it was he who once astonished Edwin Forrest by the inquiry, "I should like to know what in —— your Richard the Third would amount to, without my spangles?" Allen was partial to the play of *Abællino*, and he chose it for his benefit. One situation in it presents all its persons on the scene, and at a certain moment they are to exclaim, "Where is Abællino?" But Jefferson's sportive plan had arranged that the company, at this supreme moment, should stand immovable and speechless. Abællino, his head darkly muffled in his cloak, for a while awaited the cue. At last he was heard to mutter, several times, "Somebody say, 'Where's Abællino!'" There was no response, and the house was already in a titter. The dilemma was finally broken by Allen himself, who loudly cried out, "If you want to know where's Abæl-lino, here he is," — and threw off his disguise, amid general laughter.

In Cowell's *Thirty Years* there is a glimpse of Jefferson's last days. Cowell had repaired to Mobile, after the burning of the St. Charles theatre, New Orleans, in 1842, and he refers to the theatre which he there joined, — a property at the corner of Royal and St. Michael streets, owned by James H. Caldwell, leased in that year to Messrs. E. De Vendel and Dumas, and managed for them by Charles J. B. Fisher, brother to Clara Fisher, the once famous singer, now Mrs. Maeder. Cowell says: —

"Charles Fisher, being very desirous of proving his friendship for the Jefferson family, engaged all the immediate descendants of 'the old man' now alive, and as many of the collateral branches as were in want of situations. Mrs. Richardson had been in Mobile the season before, and therefore she was the nucleus around whom were clustered her two sisters and their husbands, Messrs. Mackenzie and Wright, her brother Joseph and his two very clever children, and her niece Mrs. Germon and husband. The company, in consequence, was literally a family, with the exception of James Thorne and myself, Mrs. Stewart, Morton, and Mr. and Mrs. Hodges: so that when poor Joe Jefferson died the theatre had to be closed two nights; for without the assistance of the chief mourners we could not make a performance." [1]

---

[1] "OLD JOE COWELL was an envious man, who looked on the actions of his fellow-men with an eye of sarcasm, and was ready at all times to pick a flaw in, and to turn to ridicule, their best efforts." — Ludlow's *Dramatic Life*, p. 528. That is found to be true in reading Cowell's book, for the spirit of the writer shines through his words. Nevertheless, he affords an occasional detail that is of advantage to this picture of the past.

Jefferson's death occurred, suddenly, at Mobile, Ala., at midnight on Thursday, ·November 24, 1842. He died of yellow fever, and his remains were buried the next day. His grave is in Magnolia Cemetery, at Mobile (Square number 6, Lot number 32), and it is marked by a white marble headstone, inscribed with his name, the date of his death, and the number of his years. He was only thirty-eight. The stone to commemorate him was erected in 1867, by his son Joseph, and at the same time a wooden grave-mark, which had originally designated the spot (the sole tribute that poverty then permitted filial reverence to offer), was brought away by him and buried in the earth, at his home in Hohokus, N.J., — an estate that has since passed out of his possession.

The subjoined reflections upon the death of Jefferson were published, at the time, in the *Mobile Advertiser*: —

"Joseph Jefferson was the second son and the namesake of that distinguished comedian so many years the pride and ornament of the Chestnut Street theatre in Philadelphia, whose unblemished private life was a moral sanction for his public reputation; and never did the unostentatious virtues of a father more purely descend upon his offspring than in the person of the deceased. He was an actor of great talent, and an artist of unquestioned excellence. Though living in the public world, it was not there that his true merit was seen; and one who has known him many years, in every relation of life, may be permitted to say that, as a son, a brother, a father, a husband, and a friend he has left none purer to lament his death or attest his virtues. Guileless as a child, he passed through life in perfect charity to all mankind, and never, by his nearest and dearest, was he known to utter an unkind word or entertain an illiberal opinion. . . . His blameless nature was as free from a thought or act of dishonour as the diamond is free from alloy."

A portrait of Joseph Jefferson appears in the Autobiography of his son, our Rip Van Winkle, published in 1889-90. A silhouette likeness of him and of his wife is also extant. A water-colour portrait of him, made by a Philadelphia artist, named Wood, was long in existence. It was in a circular frame, marked with masonic emblems. It disappeared, with other possessions of the family, in a western city, about 1840-42. Jefferson was an uncommonly handsome man, self-contained, placid, and singularly interesting. With the person, manners, and serene and gentle temperament of an Addison, the actor was an inveterate wag. That ideal is the clearest image of him that lives in memory, and various anecdotes are told, to give it proof. On an occasion, at the Washington theatre, the play of *Tekeli* was presented, under Jefferson's management, with a melodramatic actor named Dan Reed as the hero. Reed was a large man, tall and formidable, wore a tremendous wig of black hair, and spoke in tones of thunder. On that occasion he was drunk; so that, when the first curtain fell, Jefferson thought it best to withdraw him from the performance. There was a stage-struck tailor in the theatre, the keeper of the wardrobe, a little man with a small round head, entirely bald. That person, seeing his opportunity, offered himself as a substitute for the stalwart and vociferous Reed, — and the occasion instantly became one that Jefferson could not resist. He seized Reed's wig, put it on the bald head of the tailor, and, without a word of explanation to the audience, sent him on. The business requires that Tekeli shall be brought upon the scene, in act second, upon a litter, and that he presently shall declare his identity. The little tailor rose to the occasion, assuming a fine attitude, and squeaking, in a thin, shrill voice, " Hi ham Teakaylee !" At the same instant the great shaggy wig dropped from his pate, and revealed that object, hairless, and shining like a soap-bubble, while a deep voice from the gallery, improving the ensuing moment of startled silence, clearly ejaculated, "Great Gosh, what a head !" The audience shrieked with laughter. Jefferson's enjoyment of the scene would, naturally, have been profound. He kept a grave exterior, but he was ever willing to gild the dulness and drudgery of life with innocent merriment. The jocose element was commingled in him with pensive gravity and gentleness. His character had the calm beauty of an autumn landscape, of wooded hills and browning meadows, when the sun is going down : but his achievement as an actor was colourless, and he exerted no appreciable influence upon the stage.

V

CHARLES BURKE

1822–1854

It is the testimony of judicious observers who remember Charles Burke, that he was pre-eminently a man of genius in the dramatic art; but his life was so brief, his health so delicate, his temperament so dream-like and drifting, and his experience so sad, that he neither made a rightfully ample impression upon his own period, nor left an adequate memory to ours. Charles Saint Thomás Burke, deriving the name of Saint from his god-father, and that of Thomás from his mother, was the son of Thomas Burke and his wife, Cornelia Frances Thomás, and was born in Philadelphia, March 27, 1822. When three years old he was introduced upon the stage, being utilised in a line of infantile parts, according to the custom of theatrical families in those days; and from that time he was devoted to a theatrical career. As a lad he was exceedingly apt and intelligent. He saw, and, although very young at the time, he could in some measure appreciate, the acting of the second Jefferson, and of John and Thomas Jefferson, his connections, — not to speak of other worthies of the Chestnut Street theatre, — and in that good school he was carefully trained. In the summer of 1836, when in his fifteenth year, he appeared at the National theatre, New York, as the Prince of Wales, in *Richard the Third.* The elder Booth was acting Gloster. Later in the season Burke was seen as Prince John, in *Henry the Fourth*, and as Irus in *Ion*, — the former play having been produced for J. H. Hackett, as Falstaff, and the latter for George Jones, subsequently known as Count Joannes. Burke also occasionally sang in public, and he was esteemed clever in comic vocalism. Long before that time his mother had married Joseph Jefferson (they were wedded in 1826), and when, at the end of 1837, his step-father removed from New York into the West, Burke went with the rest of the family ; and he shared the vicissitudes and hardships of the wandering life which ensued, — at first in the dramatic company formed by Jefferson and his brother-in-law Alexander Mackenzie, and afterwards with Sol. Smith and others. He was not seen again in New York till 1847, when, on July 19, he appeared at the Bowery theatre, acting Ebenezer Calf, in *Ole Bull*, and Dickory, in *The Spectre Bridegroom.* There he remained about a year, and he established himself as a local favourite. In the summer of 1848 he joined his friend, Frank S. Chanfrau,[1] at the New Na-

---

[1] FRANCIS S. CHANFRAU, one of the most versatile and brilliant actors of his time, was born in New York, on February 22, 1824. His father was a French sailor; his mother an American, a native of West Chester county, N.Y. In boyhood he learned the trade of a ship carpenter. He early drifted to the stage, and I have heard him say that he profited much by the training that he received at the hands of Mitchell, at the old Olympic theatre. That house was No. 444 Broadway, and it was first opened on September 13, 1837, by Henry E. Willard and William Rufus Blake. It subsequently passed to William Mitchell (1798–1856), who

tional theatre, formerly the Chatham, which was opened on August 14, in that year, with Burke as acting-manager; and with that house he was associated, intermittently, for two or three seasons. There is a record of his having appeared at Burton's theatre, in the spring of 1849, as Billy Bowbell, in *The Illustrious Stranger:* but Burton was jealous of him, as a possible rival in popularity, and subsequently used effective influence to exclude him from the theatres of the West Side; so that Burke was banished to the Bowery, and ever since has commonly been named, not, as he should be, with Twaits, Blissett, Warren, Jefferson, Finn, Burton, and Blake, but with comedians of the somewhat less intellectual quality of Barnes, Gates, Sefton, and Hadaway.

conducted it from December 9, 1839, until March 9, 1850. Chanfrau was for some time a member of Mitchell's company,— an organisation which, first and last, included some of the most sparkling and choice dramatic spirits of the age. Among them were Benedict De Bar, James Dunn, Augustus Fenno, George Holland, John Nickinson, Charles Walcot the elder, Mary Gannon, the bewitching Mary Taylor, the beautiful Mrs. George Loder, Mrs. H. C. Timm, and Mrs. Watts, afterward Mrs. John Sefton. Chanfrau made an extraordinary hit, at the Olympic, on February 15, 1848, as Mose, the fireman, in *A Glance at New York*, by B. A. Baker, —a paraphrase of *Tom and Jerry*. Chanfrau told me that the first performance was not auspicious, and that the play was repeated only because of Mitchell's rule that every piece produced at his theatre should be acted at least twice. On the second night the success was prodigious, and shortly afterward Chanfrau was acting Mose, nightly, at two theatres, the Chatham as well as the Olympic,— the run lasting over three months, at both houses. On July 23, 1858, he married Miss Henrietta Baker, daughter of Mrs. Alexina Fisher Baker. He had a long and prosperous career. He died, suddenly, at Taylor's Hotel, Jersey City, on October 2, 1884, and was buried in the cemetery of the West End Methodist church, at Long Branch, N.J. There also rest the ashes of those esteemed actors, William R. Floyd, who died on November 25, 1880, aged 48, and George Ryer, who died on April 26, 1882, aged 74.

The last three years of Burke's life were mainly spent in professional travel. Ludlow saw him in St. Louis, in his latter days, and Edwin Booth and David Anderson entertained him at their ranch in California in 1852–53. He worked hard, and found favour and made friends; but he met with scant prosperity, and he suffered from failing health and waning spirits. His last appearance on the stage was made where his professional life began, — at the Chestnut Street theatre, Philadelphia, on February 11, 1854; and the last character that he personated was Ichabod Crane, in *Murrell, the Land Pirate*. He was twice wedded, but left no children. Both his marriages were unfortunate. His first wife, Margaret Murcoyne, a native of Philadelphia, born in 1818, died in that city, in 1849. His second wife, Mrs. Sutherland, survived him, but has since passed away. Both those ladies were on the stage. The latter was the mother of Ione Sutherland, who adopted her stepfather's name, and, as Ione Burke, had a brief theatrical career, — mostly at Laura Keene's theatre and at Wallack's, — terminating in marriage; after which she found a home in England. Charles Burke died in the old Florence Hotel, corner of Broadway and Walker street, New York, November 10, 1854, in the thirty-third year of his age, and was buried in the same grave with his mother, in Ronaldson's cemetery, at Philadelphia. He died in the arms of his brother, Joseph Jefferson, and his last words were, "I am going to our mother."

The testimonials that exist to the loveliness of Burke's character and to the strength and versatility of his genius, are touched equally with affection and tender regret.

K

"He grew up," said Elizabeth Jefferson, "to be one of the best actors we ever had. As a boy he was full of promise; and when, after fifteen years, I saw him act, in Mobile, I was struck with what seemed to me a revival of the old time. A more talented and kind-hearted man than Charles Burke never lived."

His old comrade, Frank S. Chanfrau, wrote to me in the same strain: "Burke was a great actor and a true man. One cannot say too much of his talents and his worth. He could do many things in acting, and was wonderful in all that he did."

In person Burke was tall, slender, and extraordinarily thin; and his long, emaciated figure — agile, supple, and graceful — seemed made for comic contortions and grotesque attitudes. His countenance was capable of great variety of expression, ranging from ludicrous eccentricity to pensive sadness, and he had it under such complete control that it responded, instantly and exactly, to every changing impulse of his mind and feelings; so that he had a new face for every part that he played. The boys of the Bowery pit firmly believed him to be the original of the long-legged figure in the comic almanac.

"I knew Charles Burke well, in my early manhood," — so said the lamented John T. Ford, writing to me on February 26, 1894, only sixteen days before his death, — "and saw him act, last, on April 1, 1850 (?), under singular circumstances. He was then comedian of the Richmond theatre,[1] and a very great favourite. Very

---

[1] Burke filled an engagement at the Richmond, Va., theatre, with Chippendale and John Sefton, in 1849, and acted Mose. On December 17, 1852, he received a benefit, at the Arch Street theatre, Philadelphia,

homely in the face. Much like his father in person, and his mother in artistic endowment."

In the course of thirty years many parts were acted by Charles Burke, of which a few may serve to indicate his artistic attributes and affinities : —

REPERTORY OF CHARLES BURKE

Acres, in *The Rivals*.

Billy Bowbell, in *The Illustrious Stranger*.

Baillie Nicol Jarvie, in *Rob Roy*.

Billy Lackaday, in *Sweethearts and Wives*.

Caleb Scrimmage, in *Jonathan Bradford, or The Roadside Murder*.

Clever, in *Woman's Wit*. Acted under the name of *Slander*. By Sheridan Knowles.

Clod Meddlenot, in *The Lady of the Lions*. Burlesque.

Captain Tobin, in *The Mysteries and Miseries of New York*. By H. P. Grattan. Based on a story by " Ned Buntline " (E. C. Z. Judson).

Cloten, in *Cymbeline*.

Caleb Plummer, in *The Cricket on the Hearth*.

Dromio of Syracuse, in *The Comedy of Errors*.

Deuteronomy Dutiful, in *The Vermont Wool Dealer*.

Darby, in *The Poor Soldier*. Comic Opera. By John O'Keefe. Covent Garden, 1793.

Dickory, in *The Spectre Bridegroom*. Farce. By W. T. Moncrieff. Drury Lane, 1821.

Dr. Ollapod, in *The Poor Gentleman*.

Ebenezer Calf, in *Ole Bull*. Farce.

Thomas T. Hemphill being then the manager, and was seen in *Rip Van Winkle*, *Murrell the Land Pirate*, and *The Idiot Witness*. In 1852 he applied to J. W. Wallack for an engagement, and was refused. Burke received $2655 for six nights in San Francisco, in 1852–53. His second wife, Mrs. Sutherland, had been divorced from A. B. Sutherland, an actor, who subsequently was allied with the handsome, talented, and eccentric Charlotte Crampton.

Ensign Jost Stoll, in *Jacob Leisler, or New York in 1690*.   Historical Drama.   By Cornelius Matthews.   Bowery theatre, 1848.

First Grave-digger, in *Hamlet*.

Grumio, in *The Taming of the Shrew*.

Grandfather Whitehead, in the drama of that name.   By Mark Lemon.   Henry Placide was the original in America (1843).

Horsebeam Hemlock, in *Captain Kid*.   Drama.   First acted at the Park, New York, in 1839, with Peter Richings as Robert Lester, *alias* Kid, Mrs. Richardson as Kate, and Charlotte Cushman as Elspy.

Isidore Farine, in *The Pride of the Market*.   Mary Taylor acted with Burke, as Marton.

Ichabod Crane, in *Murrell the Land Pirate, or The Yankee in Mississippi*.   Drama.   By Nathaniel Harrington Bannister (1813–1847), author of about one hundred plays.

Iago, in a travestie of *Othello*.

Jemmy Twitcher, in *The Golden Farmer*.   Gates was the original in America (1834).

Jonathan Ploughboy, in *The Forest Rose, or American Farmers*.

John Duck, in *Cavaliers and Roundheads*.

Launce, in *The Two Gentlemen of Verona*.

Launcelot Gobbo, in *The Merchant of Venice*.

Mr. McGreedy, in a burlesque, by Charles Burke, satirising W. C. Macready.

Mesopotamia Jenkins, in *The Revolution*.   Play.   By Charles Burke.   Bowery, 1847.

Mettaroarer, in *The Female Forty Thieves*.   Burlesque.   In that part Burke gave a comic imitation of Edwin Forrest, as Metamora.

Moses, in *The School for Scandal*.

Marrall, in *A New Way to Pay Old Debts*.

Mock Duke Jaques, in *The Honeymoon*.

Mark Meddle, in Boucicault's comedy of *London Assurance*.

Paul Pry, in the comedy of *Paul Pry*.   By John Poole.

Rip Van Winkle, in a drama on that subject, by himself.

Seth Slope, in the farce of *Seth Slope*.

Selim Pettibone, in *A Kiss in the Dark*.

Stitchback, in *Hofer, the Tell of the Tyrol*.

Splash, in *The Young Widow*.

Solon Shingle, in *The People's Lawyer*. Farcical play. By Dr. J. S. Jones.

Slender, in *The Merry Wives of Windsor*.

Sir Andrew Aguecheek, in *Twelfth Night*.

Sudden, in *The Breach of Promise*.

Timothy Toodle, in the farce of *The Toodles*.

Toby Veck, in *The Chimes*. Drama. Based on the Christmas story by **Charles Dickens**.

Touchstone, in *As You Like It*.

Zekiel Homespun, in *The Heir at Law*.

An instructive article by L. Clarke Davis, published in *Lippincott's Magazine*, July, 1879, entitled *At and After the Play*, incidentally shows Burke as dramatist and actor, embodies a pleasing reminiscence of him by the famous humourist and comedian John S. Clarke, and places Burke and Jefferson before the reader in their sacred relation of affectionate brotherhood. Burke made a version of *Rip Van Winkle*, and acted Rip. Mr. Davis compares the more recent Boucicault version with that of Burke : —

" Burke's play follows closely the story of the *Sketch-Book*, and lacks altogether the sweet, tender humanity and the weird spirituality which pervade the combined work of Jefferson and Boucicault : it makes nothing of the parting from, or the meeting with, the child Meenie ; but much of the dialogue, which was Burke's own, has been wisely retained. The speech containing the notable line, ' Are we so soon forgot when we are gone ? ' is Burke's, not Boucicault's, though Jefferson has transposed and altered it for the better. It is introduced in the original, when Rip, returning to his old home, is told that if he be Rip, and not an impostor, some one of his old cronies will surely recognise him. He answers : ' To be sure dey will! Every one knows me in Catskill.' (*All gather around him and shake their heads.*) ' No, no, I don't know dese peoples — dey don't know me neither ; and yesterday dere was not a dog in the village but would have wagged his tail at me ; now dey bark. Dere was not a child but would have scrambled on my knees: now dey run from me.   Are we so soon forgotten when we are gone?   Already dere is no one wot knows poor Rip Van Winkle.'

"We never saw Charles Burke play this part, though we have seen him play many others, and can testify to the greatness of his genius and the perfection of his art. . . .   How he spoke that speech we have been told by John Sleeper Clarke, who is so just a man, and so free from professional jealousy, that he could not, if he would, praise the dead at the expense of the living.   Mr. Clarke says that in the delivery of those lines no other actor has ever disturbed the impression that the profound pathos of Burke's voice, face, and gesture created: it fell upon the senses like the culmination of all mortal despair, and the actor's figure, as the low, sweet tones died away, symbolised more the ruin of the representative of a race than the sufferings of an individual: his awful loss and loneliness seemed to clothe him with a supernatural dignity and grandeur, which commanded the sympathy and awe of his audience.   Mr. Clarke played Seth with Mr. Burke for many consecutive nights, and he relates that, on each succeeding night, though he was always aware of what was coming, even watching for it, when those lines were spoken his heart seemed to rise in his throat, choking him, and his cheeks were wet with tears; for Burke's manner of pronouncing them was so pathetic that not only the audience but even the actors on the stage were affected by it.

"Mr. Jefferson, remembering how his brother spoke that speech, has adopted a different mode: 'It is possible that I might speak it as he did, but — '   He leaves the sentence unfinished, the reason untold; but it is an open secret, to those who know how deep is the reverence of the living Rip for the dead one.   They know that there are tones of Charles Burke's voice even which are held in too sacred a memory by his brother ever to be recalled by him upon the stage.   In speaking of him, Mr. Jefferson said: 'Charles Burke was to acting what Mendelssohn was to music.   He did not have to work for his effects, as I do.   He was not analytical, as I am.   Whatever he did came to him naturally, — as grass grows or water runs.   It was not talent that informed his art, but genius.'"

The memorials that remain of Burke are few and unsubstantial. Those playgoers who remember a French comedian named Leduc,[1] who acted at the theatre in Fourteenth street, New York, when *La Grande Duchesse* was first presented in America, October, 1867, possess at least a suggestion of Burke's likeness. The French actor was one of the company that Hezekiah L. Bateman brought from Paris to co-operate with Mlle. Tostée, in the introduction of Opera Bouffe upon the American stage. Leduc acted Prince Paul, and subsequently Menelaus, in *La Belle Hélène.* He was of a winning personality. He never obtruded himself. He drifted in and out of the scenic spaces like a star among the light clouds of a summer night. His art concealed every vestige of effort. He was the perfection of grace. And through all the gentle drollery of his seemingly unconscious action there ran a vein of wistful sensibility, which, without being sadness itself, produced the momentary effect of sadness. It was my fortune often to see that refined actor, with our Joseph Jefferson as a companion spectator, and to enjoy in his acting a great delight, — because of that thoroughness of dramatic art which is nature transfigured. Jefferson said that Leduc was more like Charles Burke than any man he had ever seen. But Burke, he added, had tragic power as well as humour, and would often astonish his associates and spectators, who had been thinking only of his drollery, by a sudden tragic passion, or by his marvellous poise in the realm of pathos. Burke as an actor had the mental constitution of Hood as a poet, — who, in one mood, could

---

[1] The comedian Leduc is, I am informed, still living, (1894). He was associated, not very long ago, with the Municipal theatre, at Toulon.

chuckle over the farcical theme of *Miss Kilmansegg*, and, in another, could melt the heart with *The Bridge of Sighs*, or awe the fancy with the sombre image of *Eugene Aram*, or wake the spirit of melancholy regret with *Inez*, or thrill the deep foundations of imagination with the weird, poetic atmosphere of *The Haunted House*.

In the days of his prosperity as Mose, Frank S. Chanfrau opened a theatre, in Brooklyn, called The Museum, with Charles Burke as stage-manager. On the opening night Burke acted the chief comic part in a new piece, and spoke the tag. Chanfrau, who had been acting elsewhere, hurried thither as soon as his performance was ended, impatient to learn the result of the new venture. That result was disaster. The piece had been coldly received, and all Burke's efforts had failed to save it. Chanfrau went at once to the stage. The curtain had fallen. The actors had dispersed. Burke alone remained upon the scene. He was standing in the centre front of the stage, exactly where he had stood when the curtain fell. Motionless, with head bowed, with hands clasped, unconscious of all around him, the comic genius stood there, in the shadow, with bitter grief in his heart, and with tears slowly trickling down his face. He could not speak. His sensitive spirit had taken upon itself the blame and the blight of a failure. So, transfigured by loss and sorrow, he stands forever in the pantheon of memory ; and round him the withering leaves of autumn fall, and cold winds sigh in the long grasses, and twilight slowly deepens, and the world is far away.

VI

JOSEPH JEFFERSON

RIP VAN WINKLE

1829

THE maternal ancestry of Joseph Jefferson, the present representative (1894) of the Jefferson Family of Actors, the famous Rip Van Winkle whom everybody knows and loves, is French; and of him, as of Garrick, it is to be observed that the blood of three nationalities flows in his veins. French, English, and Irish were the currents that mingled in Garrick: French, English, and Scotch are the currents that combine in Jefferson. The inquirer finds Jefferson's French ancestry in the island of St. Domingo. There, about the beginning of the nineteenth century, living in affluence upon his plantation, dwelt M. Thomás, a gentleman newly arrived from France. Little is known about him; but it is remembered that he was a person of winning manners, cheerful fortitude, and resolute mind. He had paused for a while in New York, with his wife, on their journey from France to St. Domingo to take possession of an inherited estate; and in New York, on October 1, 1796, was born their daughter, Cornelia Frances. In the next year they were established in their new home, and there they resided till the period of the negro insurrection led by Dessalines. At that crisis they had a narrow escape from murder, in the massacre of the white population by which that revolt was attended. The first rising of the negroes against the French in St. Domingo occurred in 1791–93, and it was succeeded by the temporary government of Toussaint L'Ouverture, —to whom Wordsworth addressed a sonnet, and whom Wendell Phillips canonised. The second rising, which resulted in either the murder or expatriation of the French residents, was effected in March, 1804, and it was then that M. Thomás and his family were in peril. They escaped, however, by favour of a negro slave, named Alexandre, who, impelled by affectionate fidelity, gave warning of their danger, just as it was at hand; but it was only by precipitate flight that M. Thomás was able to elude the doom of slaughter which had been pronounced against him and his household. He fled by night;[1] and, after many perils, escaped to sea, in an open boat, accompanied by his wife and daughter, and by the faithful servant who had saved their lives. The exiles were picked up by an American vessel and carried into Charleston, S.C.

M. Thomás was now poor, and the rest of his life was passed in poverty and labour. At first he attempted a minor shop-keeping industry, but that did not succeed. His wife soon died, and his daughter remained his chief care. One day, in a Charleston street, he chanced to

---

[1] Jefferson's mother told him that she could distinctly remember that night, and the dreadful moments of breathless suspense while the barbarous and bloodthirsty negroes were beating the bushes, to discover the fugitives in their concealment.

meet Alexander Placide, whom he had known in France, and who welcomed him as an old friend. Placide, popular as an athlete and a rope-dancer, — the father of Henry, Thomas, Caroline, Eliza, and Jane Placide, all known, in later days, upon the stage, — was then manager of the Charleston theatre, and in that theatre M. Thomás found employment. He never attempted acting; but his daughter, who became a pet with the Placide family, was soon brought forward, in the ballet, and presently was entrusted with minor parts in plays. That was her school, and there she grew up, an actress and a singer, early winning a good rank in the profession, — especially as a vocalist, — which she maintained almost to the end of her life.

"Possessing a fair share of ability as a comic actress," says Ireland, " with a pleasing face and person, and an exquisite voice, — which, in power, purity, and sweetness, was unapproached by any contemporary, — she soon eclipsed all rivalry in vocalism; and, till the more cultivated style of Italy was introduced, was considered the model of all excellence. She was attached to the Park, New York, for two or three seasons, and afterwards removed to Philadelphia, where she became an equally distinguished favourite."

The first husband of Cornelia Frances Thomás was the Irish comedian, Thomas Burke, to whom she was married in her girlhood. Burke was noted for his fine talents, handsome person, and ill-ordered life. He was on the Charleston stage, where Miss Thomás first met him, as early as 1802. He first appeared in New York, on April 29, 1811, at the Park, and subsequently he fulfilled several New York engagements. At a later period he resided in Philadelphia, where he became a favourite with playgoers, as the dashing

Irishman. His death was caused by delirium tremens, in 1824, in Baltimore. W. B. Wood says he died on June 6, 1825. However that may be, his demise was a relief to those who were best acquainted with him ; and on July 27, 1826, his widow became the wife of Joseph Jefferson, the third of the line of actors commemorated in this biography.

A pleasant glimpse of the mother of our Jefferson is given in N. M. Ludlow's *Dramatic Life* (1880) : —

"Finding matters so dull in New York (1826), my wife and I went to Philadelphia, to pay a visit to our much-esteemed friend, Mrs. Cornelia Burke, after whom our first daughter was named. We found the lady recently married again, to Mr. Joseph Jefferson, scenic artist, afterwards father of Joseph Jefferson, of Rip Van Winkle renown. . . . Our meeting with this lady was a very pleasant one : we had not seen her since the voyage we made with her to Virginia, from New Orleans, in the summer of 1821. We presented to her the little namesake, then five years of age, who was greatly admired by Mrs. Jefferson and her friends. (Now, 1894, Mrs. Matthew C. Field, an old lady, resident in the West.)

"We passed a very pleasant week in Philadelphia, occasionally visiting Mrs. Jefferson, who was always excellent company herself; and, in addition to this, we often met with very agreeable persons at her house, who were in the habit of visiting her. Mrs. Jefferson was of French parentage. . . . Her first efforts on the stage were in singing characters, such as Rosina, in the comic opera of *Rosina, or the Reapers*; Countess, in *John of Paris*; and Virginia, in *Paul and Virginia*, and the like. I remember with much pleasure her singing, in those English operas. She performed Blanche of Devon, in the melodrama of *The Lady of the Lake*, on the night when I made my first appearance in Mr. Caldwell's company, in New Orleans, in 1821. She also performed speaking characters very well. The first time that I remember to have seen her was at Albany (1814–15), in the character of Susan Ashfield, in *Speed the Plough*, on the occasion when I made my clandestine appearance as Bob Handy's servant, and was complimented on it by Mr. Thomas Burke."

Mr. and Mrs. Burke had one son, Charles Saint Thomás Burke. He became a fine comedian, but, as already shown, he died too soon for his fame and for the happiness of his generation. Mr. and Mrs. Jefferson had four children, two of whom died in infancy, while two have survived to the present day (1894):—

1. JOSEPH JEFFERSON.—This is our Rip Van Winkle.

2. CORNELIA JEFFERSON.—She was born in Baltimore, October 1, 1835, and went on the stage in childhood, performing in the travelling company of which her parents were members, at Chicago, Galena, and other places in the West and South, after the year 1837. She accompanied her relatives, in their various professional wanderings, during the next twelve years. On May 17, 1849, she appeared in New York, at Chanfrau's National theatre, in Chatham street, acting Little Pickle, in *The Spoiled Child*. In 1857 and 1858 she was a member of the dramatic company of Laura Keene's theatre, and she was seen on that stage after it became the Olympic,—being the second house of that name in New York,—in the autumn of 1867, as Titania, in *A Midsummer Night's Dream*. (The Olympic, which had been opened in 1863, by John A. Duff,—its first manager being Mrs. John Wood,— was, in 1867–68, managed by James E. Hayes, a noted scene-painter, who had married one of Mr. Duff's daughters, and who died in New York, May 7, 1873. Mr. Duff died, in New York, March 31, 1889.) Cornelia Jefferson visited England in 1877. She is the widow of Charles Jackson, and has one son, Charles Jackson, who is on the stage. She has long been living in retirement.

The mother of Charles Burke and Joseph Jefferson died, at Philadelphia, in November, 1849, and her grave — which, in 1854, became also that of the former of those sons—is in Ronaldson's cemetery, corner of Bainbridge and Ninth streets, in that city. In company with Joseph Jefferson, I once visited that place of rest, and found it thickly overgrown with flowering shrubs and climbing

roses. A large white stone marks the spot, inscribed
"TO OUR MOTHER AND OUR BROTHER. CORNELIA F.
JEFFERSON. CHARLES BURKE."

In that little graveyard rest other members of the
dramatic profession, admired in their day, but mostly
forgotten now. The sumptuous Josephine Clifton, who
died in 1846, is buried there, together with her sister,
Louisa Missouri Miller, and there was entombed Samuel
Chapman, the first husband of our Jefferson's aunt Elizabeth. The grave of William Jones, commonly known
as "Old Snacks," who died in Edwin Forrest's house,
in 1841, aged sixty, is also in that cemetery.

The fate of M. Thomás, the French ancestor of Jefferson, was tragic. He survived till 1827, living, toward
the last, in his daughter's household. During his latter
years he was in continual suffering, from incurable gout.
He bore his agonies patiently, till he could bear no
more : the constant torture drove him to despair. In
that condition, — frantic with pain, hopeless, and miserable, — the poor old gentleman drove out, one morning,
to the Market street bridge, over the Schuylkill river,
dismissed his carriage, and, as soon as he was left alone,
sprang over the parapet and was drowned.

JOSEPH JEFFERSON, the representative American comedian of our time, was born at Philadelphia on February
20, 1829, in a house which still is standing, — unchanged
except that a shop has been opened on the ground-floor
of it, — at the southwest corner of Spruce and Sixth
streets. In childhood he gave indications of an exceptional mind and character, and of artistic abilities. He
was reared amidst theatrical surroundings, and, in 1833,

when only four years old, was carried upon the stage, at the Washington theatre, by Thomas D. Rice, a famous delineator of negro character. That comedian, on a benefit occasion, introduced the child, blackened and dressed like himself, into his performance of Jim Crow. Little Joe was taken upon the scene in a bag, and emptied from it, with the couplet, —

> "Ladies and gentlemen, I'd have you for to know
> I've got a little darkey here, to jump Jim Crow."

A witness of that scene — the veteran actress, Mrs. John Drew [1] — says that the boy promptly assumed the attitude of Jim Crow Rice, and sang and danced in imitation of his sable companion, and was a miniature likeness of that grotesque person.

Thomas D. Rice, thus associated with Jefferson, was a remarkable man and had a singular career. He was born in New York on May 20, 1808, and died there, on September 19, 1860. When a boy, he was employed as a supernumerary at the Park theatre. Afterwards he went into the West. Cowell met him, at Cincinnati, in 1829, "a very unassuming, modest young man, little dreaming then that he was destined to astonish the Duchess of St. Albans, or anybody else ; he had a queer hat, very much pointed down before and behind, and very much cocked on one side." The same writer says that Thomas H. Blakeley was the first to introduce negro vocalism on the American stage, and adds that Blakeley's singing of the *Coal Black Rose* set the fashion

---

[1] "The first time I acted in Washington was in a company with which Joseph Jefferson made his first appearance, at the age of four, as the baby in Jim Crow Rice's negro sketch." — Mrs. John Drew, in the *Baltimore American*. Friday, February, 16, 1894. See note on p. 104.

which Rice followed. G. W. Dixon, known as Zip
Coon, and notorious as a newspaper libeller, was a
pioneer in that form of public entertainment ; and he
closed a disreputable life, in a charity hospital, at New
Orleans, in 1861. Wemyss, however, declares that
the original Jim Crow was a negro, at Pittsburgh, Pa.,
named Jim Cuff. The veteran actor, Edmon S. Conner,
in an article published in the *N. Y. Times*, June 5, 1881,
asserts that it was an old negro slave, owned by Mr.
Crow, who kept a livery-stable in the rear of the theatre, in Louisville, Ky., managed by Ludlow and Smith, in
1828–29, and that the slave adopted his master's name,
and called himself Jim Crow. Conner adds : —

"He was much deformed, the right shoulder being drawn high
up, the left leg stiff and crooked at the knee, giving him a painful
but laughable limp. He used to croon a queer tune with words of
his own, and at the end of each stanza would give a little jump, and
when he came down he set his ' heel a-rockin'.' He called it 'jump-
ing Jim Crow.' The words of the refrain were : —

> ' Wheel about, turn about,
> Do jes so,
> An' ebery time I wheel about,
> I jump Jim Crow ! '

"Rice watched him closely, and saw that here was a character
unknown to the stage. He wrote several stanzas, changed the air
somewhat, quickened it, made up exactly like the old negro, and
sang to a Louisville audience. They were wild with delight, and
on the first night he was recalled twenty times."

Rice went to England in 1836, and soon became
prominent on the London stage. He married Miss
Gladstane, daughter of the manager of the Surrey
theatre. His profession yielded him a large income.
It was one of his fancies to wear gold pieces on his coat

for buttons; and sometimes he was first stupefied with wine and then robbed of those ornaments. He was a capital actor, in such parts as Wormwood, in Buckstone's farce of *The Lottery Ticket*, Old Delf, in *Family Jars*, Ginger Blue, and Spruce Pink, in *The Virginia Mummy*. He took hints from actual life, but he was an interpreter, not a photographer; and, in that sense, he was the original of whatever he did. The moment any man accomplishes anything that is out of the ordinary rut of mediocrity, numerous observers strive to detract from his merit by impugning his originality. Well and wisely did Falstaff say that "honour is a mere scutcheon." Rice wrote the negro burlesque opera called *Bone Squash*, and also a *Travesty of Othello*.

Jefferson's beginning as little Jim Crow is mentioned, together with other matters illustrating his juvenile talent, in the *Notes from Memory* that were written for me by his aunt Elizabeth: while William Warren, his second cousin and old comrade, told me a quaint story suggestive of a certain sapient maturity in his childhood. That rare comedian, Henry J. Finn,[1] going into the green-room one night at the Washington theatre, dressed for the part he was to act, observed little Joe, wrapped in a shawl, sitting in a corner. After various flourishes of action and mimicry, for which he was admirable, he paused in front of the boy, and, not

---

[1] FINN was indeed one of the most extraordinary men that have appeared upon the stage. He was thoroughly educated, a ripe scholar, an excellent writer, — both serious and comic, — a good dramatist, a skilful painter, and a clever editor; and as an actor, he succeeded in both tragedy and comedy. He was born at Cape Breton, in 1790, had his career both in England and America, and perished in the burning of the steamer *Lexington*, in Long Island Sound, in January, 1840.

L

dreaming that such a tiny creature could make any reply, solemnly inquired, " Well, my little friend, what do you think of me ? " The child looked at him, with serious eyes, and gravely answered, " I think you are a very wonderful man." And Finn was impressed, and a little disconcerted, by that elf-like quaintness and judicial sobriety of infancy.

In 1837, when eight years old, the little lad was at the Franklin theatre, New York, with his parents, and it is recorded that he appeared upon the stage, September 30, in a sword-combat, with Master Titus.[1] Young Jefferson, on that occasion, personated a pirate, while young Titus opposed him, in the character of a sailor ; and, at the end of a spirited encounter, the miniature pirate was prostrate, and the miniature sailor bestrode him in triumph. Mr. and Mrs. Jefferson left New York at the end of the season of 1837–38,[2] tak-

---

[1] The Master Titus who figured in that scene was a bright boy, the son of an officer at the New York City Hall, but his career was prematurely ended, shortly after that time, by the accidental explosion of a gun, which blinded him. He was acting in *Matteo Falconi*, with Mr. William Sefton, when the disaster occurred.

[2] In a letter to J. H. McVicker, which got into print, Jefferson said : —

"I am not sure that I remember dates and circumstances in their exact form. My father and his family arrived in Chicago, by way of the lakes, in a steamer, somewhere about May in the year 1838. He came to join Alexander Mackenzie, my uncle, in the management of his new theatre. Mackenzie had been manager of the old one, the season before: I think the new theatre was the old one refitted. [An error.] I know it was the pride of the city and the ideal of the new managers, for it had one tier of boxes and a gallery at the back. I don't think that the seats of the dress-circle were stuffed, but I am almost sure that they were planed. The company consisted of William Leicester, William Warren, James S. Wright, Charles Burke, Joseph Jefferson, Thomas Sankey, William Childs, Harry Isherwood, Joseph Jefferson, Jr., Mrs. Mackenzie, Mrs. J. Jefferson, my mother, Mrs. Ingersoll, and Jane Germon. I was the comic singer of this party, — making myself useful in small parts and first villagers : now and then doing duty as a Roman Senator, at the back, wrapped in a clean hotel sheet, with my head just peering over the profile banquet table. I was just nine years old. I was found useful as *Albert*

ing their children, — Charles Burke, and Cornelia and Joseph Jefferson, — and went to Chicago ; and for the next twelve years the family led the life of the strolling player, wandering through the West and South, and even following the armies of the Republic into Mexico ; so that, until he came forward at Chanfrau's New National theatre, as Jack Rackbottle, in *Jonathan Bradford*, September 10, 1849, Jefferson was not again seen in New York. Those intervening years were crowded with vicissitude and privation. Often the youthful Jefferson participated in performances that were given in the dining-rooms of country hotels, without scenery, and with no adjunct to create the illusion of a stage, except a strip of board, nailed to the floor, sustaining a row of tallow candles. Not the less were those representations given with the earnestness, force, and fidelity of accomplished actors. That kind of experience, indeed, was not uncommon with the players, in the early days of the American stage, when strolling actors drifted in flat boats down the great rivers of the West, and now and then shot wild beasts upon their banks, and often performed in the barns of the frugal-minded farmer. Land journeys from town to town were made in wagons or on foot, while cold and hunger not infrequently were the harsh companions of that precarious life. Once the Jefferson company, roaming in a region far

and the *Duke of York*. In those days the audience used to throw money on the stage, either for comic songs or dances, and, oh, with that thoughtful prudence which has characterised my after life, how I used to lengthen out the verses! The stars, during the season, were Mrs. McClure, Dan Marble, and A. A. Adams. Some of the plays acted were *The Lady of Lyons, The Stranger, Rob Roy, Damon and Pythias, Wives as They Were — Maids as They Are*, and *Sam Patch*. The theatre was in Randolph street — at least it strikes me that was the name. [It was in Dearborn street.] The city, about that time, had from 3000 to 4000 inhabitants. I can remember following my father along the shore, when he went shooting, in what is now Michigan avenue."

from any settlement, had found a more than commonly
spacious barn, and a farmer of more than commonly
benevolent aspect, and it was thereupon resolved to
give a performance in that auspicious spot. Written
handbills, distributed through the neighbourhood, proclaimed the joyous design. There was a cordial response. The farmers and their wives and children,
from far and near, came to see the play. The receipts
were twenty dollars, and that treasure was viewed as
a godsend by the poor players, who saw in it the
means of food, and of a ride to the next town. But no
adequate allowance had been made for the frugality of
the genial owner of the barn. "I guess that pays my
bill," he said, as he put the money into his pocket; and
so the venture was settled, and the rueful comedians
walked away. On another occasion, in Mississippi, they
had hired a wagon to carry them from one town to
another, fifteen miles distant, and their driver, after proceeding about half way, demanded payment of his due;
when, being told that it would be paid out of the proceeds of their next performance, he turned them from
his vehicle, and left them in a forest road, in a rain-
storm; from which predicament they were rescued,
after some hours, by a friendly ox-cart. Amid scenes
of that kind young Jefferson learned to be an actor;
and, aside from barely three months at school which he
once enjoyed, that was the only kind of training he ever
received. In Mexico, when the war occurred, in 1846,
he was among the followers of the American army, and
gave performances in tents. He saw General Taylor on
the banks of the Rio Grande; he heard the thunder of
the guns at Palo Alto; he stood beside the tent in

which the gallant Major Ringgold lay dying; he witnessed the bombardment of Matamoras, and, two nights after the capture of that city (May, 1846), he acted in its Spanish theatre. Those were the days when he wore the gypsy colours, and knew the gypsy freedom, and saw the world without disguise.

The principal features of the cast of *Jonathan Bradford*, in which Jefferson acted at Chanfrau's New National theatre, when he came home in 1849, were these : —

Jonathan Bradford	John Crocker.
Dan McCraisy	Redmond Ryan.
Jack Rackbottle	Joseph Jefferson.
Caleb Scrimmage	Charles Burke.
Anne Bradford	Mrs. H. Isherwood.
Sally Sighabout	Mrs. Sutherland.

In and Out of Place was also acted, with Mrs. Charles Mestayer as Letty. That lady, formerly Miss Pray, then Mrs. C. Mestayer, and finally Mrs. Barney Williams, was in the bloom of her buxom vivacity. In *The Poor Soldier*, which completed the bill for that night, Charles Burke appeared as Darby, and Miss Lockyer as Norah. Cupid, also, seems to have been present; for Mrs. Sutherland was afterwards wedded to Burke, and Miss Lockyer to Jefferson. The season lasted from September 10, 1849, to July 6, 1850, and among the players who appeared during that time, and with whom, accordingly, Jefferson was associated, were Mrs. D. P. Bowers; Miss Sarah Crocker, afterwards Mrs. Frederick B. Conway, sister to Mrs. Bowers; Frank S. Chanfrau, then popular as Mose; Anna Cruse, afterwards Mrs. William Cowell; Fanny Herring; Emily Mestayer; Mrs. Helen Muzzy;

Wyzeman Marshall; Barney Williams; and Harry Watkins, — who died at 463 West Twenty-third street, New York, February 5, 1894, aged sixty-nine. The elder Booth acted at the National, in those days; the inveterate wag, Harry Perry, was seen there; Edwin Booth made his first New York appearance on that stage; Joseph Proctor there presented the avenging Jibbenainosay; John R. Scott exhibited there the exuberant melodrama of the past; George L. Fox began his metropolitan career in that theatre; the fascinating Julia Pelby passed across its scene, in *The Child of the Regiment;* Charles Dibdin Pitt displayed his fine figure and plastic art as Virginius; and Yankee Locke, James H. McVicker, and Jim Crow Rice there let slip the spirits of their humour, and paid their tribute to the rosy gods of mirth. In other quarters Burton, Blake, and Mitchell were the sovereigns of laughter; Hamblin, Conner, and Forrest were the kings of tragedy; and John Brougham, Lester Wallack, and George Jordan held the field of elegant comedy against all comers, and felt, with Alexander, that "none but the brave deserve the fair."

On leaving the National theatre, in the autumn of 1850, Jefferson and his wife went to Mitchell's Olympic, where they acted in November; and about that time the young comedian applied for a position in Brougham's Lyceum, — opened December 23, that year. He wished to be stage-manager; and had he been accepted the fate of that theatre, and the subsequent career of the loved and lamented John Brougham, might have been different from what they were, — an almost continuous tissue of misfortunes. In the season of 1851–52,

Jefferson was attached to the company of Anna Thillon and the Irish comedian Hudson, who gave musical plays at Niblo's Garden; and shortly afterward at that theatre he was associated with Mr. and Mrs. John Drew, William Rufus Blake, Lester Wallack, Mrs. Stephens, Mrs. Conover, afterwards Mrs. J. H. Stoddart, and Charles Wheatleigh. He then formed a partnership with John Ellsler, and took a dramatic company through a circuit of theatres in the South, — visiting Charleston, Savannah, Macon, Atlanta, Augusta, Wilmington, and other cities. After that tour was ended he settled in Philadelphia, and then in Baltimore, — first at the Holliday Street theatre, and then at the Baltimore Museum, corner of Baltimore and Calvert streets, where he was stage-manager. In the summer of 1856 he made a trip to Europe, to study the acting then visible in London and Paris. On November 18, 1856, the beautiful Laura Keene opened her theatre, afterwards the second Olympic, at 622 and 624 Broadway, New York, and Jefferson was soon added to the force, already strong, of her recruits, — a company that included, among others, James G. Burnett, George Jordan, T. B. Johnston, Charles Peters, James H. Stoddart, Charles Wheatleigh, Ada Clifton, afterward Mrs. Edward Mollenhauer, Cornelia Jefferson, Mrs. Stephens (died July 29, 1858), Charlotte Thompson, and Mary Wells. The second season opened on August 31, 1857, with *The Heir at Law*, and Jefferson made a hit as Dr. Pangloss. On the opening night of the third season (1857–58) he appeared as Augustus, in *The Willow Copse*. Charles W. Couldock acted Luke Fielding, Edward A. Sothern, Sir Richard Vaughan, and Laura Keene, Rose

Fielding. Mr. and Mrs. W. R. Blake, Sara Stevens, Effie Germon, and Charles Walcot joined the company in that season; and it was then that Blake,—a good actor, but one who had a tendency to coarseness,—being resentful of Jefferson's custom of expunging indelicate lines from the old comedies, made a vain attempt to stigmatise him as "the Sunday-school comedian." There was a scene in the green-room, and Blake was discomfited. "You take an unfair and unmanly advantage of people," said Jefferson, "when you force them to listen to your coarseness. They are, for the time, imprisoned, and have no choice but to hear and see your ill-breeding. You have no better right to be offensive on the stage than you have in the drawing-room." On October 18, 1858, for the first time anywhere, was presented Tom Taylor's comedy of *Our American Cousin*, which brought the flood-tide of fortune in Jefferson's professional life. He acted Asa Trenchard and he was famous. Seldom has an actor found a medium for the expression of his spirit so ample and so congenial as that part proved to be for Jefferson. Rustic grace, simple manliness, unconscious drollery, and unaffected pathos, expressed with artistic control and in an atmosphere of repose, could not have been more truthfully and beautifully combined. The piece ran for one hundred and forty consecutive nights, until March 25, 1859,—a long run for that epoch,—and it made the success of the year and of the theatre. It was then also that Sothern, reluctantly accepting the trivial part of Lord Dundreary, afterwards much elaborated by him, laid the foundation of his fortune and fame,—presenting, in a vein of delicate caricature, a new and perfect type of whimsical humour.

JOSEPH JEFFERSON
At the age of 28.

This was the cast of *Our American Cousin :* —

Asa Trenchard . . . . Joseph Jefferson.
Lord Dundreary . . . . Edward A. Sothern.[1]
Sir Edward Trenchard . . . . . Edwin Varrey.
Lieutenant Vernon . . . . . . Milnes Levick.
Capt. de Boots . . . . —— Clinton.
Coyle . . . . James G. Burnett.[1]
Abel Murcot . . . . Charles W. Couldock.
Binney . . . . Charles Peters.[1]
Buddicombe . . . . Henry McDouall.[1]
Florence Trenchard . . . . . Laura Keene.[1]
Mrs. Mountchessington . . . . Mary Wells.[1]
Augusta . . . . Effie Germon.
Georgina . . . . Mrs. E. A. Sothern.[1]
Mary Meredith . . . . Sara Stevens.[1]
Sharp . . . . Miss Flynn.[1]
Skillet . . . . Mrs. M. Levick.

The season of 1858–59 at Laura Keene's theatre
lasted till July 14, when Jefferson's relations with her
company were ended, and on September 14, 1859, he
appeared in the dramatic company engaged by Dion
Boucicault and William Stuart for the Winter Garden
theatre, then opened with Boucicault's adaptation of *The
Cricket on the Hearth*, entitled *Dot.*[2] That theatre,
originally called Tripler Hall, had been known as the

[2] This was the cast of characters in *Dot :* —

John Perrybingle . . . . Harry Pearson.[1]
Edward . . . . A. H. Davenport.[1]
Tackleton . . . . T. B. Johnston.[1]
Dot . . . . Agnes Robertson.
Bertha . . . . Sara Stevens.[1]
Mrs. Fielding . . . . Mrs. W. R. Blake.[1]
Tilly Slowboy . . . . Mrs. John Wood.
Caleb Plummer . . . . Joseph Jefferson.

[1] Dead.

Metropolitan, under William E. Burton's management, and later as Laura Keene's Varieties. It was in Broadway, on the west side, opposite the end of Bond street. Jefferson appeared as Caleb Plummer, and also as Mr. Bobtail; and in the course of the ensuing six months he was seen as Newman Noggs, Salem Scudder, Granby Gag, Sir Brian, and Rip Van Winkle. The first presentation of Boucicault's drama of *The Octoroon*, December 5, 1859, was an important incident of the season; and on February 2, 1860, a new theatrical version of Dickens's novel of *Oliver Twist*, made by Jefferson, was for the first time presented, — the withdrawal of Boucicault, who left the theatre suddenly, on a disagreement, having opened the way for it. James W. Wallack, Jr., a superb romantic actor and one of the most interesting of men, made an astonishing success, as Fagin, the Jew, while Matilda Heron acted with a wonderful wild power as Nancy.[1] There were in the Winter

---

[1] The chief features of the cast of *Oliver Twist* show the diversified strength of the company and the good judgment with which that strength was directed: —

Brownlow	James H. Stoddart.
Bumble	George Holland.[1]
Sikes	George Jordan.[1]
Fagin	James W. Wallack, Jr.[1]
The Artful Dodger	T. B. Johnston.[1]
Oliver Twist	Ione Burke.
Nancy	Matilda Heron.[1]
Mrs. Corney	Mrs. W. R. Blake.[1]

From October 1, 1860, till March 9, 1861, Charlotte Cushman acted at the Winter Garden theatre, giving forty-eight performances, and in the course of that engagement *Oliver Twist* was presented, and Miss Cushman acted Nancy, — a part originally played by her many years before, and in which, probably, she never had an equal.

[1] Dead.

Garden company, at one time, A. H. Davenport, George Holland, Joseph Jefferson, George Jamieson, T. B. Johnston, George Jordan, Harry Pearson, — who died in May, 1884, — James H. Stoddart, James W. Wallack, Jr., Mrs. J. H. Allen, Ione Burke, Mrs. W. R. Blake, Matilda Heron, Sara Stevens, and Mrs. John Wood. Mr. and Mrs. Boucicault had retired, — proceeding to Laura Keene's theatre, where they remained from January 9 to May 12, 1860. There Boucicault produced, for the first time, his plays of *The Heart of Midlothian*, January 9, and *The Colleen Bawn*, March 29. The Winter Garden season, meantime, was further signalised by the production, February 19, of Mrs. Sidney Frances Cowell Bateman's play of *Evangeline*, — a work based on Longfellow's poem, — in which Miss Kate Bateman began the more mature portion of her professional career, and in which Jefferson acted the humorous character — not much to the author's satisfaction. "It is the best comic part my wife ever wrote," Bateman said; and "It is the worst comic part I ever played," was Jefferson's reply. He withdrew from the Winter Garden in the spring of 1860, and on May 16 opened Laura Keene's theatre for a summer season, which lasted till August 31. The pieces presented were *The Invisible Prince, Our Japanese Embassy, The Tycoon, or Young America in Japan,* and *Our American Cousin.* Jefferson, Sothern, and Couldock reappeared, acting their original parts, in the latter piece, while Mrs. Wood enacted Florence. In Jefferson's dramatic company, at that time, were Ione Burke, James G. Burnett, Mrs. Henrietta Chanfrau, Cornelia Jefferson, James H. Stoddart, Mrs. H. Vincent, Hetty Warren, and Mrs. John Wood. In those seasons at the Winter Garden and Laura Keene's theatre, the foundations of Jefferson's fame were completed and the building of its noble structure was well begun.

Early in 1861, being much oppressed by a domestic bereavement and by failing health, Jefferson was persuaded to seek relief in travel and new scenes. He formed at that time the resolution to appear on the London stage, and he planned the career which he has since fulfilled. There has not been much of either luck or chance in Jefferson's life, and, though a fortunate man, he is pre-eminently a man who has compelled fortune, by acting with resolution upon a wise and definite purpose. At first he went to California, arriving in San Francisco on June 26, 1861, and on July 8 he made his first appearance in that city, at Maguire's Opera House, in Washington street. His California season lasted till November 4, when he made his farewell appearance. The next day he sailed for Australia,[1] and in that country — enchanted with its magnificent climate, its beautiful scenery, its progressive civilisation, and its intelligent, kindly people — he passed four prosperous and beneficial years. There he recovered his health, and there he won golden opinions by his acting of Asa Trenchard, Caleb Plummer, Bob Brierly, Rip Van Winkle, Dogberry, and many other characters. He also gained hosts of friends. Among

---

[1] Jefferson was accompanied on that expedition by Mr. James Simmonds, who remained in those colonies and died there, at Auckland, New Zealand, early in 1871. Mr. James Simmonds was well known as an actor and a manager. At one time he managed the Eagle theatre, in Sudbury street, Boston, Mass. He was the author of several songs, one of which, entitled *Speak of a Man as You find Him*, has enjoyed much popularity.

his comrades at that time were Benjamin L. Farjeon, the novelist, Henry Edwards, George Fawcett Rowe, famous as Micawber, Louis A. Lewis, the composer, and James Smith, the brilliant editorial writer. One notable incident of his professional life at Melbourne was the success of Rosa Dunn, Mrs. Lewis, who acted Mary Meredith in *Our American Cousin*, Hero in *Much Ado*, and kindred characters, and showed herself to be a lovely actress. From Melbourne he went to Tasmania, where, among what Henry J. Byron called the Tasmaniacs, he met with prodigious favour. His performance of Bob Brierly, on one occasion, at Hobart Town, drew an audience that included upward of six hundred ticket-of-leave men; and, though at first they viewed him with looks of implacable ferocity, they ended by giving him their hearts, in a hurricane of acclamation. Leaving Tasmania, he sailed for Callao, and passed a little time on the Pacific coast of South America and at the Isthmus of Panama. Daniel Symons, remembered for his piquant acting of Dr. Caius, accompanied him from Australia, and was thenceforth for a time the companion of his travels. (Mr. Symons [1] died in 1871.) At Panama Jefferson took passage for England, and on arriving at London he commissioned Boucicault to recast and rewrite the old play of *Rip Van Winkle*, for production in the English capital.

The story of Rip Van Winkle is suffused with the wildness of gypsy life, and it arouses the imagination at the same time that it touches the heart. The famili-

---

[1] For the benefit of Mr. Daniel Symons, on June 29, 1871, at the Olympic theatre, New York, Jefferson acted Mr. Golightly and George L. Fox acted Gregory Thimblewell, the Tailor of Tamworth, in *State Secrets*.

arity and the ascendency with which, in the contemporary mind, it has been endued, are attributable less to
Washington Irving's sketch than to the influence of
the actor, by whom the name of Rip Van Winkle has
been written on the tablet of human affection, all over
the world. Irving's sketch, while felicitous both in
atmosphere and style, is but a faint and dim fore-
shadowing of Jefferson's vital creation. The regnancy
of Rip Van Winkle, the fact that the character has
become a part of actual life, is due to the stage. It
had existed for centuries : it never really lived until it
was vitalised by the dramatic art. The legend is Greek.
The original Rip was a Grecian youth, named Epimeni-
des, who was sent into the mountains to hunt for a stray
sheep, and who fell asleep in a cave, at mid-day, and
slept for fifty-seven years ; so that, when he returned,
his home and his people were gone, and he was a stranger among strangers — until recognised by his younger
brother, now become an old man. That legend appears
again in remote German literature. Washington Irving
gave it a local habitation among the Catskill Mountains,
and in that way it has been known to the reading
world since *The Sketch-Book* was published, in 1819.
Irving's narrative is brief, and Irving's vagabond is
"a thirsty soul," who haunts taverns and who is by no
means the romantic and poetic vagabond of Jefferson.
The beauty of the sketch is felicity of description.
The possible element in the legend that inspired Irving's fancy was the association of a spectral presence
with the midnight storm among the mountains. No
thought, in particular, was expended by him upon the
character ; and the commendation that has from time

to time been bestowed upon Jefferson, for his fidelity to
Irving, in the delineation of Rip Van Winkle, is therefore comical. The hero of the sketch is an amiable
sot : the Rip embodied by Jefferson is a dream-like,
drifting, wandering poet of the woods. No two persons
could be more unlike. Artistic minds everywhere have
felt the influence of Jefferson's genius, and have been
stimulated to take especial note of the subject, and to
view it through a haze of the imagination. The actors,
however, were first in the field.

The first recorded play on the subject was produced
at Albany, on May 26, 1828, and the first Rip was
Thomas Flynn (1804–1849), the intimate friend of
Junius Brutus Booth, and the man from whom the late
Edwin Booth derived his middle name of Thomas (not
Forrest, as often incorrectly stated). In my former
account of the Jeffersons, 1881, I indicated Charles B.
Parsons as probably the first representative of Rip Van
Winkle upon the stage. That was an error; he was
the second ; and I am indebted to the research of that
careful theatrical scholar, H. P. Phelps,[1] of Albany, for
the conclusive evidence that Flynn was the first.

The Albany *Argus* of May 24, 1828, contained the
following paragraph : —

"MRS. FLYNN'S BENEFIT.

"This interesting and favourite actress (late Miss Twibell) takes
her benefit on Monday evening next, when will be performed for

---

[1] Mr. Phelps, in addition to his *Players of a Century*, published in
1880, being a record of the Albany stage, and a very useful book, has
begun the publication of *The Stage History of Famous Plays*, — a work of
obvious value and special interest, — of which the first volume, 1890, is
devoted to *Hamlet*, and contains numerous contemporary testimonials as
to various representatives of the character.

the first time an entirely new melodrama, written by a gentleman of this city and called Rip Van Winkle, taken from Washington Irving's novel of that name. The piece, we understand, has been several days in active preparation, and is pronounced by competent judges to be replete with wit and humour, which, added to the locality of the piece in a story which is familiar, cannot fail to draw a full house."

"I can find no notice of its production," — so Mr. Phelps writes to me, — "but it must have been played, for it is announced for the second and last time, May 28, 1828, in an advertisement in which it is called *Rip Van Winkle, or the Spirits of the Catskill Mountains.*

The principal parts were cast as follows, and the cast was advertised : —

Derrick Von Slous	Parsons.[1]
Knickerbocker	Phillips.
Rip	Flynn.
Lowenna	Mrs. Flynn.
Alice	Mrs. Forbes.

A prologue, by "a gentleman of this city," introduced the piece, with these propitiatory rhymes : —

> "If scenes of yore, endeared by classic tales,
> The comic muse with smiles of rapture hails ;
> If when we view those days of Auld Lang Syne
> Their charms with home, that magic name, combine ;
> May we not hope, kind friends, indulgence here ?
> Say, (for I speak to yonder fat mynheer,)

---

[1] Parsons became a clergyman, and it is mentioned that he preached the funeral sermon of Danford Marble, — one of the most distinctive of American comedians, — who died of Asiatic cholera, at Louisville, Ky., in 1849. Parsons was born in 1803 and died in 1871. The Phillips mentioned in this cast was Moses S. Phillips, of Philadelphia, commonly called "Nosey," for the reason that his nose was prodigious. He was born in 1798, and died in 1854, at New York.

Say, shall our burgomasters smile to-night?
Shall Sleepy Hollow's fairy scenes delight?
Shall they from woe-worn care divert one wrinkle
To crown our hero, far-fam'd Rip Van Winkle?
Shall Knickerbocker's sons, that gen'rous race,
Whose feelings always beam upon their face,
Excuse the efforts which the muse affords
And greet each buskin'd hero on these boards?
Shades of the Dutch ! How seldom rhyme hath shown
Your ruddy beauties, and your charms full blown !
How long neglected have your merits lain, —
But Irving's genius bids them rise again.

" To you, Albanians, grateful as we are,
We offer tremblingly our bill of fare.
Yours was the soil of Dutchmen. Here they trod,
When leaving Hudson's waves, fair freedom's sod.
'Twas here a Stuyvesant and Chrystyon came,
And kept their honour and their unstained name.
Oranje Boven be their motto, too,
And be their sons like them, to freedom true.
Let, then, our generous friends one smile bestow !
Friends perched aloft and you, my friends below,
Save us, we ask you, from the critic's paw :
We know your answer ; 'tis a cheering Yaw."

The second representative of Rip, Charles B. Parsons, played it at Cincinnati, in the season of 1828–29. The version that Parsons used was bought in New York, in the summer of 1828, and carried to the West by the theatrical manager, N. M. Ludlow. Still another version was presented, on October 30, 1829, at the Walnut Street theatre, Philadelphia, with William Chapman as Rip. Mrs. Samuel Chapman (Elizabeth Jefferson), Miss Jane Anderson (now, 1894, Mrs. Germon), and J. Jefferson, probably John, were in the cast. That piece is thought to have been one that was made in

M

England by a dramatist named Kerr; but possibly it may have been another draft of the same play that Ludlow had produced in Cincinnati. James H. Hackett, afterward so widely celebrated as Falstaff, produced *Rip Van Winkle* at the Park theatre, New York, on April 22, 1830, and played the chief part. His version, which he again presented on August 10, 1830, at the Bowery theatre, may have been written by himself: he was a good writer. On April 15, 1831, however, he acted Rip, at the Park, in a version "altered" by himself "from a piece written and produced in London." In 1832 he went to England, — making his second expedition to that country, — and at that time Bayle Bernard made a new draft of the play for him, in which he appeared in London; and upon his return to America, he brought out Bernard's version at the New York Park on September 4, 1833, and that he continued to present for several years. Bernard had made an earlier version for Yates, which was acted in 1831–32 at the London Adelphi, with Yates, John Reeve, J. B. Buckstone, O. Smith, W. Bennett, and Miss Novello in the cast. Flynn, acting at the Richmond Hill theatre, New York, played Rip on July 29, 1833, keeping, no doubt, the draft that he had originally offered at Albany. A version by John H. Hewitt, of Baltimore, was performed at the. Front Street theatre in that city, in the season of 1833–34, with William Isherwood as Rip.[1] Charles Burke made a play for himself on the subject, and brought it forward at the Arch Street theatre, Phil-

---

[1] Harry and William Isherwood were the managers of the Front Street theatre, Baltimore, in 1833–34. William Isherwood played leading parts, and Harry Isherwood painted the scenery.

adelphia, in 1849. Burke acted Rip, and Jefferson acted the inn-keeper, Seth. Burke's version was subsequently amended and improved by him, and on January 7, 1850, he acted in it at the New National theatre, New York. Burke's play seems to have been based upon the earliest versions, used by Flynn and Parsons, but it was largely the work of his own hands. The material appears to have been viewed as common property. Flynn, Parsons, Chapman, Hackett, Yates, Isherwood, and Burke were predecessors of Jefferson as Rip Van Winkle; but when Jefferson arose he treated the part in an original manner, lifting it into the realm of poetry, and making it substantially a new character. Down to 1866 the best known and most widely accepted Rip Van Winkle was Hackett; but, in melancholy illustration of the mutability of human affairs, the fame of Hackett declined as that of Jefferson advanced, till at last there came a time when the old actor of Rip laid aside the part, and was content to sit among the admiring spectators of the favourite of a new age. Jefferson's performance is different from Hackett's and a greater work, but not less sad was the moral of that spectacle : —

> "'Tis certain, greatness, once fall'n out with fortune,
> Must fall out with men too: What the déclin'd is
> He shall as soon read in the eyes of others
> As feel in his own fall. . . .
> The present eye praises the present object."

Thus through a period of more than two generations the stage has been illuminating and enforcing the romantic aspects of the story of Rip Van Winkle. It was the stage that suggested how much that theme contains. All the salient extremes of a representative

picture of human experience are found in it : — fact and
fancy ; youth and age ; love and hatred ; loss and gain ;
mirth and sadness ; humour and pathos ; rosy childhood
and decrepit senility ; lovers with their troubles which
will all be smoothed away, and married people with their
anxieties which will never cease ; life within doors, and
life among trees and mountains ; the domestic and the
romantic ; the natural and the preternatural ; and,
through all, the development and exposition of a humorous, cheering, romantic, restful human character.   Such
a theme cannot be too much commended to thoughtful
consideration.   It is prolific of lessons for the conduct
of life.   It teaches no direct moral ; but its power is in
its influence, — to lure us away from absorption in the
busy world, and to make us hear again the music of
running water and rippling leaves, the wind in the pine-
trees, the surf upon the beach, and, under all, the distant
murmur of that great ocean to which our spirits turn
and into which we must vanish.

Jefferson, beginning with Burke's method, but soon
veering into his own, had long acted Rip, though he did
not become conspicuous in it till the time of his visit to
England in 1865.   The piece that he put into the hands
of Boucicault, for revision, was the old piece made by
Charles Burke ; and further to stimulate the plan of
that ingenious dramatist he indicated a plan for revising
and rewriting it.[1]   In particular he suggested that the

[1] " He asked Boucicault to reconstruct it.   Many of the suggestions of
changes came from Jefferson, and one at least from Shakespeare.   Boucicault shaped them in a week, . . . but he had no faith in the success of
his work, and told Jefferson that it could not possibly keep the stage for
more than a month.   While much of the first and third act was the conception of Burke, part of each was Jefferson's. . . .   The impressive end-

spectres, in the midnight encounter on the mountain, should maintain a cold and awful silence, and that only the environed and bewildered man should speak. Boucicault adopted that idea, and contributing the scheme of Gretchen's second marriage, and annexing a diluted paraphrase of the recognition of Cordelia, in *King Lear*, he made a new version of the old play, and with that, Jefferson sought the favour of the London audience, — appearing at the Adelphi theatre on September 4, 1865. His success was great, and it has ripened into a renown as wide as the world.

On the night before his first appearance in London, Jefferson, who was nervous and apprehensive, retired to his apartment, in a house in Regent street, and, in a mood of intense thought and abstraction, proceeded to "make up" for the third act of *Rip Van Winkle*. That done, and quite oblivious of his surroundings, he began to act the part. Dominie Sampson himself was never more absent-minded. The window-curtains happened to be raised, and the room was brightly lighted, so that the view from without was unobscured. Not many

ing of the first act is wholly Boucicault's, but the climax of the third — the recognition — is Shakespeare's. . . . In *Rip Van Winkle* the child struggles to a recognition of her father, while in *Lear* the father struggles to recognise his child. Compare the two situations, — that of Lear and Cordelia with that of Meenie and Rip, — and the source of Boucicault's inspiration will be apparent; and only as Shakespeare is greater than Boucicault is the end of the fourth act of *Lear* greater than the third act of *Rip*. It is the most beautiful of all human passions, — the love between father and child, — which informs them both, and which makes them both take hold upon the heartstrings with a grasp of iron. The second act of *Rip Van Winkle*, which is remarkable as being wholly a monologue, is entirely Jefferson's conception." — L. Clarke Davis, in *Lippincott's Magazine*, July, 1879.

minutes passed before it began to be utilised, — and a London crowd is quick to assemble. Inside, the absorbed and inadvertent comedian unconcernedly went on acting Rip Van Winkle: outside, the curious multitude, thinking him a comic lunatic, thronged the street till it became impassable. The police made their way to the spot. The landlady was finally alarmed; and the astonished actor, brought back to the world by a clamour at his door, inquiring if he was ill, at length comprehended the situation, and suspended his rehearsal.

An incident kindred with this, as to comicality, attended one of Jefferson's performances of Rip, at Charleston, South Carolina. He had reached the first scene of the third act, and the venerable Rip, just awakened from his long sleep, was slowly and painfully raising himself from the earth. The house was hushed, in anxious and pitying suspense. At that moment the heavy, floundering tread of a drunken man was heard in the gallery. He descended in the centre aisle, reached the front row, and gazed upon the stage. Then, suddenly, was heard his voice, — distinctly audible throughout the theatre, — the voice of interested curiosity, tipsy gravity, and a good-natured thirst for knowledge: "What in —— is that old idiot tryin' to do?"

The British public took Rip Van Winkle to its heart. "In Mr. Jefferson's hands," wrote the liberal and kindly John Oxenford, "the character of Rip Van Winkle becomes the vehicle for an extremely refined psychological exhibition." "Mr. Jefferson achieved a triumphant success on the night of his first appearance in London" [C. E. Pascoe's *Dramatic List*, p. 190], "and he has now the reputation of being one of the most genuine artists who have at any time appeared on the English stage."

Jefferson sailed from Liverpool on July 30, 1866, arrived in New York on August 13, and on September 3 appeared at the Olympic theatre. His performance of Rip was received with delight, and the fame of its beauty soon ran over the land. During that engagement he also acted Asa Trenchard, Caleb Plummer, Mr. Woodcock, and Tobias Shortcut. It was my good fortune to witness those performances, and to make this record of them, at the time, in the New York *Tribune :* —

'*Our American Cousin* was revived (October 15) at the Olympic theatre, and it was played before a large audience. It is a favourite play with the multitude. Its half sentimental, half melodramatic story appeals to sympathy, while its central character — the magnanimous Yankee, whose outside is rough, but whose heart is noble, who does justice to an injured woman, and who copiously chaffs the British aristocrat — is a pleasing personage to many minds. The puerility of the incidents and dialogue and the exaggerations of character seem to pass unnoticed, or, if noticed, are tolerated for the sake of the hero. Mr. Jefferson as Asa Trenchard displayed winning humour, delicate sentiment, and delightful precision. The charm of his personation is the fine individuality with which he invests the character. The quality of manliness was prominently indicated, so that Asa's self-sacrifice seemed the natural act of a magnanimous man, and not the phenomenal generosity of a buffoon. In the scene with Mary Meredith, where the will is burned, Mr. Jefferson captivated his hearers by his perfectly natural expression of the pure tenderness of homely simplicity. In the comic dialogues he was irresistibly humorous. His personation is more highly polished than it was of old, but the art is well concealed and the effect is admirable. Next to Mr. Jefferson as Asa was Charles Peters as Binney, — a perfect type of the stolid British servant. J. H. Stoddart was Abel Murcott, and he played it with strong emotion and good art. Charles Vandenhoff, a new actor, made his first appearance as Lord Dundreary, following the old

model and playing well. Miss Kate Newton enacted Mary Meredith, and Miss Caroline Carson, Florence.

'Jefferson's personation of Caleb Plummer (October 17) was
worthy of his genius. The gentle old man of Dickens's story lives
again in him, and touches every heart by his sweet self-sacrifice.
Jefferson's sensibility makes him sympathetic with the character,
while his admirable art enables him to embody it with thorough
precision of detail. There is no elaboration in his acting.
Jefferson's Caleb is deeply touching, and the story of the drama
is beautiful in its purity, simplicity, and humanising sentiment.
J. H. Stoddart's Tackleton exhibited close fidelity to the original.
Charles Vandenhoff made a pleasant impression as John Perrybingle, as also did Miss Carson as Dot. Tilly was Mrs. Saunders,
who has delightful whimsicality. Blanche Gray as Bertha evinced
a quick sympathy with the part. May Fielding was personated
by Miss Telbin; Dot by Miss Alice Harrison, a charming actress;
and Edward Plummer by Charles Barron.

'Jefferson, at the Olympic (October 22), kept his audience in a
state of happy laughter for several hours. *Woodcock's Little Game*
is a cross between comedy and farce, and is very bright; and *The
Spitfire* is one of the most delicious of farces. Jefferson acted
admirably. His manner, when issuing the command to "weigh the
anchor," and then "come and tell me how much it weighs," was
ludicrous beyond description, — an assumption of sapience that no
gravity could resist, it was at once so earnest and so comical.'

Washington Irving (1783–1859) did not live to be
a witness of the success of Jefferson, in the character
of Rip; but Irving saw Jefferson upon the stage,
and remembered his grandfather, and appreciated and
admired the acting of both. The following mention
of them occurs in the Journal of the last days of
Washington Irving, kept by his nephew, Pierre M.
Irving, and published in 1862 : —

"September 30, 1858. — Mr. Irving came in town, to remain
a few days. In the evening went to Laura Keene's theatre to see

young Jefferson as Goldfinch, in Holcroft's comedy of *The Road to Ruin.* Thought Jefferson, the father, one of the best actors he had ever seen; and the son reminded him, in look, gesture, size, and make, of the father. Had never seen the father in Goldfinch, but was delighted with the son.—*Life and Letters of Washington Irving.* Vol. IV., p. 253.

The grandfather, and not the father, evidently, was meant in this reference. Irving had seen old Jefferson, in the days of *Salmagundi.* It is doubtful whether he ever saw the father of our comedian.

At the close of that engagement Jefferson departed, on a tour of the West and South; but in 1867 he was again at the Olympic, from September 9 to October 26, playing only Rip, which drew crowded houses. James E. Hayes—succeeding Leonard Grover, who was the successor of Mrs. John Wood—had then assumed management of that theatre, with Clifton W. Tayleure as his assistant, and with a dramatic company comprising William Davidge, William Daly, Charles K. Fox, T. J. Hind, Owen Marlowe, Edmund Milton (Holland), Horace Wall, Miss Bessie Foote, Miss Alice Harrison, Mrs. T. J. Hind, and Miss Cornelia Jefferson. Miss Foote, a handsome woman, from the London stage, made her first appearance on September 9. Jefferson took a benefit on October 19, and closed on October 26, leaving on the Olympic stage *A Midsummer Night's Dream* (produced on October 28), with a fine panorama by W. Telbin, which he had brought from London. Cornelia Jefferson assumed the character of Titania, giving a performance that was remarkable for poetic feeling and delicate sentiment. George L. Fox impersonated Bottom. That

beautiful play had a hundred consecutive representations. During his tour of the country in 1867 Jefferson
put into rehearsal, at the Varieties theatre, New Orleans,
then managed by the sparkling light comedian William
R. Floyd (died November 25, 1880), the comedy of
Across the Atlantic, by Robertson ; but, feeling dissatis-
fied with himself in the character of Colonel White, he
sent back the piece to its author, with a forfeit of $500,
and Robertson subsequently sold it to Sothern, by whom
it was produced at the London Haymarket, under the
title of *Home.* Lester Wallack afterward presented it
in New York, and Colonel White was one of the happiest
impersonations of that polished comedian. The summer
of 1868 was passed by Jefferson among the mountains
of Pennsylvania ; but on August 31, he began a new
season, appearing at McVicker's theatre, Chicago. *Rip*
ran for four weeks, drawing and pleasing crowds of
people, and then, on October 3, was succeeded by *The
Rivals*, in which the comedian made a marked hit, as
Acres. In 1869 he bought an estate near Yonkers, on
the Hudson river, an estate at Hohokus, N. J., in the
peaceful valley of the Saddle river, and still another,
a lonely and lovely island, ten miles west of New
Iberia, in Louisiana, hard by the prairie home of the
exiled Acadians of *Evangeline.* On May 4, 1869, he
began an engagement in Boston, and from August 2 till
September 18 he was at Booth's theatre, New York
(opened for the first time on February 3, 1869), still
acting Rip. Early in 1870 he went into the South, to
visit his Iberian plantation. He was heard of in New
Orleans about the middle of February, and towards the
end of February he was in Mobile, and quite ill. He

JEFFERSON FAMILY GROUP

At Hohokus, N. J

came north in March, acted in Boston toward the end of April, and subsequently appeared in Louisville, in Philadelphia, and elsewhere, — repairing finally to Hohokus, N.J., where, in 1869, he had established his home. On August 15 he again came forward at Booth's theatre, making his fourth visit to the capital, with Rip; and he filled an engagement lasting till February 7, 1871, — nearly five months, and steadily prosperous from beginning to end. By the middle of December, 1870, Rip had been seen, at Booth's theatre, by more than 150,000 persons. Between Jefferson and Edwin Booth — whom no man ever knew well except to honour and love, and whose great services to the stage were equally a blessing to his countrymen and a source of pure renown to himself — there existed an affectionate friendship, and the fact has its peculiar significance, that no scrap of writing was ever used between them, in the business of those engagements.

On January 19 and 21, 1871, performances were given in New York for the benefit of the widow and children of the veteran actor, George Holland (1791–1870), and Jefferson, who had delayed his departure from the capital for that purpose, participated in them. The farce of *Lend Me Five Shillings* was acted, and Jefferson appeared as Mr. Golightly. The other parts were presented by Blanche de Bar, Frank Chapman, James Dunn, Effie Germon, W. J. Leonard, Thomas E. Morris, George Parkes, and Mr. Peck. Jefferson was greeted with great delight. To note the glad faces of the multitude that gazed on him with such lively interest, and followed the current of his droll humour with so much sympathy and pleasure, was to see that he had won the affection not

less than the admiration of the public. The spirit of
his impersonation of Mr. Golightly was perfectly correct, and the method was as delicate and as precisely
adjusted as the mechanism of the finest watch; and over
all there was the charm of a genial, gentle personality.

In 1872 the comedian was attacked with glaucoma;[1]
but a skilful operation on his left eye, performed early
in June, by Dr. Reuling of Baltimore, averted blindness,
and soon restored his health. He reappeared upon the
stage, January 1, 1873, at Ford's Opera House, Baltimore, and was received with an affectionate greeting, in
which the whole country joined. On July 9, 1873, accompanied by his wife and by William Warren, the
comedian, his second cousin, he sailed for England, but
he did not act while abroad. The return voyage began
on August 16, and on September 1, Rip was again seen
at Booth's theatre. On September 3, 1874, at the same

[1] In June, 1872, Jefferson wrote to a friend as follows: —

"My left eye has been overcast by a mist, for some time; the pain became so intense
that I was alarmed, and called upon Dr. Chisolm, one of the celebrated oculists of
Baltimore, who told me that I was threatened with the loss of sight in one eye, and
possibly in both. To-day I had another examination under the ophthalmoscope, by the
eminent oculist Dr. Reuling, and I regret to say he gives me the same cheerless intelligence. Nothing can save my sight unless at once I give up my profession and submit to
an operation, which will not only keep me in bed for two days, but confine me in darkness
for a longer time. Dr. Reuling, who will at once perform the operation, gives me every
hope of recovery, by attending to my case in this its early stage, but cannot take the
responsibility if I expose my eye to the continual glare of the light, or delay in at once
submitting to an operation. I would have informed you before, but I am only just in
possession of the serious fact."

The necessary surgical operation was performed by Dr. Reuling, at
Jefferson's home, at Hohokus, N.J., on June 13, and in August the
comedian thus announced his recovery: —

"I have just returned from a visit to Dr. Reuling, at Baltimore. He made a final
examination of my eye and gives me the pleasing intelligence that all traces of the
disease have entirely disappeared. I no longer wear glasses, and in fact am as good
as new. The Doctor says I could act to-night, without the slightest risk."

house, he began his farewell engagement, and in June, 1875, he went to England, on a professional expedition. He remained abroad two years and a half, his first London engagement, at the Princess's, extending from November 1, 1875, to April 29, 1876, and his second, from Easter, 1877, to the ensuing midsummer, when he went to the Haymarket for a brief season of farces, *Lend Me Five Shillings* and *A Regular Fix*, under the management of John S. Clarke, — after which he returned to America, and here he has ever since remained.[1]

Jefferson arrived home on October 17, 1877, and on October 28, at Booth's theatre, under the management of Augustin Daly, again accosted his countrymen, as Rip. A warm welcome greeted him, and he made another successful tour of the United States. Early in 1878 he paid a second visit to California, and on December 16, 1878, he acted in New York, at the Fifth Avenue theatre, then under the direction of Daniel H. Harkins and Stephen Fiske. After that he was absent from the metropolis till October, 1879, when he appeared at the Grand Opera House. On September 13, 1880, he effected, at the Arch Street theatre, Philadelphia, a careful and brilliant production of *The Rivals*, and made an extraordinary hit as Acres, — a part in which he first gained distinction in his youth; and his professional exertions have since been divided between Acres and

---

[1] "Mr. Jefferson's departure," said the *London Telegraph*, "means the loss of one of the most interesting and intellectual forms of amusement. . . . His picture is engraven on our memories. . . . There will be no lack of smiling faces when London is once more favoured with the presence of so genial, accomplished, and sympathetic an artist."

Rip.   Those two characters, together with Asa Trenchard, Caleb Plummer, Dr. Pangloss, Dr. Ollapod, Bob
Brierly, Mr. Golightly, Tobias Shortcut, Hugh de Brass,
the First Grave-digger in *Hamlet*, and Tracy Coach are
the only parts that Jefferson has acted since 1880.
The story of his life, indeed, since that time, is mainly
a record of pleasant professional wanderings with Rip,
Acres, and Dr. Pangloss.   He has acted but a part
of each season, preferring to live mostly at home and
devote his attention to the art of painting.   All his
life he had been accustomed to sketch and to paint
in water-colours, as a diversion ; but some time after
1880 he began to manifest not only great enthusiasm
but remarkable talent for oil painting, in the department of landscape.   In that art he has found much
happiness, and his achievements have aroused the
interest and commanded the respect of many competent
judges.   Several of his works have been exhibited.
Some of them have been circulated, in etchings.   The
charm of his pictures, like that of his acting, is tenderness of feeling, combined with a touch of mystery, — an
imaginative quality, kindred with the freedom and the
wildness that are seen in the paintings of Corot.   In
that field Jefferson has accomplished more than perhaps
his contemporaries are likely to recognise, — for no
man must succeed in more than one art, if he would
satisfy the contemporary standard and retain the good-
will of the present age.

In 1869 Jefferson began to make a home for himself
upon a magnificent estate about ten miles west of
Iberia, and not far from the Gulf of Mexico, in Louisiana.   He possesses, indeed, a fine dwelling, upon a

breezy upland, at Buzzard's Bay,[1] in Massachusetts ;
but his southern plantation, which is devoted to oranges,
flowers, sheep, and sport, is his more characteristic
retreat. It is a place where any man might be happy.
It is an island in the prairie, but high and variegated,
containing more .than six hundred acres of land, and
isolated by a broad, shining, steel-blue lake, and by an
arm of one of the bayous of that well-watered country,
— the country associated with Longfellow's *Evangeline*,
and in which still may be found the race of the exiled
Acadians. Almost every kind of wood that grows may
be found growing upon that estate. Some of its trees
are nearly three hundred years old, and in summer the
great spreading boughs of those giants are profusely
draped, in many a green dell, not only with the long,
funereal moss of the South, but with brilliant and
odorous tropical flowers. Orange groves are scattered
over the island ; many kinds of wild fowl live in the
woods and swamps and on the lake ; and often the blue
waters are cleft by the rapid canoe of the sportsman.
In one wild part of that gorgeous solitude an eagle has
made its nest, on the peak of a stalwart pine-tree.

[1] Jefferson's home at Buzzard's Bay is called " Crow's Nest," and is not
distant from " Gray Gables," the home of his friend, President Cleveland.
The comedian built it in 1889, and there collected a number of excellent
paintings, a fine library, and many interesting memorials and relics. On
April 1, 1893, in consequence of an accident to a gasoline tank, the house
caught fire and was burnt down. Among the paintings that were con-
sumed was a portrait of Mrs. Siddons by Sir Joshua Reynolds; a portrait
of himself by Sir David Wilkie; a portrait of a lady by Sir Thomas Lawrence; and pictures by Corot, Daubigny, Troyon, Van Marke, Michel,
Rousseau, Diaz, A. Mauré, Coutourier, and Montecelli. An old, attached,
and much-esteemed servant, Miss Helen McGrath, perished in the flames.
" Crow's Nest " has been rebuilt, 1894.

Jefferson's dwelling, a mansion embowered by large trees, stands upon an eminence, looking southward, and commands an unbroken prospect of miles of lonely prairie, over which the dark buzzards slowly sail and the small birds flit merrily about, and on which herds of roving cattle, seen in the distance as black and formless shapes, roam lazily around, making a changeful picture of commingled motion and peace. There, with his wife and children, his books, his pictures, the art of painting for an occupation, and the memories of a good and honoured life for a solace, the veteran may reap "the harvest of a quiet mind," and calmly look onward to the sunset of life.

Jefferson has been twice married. His first wife, to whom he was wedded on May 19, 1850, in New York, was Margaret Clements Lockyer, a native of Burnham, Somersetshire, England, born September 6, 1832, and brought to America, by her parents, while yet a child. Miss Lockyer went on the stage when about sixteen years old, and early in her career was connected with the Museum at Troy, N.Y. Ireland mentions that she appeared at the Bowery theatre, New York, on November 6, 1847, on the occasion of a benefit of Thomas H. Blakeley. "Chanfrau and Mrs. Timm, from the Olympic, enacted Jeremiah Clip and Jane Chatterly, in *The Widow's Victim*, and a *pas de deux* was executed by the Misses Barber and Lockyer. The latter was young and talented." She is mentioned, on another occasion, as having acted Norah, in *The Poor Soldier*.[1] After her

---

[1] *The Poor Soldier.* Comic opera, by John O'Keefe. 1798. Altered and improved, by the author, from his earlier farce (1783) of *The Shamrock.* Wood says it was a favourite with George Washington.

JEFFERSON FAMILY GROUP

At Orange Island, La.

marriage she did not continuously pursue the dramatic profession, nor did she at any time acquire exceptional distinction as an actress. Her death occurred on February 18, 1861, in Twelfth street, New York, and she was buried at Cypress Hills, Long Island.

The children of Jefferson's first marriage are : —

1. CHARLES BURKE JEFFERSON. — Born at Macon, Ga., March 20, 1851. He adopted the stage, and made his first regular professional appearance, November 26, 1869, at McVicker's theatre, Chicago. The occasion was that of his father's benefit, and Charles, a handsome youth of eighteen, acted Dickory, in *The Spectre Bridegroom*. He has acted other parts, but has not steadily pursued the art.

2. MARGARET JANE JEFFERSON. — Born at New York, July 4, 1853. She never was on the stage. She is the wife of Benjamin L. Farjeon, the distinguished English novelist, to whom she was married, in London, in June, 1877.

3. FRANCES FLORENCE JEFFERSON. — Born at Baltimore, Md., July 9, 1855; died there, December 12, 1855.

4. JOSEPH JEFFERSON, JR. — Born at Richmond, Va., in September, 1856; died there, in 1857.

5. THOMAS JEFFERSON. — Born in New York, in 1857. In boyhood he attended school in London, and afterward, in Paris. Having adopted the stage, he made his first regular professional appearance, at Edinburgh, in the character of Coccles, in *Rip Van Winkle*, in 1877, acting in his father's theatrical company. He was engaged at Wallack's theatre, New York, for the part of Anatole, in *A Scrap of Paper*, appearing on January 5, 1880, and he again played the same part there, March 28, 1881. When his father revived *The Rivals*, September 13, 1880, at the Arch Street theatre, Philadelphia, he was cast for Fag, and in that mercurial type of bland mendacity and good-natured assurance he made a pleasing impression. On August 21, 1879, at Hohokus, N.J., Thomas Jefferson was married to Miss Eugenia Paul.

6. JOSEPHINE DUFF JEFFERSON. — Born at New York, November 10, 1859. She never was on the stage.

N

The second marriage of Jefferson occurred on December 20, 1867, at Chicago, when he was wedded to Miss Sarah Isabel Warren, a daughter of his father's cousin, Henry Warren (died 1894), brother of William Warren, the once famous comedian. The children of his second marriage are : —

1. JOSEPH WARREN JEFFERSON. — Born at New York, July 6, 1869. Married, June 13, 1891, to Blanche Beatrice Bender. Has adopted the stage and is a member of his father's company (1894).

2. HENRY JEFFERSON. — Born at Chicago, Ill. Died, at London, England, November 5, 1875. Buried at Cypress Hills, Long Island, N.Y.

3. WILLIAM WINTER JEFFERSON. — Born in Bedford House, Tavistock Square, London, April 29, 1876, and christened, on June 27, the same year, in the Church of the Holy Trinity, — the Shakespeare church, — at Stratford-on-Avon. Is on the stage.

4. FRANK JEFFERSON. — Born at New York, September 12, 1885.

The fourth Jefferson, resembling his grandfather in this as in some other particulars, has shown remarkable versatility in the dramatic art, not only by the wealth of contrasted attributes lavished by him upon Rip Van Winkle, which he has made an epitome of human nature and representative experience, but by the number and variety of the parts that he has acted. More than a hundred of them are recorded here, and in many of them his acting has been so fine that he would have been recognised as a rare and admirable comedian, even though he had not acted Rip at all. It is either ignorance or injustice, accordingly, that — with the intention of disparagement — designates him as "a one-part actor." Yet certainly he has gained his place mainly by acting one part, and that fact has been noticed by various observers, in various moods. " I am glad to see you making your fortune, Jefferson," said Charles Mathews, "but I don't like to see you doing it with one part and a carpet bag." Mathews was obliged to play many parts, and therefore to travel with many boxes of wardrobe ; whereas the blue shirt, the old, rusty leather jacket, the red-brown breeches, the stained leggings, the old shoes, the torn red and white silk handkerchief, the tattered old hat, the guns and bottle, and the two wigs for Rip can be carried in a single box. The comment of Mathews, however, was meant to glance at the "one-part" policy, and Jefferson's reply to that ebullition was alike significant and good-humoured. " It is perhaps better," he said, " to play one part in different ways than to play many parts all in one way." That sentence explains his artistic victory. A few of Jefferson's characters are designated here : —

REPERTORY OF JOSEPH JEFFERSON

[RIP VAN WINKLE.]

A.

Acres, in *The Rivals*.

Andrew, the Savoyard, in *Isabel*.

Asa Trenchard, in *Our American Cousin*. Domestic drama. By Tom Taylor. Laura Keene's theatre, New York, 1858.

B.

Beppo, in *Fra Diavolo*. Burlesque. By H. J. Byron.

Box, and also Cox, in *Box and Cox*. Farce. By J. M. Morton. London, Haymarket, 1847. Jefferson was the original Cox, in America, and Burton the original Box — at the Arch Street theatre, Philadelphia, in 1848.

Bob Trickett, in *An Alarming Sacrifice*. Jefferson's first wife played Susan Sweetapple.

Bob Brierly, in *The Ticket-of-Leave Man*. Drama. By Tom Taylor. 1863.

Bob, in *Old Heads and Young Hearts*. Comedy. By Dion Boucicault.

Bobtail, in *Bobtail and Wagtail*.

C.

C. T. Item, and also The Tycoon, in *The Tycoon, or Young America in Japan*. Burlesque. By William Brough. Adapted by Fitz-James O'Brien and Joseph Jefferson. Olympic, New York, 1860.

Caleb Plummer, in *Dot, or The Cricket on the Hearth*. Drama. By Dion Boucicault. Based on Christmas story by Charles Dickens.

Crabtree, Moses, and Trip, in *The School for Scandal*.

Caleb Quotem, and also John Lump, in *The Review, or The Wags of Windsor*. Farce. By George Colman, Jr. Haymarket. Authorised edition, 1808. Fawcett was the original Caleb Quotem. Junius Brutus Booth sometimes acted John Lump, and Jefferson acted with him as Caleb.

D.

Dr. Botherby, in *An Unequal Match*. Comedy. By Tom Taylor.

Dard, in *White Lies*. Drama. By Cyril Turner. Based on novel, of French origin, by Charles Reade.

Dick, in *Paddy the Piper*. Drama. By James Pilgrim. New National theatre, New York, October 6, 1850.

Dr. Smugface, in *A Budget of Blunders*. Farce. By Prince Hoare. Covent Garden, 1810.

Dr. Pangloss, in *The Heir at Law*.

Dan, in *John Bull*. Comedy. By George Colman, Jr. Covent Garden, 1805.

Donaldbain, Malcolm, and each of the Three Witches, in *Macbeth*.

Dickory, in *The Spectre Bridegroom*.

Dr. Ollapod, and also Stephen Harrowby, in *The Poor Gentleman*.

Dogberry, and also Verges, in *Much Ado About Nothing*.

F.

Figaro, in *The Barber of Seville*.

Fixture, in *A Roland for an Oliver*.

Fainwould, in *Raising the Wind*. Farce. By James Kenney. Covent Garden, 1803.

Francis, in Shakespeare's *Henry the Fourth*.

G.

Gloss, in *Doublefaced People*. Comedy. By H. Courtney.

Granby Gag, in *Jenny Lind*.

Goldfinch, in *The Road to Ruin*. Comedy. By Thomas Holcroft. Covent Garden, 1792.

H.

Hans Morritz, in *Somebody Else*.

Hugh Chalcote, in *Ours*. Comedy. By Thomas W. Robertson.

I.

Isaac, in *Lucille*.

J.

Joe Wadd, in *The Hope of the Family*.

James, in *Blue Devils*.

John Quill, in *Beauty and the Beast*.

Joshua Butterby, in *Victims*. Comedy. By Tom Taylor.

Jaques Strop, in *Robert Macaire*.

Joe Meggs, in *The Parish Clerk*. Drama. By Dion Boucicault. Acted at Manchester, England. Contains one excellent scene. Has not been acted in America.

K.

Kaserac, in *Aladdin*.

L.

La Fleur, in *Animal Magnetism*. Farce. By Elizabeth Inchbald. Covent Garden, 1788.

Lord Mayor, Catesby, Oxford, the Prince of Wales, and the Duke of York, in Cibber's version of Shakespeare's *Richard the Third*.

M.

Mr. Woodcock, in *Woodcock's Little Game*.
Mr. Gilman, in *The Happiest Day of My Life*.
Mr. Timid, in *The Dead Shot*.
Mazeppa, in the burlesque of *Mazeppa*. By H. J. Byron.
Mr. Fluffy, in *Mother and Child*.
Mr. Brown, in the farce of *My Neighbour's Wife*.
Mr. Lullaby, in *A Conjugal Lesson*.
Mr. Golightly, in *Lend Me Five Shillings*.

N.

Newman Noggs, in *Nicholas Nickleby*. Drama. By Dion Boucicault. Based on the novel by Dickens.
Niken, in *The Carpenter of Rouen*.

O.

Old Phil Stapleton, in *Old Phil's Birthday*.
Oliver Dobbs, in *Agnes de Vere*.
Oswald, in *King Lear*.
Osric, and also the Two Clowns, or Grave-diggers, in *Hamlet*.

P.

Pierre Rough, in *The Husband of an Hour*. Drama. By Edmund Falconer.
Pierrot, in *Linda, The Pearl of Chamouni*.
Prop, in *No Song no Supper*.
Pan, in *Midas*. Burlesque. By Kane O'Hara. Covent Garden, 1764-1771.
Pillicoddy, in *Poor Pillicoddy*. Farce. By J. M. Morton.
Peter, and also Paris, in *Romeo and Juliet*.
Peter, in *The Stranger*.

R.

Robin, in *The Waterman, or The First of August*. Ballad opera. By Charles Dibdin. Haymarket, 1774.
Roderigo, in *Othello*.
Rip Van Winkle, in the romantic and domestic drama of that name. Old version by Charles Burke. 1849. New one by Dion Boucicault. Adelphi, London, 1865.

S.

Septimus, in *My Son Diana*.

Salem Scudder, in *The Octoroon*. Drama. By Dion Boucicault.
Based on novel by Captain Mayne Reid. Winter Garden, New
York, 1859.

Slasher, in *Slasher and Crasher*. Farce. By J. M. Morton.

Sheepface, in *The Village Lawyer*. Farce. 1795.

Simon. in *The Rendezvous*.

Sir Brian, in *Ivanhoe*. Burlesque. By the Brough Brothers.

Sampson Rawbold, in *The Iron Chest*. Tragedy. By George
Colman, Jr. Drury Lane, 1796. Music by Storace. Kemble was
the original Sir Edward Mortimer. The piece was based on William Godwin's novel of *Caleb Williams*, and may be contrasted with
that tale, for an illustration of the difference between narrative and
dramatic writing.

Slender, in *The Merry Wives of Windsor*.

T.

The Steward, in *The Child of the Regiment*.

Tracy Coach, in *Baby*.

Toby Twinkle, in *All that Glitters is not Gold.*

The Infant Furibond, in *The Invisible Prince*.

The Sentinel, in *Pizarro*.

Tony Lumpkin, in *She Stoops to Conquer*. Comedy. By Oliver
Goldsmith. Covent Garden, 1773.

Tobias Shortcut, in *The Spitfire*. Farce. By J. M. Morton.
Covent Garden, 1838.

Touchstone, in *As You Like It*.

W.

Wyndham, in *The Handsome Husband*.

Whiskerandos, in *The Critic*.

Y.

Yonkers, in *Chamooni the Third*. Burlesque. By Dion Boucicault. Winter Garden, New York, 1859.

In Joseph Jefferson, — fourth of the line, famous as
Rip Van Winkle, and destined to be long remembered

by that name in dramatic history — there is an obvious union of the salient qualities of his ancestors. The rustic luxuriance, manly vigour, and careless and adventurous disposition of the first Jefferson, the refined intellect, delicate sensibility, dry humour, and gentle tenderness of the second, and the amiable, philosophic, and drifting temperament of the third reappear in this descendant. But more than either of his ancestors, and more than most of his contemporaries, the present Jefferson is an originator in the art of acting. The comedians of the Burbage and Betterton periods were rich in humour, and a few of them possessed superb artistic faculty in its display; but the inquirer will ·read many volumes of theatrical history, and traverse a wide field of time, before he will come upon a great representative of human nature in the realm that is signified by Touchstone, or Jaques, or the Fool, in *King Lear.* Wilks, certainly, must have been a great comedian. He had serious power, too, and tenderness, and his artistic method was studiously thorough; but it was in gay parts that he was best, — in Sir Harry Wildair and the wooing scene of *Henry the Fifth.* The comedians of the Garrick period, aside from its illustrious chieftain, made but little advance upon those of the Restoration. The parts that were simply humorous continued to be the parts that were acted best. Even Garrick mostly kept his pathos for his tragedy: it was the glittering splendour of vitality that dazzled, in his Don Felix, and it was the various and wonderful comic eccentricity that delighted, in his Abel Drugger. The growth of comedy-acting, nevertheless, took the direction of the heart. King, the first Sir Peter Teazle, had at least a ray of pathetic warmth. Holcroft and the younger Colman, breaking away from the influence of Congreve and Wycherley, set the example of writing in a vein that elicited the humanity no less than the humour of the comedians. The influence of tragic genius, like that of Barry, Henderson, Mrs. Crawford, and Mrs. Siddons, lent its aid to foster the development of its sister art. Munden, Dowton, and kindred spirits came upon the scene; and it was soon proved, and felt, and recognised that humour is all the more humour when it makes the tear of pity glisten through the smile of pleasure. From that day to this the stage in England and America has presented an unbroken line of comedians, who — possessed of diversified humour, ranging from that of Rabelais to that of Sterne — have also possessed the generous warmth of Steele, the quaint kindliness of Lamb, the pitying gentleness of Hood, and the sad-eyed charity of Thackeray. From that day the art of comedy-acting has been allied to a purpose that aimed higher than to make the world laugh. In the second Jefferson that growth attained to a splendid maturity, and pathos and humour were perfectly blended. It remained that a rare form of genius should irradiate mirth and tenderness with the light of poetic imagination. The fulfilment came with Jefferson in Rip Van Winkle. Most other comedians suggest their prototypes in the past. Burton, Bass, Florence, Owens, and Setchell are names that point to a fine lineage, calling up the shades of Wright, Reeve, Suett, Liston, Nokes, Kempe, and Lowin. The elder and the younger Warren, Hackett, Davidge, Parselle, and Le Moyne were descendants of Quin. The honoured name of John Gilbert was long since written with those of Webster, Farren, and Munden ; and to that family belonged the courtly Placide, the polished and commanding Sedley, the versatile and gentle Charles Fisher, and the hearty, robust, and human Mark Smith. Sothern, that prince of elegant caricature and soul of whimsical fun, was of the line of Foote, Tate Wilkinson, Finn, and Mathews; while in many attributes John T. Raymond and George Fawcett Rowe were of the same lineage. James Lewis suggests the spontaneity of Weston, the versatile humour of Estcourt, and the finish of Blissett. Lester Wallack, the most picturesque figure of a famous race, was in the brilliant comedy group of Mountfort, Elliston, Lewis, and Charles Kemble ; while John S. Clarke is the heir, in comic eccentricity, of Woodward and John Emery. But Joseph Jefferson is unlike them all, — as distinct as Charles Lamb among essayists, or George Darley among lyrical poets. No actor of the past prefigured him, — unless, perhaps, it was John Bannister, — and no name, in the teeming annals of modern art, has shone with a more tranquil lustre, or can be more confidently committed to the esteem of posterity.

VII

RIP VAN WINKLE

EVERY reader of Washington Irving knows the story of Rip Van Winkle's adventure on the Catskill Mountains, — that delightful, romantic idyl, in which character, humour, and fancy are so delicately blended. Under the spell of Jefferson's acting the spectator was transported into the past, and made to see, as with bodily eyes, the orderly Dutch civilisation as it crept up the borders of the Hudson: the quaint villages; the stout Hollanders, with their pipes and schnapps; the loves and troubles of an elder generation. It is a calmer life than ours; yet the same elements compose it. Here is a mean and cruel schemer making a heedless man his victim, and thriving on the weakness that he well knows how to betray. Here is parental love, tried, as it often is, by sad cares; and here the love of young and hopeful hearts, blooming amid flowers, sunshine, music, and happiness. Rip Van Winkle never seemed so lovable as in the form of this great actor, standing in poetic relief against the background of actual life. Jefferson has made him our familiar friend. We see that Rip is a dreamer, fond of his bottle and his ease, but — beneath all his rags and tatters, of character as well as raiment — essentially good. We understand why the children love him, why the dogs run after him with joy, and why the jolly boys at the tavern welcome his song and story and genial companionship. He has wasted his fortune and impoverished his wife and child, and we know that he is much to blame. ' He knows it too; and his talk with the children shows how keenly he feels the consequence of a weakness which yet he is unable to discard. It is in those minute touches that Jefferson denoted his sympathetic study of human nature; his intuitive perception, looking quite through the hearts and thoughts of men. The observer saw this in the struggle of Rip's long-submerged but only dormant spirit of manliness, when his wife turns him from their home, in night and storm and abandoned degradation. Still more vividly was it shown in his pathetic bewilderment, — his touching embodiment of the anguish of lonely age bowed down by sorrow and doubt, — when he comes back from his sleep of twenty years. His disclosure of himself to his daughter marked the climax of pathos, and every heart was melted by those imploring looks of mute suspense, those broken accents of love that almost fears an utterance. Perhaps the perfection of Jefferson's acting was seen in the weird interview with the ghosts. That situation is one of the best ever devised for the stage; and the actor devised it. Midnight, on the highest peak of the Catskill, dimly lighted by the moon. No one speaks but Rip. The ghosts cluster around him. The grim shade of Hudson proffers a cup of drink to the mortal intruder, already dazed by supernatural surroundings. Rip, almost shuddering in the awful silence, pledges the ghosts in their liquor. Then, suddenly the

spell is broken ; the moon is lost in struggling clouds ; the spectres glide away and slowly vanish ; and Rip Van Winkle, with the drowsy, piteous murmur, " Don't leave me, boys," falls into his mystic sleep.

The idle, dram-drinking Dutch spendthrift — so perfectly reproduced, yet so exalted by ideal treatment — is not an heroic figure, and cannot be said to possess an exemplary significance, either in himself or his experience. Yet his temperament has the fine fibre that everybody loves, and everybody, accordingly, has a good feeling for him, although nobody may have a good word for his way of life. All observers know that order of man. He is generally poor. He never did a bad action in all his life. He is continually cheering the weak and lowly. He always wears a smile, — the reflex of a gentle heart. Ambition does not trouble him. His wants are few. He has no care, except when, now and then, he feels that he may have wasted time and talent, or when the sorrow of others falls darkly on his heart. This, however, is rare ; for at most times he is "bright as light and clear as wind." Nature has established with him a kind of kindred that she allows with only a chosen few. In him Shakespeare's rosy ideal is suggested : —

> " Suppose the singing birds musicians ;
>   The grass whereon thou tread'st, the presence strew'd ;
>   The flowers fair ladies ; and thy steps, no more
>   Than a delightful measure, or a dance."

Nobody would dream of setting up Jefferson's Rip as a model, but everybody is glad that he exists. Most persons are so full of care and trouble, so weighed down with the sense of duty, so anxious to regulate the

world, that contact with a nature which is careless of
the stress and din of toil, dwells in an atmosphere of
sunshine idleness, and is the embodiment of careless
mirth, brings a positive relief. This is the feeling that
Jefferson's acting inspired. The halo of genius was all
around it. Sincerity, humour, pathos, imagination, — the
glamour of wild flowers and woodland brooks, slumber-
ous, slow-drifting summer-clouds, and soft music heard
upon the waters, in star-lit nights of June, — those are
the springs of the actor's art. There are a hundred
beauties of method in it which satisfy the judgment and
fascinate the sense of symmetry ; but underlying those
beauties there is a magical sweetness of temperament,
a delicate blending of emotion, gentleness, quaintness,
and dream-like repose, which awakens the most affectionate sympathy. Art could not supply that subtle,
potent charm. It is the divine fire.

In his embodiment of Rip Van Winkle Jefferson
delineates an individual character, through successive
stages of growth, till the story of a life is completely
told. If the student of acting would appreciate the fine-
ness and force of the dramatic art that is displayed in
the work, let him consider the complexity and depth of
the effect, as contrasted with the simplicity of the means
that are used to produce it. The sense of beauty is
satisfied, because the object that it apprehends is beautiful. The heart is deeply and surely touched, for the
simple and sufficient reason that the character and experience revealed to it are lovely and pathetic. For Rip
Van Winkle's goodness exists as an oak exists, and is
not dependent on principle, precept, or purpose. However he may drift, he cannot drift away from human

affection. Weakness was never punished with more sorrowful misfortune than his. (Dear to us for what he is, he becomes dearer still for what he suffers, and, in the acting of Jefferson, for the manner in which he suffers it. That manner, arising out of complete identification with the part, informed by intuitive and liberal knowledge of human nature, and guided by an unerring instinct of taste, is unfettered, graceful, free from effort; and it shows with delicate precision the gradual, natural changes of the character, as wrought by the pressure of experience. Its result is the winning embodiment of a rare type of human nature and mystical experience, embellished by the hues of romance and exalted by the atmosphere of poetry ; and no person of imagination and sensibility can see it without being charmed by its humour, thrilled by its spiritual beauty, and, beneath the spell of its humanity, made deeply conscious that life is worthless, however its ambition may be rewarded, unless it is hallowed by love.

There will be, as there have been, many performers of Rip Van Winkle; there is but one Jefferson. For him it was reserved to idealise the subject ; to elevate a prosaic type of good-natured indolence into an emblem of poetical freedom ; to construct and translate, in the world of fact, the Arcadian vagabond of the world of dreams. In the presence of his fascinating embodiment of that droll, gentle, drifting human creature, — to whom trees and brooks and flowers are familiar companions, to whom spirits appear, and for whom the mysterious voices of the lonely midnight forest have a meaning and a charm, — the observer feels that poetry is no longer restricted to canvas and marble, but walks forth

crystallised in a human form, spangled with the diamond
light of morning, mysterious with spiritual intimations,
lovely with rustic freedom, and fragrant with the in-
cense of the woods.

Jefferson's acting is an education as well as a delight.
It especially teaches the imperative importance, in dramatic art, of a thorough and perfect plan, which yet,
by freshness of spirit and spontaneity of execution,
shall be made to seem free and careless. Jefferson's
embodiment of Rip has been prominently before the
public for thirty years, yet it is not hackneyed, and it
does not grow tiresome. The secret of its vitality is its
poetry. A thriftless, commonplace sot, as drawn by
Washington Irving, becomes a poetic vagabond, as
transfigured and embodied by the actor; and the dignity of his artistic work is augmented rather than
diminished from the fact that he plays in a drama
throughout which the expedient of inebriety, as a
motive of action, is exaggerated. Boucicault, working
under explicit information as to Jefferson's views and
wishes with reference to the part, certainly improved
the old piece; but, as certainly, the scheme to show
the sunny sweetness and indolent temperament of Rip
is clumsily planned, while the text is devoid of literary
excellence and intellectual character, — attributes which,
though not dramatic, are desirable. The actor is im-
mensely superior to the play, and may indeed be said
to make it. The obvious goodness of his heart, the
deep sincerity of his moral purpose, the potential force
of his sense of beauty, the supremacy in him of what
Voltaire was the first to call the "faculty of taste," the
incessant charm of his temperament, — those are the

means, ruled and guided by clear vision and strong will, and made to animate an artistic figure possessing both symmetry and luxuriant wildness, that make the greatness of Jefferson's embodiment of Rip. He has created a character that everybody will continue to love, notwithstanding weakness of nature and indolent conduct. Jefferson never had the purpose to extol improvidence or extenuate the wrong and misery of inebriety. The opportunity that he discerned and has brilliantly improved was that of showing a lovely nature, set free from the shackles of conventionality and circumscribed with picturesque, romantic surroundings, during a momentous experience of spiritual life, and of the mutability of the world. The obvious defects in the structure are an undue emphasis upon the bottle, as poor Rip's failing, and an undue exaggeration of the virago quality in Gretchen. It would be easy, taking the prosy tone of the temperance lecturer, to look at Jefferson's design as a matter of fact and not of poetry, and, by dwelling on the impediments of his subject rather than the spirit of his art and the beauty of his execution, to set his beautiful and elevating achievement in a degraded and degrading light. But, fortunately, the heart has its logic as well as the head, and all observers are not without imagination. The heart and imagination of our age know what Jefferson means in Rip, and have accepted him, therefore, into the sanctuary of affection.

The world does not love Rip Van Winkle because of his faults, but in spite of them. Underneath his defects the human nature is sound and bright ; and it is out of this interior beauty that the charm of Jefferson's personation arises. The conduct of Rip Van Winkle is

o

the result of his character, not of his drams. At the sacrifice of comicality, here and there, the element of inebriety might be left out of his experience and he would still act in the same way, and possess the same fascination. The drink is only an expedient, to involve the hero in domestic strife and open the way for his ghostly adventure and his pathetic resuscitation. The machinery is clumsy; but that does not invalidate either the beauty of the character or the supernatural thrill and mortal anguish of the experience. Those elements make the soul of this great work, which, while it captivates the heart, also enthralls the imagination, — lifting us above the storms of life, its sorrows, its losses, and its fret, till we rest at last on Nature's bosom, children once more, and once more happy.

VIII

ACRES

In 1880 Jefferson complied with a desire, which had
been generally felt and frequently expressed, that he
should appear in some other part than Rip Van Winkle.
He had not tired of that character any more than the
public had tired of it ; but he felt the mental need of a
change, and he recognised the claim of a new generation of playgoers upon that versatility of art and those
resources of faculty and humour which had given enjoyment to theatrical audiences of an earlier time, and
laid the basis of his professional renown.   He was not
unwilling to correct a mistaken impression, current to
some extent, that he was only a one-part actor.   In
former days, before he adopted Rip Van Winkle, Jefferson acted many parts ; and early in his career he was
recognised, by the dramatic profession and by the more
discerning part of the public, as an actor of much versatility.   His personations of Asa Trenchard, Caleb Plummer, Dr. Pangloss, Dr. Ollapod, Salem Scudder, Mr.
Golightly, Mr. Lullaby, Newman Noggs, Goldfinch, Bob
Brierly, the burlesque Mazeppa, Dickory, and Tobias
Shortcut delighted old playgoers, and by them were
remembered only to be admired and extolled.   But
after his return from England, in 1866, he seldom

acted anything but Rip Van Winkle, so that the public
conception of him as a general actor had grown dim, or
altogether faded.   In reviving *The Rivals*, and appearing as Acres, he afforded refreshment to his mind ; he
lessened the possibility of making Rip Van Winkle
tedious ; he satisfied a craving for novelty on the part
of his admirers ; he revived a just sense of the breadth
of his scope as a comedian ; and, keeping pace with
modern taste, he gave his public a new pleasure, a new
picture in dramatic art, and a new subject for study and
thought.

The professional career of Jefferson has been marked,
all along its course, by wisdom.   He came to the capital at the right time, and in the right way.   He early
applied to the old comedies the right, because the pure
and poetic, method of treatment.   He could look far
ahead for the results of his labour and devotion, and
he made fidelity to the highest ideal of art the first
object of his life.   He understood perfectly well the
nature of the structure that he was rearing, and he
never trusted anything to chance.   It was he who
caused the production of *Our American Cousin*, at
Laura Keene's theatre, in New York, October 18, 1858,
and so made one of the best dramatic successes of
which there is a record.   He had the foresight to select,
while yet a young man, the character in which his
powers were destined to find their amplest expression,
— the character of Rip Van Winkle ; and for that he
conceived an ideal and devised a treatment so original,
poetic, and lovely, so unlike and so superior to the
man in Washington Irving's sketch and to the embodiment of previous actors, that he may be said to

have created the part. He left America and visited
Australia at a favourable period for such an expedition,
and with a practical view to subsequent success upon
the London stage. He sagaciously resorted to Dion
Boucicault, in London, when he deemed it essential
that a new play should be built upon the basis of the
old one, and he furnished to that practical dramatist a
general outline of the piece, the drift of the central
character, and the great situation in the second act of
Rip Van Winkle as it now stands, — a dramatic idea
which of itself would suffice to prove him a man of
genius. He returned home opportunely, after his extraordinary success in Great Britain ; and the fame
and fortune he has since acquired, the affection with
which his renown is cherished, and the joyous admiration with which his name is spoken throughout America amply indicate that his conduct of the artist-life,
since then, has been no less prudent and right than
kindly, modest, gentle, and sincere. It is not caprice
which shapes such a career as that of Jefferson, nor
is it accident that has crowned it with the laurels of
honour.

The sagacity of the comedian was shown in the choice
he made of a piece and a character to contrast with Rip
Van Winkle. Of all the old comedies, *The Rivals* is
obviously the best that this actor could have selected,
with a view of making his particular part in the performance the apex of the entertainment. The piece
is one that has not become antiquated. Its picture of
life and manners is as modern and as vital as it is clear,
richly coloured, humorous, and brilliant. The spirit of
it, moreover, is human, kindly, and pure. There is no

taint of indelicacy in the plot, — no blur of licentious-
ness, such as smirches the mirror of its great companion-
piece, *The School for Scandal*, — and in the style there
is but little of that elaborate, brittle wit which sometimes seems to impart to Sheridan's writings a tiresome glitter of artifice. The play is genial, sprightly,
and droll ; it has interest of story, alert movement, and
substantial and well-contrasted characters ; and its
theme, incidents, and atmosphere are suited to Jefferson's simple artistic method. He obtained in his choice
of it a means of expression by which he could seize
and hold the sympathy of the spectator, all the while
that he was scattering over him the flowers of
mirth, and waking in his heart the echoes of happy
laughter. It would be hard to find another comedy
equally sparkling with life, delightful in colour, and
merry and gentle in influence, in which a single, and
that a comic, character, — one of a group, yet drawn
and kept in harmony with its surroundings, — could
thus be made tributary to the idiosyncrasies of an actor,
and thus elevated into shining prominence, without
injury to its form or to the symmetry of the play.
After seeing *The Rivals*, as Jefferson presented it, the
spectator felt a great kindness for the old piece, and
had the conviction that, in Jefferson's performance of
Acres, he had seen a slight character made fascinating
by drollery of spirit, sincerity of feeling, and grace of
expression.[1]

---

[1] The several parts were dressed in a correct and sumptuous manner,
though with some intentional inaccuracy as to powdered hair. The representation was marked by clearness of outline, brilliancy of colour, and
harmony of effect. The characters in *The Rivals*, when Jefferson first

When *The Rivals* was first produced (1775), it had to be cut, in a ruthless manner, before it could be made to succeed.[1] The author, then but twenty-three years old,

produced his adaptation of it, September 15, 1880, at the Arch Street theatre, Philadelphia, were cast as follows : —

Acres	Mr. Jefferson.
Sir Anthony Absolute	Frederick Robinson.
Captain Absolute	Maurice Barrymore.
Sir Lucius O'Trigger	Charles Waverley.[1]
Falkland	Henry F. Taylor.
Fag	Thomas Jefferson.
David	James Galloway.
Mrs. Malaprop	Mrs. John Drew.
Lydia Languish	Rosa Rand.
Lucy	Adine Stephens.

Jefferson produced *The Rivals* and personated Acres, at the Union Square theatre, New York, on September 12, 1881. That was his first presentation of the subject in New York, subsequent to the Philadelphia revival. The cast of characters then was : —

Acres	Mr. Jefferson.
Sir Anthony Absolute	Frederick Robinson.
Captain Absolute	Mark Pendleton.
Sir Lucius O'Trigger	Charles Waverley.
Falkland	Henry F. Taylor.
Fag	Thomas Jefferson.
David	James Galloway.
Mrs. Malaprop	Mrs. John Drew.
Lydia Languish	Rose Wood.
Lucy	Eugenia Paul.

[1] The partial failure of *The Rivals*, when first acted, was due in part to its inordinate length, and in part to its incompatibility with the taste then prevalent, which preferred sentimental plays, harmonious with the manners of the time. Falkland and Julia were approved, but Mrs. Malaprop, being a humorous caricature, was condemned. An interesting reference to this subject is made by Bernard (*Retrospections*, Vol. I., p. 86), who saw

[1] Charles Waverley was a conscientious actor and notable for refinement. His perception of character was keen, and in parts of a demure or playful order he could be very agreeably droll. He was a man of steadfast principles and amiable disposition, and was modest and sympathetic. He died, in London, in August, 1883.

had written it with exuberant spirits, and it contained substance enough for several plays rather than one. Jefferson did not hesitate to cut it still further, and slightly to change its sequence of action, and here and there, in the character of Acres, to deepen traits that the author has only outlined, to add new business, — always, however, in harmony with the original conception, — and to give, by occasional new lines, an added emphasis and prolongation to the humorous strokes of Sheridan.

Those parts of plays which are not essential may well be spared, unless they can be done perfectly well. The last of the four great soliloquies of *Hamlet* is invariably omitted; and no one of Shakespeare's plays is ever acted exactly as it stands, because there are lines that cannot be spoken, and because the necessity of certain other lines is obviated by the resources of modern stage scenery. The author of *The Rivals* would, probably, have been the first to favour any change that might improve its effect, — for, as stated by Moore, on the authority of Lady Cork, he "always said that *The Rivals* was one of the worst plays in the language, and he would give anything if he had not written it." Jefferson gave the comedy in three acts, — the first curtain falling upon the exit of Sir Anthony Absolute, after his choleric scene with his son; the second upon the exit of Acres, at the words, "Tell him I kill a man a week"; and the third upon the close of the piece, with a tag that the actor added. The character of Julia was omitted and that of Falk-

the performance, and who declares that the ascription of the partial failure to the inefficient acting of Lee, as Sir Lucius O'Trigger, was unjust and ungenerous.

land considerably reduced. Those parts are only pleasant when acted by players of the first class, such as can no longer be led to undertake them. (Mrs. Siddons once played Sheridan's Julia, but a walking lady would hardly accept it now.) The loose lines, as well as what Moore called the "false finery and second-rate ornament," were shorn away. Two of the scenes of Acres were blended into one, so that the vain and timorous squire's truculence, when writing the challenge, might be made the more comical by immediate contrast with his dismay and gradually growing cowardice, as he begins to realise its possible consequences. In other respects there was no change.

Jefferson's felicity in light parts, whether of comedy, burlesque, or farce, resides in his application to them of an intense earnestness of spirit and a poetic treatment,[1] — by which is meant a treatment that interprets, illustrates, and elevates the character. In that way he embodied Acres. The first of the three scenes in which he appeared was that of the call which is made by Acres at the lodging of Captain Absolute, where he meets Falkland; the second, that of his reception of Sir Lucius O'Trigger, at his own chambers, when he writes the challenge to the mythical Beverley, is frightened by the

---

[1] In 1871, on the occasion of the Holland Benefit, in New York, Jefferson charmed a great audience with his representation of Mr. Golightly; and that exquisite work he gave later (1877), in London, on the occasion of a benefit to the impoverished and dying veteran, Henry Compton, when his success was such that John S. Clarke immediately proposed to him a season of farce at the Haymarket, — a season devoted to Mr. Golightly and Hugh de Brass, — in which, while the treasury neither gained nor lost, fastidious critics of the British capital enjoyed a kind of acting which they conceded to be kindred with the best upon the light comedy stage of Paris.

terror of his bumpkin servant, David, and, at last, with rueful reluctance, entrusts the warlike missive to Captain Absolute; and the third, that of the frustrated meeting in King's Mead meadows, when, in the extremity of fear, his "valour oozes out at the tips of his fingers," and the snarl that young Absolute has woven is happily disentangled. The variety that he evoked from those scenes was little less than wonderful. At first it seemed as if he had overladen the character with meaning and lifted it too far. But, when the work was studied, it was seen that the actor had only taken the justifiable and admirable license of deepening the lines and tints of the author, and of endearing the character by infusing into it an amiable and lovable personality That this was not clearly intended by Sheridan would not invalidate its propriety. The part admits of it, and is better for it; and this certainly would have been intended had it been thought of, — for it makes the play doubly interesting and potential. That Acres becomes a striking figure in the group, and a vigorous motive in the action, is only because he is thus vitalised. If the other parts were animated by an equal genius in the performance of them, it would be seen that he has no undue prominence.

Jefferson considered that a country squire need not necessarily reek of the ale-house and the stables; that Acres is neither the noisy and coarse Tony Lumpkin nor the "horsey" Goldfinch; that he is not less kindly because vain and vapid; that he has tender ties of home, and a background of innocent, domestic life; that his head is completely turned by contact with town fashions; that there may be a kind of artlessness

JEFFERSON AND FLORENCE IN THE RIVALS
From a photograph by Falk.

in his ridiculous assumption of rakish airs ; that there is something a little pitiable in his bombast ; that he is a good fellow, at heart ; and that his sufferings in the predicament of the duel are genuine, intense, and quite as doleful as they are comic. All this appeared in the personation. You were impressed at once by the winning appearance and temperament, and Acres got your friendship, and was a welcome presence, laugh at him though you might. Jefferson introduced a comic blunder with which to take him out of the first scene with Absolute, and also some characteristic comic business for him, before a mirror, when Sir Lucius, coming upon him unawares, finds him practising bows and studying deportment. He did not seem contemptible in those situations ; he only seemed absurdly comical. He communicated to every spectator his joy in the success of his curl-papers ; and no one, even amidst uncontrollable laughter, thought of his penning of his challenge as otherwise than a proceeding of serious import. He was made a winning human being, with an experience of action and suffering ; and sympathy with him, on his battle-field, would have been really painful but that the spectators were in the secret. The spirit of Jefferson's impersonation was humanity and sweet good nature, while the traits that he especially emphasised were ludicrous vanity and comic trepidation. He left no moment unfilled with action, when he was on the scene, and all his by-play was made tributary to the expression of those traits. One of his deft touches was the trifling with Captain Absolute's gold-laced hat, and — obviously to the eye — considering whether it would be suitable to himself. Nothing could be more humorous than the mixture of assurance, uneasy levity, and dubious apprehension, at the moment when the challenge has at last and irrevocably found its way into Captain Absolute's pocket. The rueful face, then, was a study for a painter, and only a portrait could do it justice. The mirth of the duel scene it is impossible to convey. It must be supreme art indeed which can arouse, at the same instant, as this did, an almost tender solicitude and inextinguishable laughter. The little introductions of a word or two here and there in the text, made at this point by the comedian, were very happy. To make Acres say that he does not care "how little the risk is" was an inspiration; and his sudden and joyous greeting, "How are you, Falkland?"—with the relief that it implies, and the momentary return of the airy swagger,—was a stroke of genius.

The test to which, in his success, a comedian proves equal was suggested, in all its clear and cold severity, by that extraordinary work. No tragic actor is ever so rigidly judged; or, in the nature of the case, ever can be. It may be as difficult to act well in tragedy as in comedy; but it is always easier to produce successful effect by tragedy than by comedy; and tragedy can often be made to disguise imperfect acting. The spectator of a tragedy soon becomes excited, sympathetic, and responsive, under the stress of the tragic subject itself, and out of his own imagination and feeling he will often supply the charm, and perfect the illusion, which it may happen that the tragedian can neither exert nor create. The comedian, on the contrary, derives no such aid from his subject or from his audience. The spectator of a comedy is placid : he does not laugh until something laughable occurs, and he casts no glamour of emotion or fancy around the artist before him. The expedient known as "mugging" may, indeed, beguile a vulgar taste into the mood of laughter ; but with "the judicious" it never will supply the humour that is essential in comedy, nor obtain acceptance as a substitute for art in acting. Furthermore, the composition of a piece of comedy-acting is a mosaic, — made of many details, tints, and tones, — whereas an embodiment in tragedy may be achieved with large, imposing strokes, and masses of colour. Never was a truer word spoken than that of Garrick, when he said that comedy is serious business. It may not be so noble to act Don Felix as to act Hamlet ; but, in art, it is more difficult to make a great effect with the former than with the latter. Jefferson expended rare intellectual force and exuberant humour upon the fabric of Acres, and in that respect, while giving much pleasure, taught a valuable lesson.

Mrs. Drew treated in the same earnest spirit the character of Mrs. Malaprop. The dressing was appropriately rich, and in suitable taste ; the manner decorous and stately ; the personality formidable ; the deportment elaborate and pretentious, as it should be ; the delivery of the text exquisite in its accuracy and finish, and in its unconscious grace, — the word being always matched by the right mood, and not a single blunder, in what that eccentric character calls her "orthodoxy," made in any spirit but that of fervent conviction. Merely to hear her say, " He has enveloped the plot to me, and he will give you the perpendiculars,"

was to apprehend the character in a single sentence.
Her illustrative stage business with the letter, — giving to Absolute, by mistake, one of the love-letters of
O'Trigger, instead of the intercepted epistle of Beverley, and then hastily reclaiming it, — was done with a
bridling simper and an antique blush that were irresistible. The pervasive excellence of the work was
intense sincerity, and that redeemed the extravagance
of the character and the farcical quality of its text.
For the first time it seemed as if Mrs. Malaprop might
exist. The part was finely acted, in earlier days, by
Mrs. Vernon ; but Mrs. Drew made it rational.

Frederick Robinson, as Sir Anthony Absolute, was
admirable for choler, captivating warmth of humour, and
clever management of the dubious, pausing moments of
suspicion, in Captain Absolute's hoodwinking scene with
his father. Thomas Jefferson was a gay and effective
figure, as Fag, and he made his satirical exit with skill
and effect, worthy of a comedian. Jefferson's presentment of *The Rivals* showed what thoroughness and
sincerity can accomplish in the ministry of art. Never
to slight anything, but to go to the depth and height of
the subject, and bring out all its meaning and all its
beauty, — that was the suggested moral of his splendid
success with one of the everyday plays of the theatre.
The wild flower that grows by the wayside, if you but
nurture it aright, will reward your care a hundredfold
in loveliness and bloom.

IX

CALEB PLUMMER AND MR. GOLIGHTLY

In the characters of Caleb Plummer and Mr. Golightly Jefferson touched, in his true and delicate manner, the springs of tears and laughter. There are, indeed, resources in the comedian's nature upon which neither of them makes any demand. His deep sympathy with whatever is weird, romantic, and picturesque remained unaffected by those characters. His sense of spiritual sublimity was not awakened. His imagination rested. Yet it would be difficult to select two parts more commodious or more apt for the exhibition of his humanity and his humour.

In Caleb Plummer, an infirm old man, oppressed with poverty but sustained by inherent patience and goodness, the attribute to be exemplified is the possible unselfishness of human nature, under serio-comic conditions. In Mr. Golightly, — which the comedian made a gem of comedy in a setting of farce, — the spirit is that of joyous animal mirthfulness shining through comic perplexity. Jefferson's acting has always been remarkable for tenderness of heart, which no man can convey who does not possess it, and for the spontaneous drollery, the condition of being an amusing person, which comes by nature, and which cannot be taught. His

investiture with the individuality of that character was
"a property of easiness." He has often attained to a
loftier height than is reached in those works. His
crowning excellence as a comedian is, that he can sustain himself in the realm of the ideal, — that he does
not stop at being a photographic copyist of the eccentric, the rustic, the ludicrous, and the grotesque in
human life. His scene with the ghosts, in *Rip Van
Winkle*, his night-talk in the empty schoolhouse of *The
Parish Clerk*, his letter-scene with Mary Meredith, in
Our American Cousin, each, in a different way, exemplified the power of the actor, when feeding the heart
from the fountain of the imagination, to sublimate
human feeling and to create and personify a splendid
ideal. The level upon which, however, he more habitually treads is that of humanity, in its laughable, mournful
admixture of weakness, suffering, patience, amiability,
despondency, hope, and endeavour. Simple, tender,
pensive, bright, and droll, the comedian assumes with
perfect readiness the guise of a nature kindred with his
own. And, after all, nothing is more clearly proved, by
all that is known of actors, than the truth that an actor
makes his most substantial success in a character that
implicates his essential individuality. He may display
mechanical versatility in a hundred types, but into that
type he will pour the golden life-blood of his heart.
Jefferson's achievements, which are those of the imagination, have not, perhaps, been appreciated as such,
except by a few persons. His Rip Van Winkle, to
most observers, is a young man merrily tipsy and an
old man wretchedly desolate ; and it makes them laugh
and cry, — and there is an end of the matter. They do

not consider that Rip, when confronting the beings of
another world, — the spectres that encircle him on the
lonely mountain top and in the depth and mystery of
the night, — is in a position analogous to that which in
Hamlet is awful beyond expression. They are aware,
indeed, that the illusion is sustained; but they take no
thought of the profound, exalted, tremulous, poetic sensibility which sustains it. Jefferson's achievements of
the heart are much more obvious, and those and his
humour have always been understood. In that way,
doubtless, his memory will live, in the years to come.
Many of his admirers have long regarded his Caleb
Plummer as the best of his embodiments. The right
method of estimating the full stature of an actor is to
deduce it, not from one of his works, but from all of
them. The performance of Caleb Plummer was a
touching exemplification of dramatic art applied to the
expression of simple tenderness; but it revealed only
one phase of the actor's strength. Caleb Plummer is a
more pathetic person to think about than to see. You
cannot read his story without tears. But the moment
the actor makes him visible he runs the risk of absurdity or of tediousness in the result; for he must
make the personality amusing, and he must make the
self-sacrifice beautiful. The audience must be made to
laugh at him, — and to love him while they laugh. Jefferson's sincerity was not more obvious than his consummate skill. He lived in the character. He never lapsed
out of the feeling of it. He kept, with nature's precision, the woful face and the forlorn, blighted figure, — a
being sequent on years of penury. He sustained, in a
vein of irresistible pathos, the artificial, jocular man-

P

ner. It was easy to see that the whole of that nature and experience was developed by him from within, — that in the infirmity and the grief of the heroic old man it was the heart that trembled, and not merely the fingers. And yet, behind the spontaneousness of identification, the actor must have kept his mind and nerves in repose and control. There was not a false tone, a wrong gesture, an excess, or any flaw of form in the work, and it held its audience in eager suspense. A tragedian may sometimes reach that effect with his subject; a comedian never reaches it except with his soul.

Jefferson gave a neat theatrical version of *The Cricket on the Hea th*, in three acts, using the text of Dickens, and braiding deftly together the affairs of Dot and John Perrybingle, Caleb Plummer and blind Bertha, the returned sailor-boy, old gruff Tackleton and Tilly Slowboy. In the second act occurs the pious deception of Bertha, and the old man makes merry, with his quavering song, — an effect produced with sweet and touching quaintness by Jefferson. In the third act the righteous deceit of Caleb is confessed, with a pathos certainly equal to that of the recognition scene of *Rip Van Winkle*, long peerless among scenes of domestic tenderness upon the stage.

The farce of *Lend Me Five Shillings* is notable for unflagging vivacity of incident and language. Jefferson as Golightly presented a good fellow, of vivacious manners, beset with little troubles, through which he makes his way with mirth and grace, alternating with a' most comical denotement of serio-comic perplexity.

CALEB PLUMMER.

X

DR. PANGLOSS AND THE HEIR AT LAW

ONE of the peculiarities of Jefferson as a comedian is that he thinks in an original way and strikes out for himself new pathways and new methods. The character of Rip Van Winkle had been presented by several good actors before he assumed it, but it never became a representative character —comprehensive of many contrasted elements of human nature and human experience — until it was refashioned and newly embodied by him; and the reason of his surpassing success with it is that he treated it in a poetical and not in a literal manner. The character of Acres, in *The Rivals*, had always been treated as a low-comedy character, until Jefferson, in his memorable revival of that comedy at the Arch Street theatre, Philadelphia, in 1880, embodied it in such a way as to make it rueful, sweet, and sympathetic to the feelings, as well as quaint, ludicrous, and effective to the sense of comic humour. Censors of the acted drama said, indeed, that he took an unjustifiable liberty with the old piece: William Warren, the veteran comedian, playfully remarked that he was giving *The Rivals* "with Sheridan thirty miles away" : yet it was found that the character of Acres would bear that construction, and that the practical result was a more effec-

tive performance of the part than had before been seen,
—because for the first time the auditor was made to
sympathise with Acres in his serious perplexity and
well-grounded apprehension, as well as to laugh at his
ridiculous bravado and comic cowardice. Here, then,
was an independent intellect operating in an original
manner, refreshing an old and almost worn-out stage
figure, and commending it to the practical appreciation
of the living age. Lester Wallack, re-enforced with the
great prestige of his father's name, and potential with
his own brilliant ability and reputation and his capital
stock company, could, toward the last of his career,
accomplish nothing with the old comedies ; and, seeing
himself gradually deserted by the public, he withdrew
from the field. Jefferson has kept *The Rivals* steadily
in his working repertory, and everywhere has had practical success in the presentation of it. The new time
cares not for the conventional methods of the old.
Whoever would succeed with an old stock comedy must
suffuse it with the alert, nimble, sparkling spirit of the
life of to-day, must brush away from it the moss and
lichen of the past, and so must make it appreciable by
the mood if not actually applicable to the experience of
the passing hour. That is what Jefferson has done for
The Rivals, and for Colman's still more recondite
comedy of *The Heir at Law*.

Old playgoers, familiar with this comedy, know how
far removed it is from the knowledge and from the probable liking of the present day. Its ground-plan, indeed,
would always be effective, —a plan that had frequently
been used before Colman used it, and has repeatedly
been used since. That plan comprehends the investi-

ture of a low character with the state and embellishments of high social life, and the deduction therefrom
of incongruities that are comical.   Shakespeare employed
that device in Christopher Sly.   Burton's performance
of the Parvenu was a modern example of it.   But that
well-approved expedient of humour was not handled by
Colman with exceptional brilliancy, and, aside from its
felicitous equivoke, the piece is not one of robust merit.
Sentimental comedy had not entirely gone out of fashion
in England when this play was written, and Colman —
harsh satirist though he was, and of the rough school of
Peter Pindar — deemed it still essential to temper his
satire with a little of the current popular sentiment.
The impoverished young lady who is an orphan, and
who is attended in her poverty by one faithful old servant, finds, accordingly, a place in the piece, and is at
once the occasion and the vehicle of amiable platitudes.
Nor is her devoted lover omitted from the scene, — the
rightful heir to the estate and title that have fallen to
the old tallow-chandler, who will be permitted to enjoy
them, in the company of his absurd wife and his cox-
combical son, for only a few ridiculous days.   Caroline
Dormer and the Irish Kendricks and Henry Moreland
and Mr. Steadfast are wooden persons that long had
served the English stage before Colman again enlisted
them.   But the humour of *The Heir at Law* is genuine,
and it far exceeds the conventional sentiment, while the
situations are neatly made, and frequently are droll, and
the drawing of the characters is equally true and bold.
This much might always have been said of it ; and, indeed, average modern critical opinion, reverential of
time, commonly refers with particular respect to this

piece and to many of its kindred, although the custom
of going to see them would lapse altogether, if it were
not for the occasional rejuvenating influence that is
exercised upon them by living genius.

The Heir at Law was first acted on July 15, 1797, at
the Haymarket theatre, London, and there is a certain
significance in the fact that it still lingers upon the stage
when now almost a hundred years have passed away.
The original cast is a strong one, and the performance
must have been excellent. Dr. Pangloss was played by
Fawcett ; Daniel Dowlas, *alias* Lord Duberly, by Suett ;
Dick Dowlas, by Palmer ; Zekiel Homespun, by Munden ; Henry Moreland, by Charles Kemble ; Steadfast,
by J. Aikin ; Kenrick, by Johnstone ; Cicely Homespun, by Mrs. Gibbs ; Deborah Dowlas, *alias* Lady
Duberly, by Mrs. Davenport ; and Caroline Dormer, by
Miss De Camp. Almost every name in that cast is a
famous one. On its first production the piece was acted
twenty-eight times, and on December 12, the same year,
it was revived at Covent Garden, with Quick as Daniel
Dowlas, Knight as Dick, and Munden, Fawcett, Johnstone, Mrs. Gibbs, and Mrs. Davenport in their original
characters. After that it seems to have been neglected ;
but it came again on May 2, 1808, at Drury Lane, and
the chief features of the cast were once more remarkable. Dr. Pangloss was acted by Bannister ; Dowlas,
by the elder Mathews ; Dick, by Russell ; Zekiel, by
De Camp ; Cicely, by the fascinating Dora Jordan ; old
Deborah, by Mrs. Sparks ; and Caroline Dormer, by
Mrs. H. Siddons. On February 6, 1823, the piece was
done at Drury Lane, with Harley as Dr. Pangloss, Liston as Dowlas, S. Penley as Dick Dowlas, Knight as

Zekiel, and Mrs. H. Hughes as Cicely. *The Heir at Law* was introduced upon the American stage at the old Park theatre, New York, on April 24, 1799, and it has remained a fixture, although not often produced with a great cast. Dunlap opened the season of 1799–1800 with it, November 18, 1799, at the Park, on which occasion Zekiel Homespun was acted by the present Joseph Jefferson's grandfather, Dr. Pangloss was assumed by the brilliant John Hodgkinson, and Cicely by his wife, while old Dowlas was taken by the elder Hallam, and Henry Moreland by the younger. That excellent annalist, Ireland, has preserved a notable cast with which the comedy was performed at the Richmond Hill theatre, New York, on July 6, 1832: Dr. Pangloss, Hilson; old Dowlas, John Barnes; Zekiel, Thomas Placide; Dick Dowlas, Clarke; Kenrick, Greene; Deborah, Mrs. Walstein; Caroline, Miss Smith; Cicely, Mrs. Hilson. In later times, Burton, John Brougham, John E. Owens, William Warren and John S. Clarke have gained particular distinction as Dr. Pangloss. Jefferson acted Dr. Pangloss for the first time in New York on August 31, 1857, at Laura Keene's theatre, making a decisive hit.

Jefferson has applied to Dr. Pangloss the same subtle method of interpretation that he applied to Acres.[1] The part was obviously intended as a harsh and bitter satire upon a class of unworthy persons numerous in Colman's time, — imposters in religion and morality, and more pretentious than sound in scholarship, — who, as parsons or as tutors, were willing, for a consideration,

---

[1] For further consideration of Jefferson as Dr. Pangloss, see my *Shadows of the Stage*, Vol. I.

to become the companions of wealthy vice. Dr. Pangloss possesses a smattering of learning, a little Latin, less Greek, a shrewd perception of character, and abundant knowledge of the fashionable world. He is not, however, burdened with moral principle or refinement of character. He will serve Lord Duberly for one salary and Lady Duberly for another, and the Hon. Mr. Dowlas for a third, knowing all the while that they are at cross-purposes, and meaning to be true to neither, but absolutely and entirely to serve his own interest. The quality that chiefly stamps him in the printed page is waggish alacrity. On the stage he has usually been depicted as a fantastical comicality, ludicrous but unreal. It was enough if he got the response of laughter. Jefferson, making him exceedingly comical, made him also human, natural, probable, real, and even established him in a kindly regard. You not only laughed at Dr. Pangloss, you liked him. He did not impress you as a rogue. He was never mischievous, never unamiable. He was a scholar who has had hard times; he meant to do well by all those absurd people who employed him; and his light heart, gay disposition, and jocular humour seemed to endear him to all the characters with whom he came into contact, and they endeared him to his audience.

XI

SOME OF JEFFERSON'S CONTEMPORARIES

A COMPREHENSIVE view of Jefferson's period should include certain parallel careers with which his own has been associated. One of the most important of them was that of Sothern, whose eminence as Lord Dundreary was at one time very high, and whose name assuredly will live in the history of the stage. Edward Askew Sothern was born at No. 1 Parliament street, Liverpool, England, April 1, 1826. His father was a rich colliery proprietor and ship-owner. The family consisted of nine children. Edward was the seventh, and the only member of the family that adopted the stage. His parents had died before he made choice of that profession. He was educated under the charge of a private tutor, the Rev. Dr. Redhead, rector of a church in Cheshire. Reverses of fortune which befell his father, and then the death of his parents, broke up the family and dissipated his prospects, and this led to his adoption of the stage. He was then, in 1854, a medical student in London ; but he was conscious of a strong predilection for the drama, and presently he consorted with amateurs who paid for the privilege of playing at the King's Cross theatre, and so he embarked on his career. His first regular engagement was at a theatre in Guernsey, and the first salary he ever received was fifteen shillings a week. The characters in which he there began his career were the Ghost, Laertes, and the Second Actor in *Hamlet*. To facilitate his proceedings in those three parts, which, of course, required change of dress, he wrote three slips, for identification, and pinned one on each wig. A sportive individual changed them, and the consequent mixing up of Laertes with the scenes allotted to the Ghost produced a remarkable effect, and the young actor was thereupon discharged for incapacity. He then visited the theatres of Plymouth, Weymouth, Wolverhampton, and Birmingham, and finally emigrated to America.

In 1862 he appeared at the National theatre, Haymarket Square, Boston, as Dr. Pangloss in *The Heir at Law*, and met with a failure. His stage name then was Douglas Stuart, and this he continued to use till, in 1856, by the advice of the veteran J. W. Wallack, he discarded it and took his own. The first performance that he gave under his own name was in the character of Wilson Mayne, in Lester Wallack's comedy of *First Impressions*, produced at Wallack's theatre, September 17, 1856. From Boston he removed — after his failure, which he had the sense to recognise and accept — to Barnum's Museum, in New York, 1853, where he took a utility engagement to play all sorts of parts and to appear twice every day. That was a rough school, but a good one, and he rapidly improved under the discipline of industry. Those were the times to which Artemus Ward referred, when he commended the actors as "a hard-working class of people" — visible every morning, "with their tin dinner-cans in their hands," on the way to the scene of their toil.

While at Barnum's Museum, Sothern made so good an impression that he attracted the notice of E. A. Marshall of the Broadway theatre, who presently engaged him to play light comedy and juvenile business at Washington. After a few months in the capital, he joined Laura Keene, at the Charles Street theatre, Baltimore, and thence he went to Wallack's, in New York, then in Broadway, near the corner of Broome street. His first appearance there was made as Lord Charles Roebuck, in *Old Heads and Young Hearts*, September 9, 1854, and there he remained four years, acting various parts, — walking gentlemen, heavies, and broad low comedy. In December, 1857, he was selected for Armand Duval, to the Camille of Matilda Heron, and from that time he steadily moved upward in professional rank. In the next year he joined Laura Keene's theatre, — afterwards the Olympic, destroyed August 10, 1880, — acting juvenile and comedy business. When *Our American Cousin* was brought out there, October 18, 1858, Laura Keene asked Sothern to try and do something with a "fourth-class dyed-up old man," who had about seventeen lines to speak. The actor assented, on condition that he might be permitted to try an experiment. That was the beginning of his success in Lord Dundreary. "I do and say nothing in Dundreary," Sothern once wrote, "that I have not known to be, in some form or another, done and said in society since I was five years old." [1]

[1] The subjoined statement was made by Sothern, in one of the newspapers, with reference to his design and method in his acting: —

"In Dundreary I desired to illustrate the drawling, imbecile dandy. That required the rewriting and large extension of a part originally of but a few lines. I have tried to make the type of character ridiculous, and to minister to innocent amusement in so

In 1861 he went to the Haymarket theatre, London, appearing November 11 as Lord Dundreary, and from that time onward his career was one of almost unvarying prosperity. In July, 1867, he acted in Paris, but was not much commended there. He became a favourite at the London Haymarket, where he fulfilled many engagements, and at one time he was associated with its management. He there brought out *Aunt's Advice*, adapted by himself from the French; and he there appeared as David Garrick, 1864; Frank Jocelyn, in *The Woman in Mauve*, 1865; Hon. Sam Slingsby; Marquis Victor de Tourville, in *A Hero of Romance;* Colonel John White, in *Home;* Hugh de Brass; Charles Chuckles, in *An English Gentleman;* Sidney Spoonbill, in *A Hornet's Nest*, and Fitzaltamont, in *The Crushed Tragedian.* Those, together with Frank Annerly, in *The Favourite of Fortune*, Mulcraft, Chuckfield, and Laylot, in *Barwise's*

doing; but more has happened than I at first expected. I have found the character a vehicle for many hits, conceits, and odd jumbles and devices, and I have had to vary the lines repeatedly, preserving only the characteristics and the central purpose. That purpose is intellectual, and only incidentally comical. Every speech in Dundreary is a hit at himself or at social follies. The secret of wit, which is surprise, is cultivated in the putting of things, and the purpose of satire is served by the effect of the scheme, events, and lines on the audience. There is a large superficial but sympathetic class who are mainly interested in the story; for them I bring the character to success and happiness both through and in spite of his seeming blunders. But I have them very little in mind in acting. I think of the most intellectual persons I can presume to be present and play to them. They see the inner purpose. The general effect lifts the rest.

"The purpose I have in *The Crushed Tragedian* is to portray and extinguish the much too serious and eminently ridiculous heavy striders and posers of the stage. It is not a caricature. In some parts of the English provinces, as we call the regions out of London, and in parts of America remote from great cities, the play has been taken as a serious one. They have thought The Crushed was like many actors they were used to seeing, though perhaps a very bad case himself; but they have paid me the compliment of taking me to be as poor and misplaced a person in my profession as the one I was trying to portray. My make-up in that play had no reference to George Jones, *The Count Joannes.* I acted the part over 100 nights before I ever saw him. I never modified my manner or make-up after I saw him, and never thought of him before I saw him. The resemblance was in the type. He and not I was responsible for that."

Book and *The Burrampooter*, Harry Vivian, in *A Lesson for Life*, and Robert Devlin, in *A Wild Goose*, were his characters. But his chief works were Lord Dundreary and David Garrick. These called into play his wonderful skill in caricature and his slender powers in sentiment, together with his genuine earnestness and fine artistic method.

After passing about ten years in England, Sothern returned to America in 1871. His farewell benefit at the Haymarket occurred on October 5, that year, and on October 23 he came forward as Dundreary, at Niblo's. In the fall of 1872 he played a long engagement at Wallack's theatre, — November 11, 1872, to May, 1873, a period of twenty-nine weeks. His first appearance in America as David Garrick was made on February 10, 1873. The following summer he visited California, returning to Wallack's in the autumn. On August 15, 1874, he sailed for England, but he was again in New York two years later, and filled a fine engagement at the Fifth Avenue. In the autumn of 1877 he took an active part in organising and conducting benefits for his much-loved friend and comrade Edwin Adams, — himself giving performances in New York, Philadelphia, and Boston, — and no one who was associated with him in that enterprise (as I was) will forget the persistent energy, patient kindness, and wholehearted, unselfish zeal with which he laboured for his dying comrade, or the honest pride and joy that he felt in the success of the project. The performance in New York occurred on October 12, at the Academy, when Sothern appeared as Othello, with W. J. Florence as Iago, Mrs. John Drew as Emilia, and Miss Lotta as

Desdemona, in the third act of the tragedy, and, contrary to the public expectation, gave a performance of the Moor which was just in design and good in method. Mrs. Adams received $9381. In the same year he was seen in a round of parts at the Park theatre ; and at later as well as earlier times he made prosperous starring tours of the United States and Canada. During the summer of 1879 he passed several weeks on the Restigouche River, near Quebec, in company with the Duke of Beaufort, Sir John Rae Reid, W. J. Florence, Col. E. A. Buck, and other friends. The Duke is the sole survivor (1894) of that merry company. Sothern's last engagements in New York were filled at the Park theatre and the Grand Opera House, in September and December, 1879, and his last appearance was made on December 27, 1879, at the latter house.

The acting of Sothern formed a subject of attractive and singular study. He was a thorough artist in every word and action. He laboured over his characters with a microscope. He was perpetually studying, — perpetually on the watch for peculiarities of character and of its expression, whether in himself or others. He was a master of the realm of whim, — as true and fine, within his especial field of dramatic art, as even Laurence Sterne in the wider field of creative literature. He committed to memory all the parts in every play that he acted, and he laboured to make each part complementary of the others, and thus to produce a perfect mosaic picture of human nature in social life. His particular aptitude was for comedy, and that of a whimsical character. His sentiment, though truly felt, was far less free in expression, and indeed had a forced, unnatural effect. He read many books and was fond of the hard work of thinking, which most persons shun. He wrote well, though slowly and but little; yet each of his characters owed something to his own invention. Dundreary was almost entirely his own; and he wrote in Robertson's comedy of *Home* the best part of the love scenes. He wrote a portion also of a comedy called *Trade*, which, in later years, has been acted by his son, E. H. Sothern, under the name of *The Highest Bidder*. He had studied the acting of Rachel, whom he ranked above all other actresses. His nature was deeper in human tenderness than it seemed to be in the eyes of most persons. He could be selfish, icy, and stern; but it usually was when confronted with selfishness in others. At the same time it is to be admitted that he grew cynical in his ideas of human nature as he grew older, and as he bitterly realised and condemned his own faults and saw how little there is in the world of absolutely unselfish goodness. Yet he was by nature of an affectionate, kindly disposition, and he honoured integrity wherever found. The sentiments that David Garrick utters to Ada Ingot, in the last scene of the comedy, were those in which he truly believed. His habitual mood, however, was one of levity, and he was apt to prove fickle in his superficial friendships. He loved and trusted but few persons. It suited his humour to jest and to seek excitement and distraction; first because his temperament naturally bloomed in a frolic atmosphere, and then because he wished to suppress melancholy feelings and a gloomy proneness to self-reproach and saddening introspection. In his domestic life he was unfortunate; and he lived to learn — as all must do who depart away from innocence — that the wrong that is done to the affections can never be righted on earth. Outwardly he was the gayest of the gay: at heart he was an unhappy man, and he suffered much. But he fulfilled his work and his destiny — which was his character. He made the world laugh. He exemplified anew, for artists and thinkers, the beauty of thorough artistic mechanism. He impressed the men of his time with a profound and abiding sense of the power of intellectual purpose. And he left to his friends the remembrance of a strange, quaint, sweet comrade, at whose presence the sunshine sparkled and the flowers bloomed, and life became a holiday of careless pleasure. He died at No. 1 Vere street, London, January 20, 1881, and was buried in the cemetery at Southampton.

Laura Keene, with whom Jefferson was conspicuously associated in the production of *Our American Cousin*, was of English origin, and was born in 1820. At an early age she acted, under the management of Madame Vestris, at the London Olympic theatre, where she attracted attention and esteem for various efforts in light comedy. One of her most pleasing personations was Pauline in *The Lady of Lyons*. In 1852 she was engaged by J. W. Wallack for his new theatre, then just opened, near the corner of Broome street and Broadway, New York; and on October 20, that year, she made her first American appearance, acting Albina Mandeville, in *The Will*. Her success was immediate and decided. She soon left Wallack's theatre, though, and took to strolling as a star. In 1854 she visited San Francisco, and, in company with Edwin Booth,

D. C. Anderson, and others, made a trip to Australia. In November, 1855, she was again in New York, and managed the Metropolitan theatre, afterwards called the Winter Garden, styling it the Varieties. A little later she took the management of the Olympic, which was then newly built, in Broadway, on the east side, between Bleecker and Houston streets, and she opened it on November 18, 1856, with *As You Like It*. That house, known as Laura Keene's theatre, she continued to direct for four or five years, but with dubious judgment and variable success. At times its fortunes sank to a low ebb. At one of those times *Our American Cousin* was brought out, and Jefferson made a great hit, and averted disaster, by his performance of Asa Trenchard. In 1860 Miss Keene became the wife of Mr. John Lutz, with whom she had been for some time associated. One of her last ventures at Laura Keene's theatre was a spectacle play, called *The Seven Sisters*, by Thomas Blades de Walden, which was considered rubbish, but which ran, from November 26, 1860, one hundred and sixty-nine nights. For a long time after leaving that theatre Miss Keene was inconspicuous in theatrical life, but it was vaguely known that she was roaming the country with a travelling company. She was acting at Ford's theatre, Washington, on April 14, 1865, in *Our American Cousin*, at the time of the dreadful and afflicting tragedy which bereaved the Republic of Abraham Lincoln. In 1870 she united with William Creswick in the production of a piece called *Nobody's Child*, at the Fourteenth Street theatre, but her presence upon the stage was not propitious to the success of that effort, and it was speedily

Q

discontinued.   Her latest success in New York was
obtained in Boucicault's drama of *Hunted Down*, which
she produced at the theatre in Broadway known for
a while as Lina Edwin's, and ultimately burnt down.
Her last New York engagement was played at Wood's
Museum.

In person Miss Keene was slender and graceful.
She had an aquiline face, delicate features, dark eyes,
and a musical voice.   She was lovely to see, in statuesque
characters and attitudes.   She often dressed in white
garments, and she seemed to enjoy heightening as
much as possible the effect of the spiritual attribute in
her personal appearance.   She had a swift, gliding
motion, and a strange trick, in the expression of feeling,
of continually winking both her eyes.   As an actress,
she was best in the utterance of despairing delirium.
Moments of woe and of pathetic recklessness commended themselves to her temperament.   One of her
most successful performances was that of Marco in *The
Marble Heart.*   She was very good as Becky Sharp, in
Vanity Fair.   At the highest she was a clever actress
of brilliant comedy; but she wasted her talents, and
came at last to be only an experimenter in the hydraulic
emotional school.   She died of consumption, at Mont-
clair, N.J., on November 4, 1873, in her fifty-fourth
year.   To old playgoers her death was a mournful
reminder of the flight of time and the rapid extinction
of their favourites.   In the prime of her beauty and
talent, she enjoyed almost boundless favour with the
public, but she outlived her popularity and sunk into
comparative oblivion; so that the news of her death
scarcely caused a ripple of feeling, outside of a narrow

circle of professional contemporaries and theatrical followers. The moral of her experience was not wholly the
evanescence of popularity. Public life may be mutable,
but solidity of character and talents well used upon
the stage do not fail to win for their possessor a place
of permanence, at least in the memory of the passing
generation. Neither was possessed by Laura Keene,
and hence her contemporaries scarcely heeded the
sound of her passing bell.

Another conspicuous career, contemporary with that
of Jefferson, was that of Raymond, a comedian with
whom Jefferson sometimes acted, and whose friendship
he possessed to the last. John T. Raymond, long and
widely distinguished as Colonel Sellers, was born at
Buffalo, N.Y., on April 5, 1836, and died at Evansville,
Ind., on April 10, 1887, having just entered on his
fifty-first year. His family name was O'Brien. He
received a common-school education, together with some
training in mercantile pursuits ; but at the age of seventeen he ran away from home to go upon the stage. "I
knew no more about the theatre then," he once said,
"than I did about the moon." His first appearance
was made on June 27, 1853, at a theatre in Rochester,
N.Y., under the management of Carr and Henry
Warren, and he came forward in the part of Lopez in
The Honeymoon. He was almost paralysed with stage
fright on that occasion, and as the condition of Lopez
is mostly that of comic vacuity, he made an accidental
hit in the part; but on the following night, when he
undertook to play one of the soldiers in *Macbeth*, his
inexperience was painfully revealed. From Rochester
he went to Philadelphia, where he appeared as Timothy

Quaint, in *The Soldier's Daughter*, on September 20, 1854. A little later he was engaged by John E. Owens for the Charles Street theatre, Baltimore, and for several seasons after that he was employed on the circuit of the Southern theatres, acting in Charleston, Savannah, Mobile, and New Orleans.

Raymond first became known in New York in 1861, when he appeared at Laura Keene's theatre, as the successor to Jefferson, in low comedy and character parts. He acted Asa Trenchard in *Our American Cousin* at that time. On July 1, 1867, he appeared in London, at the Haymarket theatre, acting that part in association with Sothern, and in company with that famous actor he subsequently visited Paris and acted there, and likewise made a tour of the British provincial theatres. In the autumn of 1868 he reappeared in New York, playing Toby Twinkle in *All that Glitters is not Gold*. A little later he went to San Francisco, where, on January 18, 1869, he made his first appearance at the California theatre, acting Graves in Bulwer's comedy of *Money*. There he remained for several seasons, steadily advancing in public favour and appreciation. He was, in fact, a great favourite in California, but being ambitious to extend the field of his activity and conquest, he presently left the stock company, returned to the eastern seaboard, and, after various efforts, at length made a conspicuous and brilliant hit in the character of Colonel Sellers, in a play based on Mark Twain's story of *The Gilded Age*. That piece was brought out at the Park theatre, Broadway and Twenty-second street, which was burned down in the fall of 1882. With that character Raymond made himself known throughout the

Republic and Canada, and in that part he appeared, but not with success, before the public of London in 1880.

For several seasons Colonel Sellers prospered abundantly, but after a time it began to grow hackneyed, and Raymond was constrained to seek a new character. He played at Wallack's theatre as Ichabod Crane, in a drama by George Fawcett Rowe, on the basis of Washington Irving's story of *Wolfert's Roost*, and this is justly remembered as one of the most quaint, humorous, and touching performances that have graced the comedy stage in our time. After that he travelled every season with more or less success throughout the country, varying his performances of Colonel Sellers with such parts as the old shoemaker, in *My Son;* the politician, in D. D. Lloyd's *For Congress;* and Montague Joliffe, in Pinero's *In Chancery.* In 1886 he played in the principal cities of the Union in Pinero's amusing farce of *The Magistrate.* His professional career extended over a period of thirty-two years, and in the course of that time he acted all the parts that usually fall to the lot of a low comedian. He was seen in Acres, Asa Trenchard, Dickory, Goldfinch, Lullaby, Ollapod, Pangloss, Pillicoddy, Roderigo, Salem Scudder, Toby Twinkle, Tony Lumpkin, Toodle, and many kindred characters. By nature and by purpose he was a thoughtful comedian, — one who desired to identify himself with important eccentric characters in rational drama ; but his excessive animal spirits and a certain grotesque extravagance in his temperament and manner affected the public more directly and powerfully than anything that he did as a dramatic artist. " When I remain in the picture," he said to me, "the public will not accept me, but the moment I get out upon the frame they seem to be delighted." For this reason Raymond usually got "out upon the frame." His humour was rich and jocund. He had a peculiar and exceptional command over the composure of his countenance. He could deceive an observer by the sapient gravity of his visage, and he exerted his facial faculty with extraordinary comic effect. He was possessed of consummate audacity in the perpetration of practical jokes. His mood was eager, sanguine, and hopeful, and it sometimes painted the future in rosy hues ; but he was subject to melancholy, which he carefully concealed. He was impetuous in temper but affectionate in disposition, and his private life was marked by acts of kindness and generosity. As an actor he gave innocent pleasure to thousands of people, and lightened for many hearts the weary burden of care. His professional lineage is that of such ancestors as Foote, Finn and Sothern, though to some extent he lacked the artistic finish of those renowned models. Raymond was twice married, his first wife being Marie E. Gordon, an actress known upon the stage since 1864, now dead. They were legally separated. His second wife was the daughter of Miss Rose Eytinge, long a prominent and successful actress. At the time of his second marriage, the comedian obtained legal authority for the change of his name from John O'Brien to John T. Raymond.

A most interesting comedian, one of Jefferson's prominent contemporaries, and one of his prized and honoured friends, was Mark Smith. That actor was the son of the veteran Sol Smith (1801–1869), and was born at New Orleans on January 27, 1829. He played juvenile

characters at his father's theatre while yet a boy. At
fifteen he went to sea, but he soon grew weary of marine
toil, and in 1849 he formally adopted the profession of
the stage, and that he followed all his days. On March
18, 1862, he appeared at Wallack's theatre, New York,
as Sir William Fondlove, in *The Love Chase*, and made
a brilliant hit, and from that time onward he maintained
a high professional rank, and had the cordial esteem of
the public. In 1863 he was associated with the English
actress Emily Thorne in performances of musical burlesque at the Winter Garden. In 1866 he was a partner
with Lewis Baker in the management of the New York
theatre. In 1869 he was a member of Edwin Booth's
company, at Booth's theatre, and later he was connected
with the St. James theatre in London, and with Albert
M. Palmer's Union Square theatre, New York. He
died suddenly in Paris, France, on August 11, 1884, and
his remains were sent home and buried in the Belle-
fontaine cemetery, at St. Louis.

Mark Smith was a man of unique individuality and
large intellectual resources. He had developed slowly
and thoroughly, — though not yet entirely, — and had
steadily risen, and was fitted still to rise, in an art-growth
that never paused. He was a student and a thinker.
He aimed high, and he was content with nothing less
than superlative excellence. He possessed by nature
both the actor's faculty and the literary spirit. An
atmosphere of art surrounded him as naturally as foliage
surrounds a tree. No one could be, even temporarily,
his companion without perceiving in him an innate and
profound love for letters; a rare and subtle apprehension of the beauty and the significance of artistic forms;

an ample and exact knowledge of many books; keen
intuition combined with wide store of wise observation
upon human nature; and the spontaneous delight alike
of the child and the philosopher in things that make
human life radiant and lovely. Those faculties and
qualities he had done much to cultivate. The influence that radiated from his character was singularly
charming. It was the sympathetic force of a thoroughly
honest nature, good, tender, cheerful, responsive to
virtue and simplicity, and exalted and made picturesque
and zestful by the thrill of imaginative and aspiring
intellect. Mark Smith was not the kind of good man
whose worth is tedious and stupefying, — and therein
may injure virtue almost as much as if he were a profligate. In him the every-day virtues grew brilliant, —
taking on a rosy grace from the piquant loveliness of
his character, — and his comrades not only rested on his
perfect probity, but found continual delight and comfort in his presence.

No one could see him act without being, in quite an
equal degree, conscious of this personal charm. The
attribute of winning goodness that endeared him in
private life was the attribute that shone through his
acting and endeared him upon the stage. As an actor,
he was the Cheeryble Brothers rolled into one, — and
that one was endowed with a commanding intellect and
polished taste as well as with helpful and lovable benignity. When Mark Smith was upon the scene, — as Squire
Broadlands, or April, or Harmony, or Col. Damas, or
Sir Oliver Surface, — the spectator involuntarily felt that
every ray of manly worth, joyous serenity, and human
feeling that flashed through the character had its native

source in the heart of the man himself. This was the attractive power of his heart; and the attention which he thus captivated his versatile mimetic talents and his fortunate personal characteristics never failed to repay. It would be almost impossible to name an actor so thoroughly satisfactory as Mark Smith was, in many sorts of character. His range of Shakespearian parts included Polonius, Friar Lawrence, Kent, Brabantio, Duncan, Hecate, Casca, Autolycus, the Host of the Gartar, the Duke of Venice, Adam, Dromio, Shallow, Verges, Sir Toby Belch, Bardolph, and Dogberry. He did not play them all equally well, but in each one of them he was an artist; and outside of Shakespeare, his range touched at one extreme Sir Peter Teazle and at the other Diggory and Powhatan. One of the most complete pieces of acting that have adorned our stage was his impersonation of the vain, amorous, rickety, polished old coxcomb, Sir William Fondlove, in which he made his first appearance at Wallack's theatre, on March 17, 1862. Another characteristic and charming work was his Doctor Desmerets in *The Romance of a Poor Young Man*. Old Rapid, Hardcastle, Sir John Vesey, Stout, Haversac, De Blossiere, in *Henriette*, Lord Plantagenet, Solomon, Bob Tyke, Mr. Ironsides, Lord Duberley, and many more testified to his versatile abilities, and afforded channels of observation through which might be traced the peculiarities of his mind and the springs of his art.

Whatever defects there were in his acting arose from over-correctness and inflexibility. He was a formal actor, and sometimes he was hard and dry. But that was a good defect, since it arose out of his profound desire and scrupulous care, first of all, to be true; and it was a defect he was outgrowing, and would inevitably have outgrown, with the acquisition of perfect mastery of himself and of the methods of his art. Those who saw his stately, sweet, and tender personation of Jaques Fauvel, at the Union Square theatre, saw clearly enough how much the angular precision and set utterance of earlier days had faded away, and how richly his nature was developing in the direction of flexible and free humour and pathos. It is easy to go astray in attempting to define a human being and to indicate the results of circumstance likely to flow out of the tendencies of a character; but there is no doubt that Mark Smith was richly endowed, and there seems reason to say that if he had lived to complete his experience he would have become one of the great actors of his time. His fidelity to nature was as accurate as a reverent intention could make it. He was a graphic delineator. He was a rosy and jolly and yet a human and refined humourist. He possessed unusual natural dignity of mind; so that, while he respected the real worth of old models, he thought for himself and struck out a pathway of his own. His human sympathies were comprehensive and warm. He had a remarkably keen intuitive perception of the shades of character, and, as his Country Squire alone was sufficient to prove, he had the delicate and trained capacity to make them seen and felt. That hard, genial, stubborn, yielding, eccentric, simple, bluff, hospitable, peremptory English gentleman has no representative on the American stage now that Mark Smith is gone. If any actor known to this country could have put Sir Roger de Coverley into the theatre, and made him as fine and as lovable there as he is in the pages of Addison, Mark Smith was the man. This points to his quality and his rank, and explains the affectionate remembrance in which he is held. He belonged to the school of actors that Munden made distinctive, and that Burton, Blake, Gilbert, and Warren illustrated so well. He was not as droll as Blake, nor did he possess as juicy a humour; but in serious moments he resembled him; and as to severe accuracy of form, he often surpassed him.

The breadth of his scope is indicated in the number and variety of parts that he could adequately play. The field of art in which he stood alone is that which English literature has peopled with characters representative of ambient, large-hearted hospitality, tinged with sentiment and eccentricity. His imagination took delight in images of good-cheer and scenes of kindness. The prattle of children and the soft laughter of young lovers sounded in his mind and gladdened it. He was at home on the green lawn of the ancient manor-house, under the immemorial elms, crowning the feast with welcome, amid the blessings of music and sunshine, and fragrant summer wind, with, over all, a hazy, tranquil air of restful antiquity and gentle romance. So he has passed into the region of storied memories and taken his place forever, — the noblest type our stage has presented of the pure and simple country gentleman! Scott and Irving would have loved that healthful nature, and honoured it and anchored by it, amidst the shams and fevers of a weary world. Primrose and the Village Preacher lived again in him, — with other manners, indeed, and wearing another garb, and fettered and

veiled; but the same in soul. He adorned the stage;
he comforted and benefited his fellowmen; he won an
affection and left an ideal that will not die; and he rests
after an honest, useful, stainless life.

At a meeting of the friends of Mark Smith, held at
Booth's theatre, on September 1, 1884, A. Oakey Hall
presiding, arrangement was made for a performance for
the benefit of his widow and children, — which subsequently occurred, — and the following resolutions,
written by me, were adopted: —

Whereas, In the wisdom and love of God, — which, whether it
bless us or whether it afflict, we but dimly understand and can
never fathom, — our beloved friend and comrade, Mark Smith,
has been taken from the life of this world into the life that is
eternal; and

Whereas, We, his friends, members of the stage and the press,
amidst our personal sorrow under a bitter bereavement and
affliction, are mindful that, in the death of Mark Smith, the profession which he adorned, and this community, which he so often
charmed and benefited, have sustained a loss so grievous and
extraordinary that some formal commemoration of it ought to be
made; therefore, be it

Resolved, That while we bow in humble reverence before the
awful will of heaven, — striving to keep in mind the belief that all
things are ordered for the best, — we yet deplore, in this death, the
loss of one of the best and dearest of our fraternity, in the removal
of whom from the scenes of his usefulness and from our companionship we feel the pangs of a calamitous and overwhelming affliction.

That we remember Mark Smith as one who wore with purity and
honour the noble name of gentleman; whose character was lovely
in its simplicity and modest worth; whose life was virtuous; whose
mind was well stored; whose talents were unusual and brilliant,
and were always used for good and never for evil; and who did his
duty faithfully, thoroughly, and cheerfully, under every condition.

That, when we recall Mark Smith as an actor, we think of one
who loved his profession with all his heart, and served it with

all his strength; whose versatility and thoroughness were extraordinary; who enriched the stage with many delightful personations of humorous and eccentric character; and who was especially noble and impressive in parts emblematic of manly worth, human sentiment, rosy and jolly humour, and the graces of domestic life.

That, equally in his profession and his private walks and ways. Mark Smith illustrated integrity of principle that never swerved. and gentleness of life that never tired, — setting an example of honour and goodness, and leaving, now that he is dead, the memory of a character and a career that were founded on justice and kindness and hallowed by virtue, humanity, charity, and good fellowship.

That we deeply sympathise with the afflicted widow, children. and relatives of the deceased actor, — commending them to seek comfort, as we do, in the thought of his goodness, and of the universal esteem in which he was held and in which he is remembered, and to rest with patient trust upon the Divine will.

George Holland, still another of Jefferson's comrades, was born in London, England, on December 6, 1791. His father was a tradesman. The boy was first sent to preparatory schools in Lambeth, and afterwards to a boarding-school, kept by an eccentric scholar, Dr. Duprée, at Berkhampstead, Hertfordshire. He did not prove a devoted student. He was more remarkable for his pranks than for his proficiency in learning. But he became distinguished as a cricket-player, and he laid the foundation of good health by abundant indulgence in that sport. At Dr. Duprée's school he passed two years, at the end of which time he was taken home by his father and set at work in the silk and ribbon warehouse of Hill & Newcombe, Wood street, Cheapside, London. Prior to going thither, though, he enjoyed a vacation of six weeks and had his first experience of the stage. Astley's amphitheatre existed then, and was conducted by Crossman, Smith & Davis.

One of those managers, Smith, happened to be a friend of the Holland family, and by him young George was frequently taken to the rehearsals. *Les Ombres Chinois* was the name of the entertainment, — a show consisting of pasteboard figures of men and animals, worked with wires, behind an illuminated screen. An incidental dialogue was delivered, correspondent to the action of those dummies. That exhibition so delighted the boy that he made an imitation of it, and so good a one that it made a hit in the home circle. With the silk mercers young Holland passed six months, selling silk and ribbons and silk hats, the latter articles having then only just come into fashion. Not liking that pursuit, he next procured work in a banking house in Cornhill. His post was that of an out-of-door clerk, and his duty required him to walk ten miles a day. This made an invalid of him and laid him up for two months. After that he passed six months in a bill-broker's office and acquired acquaintance with the volatile art of "kite-flying." Then came another illness, on recovering from which he found himself a wanderer in London. Accident now brought him into association with the once famous Newman, who established *Newman's Echo*, — a cheap sheet, presenting an epitome of the advertisements of "wants" and "situations" originally published in the expensive newspapers of the day. Reading was costly in those days, and poor men could get the news only by dropping into an alehouse and paying for the privilege of taking a turn at the paper. This was the cheapest way. *Newman's Echo* placed a certain class of information, gleaned from all the current journals, within everybody's reach. So good an idea could not fail at the start. Holland worked at it with equal fidelity and energy, and Newman soon grew rich. Then he speculated with his money and was ruined, and the *Echo* ceased to be heard.

Once more at leisure, and waiting for something to turn up, young George now devoted some time to the art of fencing. This he learned from his brother, who was under the tuition of Professor Roland, then a distinguished practitioner with the sword. At the age of nineteen George was apprenticed to Thomas Davison, at Whitefriars, to learn the trade of a printer; and in a somewhat vain pursuit of skill in that vocation the unfledged actor spent two years. While the boy did not perfect himself as a printer, he gained positive distinction in sparring and rowing. He was a member of a boat-club; he could — and frequently did — row from London Bridge to Richmond and back again, twenty miles each way; he frequented the Free and Easy, and learned and sang comic songs therein; he made the illustrious acquaintance of Tom Cribb, Molineaux, Tom Belcher, Dutch Sam, Iky Solomons, and other champions and bruisers; and he was himself known in that peculiar society as "the Comic Chattering Cove." Thus early did those vigorous animal spirits and that overwhelming propensity to fun find vent, which afterward, for so many years, gave brightness to the stage and pleasure to multitudes of its supporters. Young Holland's way of life, however, did not prove salutary to the printing business, and when twenty-one years of age he was fortunate enough to get his indentures cancelled, and thereafter

he followed a natural and independent course, which
is the only sure road to genuine success. His wanderings first took him to Liverpool. There he found
no employment, but had a sharp experience of poverty.
From Liverpool he took passage for Dublin, where he
found his father's old friend, Smith, of Astley's amphitheatre, — now riding-master at the Castle School,
a noted institution of the Irish capital. By Smith
he was kindly received, and under his direction he
made himself useful in the riding-school, and became
proficient as a rider and a manager of horses. The
evenings he passed at the Crow Street theatre. This
equestrian and dramatic period of his life was brief, as
he now became a commercial traveller, in the employment of Nunn & Co., dealers in thread-lace. For
two years George Holland drove a mercer's cart
through Ireland ; and in every town he was successful
and popular. One can readily imagine that, as a wit
on the box and a songster in the tavern parlour, he
would have a great success ; for good humour is a
greater conqueror in the battle of life than Cæsar in
the battle of nations. In 1816, Holland, at the age of
twenty-five, was set up in business for himself, to sell
bobbinet-lace, manufactured in Nottingham. His shop
was in Crow street, Dublin, near the Crow Street
theatre, and immediately opposite to a favourite haunt
of jolly boys, called Peter Kearney's Inn. To that
resort George frequently repaired, and there he made
many theatrical acquaintances. The bobbinet-lace business lasted six months, when George settled his affairs,
took down his sign, and returned to England, — to
embark on that theatrical current which continued,

through many vicissitudes of fortune, to the end of his days. George Holland was fifty-three years an actor. More than half a century of entrances and exits!

The first engagement that Holland secured was made with Samuel Russell, familiarly known as "Jerry Sneak Russell," the stage-manager for Robert William Elliston, — that Elliston, the Magnificent, for whom, as Charles Lamb wrote, "the Pauline Muses weep." The engagement was to last six weeks, till the close of the season at the London Olympic. Elliston then offered Holland an engagement at the Birmingham theatre, to begin six weeks later. That interval the actor, now regularly embarked, spent in travelling, on foot, from London to Birmingham, in company with a friendly Lanville, or Folair, and exhibiting *Les Ombres Chinois* at towns on the way. This enterprise, carried on in frolic, beguiled the tedium of the journey, and ended in a good supper. Arrived at Birmingham, Holland found Elliston grandly forgetful of the promised engagement, but ultimately he succeeded in getting a post in the great manager's company, with a salary of fifteen shillings a week. On May 19, 1817, the theatre opened with *Bertram* and *The Broken Sword.* Holland was cast as one of the monks in the former play, and as the Baron in the latter. With the monk he prospered well; but, having permitted a couple of brother actors to "make up" his face and head for the Baron, — which they did with a pantaloon wig and all the colours at hand, — he went on in the second piece an object of such absurdity that he was literally laughed and hooted from the stage. A dark Baron would have answered every purpose; but a red, white, and blue

R

one was too much for the British public. For a long time after that adventure the unlucky comedian was known as "Baron Holland." For many days — so great was his mortification — he kept away from the theatre, having, indeed, set up a school for teaching fencing and boxing. So at length the old sports became useful auxiliaries in the serious labour of life. At last Holland had an explanation with Elliston, was reinstated in the company, and was made prompter. Brunton was then the stage-manager of the Birmingham theatre, — the father of the afterwards famous Miss Brunton, who finally became the Countess of Craven, and of that other Miss Brunton, Anne, who married in succession, Merry, Wignell, and Warren, and was once the chief actress of the American stage. While Holland was prompter, Macready came to the Birmingham theatre, and played Rob Roy. Other stars came also, and among them Vincent de Camp, with whom he formed an acquaintance that was destined to be of much value to him. Holland was now offered an engagement at the theatre in Newcastle-on-Tyne, accepting which he went to London, and thence proceeded to Newcastle by a sailing vessel, that being the cheapest route. On that voyage he met Miss Povey, afterwards Mrs. Knight, and Junius Brutus Booth, together with other theatrical performers, bound to the same place. With Booth he formed a friendship which lasted all the days of the latter actor's life, and which the comedian always cherished in tender recollection. After finishing his engagement at Newcastle, Holland went to Manchester, with Usher, and there played as Harlequin. That was in 1819, the year of certain local disturbances known and remembered as the Peterloo riots. In December of that year Holland returned to Newcastle, which thenceforward, during five seasons, he made his home. The season in those times began in December and ended in May. During the summer Holland travelled, acting wherever occasion offered. While he was acting at the Newcastle theatre, in one of his annual engagements, his fondness for practical jokes and deviltry of all sorts — frequently illustrated in mischievous adventures — brought a temporary disaster upon him; for, snipping at his nose one night, with a large pair of shears, for the amusement of an enlightened public, he cut that useful organ very nearly into two pieces. It was well mended, though, and the wound left no visible scar. Holland's exceedingly natural acting on this occasion, nobody in front knowing what ailed him, was the subject of universal commendation, particularly from the manager, who sent an urgent request that the comedian would nightly repeat his spirited and remarkable performance.

In the season of 1825–26 Holland was engaged at the London Haymarket theatre, under the management of T. P. Cooke. At a later period he fulfilled an engagement at the Surrey theatre. But his English career was now drawing to a close. At Christmas, 1826, Junius Brutus Booth, then stage-manager of the Chatham Street theatre, New York, sent a letter offering him an American engagement. That epistle — in the earnest, simple style characteristic of all the writings of the great tragedian — gives interesting details with reference to the condition of the New York stage in 1826, when Edwin Forrest was a rising young actor, and Lester and J. W. Wallack, Jr., were boys, and Joseph Jefferson and Edwin Booth were yet unborn. (It is reprinted among the memorials in this volume, see p. 293.) Holland did not at once come over, but the allurement proved strong, and in the following year he accepted an engagement at the Bowery theatre. It was in August, 1827, in the ship *Columbia*, that he sailed for New York.

The Bowery theatre, then called the New York theatre, was an important institution in the dramatic world when Holland came to America, and his appearance there, on September 12, 1827, naturally attracted attention. He acted in *A Day After the Fair*, then a favourite farce, and made a decided hit. It was a long time, though, before the comedian settled into a permanent position. For years after he arrived in America he led the nomadic life of his tribe. I trace him to the Tremont theatre, in Boston, then managed by Pelby. Afterwards he played at the Federal Street theatre, in the same city, — long a favourite shrine of the dramatic muse, but now gone. Then he returned to New York, and established his residence at Yorkville. Then he performed at Albany. On January 21, 1829, he made his first appearance at New Orleans, in the Pearl Street theatre, afterwards called the Academy of Music. In the same year he acted at Louisville, Cincinnati, Natchez, Vicksburg, Montgomery, Mobile, Philadelphia, Boston, Salem, and Providence. This record shows how an actor was obliged to flit about in old times, and how hard he had to work; for travelling was not then what it is now, nor could the country boast such theatres anywhere as now adorn it in almost every city. On September 30, 1829, Holland took a benefit at the Bowery theatre, New York. Immediately afterwards I trace him on another expedition, this time in company with Mr. and Mrs. Blake, with T. A. Cooper as manager, — and a powerful combination it was, and a jovial time they must have had. In June, 1830, the comedian occupied what was known as Holland's Cottage, at Yorkville, N.Y. That was a snug suburban inn and one that enjoyed much favour. Holland, indeed, was always a popular man, and if his business capacity had kept pace with his professional success he would have gained a fortune. That success never waited on his efforts. As a worker he began, and to the last he lived in harness and ready to do his best. Leaving the Yorkville cottage in the fall of 1831, he once more went out with Cooper. That season of roving began on October 10, in that year, and lasted till April 10, 1832. Hamblin and John Henry Barton accompanied the party, and they played at Augusta, Savannah, Charleston, and New Orleans. Holland's portion of the entertainment was entitled *Whims of a Comedian*. It was a medley and included feats of ventriloquism, for which this actor was celebrated. "The whole of this performance," said the programme, "will be recited, acted, sung, and gesticulated by Mr. Holland alone." The bill of the play contained eight distinct features, and the price of admission was fixed at $1, which was a high price in those days.

From New Orleans the party went up the Mississippi, and so to Pittsburg, where Holland's engagement terminated. He then went to Cincinnati and to Louisville, and, in association with N. M. Ludlow, gave enter-

tainments in the principal towns of Kentucky and
Tennessee. Subsequently, combining forces with Mr.
and Mrs. Knight, he visited Nashville, and gave performances during one week, which were successful.
This was in the cholera season of 1832, and here, as
afterwards at New Orleans, the performances given by
Holland exerted a cheering and reassuring influence
over the public mind, inclined as it was to panic, in the
presence of the baleful disease. In 1834 Holland was
associated with old Sol Smith in the management
of the theatre at Montgomery, Ala. Allusion is
made to this fact on p. 103 of Sol Smith's *Theatrical
Management:* "The season in Montgomery this year
(1834) commenced on the 16th of January. The celebrated George Holland joined me in the management,
and the firm was Smith & Holland. . . . My business
connection with George Holland was a very pleasant
one. We parted at the close of the season with mutual
good feelings." Jane Placide and George H. Barrett
were members of the company at the Montgomery
theatre. Holland went back to New Orleans on
leaving Sol Smith, and was there made secretary of
the New Orleans Gas-light and Banking Company.
Not long afterward he accepted the post of private
secretary to J. H. Caldwell, and treasurer of the St.
Charles theatre. That was in the season of 1835–36,
which began on November 30, 1835, with Miss Cushman as the star. She played Patrick, in *The Poor
Soldier*, Helen Macgregor, in *Rob Roy*, Peter Wilkins,
Lady Macbeth, and other characters. During the same
season Mr. and Mrs. Keeley, J. W. Wallack, C. K.
Mason, Finn, A. A. Adams, and Madame Celeste

filled engagements at the St. Charles, and with all those theatric luminaries Holland had friendly relations in his capacity as treasurer. An opera troupe, including Adelaide Pedratti, G. B. Montressor, Antonio de Rosa, and others, came on Sunday, March 6, 1836, and again on December 4. In the mean time Holland had been very ill, so ill, indeed, that he was not expected to recover, but a trip to Havana restored him to health, and after six months in that lovely island he came back with renewed vigour to his labours at the St. Charles. *The Jewess*, after fifteen months of preparation, was produced with success on December 25, 1837, and the season closed on April 29, 1838. During the following season performances were given there by Forrest, Booth, J. R. Scott, Finn, J. M. Field, Farren, Sam. Cowell, Ellen Tree, Celeste, and Josephine Clifton. Those details suggest what the theatre was, in old days, in the matter of acting, and they also suggest the associations into which George Holland was thrown, — associations whereby, when old, he was a "mine of memories." On one of the bills of the St. Charles appeared these notices, which may indicate what were the manners of the time, among theatre-going people : "It is particularly requested that dogs will not be brought to the theatre, as they Cannot be admitted. Peanuts are proscribed." In the season of 1840 Fanny Ellsler appeared at the St. Charles, engaged for $1000 a night, and a benefit, on which latter occasion she was to have all the receipts except $500. Those terms were made by Holland, in the absence of Caldwell, to secure the great attraction and keep it out of the rival theatre. On the first night the receipts were $3446.50, and for the ten nights of Fanny Ellsler's engagement the average receipts were $2597.35. The benefit brought in $3760. Holland paid to the great dancer $10,000 for the ten performances; $3260 for her benefit; and $1192 for half benefit to Avalini and Silvani, her companions, — in all, $14,453. Yet this enterprise was a thorough success to the theatre. On March 13, 1842, the St. Charles theatre was burned, and so ended Holland's connection with the most prosperous establishment in which he had ever been engaged. Caldwell, the manager, survived his losses, and was a wealthy man to the last, dying in New York in the autumn of 1863.

After the St. Charles had been destroyed, Holland made a trip with Dr. Lardner, who gave a series of lectures and illustrated them with pictures. The party visited Mobile, Natchez, Vicksburg, Jacksonville, Nashville, St. Louis (at which place they found Gentleman George H. Barrett keeping a restaurant), Louisville, Cincinnati, and Buffalo. From the latter place to Troy, Holland sailed in a canal-boat. Arrived in New York, he found his old acquaintance, Mitchell, engaged in the management of the Olympic theatre. He had known Mitchell since the year 1818, when both were members of De Camp's theatrical company at Newcastle. By Mitchell he was engaged, and in the Olympic company he remained, constantly acting and always a public favourite, from 1843 to 1849. His first appearance at the Olympic was made on September 4, 1843, in *A Day After the Fair* and *The Bill of Fare*. In the summer of 1844 he acted, with Mitchell's company, at Niblo's, as Lobwitz, in *The Child of the Regiment*, Hassarac in

Open Sesame, and divers other characters. In 1849
Holland accepted an engagement at the Varieties
theatre, New Orleans, and there, says Sol Smith, "he
enjoyed a popularity never perhaps achieved by any
other actor in that city." Thomas Placide was then
the manager of the Varieties. In 1853 Holland was a
member of Burton's company, in New York. On
August 10, that year, on the occasion of the opening
of the theatre, he acted Sunnyside, in *A Capital
Match*, and Thomas, in *The Secret*. In the mean time,
Wallack's theatre, at first called Wallack's Lyceum,
had been opened, on September 8, 1852; and in the
third season Holland was added to the company, appearing on September 12, 1855, as Chubb, in John
Brougham's *Game of Love*. With Wallack's he remained connected — seceding only once, which was in
the panic days of 1857, when he joined Christy's Min-
strels — until the end of the season of 1867–68. His
last engagement was made with Augustin Daly, and
in the season of 1869–70 he acted several times at
the Fifth Avenue theatre. His last professional appearance was made there on January 12, 1870, as the
Reporter, in Miss Olive Logan's farcical comedy of *Surf*.
Subsequently, on May 16, on the occasion of his benefit,
the veteran appeared before the curtain, not having
taken part in the presentation (the play was *Frou-
Frou*), and made a brief but touching speech, consisting of three words, "God bless you!" He died,
at 309 Third avenue, New York, on Tuesday, December 20, 1870. His death had been expected for a long
time. During many months he clung to life by the
slenderest thread. When at last, about five o'clock

in the morning of December 20, he fell into his final
sleep, he sunk away so calmly that his friends who
surrounded him were unaware of his decease. He was
eighty years old. The most of his long life was passed
in active industry. His last days were much oppressed
by the suffering incidental to infirmity. He bore those
trials well, however, and flashes of his characteristic
drollery and delightful humour often enlivened the
gloom of the closing scenes. The refusal of a prominent clergyman of New York to allow Holland's funeral
in his church, for the reason that he had been an actor,
coupled with a mention of a "little church around the
corner," prompted Jefferson's exclamation, "God bless
the little church around the corner," and made that the
church of the actors, for all time. Holland was buried
from the church of the Transfiguration, in Twenty-ninth
street, New York, the Rev. George H. Houghton
reading the service. Performances for the benefit of
his widow and children, given at the instance and
mainly under the care of the present writer, produced
a fund of $13,608.41.

Holland's life was full of strange vicissitudes; but it
was animated by honest principle and characterised by
faithful labour and spotless integrity. Holland was a
good man. He attained a high rank in his profession,
largely by reason of his skill as an artist, but more
largely by reason of his natural endowments. He was a
humourist of the eccentric order. To the comedian
is accorded the happy privilege of casting the roses of
mirth on the pathway of his fellowmen, making glad
their hearts with cheerful and kindly feeling and light-
ing up their faces with the sunshine of innocent pleas-

ure. In the exercise of that privilege George Holland added in no inconsiderable degree to the sum of human happiness. He honoured his vocation. He respected himself. He performed his duty. This is no slight victory, in a world of strife, vicissitude, care, and pain; but it is the rightful reward of goodness, devoted labour, and genuine talent. It is the crown of honour, and that veteran actor wore it with equal right and grace.

One of Jefferson's special friends, and one whose name occupies a conspicuous place in the annals of the American stage, was John T. Ford, long the leader of theatrical management in the Southern States of the American Union. He was not an actor, but as the friend and companion of actors throughout the generation now closed or closing, and as one of Jefferson's comrades from the first, he should be commemorated in this chronicle.

John T. Ford was born in Baltimore, Md., April 16, 1829, and his youth was trained in the public schools of that city. It is remembered that he was a pupil at Grammar School No. 6, in Ross street, now Druid Hill avenue, and that William R. Creery, now dead, was his teacher, a gentleman and a scholar, who afterward became superintendent of the Baltimore public schools, and, to the last, enjoyed honour in that community. Successful men owe much to their good teachers, and the name of such a teacher should not be forgotten. While yet in his teens, the youthful Ford was employed by his uncle, William Greanor, a prosperous tobacco merchant of Richmond, Va.; but the boy did not like that business, and he relinquished it and went into the book trade. That, too, was presently abandoned, and in 1851, having returned to Baltimore, he became the agent for the Nightingale Serenaders, a minstrel troupe organised by George Kunkel. With that he travelled during several seasons, visiting all the cities between the Atlantic and the Mississippi, the St. Lawrence river and the Gulf of Mexico. At that time, also, he wrote, as correspondent of *The Baltimore Clipper*. In 1854–55 Ford became manager of the Holliday Street theatre, Baltimore, — a house with which, fifty years before, his maternal grandmother had been associated, when Warren and Wood first managed it, — and that field of labour he continued to cultivate for more than twenty years. Louisa Pyne, Adelina Patti, Edwin Forrest, Charles Kean, and many other artists were there presented, under his management. Rachel was engaged by him to act there, but when the time arrived she was too ill to appear. Jefferson, Edwin Adams, and John McCullough won early successes in the old Holliday Street theatre, and many new plays — by George H. Miles, Edward Spencer, Clifton W. Tayleure, Annie Ford, and other distinctively Southern authors — were originally produced there. In 1871 Ford built the Grand Opera House, Baltimore, and there his attention and labour were centred, though not to the neglect of many important outlying enterprises. Baltimore was always Ford's home, and in that city he filled many offices of trust and honour. He served as acting mayor of Baltimore, member and president of the city council, president of the Union Railroad Company, many times foreman of the grand jury in both the state and county courts, president of a land association, director of the

Maryland Penitentiary, and president of the Society for providing Free Summer Excursions and Food for the Poor. Every year he gave a performance in aid of the latter association, and the proceeds each year exceeded $2000. Ford always had the esteem and affection of his neighbours, as a just, generous, public-spirited man.

Ford's first theatrical venture in Washington was undertaken in 1854, and from that time he conducted dramatic enterprises in that city. He built three theatres in Washington, — two in Tenth street, and one at the corner of Ninth street and Louisiana avenue, named Ford's Opera House. His first theatre in Tenth street was burned down, and on the site of it he built the house known as Ford's theatre, and associated with one of the most terrible and afflicting tragedies of modern times. At the time of the murder of Lincoln, Ford and his brother Henry were for thirty-nine days detained in the Capitol prison ; but, having been fully exonerated, they were released. The theatre was seized by the United States government, and an order was issued prohibiting forever its use as a place of amusement. Ford received from the National Treasury $100,000 in payment for the building. It was used for public offices, and in 1893 it fell and killed many persons. After his twenty years of theatrical management in Washington, *The Evening Star*, a leading journal of the Capitol, described Ford's business proceedings there as having been marked by "rare integrity, indomitable will, and great sagacity."

Previous to the establishment of his theatre in Washington, Ford had often visited the city as an itinerant manager, and at a very early time in his theatrical career he had broken ground for enterprises along the Southern circuit. As long ago as 1857 he was associated with the management of the theatre in Richmond, Va., and had Joseph Jefferson for stage-manager and Edwin Adams for leading man. John Wilkes Booth was a member of his company at that theatre in 1858. For nearly thirty years Ford furnished the Southern people with theatrical exhibitions. Edwin Booth, Joseph Jefferson, Charlotte Cushman, Madame Janauschek, Madame Modjeska, Mary Anderson, and many other celebrated actors travelled through the South under his guidance. In 1878 he assumed the management of the Broad Street theatre, Philadelphia, owned by John S. Clarke, the comedian. The place had been thought unfortunate. Heavy losses had been incurred there by previous managers. The season of 1878–79 was, generally, bad; but Ford prospered, and the engagements of Booth, Jefferson, the Hess English Opera Company, and finally the *Pinafore* carried him buoyantly through the year. Ford's production of *Pinafore* was the earliest, after that of Montgomery Field at the Boston Museum. Attentive care was bestowed upon its musical requirements, and Ford was the first manager in America to offer compensation to the authors of the piece. Their pleasant memory of that proceeding doubtless prompted Gilbert and Sullivan, in coming to America with a new opera, to entrust their business interests to his hands, whereupon he leased the Fifth Avenue theatre, New York, and there produced *The Pirates of Penzance*, in the season of 1879–80.

The death of Ben de Bar, August 28, 1877, left Ford the oldest living manager in America. For thirty years the entire line of theatres on the Southern circuit, from Baltimore to New Orleans, was largely subject to his administration of affairs. He wielded a greater power than was possessed by either Caldwell or de Bar. He was the last of the former generation of theatrical directors, — the Hodgkinsons, Hallams, Warrens, Woods, and Barrys of long ago. Ford was married when young, and he reared a family of eleven children. The sudden death, in 1878, of his daughter Annie, a lovely and talented lady, was a heavy affliction. His children, educated in close association with the theatre, are an honour and credit to their parents and their vocation. His son, Charles E. Ford, worthily succeeded to his father's dramatic enterprises. Beginning business life with scarcely a dollar, Ford lived to control some of the wealthiest interests of his State, and where he once worked for a pittance built houses costing half a million. Baltimore was never accounted a good theatrical city, its inhabitants being largely engrossed with social pleasures and home life; yet there Ford reared and sustained the stage, as one of the first and best of contemporary institutions. He long resided in a fine mansion, in the northwest part of his native city, overlooking the town, the forest, and the distant bay; and there, surrounded by books and friends, he viewed serenely the results of a well-spent life and the advance of an honourable, peaceful age. He died suddenly on March 14, 1894, and was buried at Greenmount.

XII

STAGE ART

JEFFERSON is an actor in whom the romantic ardour of devotion to the dramatic art has never languished. Youth is gone, but neither its enthusiasm, its faith, nor its fire. He still embodies Rip Van Winkle with a sincerity as intense and with an artistic execution as thorough and as fresh as if the part were new, and as if he were playing it for the first time. The spontaneous drollery; the wildwood freedom; the endearing gentleness; the piquant, quizzical sapience; the unconscious humour; the pathetic blending of forlorn, wistful patience with awe-stricken apprehension; the dazed, submissive, drifting surrender to the current of Fate; and the apparently careless but clear-cut and beautiful method, — all those attributes, that bewitched the community long ago, remain unchanged, and have lost no particle of their charm. The details of those familiar attractions — the discomfiture of craft by simplicity, the expulsion from a desolated home, the flight into the night and the tempest, the aged wanderer's return, the recognition between father and daughter — are matters of general knowledge. Irradiated as they long have been by the genius of Jefferson, they could not be forgotten. It is forty years since he played the part for the first time;

RIP VAN WINKLE

From a photograph by Sarony.

and although at the outset his performance was viewed
with indifference, it is now recognised throughout the
world as a great achievement. Most persons who have
seen Jefferson as Rip would probably name that achievement as essentially the most natural piece of acting ever
presented within their observation. In its effect it is
natural; in its method, in the process by which it is
wrought, it is absolutely artificial. In that method
— not forgetting the soul within that method — will be
found the secret of its power ; in the art with which
genius transfigures and interprets actual life ; and in
that, furthermore, dwells the secret of all good acting.
If you would produce the effect of nature, in dramatic
art, you must not be natural ; you must be artificial, but
you must seem to be natural. The same step, the same
gesture, the same tone of voice, the same force of facial
expression that you involuntarily use in the proceedings
of actual, every-day life will not, upon the stage, prove
adequate. They may indicate your meaning, but they
will not convey it. Their result will be tame, narrow,
and insufficient. Your step must be lengthened ; your
tone must be elevated ; your facial muscles must be
allowed a freer play ; the sound with which you in-
tend to produce the effect of a sigh must leave your
lips as a sob. The actor who is exactly natural in his
demeanour and speech upon the stage — who acts and
speaks precisely as he would act and speak in a room —
wearies his audience, because he falls short of his object
and is indefinite and commonplace. Jefferson, as Rip,
has to present, among other aspects of human nature, a
temperament that, to some extent, is swayed by an infirmity, — the appetite for intoxicant liquor. That, in

s

actual life, is offensive ; but that, as shown by Jefferson, when it reaches his auditors reaches them only as the token or suggestion of an amiable weakness ; and that weakness, and not the symptom of it, is the spring of the whole character and action. The hiccough with which Rip looks in at the window of the cottage where the offended Gretchen is waiting for him, is not the obnoxious hiccough of a sot, but the playful hiccough of an artist who is only suggesting a sot. The effect is natural. The process is artificial. Jefferson constantly addresses the imagination, and he uses imagination with which to address it. In actual life the garments worn by Rip would be soiled. In Jefferson's artistic scheme the studied shabbiness and carefully selected tatters are scrupulously clean ; and they are made not only harmonious in colour,—and thus so pleasing to the eye that they attract no especial attention,—but accordant with the sweet drollery and listless, indolent, drifting spirit of the character. No idea could easily be suggested more incongruous with probability, more unnatural and fantastic, than the idea of a tipsy vagabond encircled by a ring of Dutch ghosts, on the top of a mountain, in the middle of the night ; but when Jefferson—by the deep feeling and affluent imagination with which he fills the scene, and by the vigilant, firm, unerring, technical skill with which he controls his forces and guides them to effect—has made that idea a living fact, no spectator of the weird, thrilling, pathetic picture ever thinks of it as unnatural. The illusion is perfect, and it is perfectly maintained. All along its line the character of Rip— the impossible hero of an impossible experience—is so essentially unnatural that if it were impersonated in the

literal manner of nature it would produce the effect of
whirling extravagance. Jefferson, pouring his soul into
an ideal of which he is himself the creator, — an ideal
which does not exist either in Washington Irving's
story, or Charles Burke's play, or Dion Boucicault's
adaptation of Burke, — and treating that idea in a poetic
spirit, as to every fibre, tone, hue, motion, and attitude,
has made Rip as natural as if we had personally participated in his aimless and wandering life. So potent,
indeed, is the poetic art of the actor that the dog
Schneider, who is never shown, possesses, all the same,
a positive existence in our thoughts. The principal
truth denoted by Jefferson's acting, therefore, is the
necessity of clear perception of what is meant by
"nature." The heights are reached only when inspiration is guided by intellectual purpose and used with artistic skill. Shakespeare, with his incomparable felicity,
has crystallised this principle into diamond light : —

> " Over that art,
> Which you say adds to nature, is an art
> Which nature makes."

The same law should decide the question of correctness in the staging and dressing of plays. Correctness
is essential, but it can be carried too far. Cardinal
Wolsey had only one good eye, — a peculiarity that is
thought to account for the fact that he was always
painted in profile ; but the stage representative of Cardinal Wolsey could scarcely be expected to extinguish
an optic for the sake of perfecting his resemblance to
that historical person. It would be natural and correct
for Queen Katherine to resort to her pocket-handker-
chief. Few ladies have been furnished with better

reason for tears. But if that deposed and afflicted monarch were to sound a bugle note in the vision scene of *King Henry VIII.* it is obvious that the illusion would be destroyed. If the plays of *Macbeth* and *Lear* were to be dressed in strict accordance with the custom of their respective periods, some of the persons in them would appear in skins,—chiefly their own. There is no wisdom in an over-scrupulous fidelity to fact. When Henry Irving accomplished his beautiful production of *Charles the First,* which opens with a scene at Hampton Court, showing the artificial lakes girded with superb trees, as they are at present, one sapient observer promptly advised him, by post, that he had made a serious mistake, because there were no trees at Hampton in Charles's time. No such consideration is of the least importance. Upon the stage, where the story of a life or of a long historic period must be told in two or three hours, the essential result is effect. To that must be sacrificed correctness and all that is ordinarily meant by "nature." The actor will not make his audience cry, if he unrestrictedly cries himself. He will not make his audience feel, if his own feeling escapes from his control. Munden's answer to the youthful aspirant who had announced his purpose to be "natural" in comedy was peremptory, but sensible: "Nature be damned! You make your audience laugh!" Garrick, when playing King Lear, would walk up the stage, while waiting for the applause to subside after one of his tempestuous outbursts in that character, and with a grimace and a chuckle, whispering to the Fool,—played by Austin,— would say, "Joe, this is stage feeling." Yet Garrick had a command over the emotions of his auditors such

as no other actor has surpassed, and few have ever
equalled. Mrs. Siddons, when playing Constance, wept
over Prince Arthur to such an extent that his collar was
wet with her tears ; yet when she rushed from the stage,
in the full tide of overwhelming anguish, as Constance
or Belvidera or Mrs. Beverley, she would walk placidly
to the green-room, taking snuff with the utmost composure. Once, addressing an associate who was performing with her, in *The Deserter*, she gravely added,
after praising his performance : "But, Kelly, you feel
too much. If you feel so strongly you will never make
an actor." One of Talma's best effects in acting was
obtained by his use of a cry of anguish which he had
first uttered on suddenly hearing of his mother's death,
— and which he had immediately committed to memory.
Edmund Kean gave a certain sob, when he said,"Othello's
occupation's gone," which was irresistibly affecting,
until he fell into the custom of using it too often.
"They have found me out," he said, on one occasion,
when it was hissed. Mrs. Mowatt records that once
when she was acting Mrs. Haller, with Mr. Moorhouse
as the Stranger, in the most pathetic passage of that
play, the audience being in tears, the afflicted Stranger murmured in her ear, "They are sending round
umbrellas." The most comical wink I ever saw was
bestowed upon me, as an auditor on the front seat, by
that great actor Edwin Booth, who, in the terrible character of Richard III., was standing upon the stage and
just about to interrupt the funeral procession of King
Henry VI. Those illustrations indicate the first principle of dramatic art, — absolute self-command. Those
players were not insincere. Mrs. Siddons was not less

in earnest because she did not allow herself to be swept away by her feelings. There never was a greater artist. "Cooke," said Lord Byron, "was the most natural actor, Kemble the most supernatural, Kean the medium between the two; but Mrs. Siddons was worth them all put together."

In dramatic writing the primal necessity is the same. The first things to be considered are action and effect. Dion Boucicault — who was not remarkable as a writer, and who, as an actor, was technical, mechanical, and imitative — possessed a rare and fine talent for composition essentially dramatic. His little play of *Kerry* is an alteration and rearrangement of a well-known French comedy, *Le Joie Fait Peur*, and his performance of *Kerry* was an Irish copy of an embodiment that he saw given by a good French comedian. His fine drama of *Daddy O'Dowd* was deduced from the much older play of *The Porter's Knot*, and his performance as O'Dowd was an Irish copy of Benjamin Webster. His excellent impersonation of the Shaughraun — by which he was best known and by which, probably, he will be best remembered — was an Irish copy of Jefferson's Rip Van Winkle, in the youthful part of it. If Boucicault had not known the one — originated and suggested to him by Jefferson — he would not have thought of the other. There is abundant discrepancy between the two figures, but the spirit and the dramatic purpose are the same in both. Boucicault almost always knew a good thing when he saw it, and his instinct as to dramatic effect was inerrant. In his play of *The Octoroon,* — based on one of the stories of Captain Mayne Reid, — the action is so copious and so incessant that the piece may be said actually to lack the relief of sufficient words. It was in that piece that the daguerreotype was first used as a dramatic expedient. It is left for a moment exposed in a lonely place, and in that moment it catches the visage of a murderer in the very act of his crime, — a picture to be subsequently used with fatal, irresistible effect. No one who ever saw that piece will forget the sudden parting of the cane-brake in the swamp, the swift appearance of the avenging Indian, his momentary pause, and then his stealthy, implacable, terrible exit, upon the track of the assassin. In his play of *Jessie Brown*, — which illustrates that fictitious story, wholly a newspaper invention, about the Scotch girl who heard afar off, and before any one else could hear it, the slogan of the Macgregor, at the Relief of Lucknow, — there is a wonderful dramatic moment, and it is a moment entirely without words. It is the moment when the suspicious Nana Sahib, impassive but malignant and sinister, pauses watchfully beside the captive Jessie, who is sitting upon the floor, upon a bit of carpet that covers the hole through which the English soldiers are presently to make their entrance. Those soldiers have mined a passage beneath the palace, and the desired relief is close at hand. The least symptom of discomposure on the part of the girl would now be fatal. She sits there, upon the brink of the deadliest peril, and as she sways her body gently to and fro, she softly sings the melody of the *Blue Bells of Scotland*, while the fateful eyes of the impacable Indian gaze on her in mute deliberation and reptile menace. The suspense of that situation cannot be conveyed in words, — it must be felt. That is true drama. Another illustration of it

would be found in Boucicault's play of *Belle Lamar.*
That piece opens with a moonlit, rustic scene on the
banks of the Potomac. A Federal soldier is pacing up
and down in the silence,—a sentry at his post. Presently, thinking perhaps of his sweetheart at home, he
breaks into song, and then he is again silent. In the
stillness that follows, high, clear, vibrant, the voice of
an unseen Confederate sentinel, across the river, peals
out the silver melody of *Maryland, My Maryland,* while
the Federal picket stops on his beat and listens. In
that effect was instantly crystallised the whole idea of
opposition and contrast in the Civil War. It was, in a
modified form, an application of Shakespeare's thought,
in the prelude to Act IV. of *Henry V.:* —

> " Now entertain conjecture of a time
>   When creeping murmur and the poring dark
>   Fills the wide vessel of the universe.
>   From camp to camp, through the foul womb of night,
>   The hum of either army stilly sounds,
>   That the fixed sentinels almost receive
>   The secret whispers of each other's watch.
>   Fire answers fire : and through their paly flames
>   Each battle sees the other's umber'd face.
>   Steed threatens steed, in high and boastful neighs,
>   Piercing the night's dull ear ; and from the tents
>   The armourers, accomplishing the knights,
>   With busy hammers closing rivets up,
>   Give dreadful note of preparation."

In another of Boucicault's plays, *The Long Strike,* —
which was based on a novel by Mrs. Gaskell, — there is
a remarkably felicitous illustration of the dramatic principle. A benevolent but crusty old bachelor lawyer,

Mr. Moneypenny, — beautifully acted by James H. Stoddart,[1] — is disturbed at his evening fireside by the visitation of a poor girl, who has been waiting at his door for some hours in the cold, who seems very wretched, and who will not go away. For a brief time he is resolute, and he will not allow her to come in. But he cannot compose himself and, after much grumbling, he permits her approach. The girl is in great trouble. Her sweetheart is accused of murder. He is innocent. The tes-

[1] James H. Stoddart, a native of Barnsley, Yorkshire, England, was born October 21, 1827. His father was an actor, and for twenty-five years was associated with the Theatre Royal at Glasgow, under the management of John Henry Alexander. In that theatre Stoddart began his career, while yet a boy, — going on as page, peasant, juvenile lord, or other such subsidiary person, receiving one shilling a night when he had a speaking part, and sixpence a night when he was not required to speak. He did not, however, long remain there, but, in association with a younger brother, formed a company at Aberdeen, and thence wandered for a time through the north of Scotland. At Aberdeen, in November, 1848, he played Hamlet. He was subsequently associated with theatres in Yorkshire, and thence he went to Liverpool, and in 1854 he came to America. His first appearance was announced at Burton's theatre, September 6, 1854, as Sir Anthony Absolute, but he appeared at Wallack's, September 7, as Sowerberry, in *A Phenomenon in a Smock Frock*. He has been associated with Laura Keene's theatre, the Olympic, the Winter Garden, the Union Square, the Madison Square, and Palmer's theatre. In a letter about his early days Stoddart wrote (December 3, 1892) as follows: —

"Alexander in the course of his seasons played a great many patriotic Scotch dramas in which my oldest brother and myself were often opposed to each other in deadly strife. We were quite celebrated for our combats, two up and two down sort of thing. He being the older, always killed me, but even in defeat I came off with the honours, for when I was stabbed I used to pause for a moment, make myself quite rigid, and then fall backwards; it always got a recognition, and I obtained quite a reputation for my back falls: so much so that my brother wanted to be the defeated party, but I would not have it. My brother and I were together in Glasgow for many winters, wandering through the smaller places in the north of Scotland the other portion of the year. The dear lad is long since dead. I still look back to the wanderings of my boyhood life as the happiest of all my theatrical career."

timony of one man, and that only, can save his life. The
man is a sailor, on board of a ship that has just sailed
from Liverpool. If that sailor can be recalled, the girl's
lover can be vindicated and rescued. The old lawyer
becomes interested. There is, he explains, one chance.
The telegraph from Liverpool may stop that ship at the
mouth of the Mersey. That chance shall be taken. The
scene changes to the office of the telegraph. The old
man and the girl enter, among others, and the lawyer
offers his dispatch. The clerk declines it. The station
at the Heads, he declares, has long been closed for the
night. The dispatch of a message would be useless.
The lawyer pleads. The operator, at first impatient,
then more considerate, finally assents to his request.
He will signal the seaside station. This he proceeds to
do. There is no response. The office is about to close.
All the people are gone, except the operator, the lawyer,
and the girl. There is a moment of dead and despairing
silence. In that moment, suddenly, — vibrating through
the stillness with a quick, sharp, decisive sound that
makes every heart leap with joy, — comes the click of
the telegraph, answering from the coast. The operator
is by chance still there ; the message can be sent, and
the ship can be stopped. What follows is, of course,
happiness. No other effect in any of Boucicault's plays
is commensurate with that of the telegraph, and it would
be hard to find any other effect so dramatic in any modern play. It applies to domestic drama the principle so
superbly denoted by Shakespeare in the knocking at the
gate in *Macbeth*.

It is not pretended that excellence in the drama is
dependent upon mechanical devices. The stage-carpen-

ter cannot take the place of the dramatist. It is only
meant that there is a dramatic way of telling a story,
and that the narrative way — which is the way natural
to most writers — does not produce a dramatic effect.
If everything could be put into words there would be
no need of the stage, and the occupation of the actor
would be gone. Dramatic art supplies an element that
nothing else can give. You can read and enjoy *Hamlet*
in your library; but you will enjoy it much more if,
having read it, you see it rightly acted. Consider, for
example, the startling significance of the first line in
that tragedy. In *Hamlet* the ghost of a king, who has
been murdered, haunts the castle of Elsinore. That
ghost is supposed to have been seen before the piece
opens. The time is midnight; the place, a platform in
the castle. A sentinel, Francisco, is alone, on guard.
We do not know that he has seen the spectre. We do
not know that he has heard of it. His fellow-soldiers,
Bernardo and Marcellus, however, have seen it, and
they may have whispered of it. There is an influence
about the place, an atmosphere, — a brooding, ominous,
stealthy, sinister dread. Francisco feels that influence.
The night is cold. There is no light but that of stars,
and there is no sound but that of the moaning wind.
Suddenly something like a footstep startles the sentry,
and his quick challenge is the first line of the play,
— "Who's there?" In those two words Shakespeare
strikes the key-note of his tragedy. The whole opening
colloquy is thrilled with "supernatural soliciting." It
is Bernardo who approaches, who has seen the ghost,
and who has no mind to be left alone. "Have you had
quiet guard?" he says; and, later, —

"If you do meet Horatio and Marcellus,
The rivals of my watch, bid them *make haste.*"

The full effect of that scene can only be communicated
by interpretation. The moment is an awful one.
Words cannot express it. Action, and that only, can
awaken the awe and terror that it ought to inspire.
That is stage art.

In the production of *Twelfth Night*, as that was
accomplished at Daly's theatre, in the season of 1892-
93, — a production of extraordinary beauty, in which
Miss Ada Rehan attained to the summit of excellence
as a poetic actress, presenting the beautiful character of
Viola, — there was a striking illustration of the dramatic
method, as contrasted with that of words. The scene
is Olivia's garden. The time is evening. Viola, disguised as the minstrel, Cesario, having received an
intimation that perhaps her brother, Sebastian, has not
been drowned, has spoken her joyous soliloquy upon
that auspicious thought, and has sunk into a seat, in
meditation. The moon is rising over the distant sea,
and in the fancied freshness of the balmy rising breeze
you can almost hear the ripple of the leaves. The love-
lorn Orsino enters, with many musicians, and they
sing a serenade, beneath the windows of Olivia's palace.
The proud beauty comes forth upon her balcony, and,
parting her veil, looks down upon Viola, — whom she
loves, supposing her to be a man. Meantime, Orsino is
gazing up at Olivia, whom he worships; while Viola
is gazing on Orsino, whom she adores. Not a word is
needed. The garden is all in moonlight; the delicious
music flows on; and over that picture — entirely dra-

matic, crystallising into one diamond point the whole meaning of the comedy — the curtain slowly falls.

It will be observed that these expedients of dramatic treatment derive their force from their harmony with the purpose of the play. One of the most touching and beautiful effects that I ever saw accomplished in acting was accomplished by Charles Dillon, an actor almost forgotten now, who came to America many years ago (1866), and represented, among other characters, Belphegor, in *The Mountebank*. Belphegor is a strolling player, a good fellow, very poor, who has married a girl of good family, whom he loves to idolatry. It is his wife's birthday. He wishes to signalise it, and he has saved a few bits of money and bought a shawl. On this day his wife — persuaded by her wealthy relatives, and because her little daughter is starved — leaves in their lodging a letter of farewell for her husband, and goes away. The room is empty. Dillon came into that room, eager, exultant, bringing his gift, and guarding it as if it were the treasure of the world. He was in ecstasy at being able to offer that little token of love and remembrance. He found the letter and read it : his figure drooped ; the whole man seemed to collapse ; the light faded out of his face ; he said nothing, but, as he walked feebly up the room, the shawl, or mantle, dropped from his arm, unrolling itself as it fell, and was negligently trodden under his feet. It is impossible to express the pathos of that simple action. There was the touch of genius in it, that captures every heart.[1]

---

[1] Poor Dillon had the infirmity of drink, and his life was in a great degree wasted. He was born in 1819, and he began as an actor in Richardson's Show. He fell dead in the street, at Harwick, England, in 1881.

A companion effect to that was wrought by Jefferson, in a play by Boucicault, called *The Parish Clerk*,—never acted in America, but presented by Jefferson, many years ago, at Manchester, England. The Parish Clerk is a gentle, generous young fellow, a teacher in an English village school. He loves a girl of the village, and he wishes to ask her to become his wife; but the local Doctor—who also loves that beautiful girl, and who wishes to get his rival out of the way—apprises the Parish Clerk that his health is broken, and that he will, probably, die within a year. The poor teacher, believing this, and knowing his health to be frail, determines that it would be wrong for him to ask the girl to share his lot, and decides that he must remain silent and go away. Then comes a scene intrinsically dramatic and of great value. The time is night. The stage displays the rough and simple interior of a rustic school-house. Through a large window at the back the moonlight streams in upon the scrawled and notched benches, the ink-stained forms, the school-master's desk, the coarse floor, and the common walls. The room is vacant. Soon the figure of the teacher, visible through the window, appears in the road, outside. He comes to the door, unlocks it, enters, and takes his place at the desk. He has come there to take his last look at the room, and to say his farewell words to the children whom he loves. Those children are present only in his fancy. He calls them, one by one; he speaks of their pranks and mischief, their toys and their play, their studies and their future; he bids them good-bye; he breaks down, sobbing, and rushes away into the night; and over his exit the curtain falls. There are but two or three lines in the text for the Parish Clerk to speak. Jefferson said whatever he happened to think of and to feel. It was not essential to be coherent. There was the situation for the actor, and there was the actor to fill it. No narrative, no literary style, no language. But there was the dramatic presentment of character and life, under ideal conditions; and the audience was overwhelmed by it. The same cause will always produce the same effect. The play of *Rip Van Winkle*, as interpreted by Jefferson, contains that same dramatic quality; and it produces, accordingly, the same potent result.

The province of stage art is not to interpret and glorify the artist, ministering to his vanity and ending in the barren commodity of human admiration, but to spiritualise and ennoble the auditor. That province it fulfils by the communication of beauty and power. The true artist cares not for either censure or praise. His object is expression, and in the pursuit of that object he obeys an impulse as deep as the centre of the world. He is the minister of beauty and power, and precisely in proportion to his fidelity is the value of his utterance to others. The songs of Burns are precious to our hearts forever, not because they are the expression of the poet, but because they are the expression of ourselves. The emotion of Gray's immortal *Elegy* is elemental in the human soul, and hence that superb and supreme utterance of it is the fulfilment of our desire. Those artists and others of their kindred have spoken for us, fully and finally, and in a manner far beyond our faculties of speech, the feeling that we should like to have uttered for ourselves. When you read Wordsworth's great *Ode on Immortality* the mists are dispersed from your mind, and you hear, in the temple of your soul, the voice not only of serene spiritual hope but of exultant conviction. While I listened to the funeral sermon on General Grant, in Westminster Abbey, I was unmoved; but when, at the close of that discourse, the glorious strains of Handel's *Dead March* burst forth from the great organ and soared beneath the fretted vault of that sublime cathedral, my spirit seemed borne away to heaven, and all that I could feel or dream of glory was expressed. The great composer, the artist in music, had fulfilled his mission. Emerson, in his large, fine manner, has designated the poet as "a man without an impediment." It is a definition that covers all the arts, — for they are sisters and inseparable, — and it is because so many spirits are imprisoned in silence that the vocal spirit is so gratefully and gladly heard. The poet Holmes has said this, in words of tender grace : —

> " A few can touch the magic string,
>   And noisy fame is glad to win them :
> Alas for those that never sing,
>   But die with all their music in them!"

As with the arts of poetry and music, so also is it with the art of acting, — the art not simply of imitating human nature and human life, but of transfiguring and interpreting them in forms of beauty and power. The actor who presents himself merely from the impulse of personal vanity, and whose quest is merely the admiration of others, is like a painter who offers a gilded frame instead of a picture. He brings no message. He has nothing to communicate. Like a bubble he floats and glistens, and like a bubble he disappears. But the actor of authentic genius, the actor who is faithful all his days to the service of ideal beauty, comes upon our lives as a joy and a comfort, and lives in our memories as a perpetual benediction.

> "The music in my heart I bore,
> Long after it was heard no more."

T

MEMORIALS

MEMORIALS

OUR STAGE IN ITS PALMY DAYS

Upon the state of the stage in America, early in the nineteenth century, — viewing it as an institution existing broadcast
and only prosperous at special places, and making allowance
for the eccentricity of the writer, — some useful light is thrown
by a letter which was addressed by Junius Brutus Booth, father
of Edwin Booth, to the comedian George Holland, in 1826.
A copy of that manuscript was given to me by Holland, in
1870, and by me was first published, in July of that year.

J. B. BOOTH TO GEORGE HOLLAND.

NEW YORK, Xmas Eve, 1826.
but direct y'r letter to the Theatre Baltimore U States.

MY DEAR SIR: Messrs. Wallack and Freeman, a few days since, shewed
me your letter, with the inclosure sent last winter to you at Sheffield.

It is requisite that I inform you Theatricals are not in so flourishing a
condition in this Country as they were some two years ago. There are
four Theatres in this City each endeavoring to ruin the others, by foul
means as well as fair. The reduction of the prices of admission has
proved (as I always anticipated from the first suggestion of such a foolish
plan) nearly ruinous to the Managers. The Publick here often witness a
Performance in every respect equal to what is presented at the Theatres
Royal D. L. and C. G. for these prices. *Half a Dollar to the Boxes* and a
quarter do. to the *Pit and Gallery!*

The Chatham Theatre of which I am the Stage-Manager, at these low
prices [holds] one thousand Dollars. — Acting is sold too cheap to the
Publick and the result will be a general theatrical bankruptcy.

Tragedians are in abundance — Macready — Conway — Hamblin —
Forrest (now No. 1) Cooper, Wallack — Maywood and self with divers

others now invest New-York. But it won't do; a diversion to the south must be made — or to Jail three-fourths of the Great men and Managers must go.

Now Sir, I will deal fairly with you. If you will pledge yourself to me for three years, and sacredly promise that no inducement which may be held out by the unprincipled and daring speculators which abound in this country shall cause you to leave me, I will, for ten months in each year, give you *thirty dollars per week*, and an annual benefit which you shall divide with me. Beyond this sum I would not venture, the privilege of your name for Benefits Extra to be allowed me — and I should expect the terms on which you would be engaged to remain secret from *all* but ourselves.

Mind this — whether you play in my Theatres or elsewhere in the U States, I should look for implicit and faithful performance of your duty toward me or my colleagues! In case I should require you to travel, when in the United States, which is most probable, I will defray all the charges of conveyance for you and your luggage — your living would not be included either by land or water — Boarding (three meals a day,) and your Bed room, may be had in very respectable houses here & in Baltimore at from four to six dollars per week — " Lodgings to let " are very scarce and expensive, and the customs of this country, in this respect, are essentially different to those of the English.

The M. S. and music of Paul Pry, with Faustus's music Do. and Book of the Pilot, the M. S. and Do. of a piece played some few years back at Sadlers Wells, call'd " the Gheber or the Fire Worshippers," two or three of Liston's new pieces I should advise you to bring. And particularly the *Gheber*, for me. The Mogul Tale here is out of print.

In the Exeter Theatre last January were two actresses that I should like to engage. Miss P—— (not the Miss P. formerly of Drury Lane) and Miss H. If you will inquire after them — I will thank you. To each of these ladies a salary of fifteen dollars a week I can venture offering — 15 dollars are upward of three Guineas and Benefit annually.

Now, Sir, I have offered to you and those Ladies as much as I can in honesty afford to give, their travelling expenses to and from Theatres in the United States (not including board) I should defray, as I told you respecting your own — and the use of their names for benefits on Stock nights. — Your line of business would be exclusively *yours*. For the ladies I would not make this guaranty — The greatest actress in the World I may say is now in this city (Mrs. D——) and several very talented women — besides I would endeavor to make such arrangements for Miss P—— and Miss H—— as would not be very repugnant to their ambition.

The reason Mrs. D—— does not go to London is my strenuous advice to her against it.—The passages from Europe I should expect repaid to me out of the salaries, by weekly deductions of three dollars each. The captain of the ship would call upon the parties or you might write to them on his visit to you. Everything on board will be furnished that is requisite for comfort, and the expenses I will settle for here previous to starting. Mind the ship you would come over in is one expressly bargained for, and will bring you where I shall (if living) be ready to welcome you—

Let me recomend you to Economy—see what a number of our brethren are reduced to Indigence by their obstinate Vanity—I have here Mr. D—— who was once in London the rival of Elliston, and is now a better actor—approaching the age of sixty, and not a dollar put by for a rainy day—too proud to accept a salary of twenty dollars per week in a regular engagement—he stars and starves. Many have been deceived and misled in their calculations in coming to this country—some have cut their throats &c from disappointment—Mrs. Romer (once of the Surrey) Mrs. Alsop Mr. Entwistle—Kirby the Clown—are all on the felo de se list—with others I now forget—

The temptations to Drunkenness here are too common and too powerful for many weak beings who construe the approval of a boisterous circle of intoxicated fools as the climax of everything desirable in their profession—What do they find it, when a weakened shattered fraim, with loss of memory and often reason, are the results—The hangers on—drop astern—and the poor wreck drives down the Gulf despised or pitied, and totally deserted.

If you choose accepting my offer—get for me those ladies. Sims can perhaps tell you where they are, and I will on the first occasion send for you and them, with the articles of agreement to be signed in London and legally ratified on your arrival in America—recollect this—the Passages in Summer, owing to the calms are longer in performing, but they are much safer, and the Newfoundland Bank is an ugly place to cross in Winter, though it is often done, yet still it is a great risk.

The *Crisis* which left London Docks, last January, with all her passengers, after being out for 68 days, and being spoken to on the banks by another vessel—is not yet come or will she ever—The icebergs no doubt struck her, as they have many—and the last farewell was echoed by the waves.—

Write to me soon and glean the information I ask for—

The letter bag for United States vessels, from London, is kept at the North American Coffee House near the Bank of England.

Yours truly,   BOOTH.

MR. H

Notice of the *First* Performance of Charles Lamb's Farce, Mr. H, at Drury Lane Theatre, London.

December 10, 1806. MR. H. Under this singular title a farce was produced on this evening, preceded by an excellent prologue. . . . It is a farce of very broad humour, and quite *sui generis*. The decision, though ultimately unfavourable, should not discourage the writer, who, as we understand, is a gentleman in the India house. The whole turns upon a man's dislike to his own name, and after numerous whimsical embarrassments, occasioned by his persisting to call himself MR. H., with his servants, the lady to whom he is attached, and in public company, he inadvertently discovers that his name is HOGSFLESH. The house was convulsed with laughter through the whole of the first act. In the second the incidents increased in extravagance, and, a few coarse expressions occurring, those who came to laugh, and had laughed most immoderately, exercised their remaining privilege, less grateful to an author's feelings, and the curtain dropped amidst so much disapprobation that the piece was withdrawn by the writer, after having been a second time announced in the bills. — *The Monthly Mirror*, Vol. XXII., p. 420, London, 1806.

Lamb's Prologue to his farce of Mr. H.

Spoken by Elliston.

If we have sinn'd in paring down a name,
All civil well-bred authors do the same.

Survey the columns of our daily writers —
You'll find that some initials are great fighters : —
How fierce the shock, how fatal is the jar,
When Ensign W. meets Lieutenant R.,
With two stout seconds, just of their own gizzard,
Cross Captain X. and rough old General Izzard !
Letter to letter spread the dire alarms,
Till half the alphabet is up in arms.
Nor with less lustre have initials shone,
To grace the gentler annals of Crim — Con.,
Where the dispensers of the public lash,
Soft penance give — a letter and a dash —.
Where vice, reduced in size, shrinks to a failing,
And loses half its grossness by curtailing.
Faux-pas are told in such a modest way —
" The affair of Colonel B. with Mrs. A."
You must excuse them — for what is there, say,
Which such a pliant vowel must not grant
To such a very pressing consonant !
Or who poetic justice dares dispute
When, mildly melting at a lover's suite,
The wife's a LIQUID — her good man, a MUTE !
Even in the homelier scenes of honest life,
The coarse-spun intercourse of man and wife,
Initials, I am told, have taken place
Of deary, spouse, and that old-fashioned race :
And Cabbage, ask'd by brother Snip to tea,
Replies, "I'll come — but it don't rest with me —
" I always leaves them things to Mrs. C——."
O should this mincing fashion ever spread
From names of living heroes to the dead,
How would ambition sigh and hang her head,
As each lov'd syllable should melt away,
Her Alexander turn'd into great A.
A single C—— her Cæsar to express —
Her Scipio shorten'd to a Roman S —
And, nick'd and dock'd to these new modes of speech,
Great Hannibal himself a Mr. H——.

WILLIAM WARREN

1812–1888

My chronicles of the Jefferson Family of Actors, when, in another form, they were first published (1881), were dedicated to the comedian William Warren, now dead and gone. That dedication, together with Warren's letter accepting it, may appropriately be preserved in this place.

✠

This Memorial of the Jeffersons

IS DEDICATED BY ITS AUTHOR

TO THEIR FAMOUS KINSMAN

WILLIAM WARREN,

ACTOR, SCHOLAR, AND COMRADE,

WHOSE

QUAINT AND TENDER GENIUS

IN DRAMATIC ART

HAS GIVEN HAPPINESS TO THOUSANDS,

AND

WHOSE EXALTED VIRTUES AND GENTLE LIFE

HAVE MADE HIM

AN EXAMPLE AND AN HONOUR

TO THE STAGE AND THE COMMUNITY.

✠

"AUGUSTA, MAINE, May 31, 1881.

"MY DEAR WINTER: Your kind letter came to me last night, at Bangor. I do accept, with my best thanks, the proffered courtesy of the dedication of your coming book, the Biography of the Jefferson Family of Actors. Wishing you every success, in that, and all things,

Believe me, ever yours,

WILLIAM WARREN."

WILLIAM WARREN.

Some account of Warren has been given in this book (see pages 56, 57). On October 27, 1882, the comedian completed his fiftieth year upon the stage. Commemorative performances were given at the Boston Museum, on Saturday afternoon and evening, October 28. Warren played Dr. Pangloss in the afternoon and Sir Peter Teazle at night; and after the public ceremonials were ended a party of his friends waited upon him, at his lodgings, No. 2 Bulfinch place, and conveyed to him a loving-cup, made of silver and gold, bearing this inscription : —

TO

WILLIAM WARREN,

ON THE COMPLETION OF HIS FIFTIETH YEAR

UPON THE STAGE,

OCT. 27, 1882.

FROM

JOSEPH JEFFERSON	JOHN McCULLOUGH
EDWIN BOOTH	LAWRENCE BARRETT
MARY ANDERSON	

The committee having charge of this gift comprised James R. Osgood, Nathan Appleton, F. G. Vinton, R. M. Field, T. R. Sullivan, and the writer of this biography, who spoke as follows :

SPEECH AND POEM BY WILLIAM WINTER.

It is our desire that the ceremonial to which we now ask your attention, while it possesses all the earnestness appropriate to a manifestation of affectionate friendship, shall not be embarrassed by even the slightest tinge of painful formality. For this reason we have sought you in your home, instead of accosting you upon the stage, amid the festivities of this brilliant and auspicious day. Your friends in Boston (which is equivalent to saying Boston itself) have had a golden opportunity, and have improved it in a glorious manner, of expressing their personal good-will, their esteem for your character, their appreciation of your achievements, and their just and natural pride in your renown. It is no common triumph to have gained such a reputation as yours, in such a city as Boston. But the fame of your genius and the knowledge of your deeds and virtues are not confined to the city of your residence. A great actor belongs to the nation and to the age. In every theatre in the United States, and at thousands of hearthstones, alike in your own country and in the lovely motherland beyond the sea, — where your line was so honourably and famously founded, — your name, to-night, has been spoken with tender respect and unaffected homage. In order that you may be reminded of this, and may be cheered, not alone with present plaudits, but with happy remembrance of the absent friends who are thinking of you now, I have been commissioned by five of the leading members of your profession, — Joseph Jefferson, Edwin Booth, Mary Anderson, Lawrence Barrett, and John McCullough, — to come into your presence and, in their names and with fervent assurance of their affection and sympathy, to beg your acceptance of this loving-cup, which is their gift. It is less bright than their friendship ; it is less permanent than their sense of your worth and their esteem for your virtues. Accept it, with all that it denotes, of joy in the triumph of the actor and of pride in the gentle, loving, blameless character and life of the man.

Roses have ever been esteemed the pledges and emblems of faithful love. In the name of your absent friends, in the name of the thousands whom in time past you have delighted and cheered, in the name of your comrades of the Boston Museum, with whom you have been so long and so pleasantly associated, and finally, in the name of the friends now clustered around you in affection and gladness, I cast these roses before you ;

and I am bold enough, — presuming on your patience, and remembering the many years through which we have been friends, — to add my personal tribute, in the lines which I now read.

> Red globes of autumn strew the sod,
>   The bannered woods wear crimson shields,
> The aster and the golden-rod
>   Deck all the fields.
>
> No clarion blast, at morning blown,
>   Should greet the way-worn veteran here,
> Nor roll of drum nor trumpet-tone
>   Assail his ear.
>
> No jewelled ensigns now should smite,
>   With jarring flash, down emerald steeps,
> Where sweetly in the sunset light
>   The valley sleeps.
>
> No bolder ray should bathe this bower
>   Than when, above the glimmering stream,
> The crescent moon, in twilight's hour,
>   First sheds her beam.
>
> No ruder note should break the thrall,
>   That love and peace and honour weave,
> Than some lone wild-bird's gentle call,
>   At summer eve.
>
> But here should float the voice of song —
>   Like evening winds in autumn leaves,
> Sweet with the balm they waft along
>   From golden sheaves.
>
> The sacred past should feel its spell,
>   And here should murmur, soft and low,
> The voices that he loved so well, —
>   Long, long ago.
>
> The vanished scenes should give to this
>   The cherished forms of other days,
> And rosy lips that felt his kiss
>   Breathe out his praise.

The comrades of his young renown
    Should proudly throng around him now,
When falls the spotless laurel crown
        Upon his brow.

Not in their clamorous shouts who make
    The noonday pomp of glory's lord
Does the true soul of manhood take
        Its high reward.

But when from all the glimmering years
    Beneath the moonlight of the past
The strong and tender spirit hears
        " Well done," at last;

When love looks forth from heavenly eyes,
    And heavenly voices make acclaim,
And all his deeds of kindness rise
        To bless his name;

When all that has been sweetly blends
    With all that is, and both revere
The life so lovely in its ends,
        So pure, so dear;

Then leaps indeed the golden flame
    Of blissful pride to rapture's brim —
The fire that sacramental fame
        Has lit for him !

For him who, lord of joy and woe,
    Through half a century's snow-white years
Has gently ruled, in humour's glow,
        The fount of tears.

True, simple, earnest, patient, kind,
    Through griefs that many a weaker will
Had stricken dead, his noble mind
        Was constant still.

Sweet, tender, playful, thoughtful, droll,
  His gentle genius still has made
Mirth's perfect sunshine in the soul,
    And pity's shade.

With amaranths of eternal spring
  Be all his life's calm evening drest,
While summer winds around him sing
    The songs of rest!

And thou, O Memory, strange and dread,
  That stand'st on heaven's ascending slope,
Lay softly on his reverend head
    The wreath of hope!

So softly, — when the port he wins,
  To which life's happiest breezes blow, —
That where earth ends and heaven begins
    He shall not know.

HACKETT IN ENGLAND

JEFFERSON'S most popular predecessor in the character of Rip Van Winkle was James H. Hackett. Mention has been made of his visit to England in 1832. He returned to America in the summer of 1833. A memento of that English visit — being also an illustrative document of a distant time — may not be deemed inappropriate here. This is one of the Hackett playbills of 1832–33, and it is a curiosity : —

THEATRE ROYAL, COVENT GARDEN.
To-morrow, THURSDAY, March 14, 1833, (36th time) the Drama of
NELL GWYNNE
The Scenery painted by Mr. GRIEVE, Mr. T. GRIEVE, Mr. W. GRIEVE, and assistants.

King Charles the Second, Mr. JONES,   Sir C. Barkeley, Mr. FORESTER
 Charles Hart, ⎰ *Managers of the King's Theatre,* ⎱ Mr. DURUSET,
 Major Mohun, ⎱   *Drury-Lane, 1667,*   ⎰ Mr. PERKINS.
Betterton (*Manager of the Duke's Theatre, Lincoln's-Inn*) Mr. DIDDEAR

Joe Haines (*late of Drury-Lane*) Mr. MEADOWS,
Counsellor Crowsfoot, Mr. BLANCHARD, Stockfish, Mr. F. MATTHEWS
Nell Gwynne, Miss TAYLOR,
Orange Moll, Mr. KEELEY   Mrs. Snowdrop, Mrs. DALY.
Scenery painted for this Piece—
EXTERIOR OF DRURY LANE THEATRE in the TIME OF CHARLES II.
LOBBY LEADING TO THE PIT OF DRURY-LANE THEATRE.
INTERIOR OF THE MITRE TAVERN.
PROSCENIUM, AND ROYAL BOX AT DRURY LANE.
Preparatory to "*The Prologue by Mrs. Ellen Gwynne, in a broad-brimmed
Hat and Waist Belt.*"……(Vide Dryden's Conquest of Granada.)
After which, (4th time) A NEW FARCE, called The

KENTUCKIAN;
Or, A Trip to New York.

Col. Nimrod Wildfire, (*a Kentuckian*) Mr. HACKETT,
(*Performed by him with universal applause throughout the United States of America*).
Freeman, (*a New York Merchant*) Mr. F. MATTHEWS,
Percival, (*an English Merchant*) Mr. DURUSET,
Jenkins, (*under the assumed name of Lord Granby*) Mr. FORESTER,
Cæsar, (*a Free Black Waiter at the Hotel*) Mr. TURNOUR,
Tradesman, Mr PAYNE, Countryman, Mr ADDISON, Servant, Mr HEATH
Mrs. Luminary (*a Tourist and Speculator*) Mrs. GIBBS,
Mrs. Freeman, Mrs. VINING,   Caroline, Miss LEE,
Mary,   Mrs. DALY,   Waiting Woman,   Mrs. BROWN
To conclude with the Opera of

FRA-DIAVOLO:
Or, *THE INN OF TERRACINA*

With the Whole of the MUSIC, composed by Auber,
Arranged and adapted to the English stage by M. ROINO LACY.
Fra-Diavolo (disguised as *the Marquis of San Carlo*) Mr. WILSON,
Lord Allcash,   Mr. DURUSET,
Lorenzo, (*Captain of Carbiniers*) Mr. I. BENNETT,
Matteo, Mr. MORLEY,   Beppo, Mr. G. STANSBURY,
Giacomo,   Mr. RANSFORD.
Francesco, Mr. CHICKINI,   First Carbinier, Mr. MEARS,
Second Carbinier, Mr. HENRY,   Third Carbinier, Mr. IRWIN,
Lady Allcash,   Miss INVERARITY.
Zerlina, (*Matteo's Daughter*)   Miss E. ROMER.
In Act III.

AN INCIDENTAL BALLET,
in which **Mons. A. ALBERT**, and **Mad. PROCHE GIUBILEI** will appear.
PLACES for the BOXES to be had of Mr. NOTTER, at the Box-Office, Hart-Street,
from Ten till Four.
OPERA GLASSES lent in the Theatre, by Mr. HUDSON, 28, *Henrietta-street,
Cavendish-square.*

REPUTATION; or the State Secret,

having been again received with the most enthusiastic applause, will
be repeated on *Saturday* and *Tuesday* next.

Hugo Istein,   **Mr. CHARLES KEAN**.

MR. HACKETT

continuing to be honoured with rapturous approbation in the character
of *Colonel Nimrod Wildfire,* and the whole performance having
been received with incessant bursts of laughter and applause,

The New Farce of The

KENTUCKIAN or A Trip to New York,

will be repeated *To-Morrow, Saturday,* and *Monday next.*

On Friday, (**Last Night but Four**) the highly popular New Dramatic Oratorio, called
The Israelites in Egypt; or, the **Passage of the Red Sea.**
Moses, Mr. H. PHILLIPS,   Aaron, Mr. WILSON,   Pharaoh, Mr. F. SEGUIN,
Amenophis, Mr. WOOD,   Siunïde, Miss SHIRREFF,   Annaï, Mrs. WOOD.
On Saturday, (7th time) **REPUTATION, or the State Secret.**
After which, the New Farce of **The Kentuckian, or A Trip to New York.**
With **The WATERMAN.**   Tom Tug, Mr. H. PHILLIPS.
On Monday, the Play of **The HUNCHBACK.**
With (6th time) The New Farce of **The Kentuckian, or A Trip to New York.**
To conclude with the Grand Ballet of **MASANIELLO.**
Printed by W. REYNOLDS, 9, Exeter-street, Strand.

NOTABLE EARLY CASTS OF RIP VAN WINKLE

The Kerr version of *Rip Van Winkle* was presented at
the Walnut Street theatre, Philadelphia, on October 30,
1829, with this announcement and cast:—

"Positively for the last time, a new melodrama, founded on Washington
Irving's celebrated tale of *Rip Van Winkle, or the Demons of the Catskill
Mountains.*

CHARACTERS IN ACT I.

Derrick Van Slous	. . Mr. Porter	Swag de Grain	Mr. Wells
Herman (his son)	. . . Mr. Read	Gustaffe (aged 7) .	. Miss Anderson
Knickerbocker	. Mr. J. Jefferson	Lowenna (aged 5) .	. Miss Eberle
Rory Van Clump.	. . Mr. Greene	Rip Van Winkle	Mr. W. B. Chapman
Nicholas Vedder .	. Mr. (J.) Sefton	Dame Van Winkle	Mrs. B. Stickney
Clausen	. Mr. James	Grubba	. Miss Hathwell

Dancers of the Mountain { Messrs. Garson, Thompson, Bloom, Miller, James,
Jones, Williams, and Johnson.

U

CHARACTERS IN ACT II.

Allemaine (Grand Judge) Mr. James		Rip Van Winkle Mr. W. B. Chapman	
Herman . . . . Mr. Greenwood		Lowenna . . . . Miss Chapman	
[probably this should be Read]		Jacintha . . . . . Miss Hathwell	
Van Knickerbocker Mr. J. Jefferson		Alice (now Mrs. Van ⎱ Mrs. S. Chap-	
Nicholas Vedder . . . Mr. Sefton		Knickerbocker) ⎰ man	
Gustaffe . . . . Mr. Greenwood			

The J. Jefferson was the father of the present Rip.
Miss Anderson was Jane, now Mrs. G. C. Germon. A letter
to me from that venerable lady, dated Baltimore, April 29,
1894, says: "I was the child. My sister Elizabeth, now
Mrs. Saunders, did not go upon the stage till some time after,
although older than myself. I played all the children that
season, 1829–30, and then joined my mother, in Baltimore,
playing the Duke of York, with the elder Booth, in *Richard
the Third.*"

The characters in *Rip Van Winkle*, when it was acted for
the first time at the Park theatre, New York, on April 22,
1830, were cast thus : —

Rip Van Winkle . . Mr. Hackett		Herman . . . . . Mr. Richings	
Knickerbocker . . . Mr. Placide		Dame Van Winkle . Mrs. Wheatley	
Nicholas Vedder Mr. Chapman, Sr.		Alice . . . . Mrs. Hackett	
Von Slous . . . . . Mr. Blakeley		Lowenna . . . . . Mrs. Wallack	

Hackett brought out the old version of *Rip Van Winkle* at
the Bowery theatre, New York, on August 10, 1830, when he
was joint manager of that house with T. S. Hamblin, casting
the parts as follows : —.

Rip . . . . Mr. Hackett		Derrick Van Slous . . . Mr. Wray	
Knickerbocker . . . Mr. Roberts		Dame Van Winkle . Mrs. W. Jones	
Nicholas Vedder . . Mr. C. Green		Alice . . . . . . Mrs. Hackett	
Herman . . . . . Mr. Lindsley		Lowenna . . . . . Miss Waring	

A bill of the Park theatre, for April 15, 1831, makes this
announcement : —

"To conclude with the popular melodrama of *Rip Van Winkle, or the
Legend of the Catskill Mountains,* altered by Mr. Hackett from a piece

written and produced in London, and founded on Washington Irving's well-known tale of that name."

CHARACTERS IN ACT I.

Derrick Van Slous . .	Mr. Blakeley	Swag de Grain	Mr. Collet
Herman (his son) . .	Mr. Nexsen	Rip Van Winkle . .	Mr. Hackett
Knickerbocker . . .	Mr. Richings	Gustaffe (aged 7)	Miss Emma Wheatley
Nicholas Vedder .	Mr. Woodhull	Lowenna (aged 5)	Miss Julia Turnbull
Rory Van Clump . . .	Mr. Povey	Dame Van Winkle	. Mrs. Wheatley
Claussen	Mr. Hayden	Alice	Mrs. Hackett

CHARACTERS IN ACT II.

Allemaine (Grand Judge) . . . }	Mr. F. Wheatley	Rip Van Winkle . .	Mr. Hackett
Herman	Mr. Nexsen	Alice (now Mrs. Van Knickerbocker) . }	Mrs. Hackett
Van Knickerbocker .	Mr. Richings	Lowenna	Mrs. Wallack
Nicholas Vedder . .	Mr. Woodhull	Jacintha	Mrs. Durie
Gustaffe	Mr. T. Placide		

A version of Rip Van Winkle by John H. Hewitt was presented at the Front Street theatre, Baltimore, in 1833, with this cast : —

ACTS I. AND II.

Rip Van Winkle (aged 35)	William Isherwood
Brom Dutcher (aged 35)	C. Durang
Peter Vanderdonk (aged 23)	— Lear
Derrick Van Brummel (aged 30)	Joseph Jefferson
Rip Van Winkle, Jr. (aged 8)	Master Rogers
Nicholas Vedder	J. Stickney
Capt. Hendrick Hutson } Mountain Spooks	— Garner
Hans Dundervelt . }	— Lawson
Dame Van Winkle (aged 30)	Mrs. Anderson
Judith Van Winkle (aged 6)	———

ACT III.

Rip Van Winkle (aged 55)	William Isherwood
Brom Dutcher (aged 55)	C. Durang
Peter Vanderdonk (aged 43)	— Lear
General Van Brummel (aged 50)	Joseph Jefferson
Capt. Van Winkle (aged 28)	— Greenwood

Jonathan Doolittle . . . . A. Byrnes
Judith (aged 26) . . . . Mrs. Durang
Capt. Hutson and Spooks . . . . ———

The Joseph Jefferson in this cast was the father of our Rip.
Mr. Hewitt, in a letter written at Baltimore, May 18, 1887,
says : —

"My adaptation differed from all others that I have since witnessed.
I introduced Captain Hutson and his elfin crew upon the stage, and gave
them excellent exercise in their game of bowls amid sheet-iron thunder,
rosin lightning, and weird music. Their chorus, led by Mr. Garner, then
a well-known Baltimore vocalist, was descriptive of the noisy game. The
managers, not being able to raise a chorus of dwarfs, were compelled
to substitute a ship's crew of jolly jack-tars, picked up in the neighbourhood of Fell's Point."

Flynn, the original performer of the part, played Rip Van
Winkle at the Richmond Hill theatre, New York, on July 29,
1833.

On September 4, 1833, when Mr. Hackett, at the Park
theatre, presented the drama, as altered and improved for
him, in London, by Bayle Bernard, the characters were
cast as follows : —

Rip Van Winkle (1st appearance since return from Europe) . Mr. Hackett
Derrick Van Tassell . . Mr. Clarke | District Judge . . . Mr. Blakeley
Nicholas Vedder . Mr. John Fisher | Perseverance Peashell . Mr. Povey
Brom Van Brunt . . Mr. Harrison | Dame Van Winkle . Mrs. Wheatley
Herman . . . . . Mr. Keppell | Alice . . . . Mrs. Wallack
Arthur . . . . Mr. Rae | Gertrude . . . . Miss Rae

The cast subjoined is from a bill of the Park theatre,
for October 16, 1834 : —

ACT I.

Rip Van Winkle . . Mr. Hackett | Hendrick Hudson . . Mr. Hayden
Derrick Van Tassell . . Mr. Clarke | Richard Juet . . . . . Mr. Harvey
Nicholas Vedder . . Mr. Blakeley | Dame Van Winkle . Mrs. Wheatley
Brom Van Brunt . Mr. John Fisher | Alice . . . . Mrs. Gurner
Rory Von Clump . . Mr. Russell |

ACT II.

Rip Van Winkle . . . Mr. Hackett	Perseverance Peashell . Mr. Povey
Young Rip . . . . . Mr. Bancker	Hiram . . . . Mr. Collett
Herman Van } Tassell } Mr. Wm. Wheatley	Ebenezer . . . . . Mr. Russell
	District Judge . . . Mr. Blakeley
Abram Higginbottom } (late Van Brunt) } Mr. J. Fisher	Dame Higginbottom . Mrs. Gurner (formerly Alice Van Winkle)
Bradford (probably } Gustaffe) . . } Mr. T. Placide	Gertrude . . . . . Miss Turnbull

Rip Van Winkle was announced at the New National or New Chatham theatre, New York, January 7, 1850, with this cast : —

Rip Van Winkle . Mr. Charles Burke	Van Slous . . . Mr. C. W. Taylor
Knickerbocker . . . Mr. Jefferson (the Rip of our day)	Ganderkin . . . . . Mr. Seymour
	Dame Van Winkle . . Mrs. Muzzy
Nicholas Vedder . . Mr. J. Herbert	Alice . . . . . Mrs. Sutherland
Herman . . . . . . Mr. Crocker	Lowenna . . . Mrs. H. Isherwood

On September 27, 1855, an opera on the subject of *Rip Van Winkle*, — the music by George Bristow, the words by J. H. Wainwright, — was produced by the Pyne and Harrison Opera company, and it was much liked and admired. The parts were cast thus : —

Rip Van Winkle . . Mr. Stretton	Van Brummell . . . Mr. Setchell
Gardinier . . . . . Mr. Harrison	Dame Van Winkle . Miss S. Pyne
Villecour . . . . Mr. Horncastle	Alice . . . . . . Miss L. Pyne
Nicholas Vedder . . . Mr. Hayes	

JEFFERSON AS A LECTURER

On April 27, 1892, Jefferson appeared for the first time as a lecturer. The place was the Art Gallery of Yale University, at New Haven. The subject was Dramatic Art. The present biographer was in the audience, and subsequently wrote the following dispatch, which was printed in the *New York Tribune* the next morning : —

'When the popularity of Sir Walter Scott as a poet began to be affected, by the sudden advent of Byron with *Childe Harold*, the Wizard of the North waved his wand in another direction and presently produced the *Waverley Novels*. It is good to have resources. Jefferson, in his delivery of his discourse on acting, made it evident that, if he were to leave the stage, he would still have at his command the influences of the lyceum. He spoke for more than an hour, in a fluent and sparkling strain of clear comment on the art that he represents, always wise and often humorous, — giving evidence of the versatility of his mind, while affording conclusive illustration of the importance of his profession. The manner of his discourse can be but faintly noted in descriptive words. His instinct as to effect guides and sustains him equally as a speaker and an actor. The foreground of his speech was chiefly composed of comic anecdote, — apt, pungent, and effective. When he reached the more serious portion of his address, the geniality of the actor gave unconscious emphasis to every truth he uttered. His distinction between oratory and acting was incisively made, and every auditor must have appreciated the subtle discrimination as to the relative value of tragedy and comedy, viewed with regard to the question of difficulty. How much may be achieved by a glance, or by an inflection of the voice, was no less potently shown than deftly urged. In response to questions that were asked, after his lecture had ended, he dwelt instructively upon the position of the actor, who must at once please at least three orders of the public intelligence, and whose dilemma is that he can neither be too refined for one class, nor too crude for another, nor too unconventional for a third. Much instruction was imparted by Jefferson, and still more of suggestion was given, — and all with the simplicity which is the crowning grace of his art. No surrounding could have been desired of a more felicitous character than was provided in the Art Gallery of Yale, hung with portraits of old renown ; nor could a more learned or a lovelier audience be anywhere assembled than was provided by New Haven on this occasion. The incident is not without a special significance. Neither theatre nor actor was permitted in Connecticut until within about fifty years. Jefferson was introduced to his audience by President Dwight, of Yale, and a speech in his honour, spoken by Prof. John Weir, was heartily cheered. The ancient social prejudice against the stage is melting away; more and more the learned and the thoughtful classes of society feel its potency and realise the importance of guiding it aright, and of utilising for the public benefit its subtle, comprehensive, far-reaching influence. The practical example and the monitions of such men as Jefferson stimulate that tendency and help to neutralise the base influence of the speculators and triflers, whose unrestricted exertions would soon bring it into irretrievable disgrace. From Jefferson's doctrine that acting is more a gift than an art, many listeners might be disposed to dissent ; but the capacity for any art is a gift, and that, probably, is all that he intended to maintain. The true actor is born, not made ; yet, on the other hand, if he have not art, he is a natural force wasted. No actor ever gave a more decisive proof than Jefferson himself afforded of the power that genius derives from command of the resources of art. He closed his discourse with some playful verses, in satire of Ignatius Donnelly's crazy theory [1] that Shakespeare's works were written by Francis Bacon.'

---

[1] Every reader who happens to be specially interested in the question of Shakespeare's authorship of his works should read the refutation of *Donnelly's Cryptogram*, written by Rev. A. Nicholson, of St. Alban's church, Leamington, and published under the title of *No Cipher in Shakespeare*. It completely destroys, upon mathematical grounds, the whole structure of Donnelly's argument. A reply was attempted by Donnelly, but it was so effectually answered by Mr. Nicholson that the cryptogram has been a laughing-stock ever since. There never was the

CHRONOLOGY OF THE LIFE OF JEFFERSON

1829 . . . Joseph Jefferson born, February 20, in Philadelphia.

1833 . . . Made his first appearance on the stage, at the theatre in Washington, with Thomas D. Rice, as Jim Crow.

1837 . . . Acted at the Franklin theatre, New York.

1838 . . . Was removed to Chicago.

1846 . . . Acted at Matamoras, Mexico.

1849 . . . September 10. Appeared in New York, at Chanfrau's New National theatre, as Jack Rackbottle.

1850 . . . May 19. Married to Margaret Clements Lockyer, who died on February 18, 1861.

Appeared at Mitchell's Olympic.

Acted in the South with John Ellsler.

1856 . . . Made voyage to Europe.

Joined Laura Keene's theatre, New York.

1857 . . . August 31. At Laura Keene's theatre made a hit as Dr. Pangloss.

1858 . . . October 18. First time of *Our American Cousin*, at Laura Keene's theatre. Jefferson won distinction as Asa Trenchard. Piece ran till March 25, 1859.

1861 . . . Appeared for the first time in San Francisco, July 8.
November 5. Sailed for Australia, where he passed four years.

1865 . . . Appeared as Rip Van Winkle at the Adelphi theatre, London, September 4.

1866 . . . September 3. Reappeared in America, at the Olympic theatre, New York, as Rip.

1867 . . . December 20. Was married to Sarah Isabel Warren.

---

least reason to suppose that Shakespeare did not write the works ascribed to him, or that Francis Bacon was concerned with them in any way. Donnelly's pernicious defamation of the dead, — for his book casts a blight of obloquy as well upon Bacon as upon Shakespeare, — could affect only the ignorant, the credulous, and the mean. Most scholars have naturally viewed it with contempt. It is, however, pleasant to know that, in a scientific point of view, that fabric of folly has been completely demolished.

1869 . . . Appeared at Booth's theatre, New York, as Rip, August 2. Bought Orange Island, Iberia, La., and estate at Hohokus, N.J.

1870 . . . Appeared at Booth's theatre, as Rip, August 15, and acted that part till February 7, 1871.

1871 . . . January 20. Acted for benefit of George Holland's family.

1872 . . . Cured of glaucoma by surgical operation.

1873 . . . January 1. Reappearance at Ford's theatre, Baltimore.
July 9. Sailed for England.
September 1. Reappeared at Booth's theatre, New York, as Rip.

1875 . . . Acted at the Princess's theatre, London, from November 1, 1875, to April 29, 1876, as Rip.

1877 . . . Midsummer engagement with J. S. Clarke, at the London Haymarket theatre, in farces.
October 28. Reappeared at Booth's theatre, New York, as Rip, under management of Augustin Daly.

1878 . . . Revisited California.

1880 . . . Produced *The Rivals*, at the Arch Street theatre, Philadelphia, and made a hit as Acres.

1889 . . . Established, at Buzzard's Bay, his home, called Crow's Nest.

1891 . . . April 1. Crow's Nest was burnt down. It has been rebuilt.

1892 . . . April 27. Made his first appearance as a lecturer, at Yale University, delivering address on acting. Received degree of LL.D. from Yale.

1893 . . . March 1. Delivered discourse on the Drama, at Carnegie Music Hall, New York, for the benefit of the Kindergarten Association.
Elected President of The Players, succeeding Edwin Booth.

Jefferson's AUTOBIOGRAPHY, originally published [1889–1890] in the *Century Magazine*, fills a handsome volume, of about 500 pages, from the press of the Century Company. Its characteristics are those of its writer, — originality, simplicity, gentleness, humour, and charm. A disquisition upon that book may be found in my SHADOWS OF THE STAGE, Vol. I., Chapter vii., together with essays on Jefferson's Acting.

The Works of Mr. William Winter.

THE LIFE AND ART OF EDWIN BOOTH.

Crown 8vo. Cloth. Gilt top. $2.25.

Uniform with "The Life and Art of Joseph Jefferson." With Portraits in Character and Other Illustrations.

Also an Edition in Cloth. 18mo. 75 cents.

Uniform with the 18mo. edition of Mr. Winter's Works. With a Portrait.

"Mr. Winter's book, aside from the great interest of its subject proper, and without considering its beauties of style and richness of material, is valuable for the many fine glimpses it gives of Booth's contemporaries in this country and in England. Nor are these glimpses confined to the theatrical life. Many of the most distinguished artists, literary men and women, editors, statesmen, and scholars were his friends, and delighted in his company. The frontispiece of the book is a striking full-length portrait of Booth." — *The Independent.*

MACMILLAN & CO.,
66 FIFTH AVENUE, NEW YORK.

SHAKESPEARE'S ENGLAND.

With numerous full-page and vignette illustrations and a photogravure
portrait of the author by ARTHUR JULE GOODMAN.

12mo. Full gilt, ornamental cover. $2.00.

Also without illustrations in the

Uniform Edition of Mr. Winter's Works.

18mo. Cloth. Gilt top. 75 cents.

"Mr. Winter's sympathy with English antiquity is profound; he writes
reverently, meditatively, and eloquently. As an interpreter of the thoughts
and feelings of Americans who approach historic and literary England
with intelligent appreciation of what it all stands for to them, he is delightful,
wise, and impressive." — *New York Times.*

"In the graceful English of which Mr. Winter is a master, he discourses
as only a poet could, and surely as Shakespeare himself would have
desired, on Stratford-on-Avon and its environs — the most satisfactory
account of the place we recall — and on the kindred topic, 'The Shrines of
Warwickshire.' Other chapters describe with the same enthusiasm and
delicate appreciation the old churches and literary shrines of London,
Westminster Abbey, Canterbury, Stoke-Pogis, Windsor, and other historic
places. Every lover of Shakespeare should own, or at least read, the
book." — *Art Amateur.*

"He offers something more than guidance to the American traveller.
He is a convincing and eloquent interpreter of the august memories and
venerable sanctities of the old country." — *Saturday Review.*

"Enthusiastic and yet keenly critical notes and comments on English
life and scenery." — *Scotsman.*

"The book is delightful reading. . . . It is a delicious view of England
which this poet takes. It is indeed the noble, hospitable, merry, romance-
haunted England of our fathers, — the England which we know of in song
and story." — *Scribner's Monthly.*

GRAY DAYS AND GOLD.

New Edition.   18mo, cloth, gilt top, 75 cents.

"This book, which is intended as a companion to 'Shakespeare's England,' relates to the gray days of an American wanderer in the British Islands, and to the gold of thought and fancy that can be found there. Mr. Winter's graceful and meditative style in his English sketches has recommended his earlier volume upon [Shakespeare's] England to many readers, who will not need urging to make the acquaintance of this companion-book, in which the traveller guides us through the quiet and romantic scenery of the mother-country with a mingled affection and sentiment of which we have had no example since Irving's day."—*The Nation*.

"No more delightful guide to the homes and haunts of genius could any reader desire."—*Kilmarnock Journal*.

"For those who are unable to visit the scenes, and have to be content with seeing through the eyes of others, a better description would be difficult to find ; and to those who propose to visit the districts no more useful, informing, and pleasant companion could be recommended."—*Glasgow Herald*.

"Mr. Winter, whether he writes in simple prose or tuneful verse, is always poetical, and it is one of his chief characteristics, as it is his greatest charm as a writer, that he not only perceives the poetic beauty of the scenes he visits, but that he makes his readers perceive it. There are more golden than gray days in this book, for Mr. Winter's thought is like to an Eldorado in its natural opulence of wealth ; it is always bright, warm, glowing with color, rich in feeling. . . . They who have never visited the scenes which Mr. Winter so charmingly describes will be eager to do so in order to realize his fine descriptions of them, and they who have already visited them will be incited by his eloquent recital of their attractions to repeat their former pleasant experiences."—*Public Ledger, Philadelphia*.

"They show at their best their author's quick sympathy and clear insight into the essential in the works and the lives of those who have made recent English literature what it is—Burns, Scott, Byron, Matthew Arnold, Clough, and many others. He has followed where they walked, has sat beside their graves, has entered into their spirit."—*Evangelist*.

"Much that is bright and best in our literature is brought once more to our dulled memories. Indeed, we know of but few volumes containing so much of observation, kindly comment, philosophy, and artistic weight as this unpretentious little book."—*Chicago Herald*.

"Is as friendly and good-humoured a book on English scenes as any American has written since Washington Irving."—*Daily News, London*.

OLD SHRINES AND IVY.

18mo, cloth, gilt top, 75 cents.

"This volume, in harmony with the edition of Mr. Winter's selected essays and poems published by Macmillan during this past year, contains some of his most charming work. The essays he lays as offerings upon the shrines of history and of literature. Mr. Winter may have gone in search of history, but his offerings—praise be to history that they lie upon her shrine—are bits from his wanderings in England, Scotland, and France, and of his 'lingering in lovely Warwickshire.' Here he meditated—and the thread runs through all the book—upon the divine poet with whose story and spirit the region is hallowed."—*Journal of Education.*

"It is a thoughtful book, full of tender and reminiscent ideas strung together on the thread of history."—*Appeal Avalanche.*

"We are glad to have these gatherings and meditations of a pure and classic dramatic scholar saved from the fate of what are aptly called 'fugitive' productions."—*New York Observer.*

"The sketches are written with the grace and sentiment that characterized so happily 'Gray Days and Gold,' and the shining thread of the author's Shakespearianism runs through them."—*Nation.*

"A decidedly choice specimen of good literature is 'Old Shrines and Ivy,' by William Winter, devoted at the outset to English Cathedrals, the pleasing views along the road to them, the historical associations of the great buildings and their relations to Shakespeare's plays, and adding instructive critical notes on some of the plays and on Sheridan's 'School for Scandal,' and closing with a very hearty personal tribute to Mr. Longfellow."—*Christian Intelligencer.*

"It is pleasant to visit Arden in such sympathetic company as that of William Winter."—*St. Paul Pioneer Press.*

"Those loving Shakespeare and his lovers should certainly see to it that this dainty little book is not only on their shelves, but thoroughly read and re-read."—*American Hebrew.*

"No one else could have written these letters and essays. They are instinct with poetry, and they breathe that reverence for the great names of history and literature which seems almost to have been crushed out by the present idolatry of material achievement."—*San Francisco Chronicle.*

SHADOWS OF THE STAGE.

FIRST SERIES.

18mo, cloth, gilt top, 75 cents.

**** Also a limited large-paper edition, $2.00.

" His stage memories are models of the best dramatic criticism, not only in sympathetic understanding of the subject, but in perfect courtesy and appreciation."—*Journal of Education.*

" Mr. William Winter's impressionable genius has seized upon the 'shadows' of the stage, transforming them into enduring pictures of reality in this charming little book, in which we find chapters on Jefferson, Edwin Booth, McCullough, Adelaide Neilson, Irving, Ellen Terry, Mary Anderson, the Florences, Ada Rehan, and others ; and the volume is one of present interest and future value."—*Boston Budget.*

" Taken one by one, and regarded in the light of their original intention, Mr. Winter's essays present features of very high merit. He possesses a full vocabulary, and uses it with freedom and vigour. His impulsive eloquence gives powerful and picturesque expression to catholic sympathies and cultured taste."—*Saturday Review.*

" Mr. Winter has long been known as the foremost of American dramatic critics, as a writer of very charming verse, and as a master in the lighter veins of English prose."—*Chicago Herald.*

" He has the poise and sure judgment of long experience, the fine perception and cultured mind of a *littérateur* and man of the world, and a command of vivid and flexible language quite his own. One must look far for anything approaching it in the way of dramatic criticism ; only Lamb could write more delightfully of actors and acting. . . . Mr. Winter is possessed of that quality invaluable to a play-goer, a temperament finely receptive, sensitive to excellence ; and this it is largely which gives his dramatic writings their value. Criticism so luminous, kindly, genial, sympathetic, and delicately expressed fulfils its function to the utmost."—*Milwaukee Sentinel.*

" This little book is in every way delightful. It gives us charming glimpses of personal character, exquisite bits of criticism, and the indefinable charm of stage life. . . . No transcript of American life of to-day would be complete without these pictures, and Mr. Winter has in a sense done a service to history in this exquisite little book."—*Appeal Avalanche.*

WANDERERS.

GEORGE WILLIAM CURTIS.

With Portrait. 18mo, cloth, 75 cents.

"Mr. Winter easily ranks among the most justly appreciative of critics and the most graceful of writers, and also was intimately acquainted with Mr. Curtis. From any point of view this eulogy commands a high degree of admiration, and will be read with wide attention and interest. It is a literary treasure in itself apart from its theme." — *Congregationalist.*

"It is the affectionate tribute of one who was a firm and intimate friend of the dead scholar and who knew the good qualities which were his. It is eloquent and pathetic in many instances, and full of reminiscence." — *Chicago Times.*

"A splendid tribute to one of the foremost men of letter America has produced." — *Chicago Herald.*

"William Winter's tender, appreciative, eloquent, and just eulogy on George William Curtis is rightly published in book form and will be read and cherished by thousands of earnest Americans. . . . Mr. Winter has drawn a portrait full of color and feeling." — *Boston Beacon.*

"A fragrant tribute that now, embalmed between the covers of a book, will shed lasting sweetness." — *Philadelphia Record.*

"Mr. Winter's tribute to the memory of his lifelong friend is not a task done perfunctorily. Manifestly his heart inspired the words that he spoke. The verdict of the future respecting Curtis's rank as an author, as a man of letters, as an orator, and as a citizen, can hardly be made up without a reference to this tiny volume; for it embodies from the experience and observation of a clear-sighted contemporary a summary of the moral and intellectual forces that environed Curtis from his youth up. It shows that a thorough-going biography of the man would mean a history of the literature and politics of the nation during a most important period." — *New York Tribune.*

MACMILLAN & CO.,
66 FIFTH AVENUE, NEW YORK.